FORGED IN FROST

OF DRAGONS AND FAE, BOOK TWO

JASMINE WALT

DYNAMO PRESS

IMPORTANT NAMES AND PLACES

This is a list of some of the character names and locations mentioned in Book One, to help refresh your memory.

MAIN CHARACTERS

ADARA: Half-dragon, half-water fae, Adara is a rare fae who can wield both fire and water magic. According to a prophecy, she is the only one who can save Ediria, but only if she can master her powers and complete the sacred ritual that will allow her to unlock her final form.

EINAR: The last dragon in Ediria. The fae hunted his kind to near extinction, so he harbors a deep hatred for nearly all of them except Adara, who is his fated mate.

SECONDARY CHARACTERS

LEAP: an orphaned air fae with the rare ability to wield lightning magic. His mother was Lord Oren's sister, and Leap was raised by him for a few short years until he ran away and fell in first with a gang of street thieves, then later was adopted by harpies. He joined Adara and Einar's band after the two of them saved one of his harpy friends.

MAVLYN: An earth fae with the ability to manipulate plant life. Mavlyn was raised in the same village Adara grew up in, and the two of them have been best friends for as long as they can remember. She is also a distant relative of Lady Mossi's.

SIDE CHARACTERS

DUNE TERRAN: an earth fae, and Adara's ex-boyfriend.

GELSYNE: Adara's adoptive mother, formerly the late Princess Olette's lady-in-waiting. Her body has been possessed by Nox.

GENERAL SLAUGH: Leader of the Shadow Guard, formerly the right hand of King Aolis.

KING AOLIS: the recently deceased king of Ediria.

KING CYRIAN: Adara's grandfather, and King Aolis's predecessor.

LADY AVANI: Lady Mossi's granddaughter, and one of the three hostages taken by King Aolis to control the other houses. They helped Adara and her friends escape Kaipei Castle after defeating Aolis.

LADY AXLYA: Ruler of House Usciete and Lochanlee.

LADY CASCADA: Lady Axlya's daughter, and one of the three hostages taken by King Aolis to control the other houses. They helped Adara and her friends escape Kaipei Castle after defeating Aolis.

LADY MOSSI: Ruler of House Ithir and Domhain.

LADY TEMPEST: Lord Oren's daughter, and one of the three hostages taken by King Aolis to control the other houses. They helped Adara and her friends escape Kaipei Castle after defeating Aolis.

LORD OREN: Ruler of the House Reatha and the Gaoth Aire.

NOX, MOTHER OF SHADOWS: A powerful shadow demon who gifted King Aolis with powerful shadow magic, and who has been trying to possess him for decades. She now possesses Gelsyne instead, who she has full control over.

PRINCESS OLETTE: Adara's late mother, and the daughter of King Cyrian.

PRINCE DARYAN: The dragon prince, and Adara's late father.

QUYE, THE ORACLE: Quye is a powerful air fae who can see the past, present, and future. The winds bring her whispers from all corners of the realm, and she also has a close connection with both the dream realm and the spirit realm. She is also a niece of Lord Oren, and Leap's cousin.

PLACES

DOMHAIN: the earth fae realm, ruled by Lady Mossi. Also where Adara grew up.

EDIRIA: the kingdom this story is set in. It is made up of four realms—Domhain, Lochanlee, Hearthfyre, and The Gaoth Aire.

THE GAOTH AIRE: the air fae realm.

HEARTHFYRE: formerly the fire fae realm before it was taken over by the dragons. After King Aolis used shadow magic to defeat the dragons, Hearthfyre became a wasteland overrun by shadow creatures. Edirians now refer to it as the Deadlands, and few dare to travel there.

LOCHANLEE: the water fae realm.

MOUNT FURIAN: a sacred mountain in Hearthfyre, where the portal the dragons used to escape is hidden.

TALAMH: The capital of Domhain, where Lady Mossi resides, and where Mavlyn was set to go to university.

WYNTH: a major city in the Gaoth Aire, where Leap is from, and where the Oracle makes her home.

Leap

"*How could you lose the girl, Slaugh?*"

Leap winced as the woman's shriek pierced his ear —he tugged on the thread of wind a little, moving it away from his ear so her rage wouldn't deafen him. Perched on one of the castle towers, he had a perfect view of the courtyard below, and more importantly, the quarrel taking place.

It had only been a few hours since he, Einar, and Mavlyn had stormed Castle Kaipei to rescue Adara. Leap hadn't witnessed what had taken place inside the castle—he'd been too busy distracting the guards outside, dropping bombs on the battlements and hurling lightning bolts at the soldiers while Mavlyn and Einar had flown in through an open window. He'd taken shelter in a nearby cave and waited for a sign from his friends—Einar was supposed to send up a smoke signal from the nearby forest—but he'd yet to see anything, so he'd snuck back to the castle, intending to find out what had happened.

"I apologize, my lady," Slaugh said in a low voice Leap would have been unable to hear if not for his ability to eavesdrop with the wind. The general's posture was subservient—head bowed, shoulders rounded, looking for all the world like a dog with his tail tucked between his legs. You would have thought he was cowering before some mighty beast, ready to rip his jugular out with her fangs.

Instead, he stood before a willowy female Leap had never seen before. Leap narrowed his eyes as he studied her. She was tall, with glossy, dark green hair and coppery skin. And though she wasn't Slaugh's height, she carried herself as if she was— chin raised, chest out, shoulders back, a proud tilt to her head that proclaimed her better than everyone and everything else, that the only commonality they shared was that they both walked the same earth, and breathed the same air.

He knew the type very well, and he loathed them. But it wasn't any of these things that scared him. It was her eyes that gave him the heebie-jeebies—they were pure black, like the surface of a frozen lake at midnight, with not even a hint of white at the edges. Impenetrable, unfathomable, unknowable.

And undoubtedly full of dark magic.

"Your apologies are worthless," the female snapped, folding her arms over her chest. Twilight crept into the sky behind her, suffusing the deep, velvet blue with pearly hints of dawn. Leap knew he couldn't stay for long—they would spot him for sure once the sun rose—but he needed to know what happened, where his friends were.

"Adara was at her weakest, her magic depleted. It should have been child's play for you to lock her up in the dungeons, or even kill her. I handed both her and the dragon to you on a silver platter!"

"I wasn't expecting the hostages to put up as much of a fight as they did," Slaugh growled. "They proved to be a formidable force, as you saw. It took all of us to contain them, and that's only because you told us we couldn't kill them."

"Yes, and you nearly bungled that, too." The mystery fae rolled her eyes. "Are you certain you've searched the entire castle? How did they escape without being seen, anyway? I thought I told you to make sure all the exits and entrances were covered."

"I did," Slaugh insisted, bunching his hands together at his sides. "But that air fae boy was creating havoc out there, using his lightning strikes to blow up the parapets, and air currents to blind and confuse the guards. He maimed and killed many of them before he fled—it would have been all too easy for Adara and her friends to sneak past. Also, I don't mean to be impudent, my lady, but you were there. Why didn't you use your shadow magic to bind Adara and her friends?"

"Because, you imbecile, shadow magic has no effect on Adara!" the fae spat. "Not yours, not mine, not anyone's! Besides," she added, her lips thinning with displeasure, "this earth fae bitch's body is proving to be more troublesome than I anticipated. Gelsyne isn't nearly as strong as King Aolis was, but she is putting up a fight, and I only just took possession of her body. It will take some days before I'm fully able to control her and use my abilities without her interference."

Leap nearly fell off the roof. He gripped the spire hard as his head spun, trying to make sense of these revelations. The female down there was Gelsyne, Adara's mother? And she was being possessed? And what was this about King Aolis being stronger than her? Was he still alive?

He has to be dead, Leap told himself. Why else would Slaugh be taking orders from this fae? And who was she, anyway?

"I see." Slaugh raked a hand through his sparse red locks,

briefly exposing the grotesque burns bubbling along his scalp. He gave a deep sigh, his shoulders slumping a little. "It's possible they took one of the two secret escape routes in the castle."

"And you're just mentioning this now?" The mystery fae looked like she was two seconds from stringing the general up from the parapets by his balls. "What are these secret entrances, and where do they lead?"

"One leads to into a cavern in the Wistful Woods, just inside Lochanlee. The other leads to the base of the Gaoth Aire."

"Well, what are you waiting for? Send your men to check them both!"

Slaugh sketched a curt bow, then whirled on his heel and stalked out of the courtyard, his cape flapping behind him. The bossy fae pinched the bridge of her nose as she watched him go, irritation souring her features. As the sky lightened further, Leap noticed the shadows around her writhing, as if mirroring her emotions.

She sighed a little, sitting down on a stone bench. Reaching out with a slender hand, she traced the edge of a blossom from one of the flowering vines crawling along the wall behind her. The flower blackened instantly, and Leap watched in horror as the rot crawled up the entire wall.

"Soon," she crooned to the shadows as they wrapped their tendrils around her limbs. "Soon."

"Cirra," Leap whispered under his breath, calling for his cloud familiar. Squalls, he needed to get out of here before he got caught in whatever *that thing's* clutches were. Turning away, he rolled down the slope of the roof and straight off the edge, free falling for just a few seconds before landing on top of her fluffy, golden form.

Where should he go first? Toward Lochanlee? Or back to Wynth?

Cirra hummed beneath him, sensing his distress. Leap closed his eyes for a moment, letting her vibrations soothe him and clear his head. Cirra might not be able to speak to him using words, but she always knew exactly what he was feeling, and had her own way of offering comfort or advice when he needed it.

"You're right," he murmured. "We should try Lochanlee first."

Cirra needed no further encouragement. She zipped away from Kaipei Castle, heading south to the water fae lands. If Leap was wrong, he would never make it to Adara and the others before Slaugh's men did, but his gut told him Adara would head toward Lochanlee. She was, after all, a water fae, and besides, they'd made too many enemies in Wynth with their recent stunts for her to want to return there.

As Cirra carried him above the cloud cover and away from prying eyes, Leap replayed the conversation between Slaugh and the mystery fae. Adara and Einar, at least, appeared to have gotten away. But what about Mavlyn? And what exactly had happened to King Aolis? The female had said Adara had been at her weakest, her magic depleted... did that mean she'd used all her power fighting Aolis?

Leap desperately wished he hadn't been separated from the others, that he'd gone into the castle with them so he could have seen firsthand what happened. But he'd used nearly all his magic reserves to keep the guards occupied so Adara and Einar could confront King Aolis without interference, and had been forced to go into hiding. The only reason he even knew it had been safe to return to the castle was because the noxious cloud of shadow magic that had hovered over Kaipei Castle for as long as Leap could remember had finally vanished.

But if King Aolis was dead, and the cloud had vanished, why

was that female using shadow magic? Shouldn't it have vanished from all of Ediria?

Cirra dipped beneath the cloud cover, revealing a scattered forest surrounding a deep blue lake. The sun had crested the horizon, sending ripples of gold across the lake's surface and gilding the verdant tops of the trees. It would have been a peaceful scene if not for the sound of a female screaming.

Leap narrowed his eyes. Wait. A female screaming?

His heart rate tripled, and he tugged on the wind, demanding it to bring the sound closer to him. The words exploded in his ears, sending his heart straight into his throat.

"Adara! Einar! Where are you?"

"Squalls!" Leap swore under his breath. That was Mavlyn's voice! Cirra put on a burst of speed, hurtling them past the lake and deep into the forest. The sound of Mavlyn's desperate shouts got louder and louder, and when Leap was almost certain they were on top of her, he jumped off Cirra and crashed through the treetops, catching a wind current to buffer his fall.

Mavlyn jumped as Leap landed right in front of her, clapping a hand to her chest. "Leap!" she cried, her eyes wide with a firestorm of emotions—relief, terror, guilt. Strewn around her in the clearing they stood in were obvious signs of battle—broken branches, chaotic footprints, the remnants of a fire that had been trampled, and even traces of blood.

"What in the skies happened here, Mavlyn?" Leap grabbed her by the shoulders, forcing her panic-stricken gaze on him. "Where are Adara and Einar? What happened to King Aolis? And why does Gelsyne seem to be running the show back at the castle?" Had all this effort been for nothing? Anger boiled in his veins as his heart sank into his gut. How could Slaugh have possibly beaten him here?

Mavlyn sucked in a shuddering breath. "I was foraging for herbs when I heard the shouts," she said in a choked voice. Her entire body trembled as tears streamed down her face, and she clenched her hands into fists to keep them from shaking. Roots burst from the ground in response to her emotions, and they writhed in the dirt, as impotent as Leap's anger. "I ran as fast as I could, but I was too late. They took Adara and Einar, Leap. They're gone."

2

Adara

Some hours earlier...

The tunnel seemed to go on forever.

On and on we walked in total darkness, the sounds of our breath and the scrapes of our shoes the only sounds echoing in the close-knit space. The scents of sweat and dirt and fear clogged my nostrils, making it difficult to breathe, and my limbs dragged, heavy with exhaustion and throbbing with the wounds from my battle against Aolis.

Fear was the only thing that kept me going. Fear of being caught by Slaugh and his men, and fear of being trapped under the earth forever, never to breathe fresh air or feel the sun on my face again.

I'd never considered myself claustrophobic, but the lack of sunlight and space in this cramped tunnel made my skin crawl. Perhaps that was because it reminded me of the time Mother had used her magic to seal me into another earth tunnel, one that had spirited me far away from her, and led me straight to Einar.

Mother.

My heart pulsed in my chest like a throbbing wound at the thought of her, and I sucked in a sharp breath. Tears slipped down my cheeks as the memory of that terrible shadow being invading my mother's body burst into my mind's eye. The way that noxious evil had risen from King Aolis's body and poured into hers... it had been the ultimate invasion of body, mind, and soul.

Was Mother still in there? Was she fighting tooth and nail to regain her bodily autonomy? Or had Nox crushed her into a shadow of her former self, forced to inhabit the darkest recesses of her mind while another took control? The thought was more than I could bear, and the tears came faster, pouring down my face until I felt like I was drowning. My shoulders began to shake, and it took everything I had not to burst into audible sobs.

No matter what lies she had told, what aliases and roles she had assumed, Gelsyne was still my mother. Everything she'd done had been to protect me... and she'd lost everything trying to keep me safe.

A warm hand curled around my shoulder from behind, radiating strength and solidarity. I closed my eyes and allowed Einar's comforting touch to seep into my soul and take the edge off my grief.

Slowly, I reached up and threaded my fingers through Einar's. His hand jerked beneath mine, as if startled, then gently wrapped around my fingers and squeezed tight.

Never in my life had I wanted to throw myself into someone's arms more, to let them wrap me up and hold me so my pain might evaporate beneath the heat of their embrace.

And never had I imagined it would be Einar's arms I would want to throw myself into.

Pull yourself together, Adara, I told myself. I let go of Einar's hand so I could swipe at the tears on my cheeks. Grief was an acknowledgement of loss, and I hadn't lost Mother yet. There was still a chance I could save her. All I needed to do was find a water fae priestess to perform the coming-of-age ritual on me, and unlock the hidden light magic inside me. Then I could use it to drive Nox from Mother's body and vanquish shadow magic from the realm once and for all.

It seemed impossible to me I could wield such power. After all, just a few short weeks ago, I'd been deemed magically impotent, unable to command so much as a thimbleful of magic. But that was before I'd discovered that the 'amulet' I'd worn around my neck my entire life had actually been suppressing my true abilities, and that I not only could wield ice magic, but fire as well.

Which was also impossible. No fae had ever been born with the power to wield both of those elements at once. So if I could do that, why not shadow magic, too?

A laugh threatened to burble at my lips at the absurdity of it all, and I choked it back down, shaking my head. I was clearly losing it. Were we ever going to get out of here? Had I been right to trust that faux shadow soldier to lead us to safety? Or were we being herded into a trap?

The path we treaded grew steeper, and my heartbeat picked up as the sounds of chirping crickets filtered through the earth above our heads. The ceiling grew lower and lower, until we were crawling on our bellies in the dirt, and my chest grew tighter as the earth closed around us.

I was just beginning to wonder if we might be crushed when we finally emerged from the tunnel into a cave. The small stone opening was barely large enough to crouch, so I scrambled out from behind Mavlyn and the faux shadow soldier as fast as I could, until I was sucking in gulps of forest air.

"You okay?" Mavlyn asked, her expression pinched with

concern. Clumps of dirt clung to her clothing, and tiny, thread-like roots infested her auburn hair. Einar was in similar shape, and I'm sure I looked no better. "You ran out of there like you were being chased by a murder of harpies."

"I'm not a fan of small spaces," I panted, doubling over so I could rest my hands on my knees. I glanced around at the three of them, noting that they were far less perturbed than I was. And the shadow soldier barely even had a hair out of place! "How are the three of you so calm?"

Mavlyn shrugged. "I'm an earth fae. Being down there felt like home."

"I don't know about home," Einar said with a dark scowl as he glanced back at the cave, "but as a soldier, I'm no stranger to being stuck in tight places. I've been in much, much worse situations." His scowl grew thunderous as he jabbed a finger at the faux shadow guard. "I know who you are, so don't pretend otherwise. What are you doing here, *Kiryan*?"

"Kiryan?" Mavlyn scrunched her nose as she looked between the two males. "Do the two of you know each other?"

I stared at Kiryan, taking in the shimmer of his green-gold irises. "You were the traveler who bought the everbright potion from my mother's shop that day."

Kiryan smiled, the expression softening his brutish features. "Yes indeed."

"And you were also the elder in the woods who told me to follow the aural lights to Einar."

"I was."

"And the male at the air temple?

"Also yes."

"What the frogs?" Mavlyn scowled. "How could he possibly be all four of those people at once? Does he just have a really good disguise?"

"No," Einar growled, his golden gaze trained on Kiryan with

a death glare. "He's just really good at hopping from body to body, taking possession of whoever will best serve his needs. A bit like someone else we know, or rather, just met."

"I sincerely hope you did not just compare me to the Mother of Shadows," Kyrian said stiffly, drawing himself up to his full height. "Not after everything I've done for you and your people."

"Everything you've done!" Einar took a step toward Kiryan, his fingers twitching as though he wanted to wrap his hands around the other male's throat. The entire forest went preternaturally still, and Einar paused, seeming to remember himself. "I only asked for one boon—that you put me into an enchanted sleep."

"Which I did," Kiryan said calmly. "But I did not promise the enchantment would remain unbroken."

"I'm sorry, but I need you two to slow down a bit." I raised my hands as Einar opened his mouth, ready to spew more vitriol at our would-be-savior. "How, exactly, did you put Einar into an enchanted sleep? Only the witchlings have the power to cast enchantments, and they're all dead."

"Not only the witchlings." Kiryan smiled. "The Radiants have that power, too."

Mavlyn looked like she was about to topple over. "*Radiants?*" she squeaked, her eyes bugging out as she stared at Kiryan. "Are you seriously telling us you're a *Radiant?*"

"That is exactly what he is telling you," Einar said tersely.

"I don't understand." I pinched the bridge of my nose, trying to stave off the headache brewing behind my eyes. "I thought Radiants were beings of light?"

"We are, just as Shadows are beings of darkness," Kiryan said patiently. He ignored Einar's glowering expression, turning his attention fully toward me. "We cannot exist in corporeal form in this world, so in order to interact with sentient beings, we must inhabit one of you. Unlike Nox, the shadow being who is currently inhabiting your mother's body, I only possess people temporarily. Doing so for prolonged periods of time can cause mental and spiritual damage, eventually leading to insanity."

"I assume that's what was happening to King Aolis," I murmured, thinking back to the king. He'd seemed like he was tee-tottering on the edge of sanity, sometimes in control of his faculties, while at other times gripped in the throes of madness. My heart sank at the thought—is that what would happen to Mother? "But how was he able to maintain control?"

"King Aolis was much stronger than Gelsyne," Kiryan said, a note of sadness entering his voice. "So strong, in fact, we chose him as a champion."

"A champion?" Mavlyn exclaimed. "But King Aolis wielded shadow magic. Aren't champions supposed to be gifted with radiant magic?"

Kiryan shook his head. "Once every millennium, the Shadows and the Radiants come to a single fae they deem worthy during their coming-of-age ceremony, and offer him or her the boon of shadow or radiant magic. Usually, the fae chooses radiant magic, which is why your stories always depict the champion as a warrior of light, leading their people through golden age after golden age. But some fae choose a darker path, and when King Aolis went through his ritual, he was wracked with grief and anger at the recent loss of his mother to the dragons. Vengeance was the only thought that consumed him, and he felt that shadow magic would allow him to enact a greater revenge against the dragons.

"However," Kiryan continued, a small smile curling his mouth, "the first time King Aolis used shadow magic, he was so horrified at the results that he sealed it away inside himself and vowed never to use it again. The Shadows were furious at this turn of events, let me tell you. They had been hoping to disrupt the balance of shadow and light in their favor so they could finally gain entry into your world."

"But if King Aolis was so perturbed by the effects of shadow magic, then why did he use it again?" Mavlyn asked, but I already knew the answer.

"Aolis was in love with Princess Olette," I said, thinking back to the conversation I'd had with the king at the dining table. "He was betrothed to her before she met my father, and she chose to marry the Dragon Prince instead. That must have driven him off the edge."

"Indeed," Kiryan said darkly. "Aolis was incensed. He viewed the broken betrothal as a betrayal—after everything he had done to serve his country, after all he had lost, his bride-to-be was taken from him, too. Nox had already been whispering to him in his dreams, and she came to him with promises of power, triple-fold what he'd already been granted, enough to eradicate all dragons. All he had to do was let her inside his head."

Einar shook his head, disgusted. "All that death and destruction, and he didn't even get his precious Olette in the end."

"Okay, but where do you come in?" Mavlyn asked the Radiant. "Why did you put Einar to sleep?"

"It was his last request," Kiryan said simply. "I couldn't stand by and let Nox and King Aolis kill all the dragons, so I used Einar's blood to open a portal and send the remaining dragons to a new realm, then sealed it behind them. Einar is the keeper of that portal—it is tied to his blood, and will remain closed so long as he or one of his descendants remains alive."

"Which was why I asked you to put me to sleep," Einar said pointedly. "It wasn't just so I wouldn't have to suffer the rest of my existence alone. It was so I could remain out of harm's way, so the lives of my people would not be at risk." He raked a hand through his hair as he glanced at me, a torn expression on his face. "I don't understand why you would jeopardize that, after all you've done to help us."

I took a step back, hurt ricocheting through my chest. After everything we'd been through, did Einar still regret that I woke him up?

"Then you are a fool," Kiryan snapped, echoing my exact sentiments. Einar blinked, drawn up short by the ire in the Radiant's voice, but Kiryan didn't give him a chance to respond. "I put you to sleep at the time because there was nothing more you could do, but I never intended for you to remain that way."

"Funny," Einar sneered, his lip curled. "I don't remember you mentioning that before you cast the enchantment."

"So you truly would have preferred to remain asleep, then?"

Einar whipped his head toward me, shock slackening his face like he'd forgotten I was there. "I—"

"You would have rather stayed in that crumbling ruin I found you in, while I faced King Aolis on my own?" I fisted my hands at my sides, my voice rising as the anguish I'd stoppered up inside me bubbled over, scalding the corners of my eyes and choking my voice. "To end up enslaved to him by marriage, while you peacefully dream away, safe and sound and untouched, as shadow magic destroys the world around you?"

"No, of course not," Einar said, looking stricken. He took a step toward me, hand extended, expression pleading. "I don't regret anything that happened between us, Adara."

"I don't buy that for a second." My voice warbled slightly, and I gritted my teeth, refusing to cry. I didn't know what Einar's game was, but I'd made the mistake of turning a blind eye to red flags in a male before, and I refused to do it again. "The only reason you even agreed to help me was so my mother would make a potion to put you back to sleep. You made that clear on multiple occasions."

An exasperated look darkened Einar's features. "Yes, that was true in the beginning, but—"

"Can we put this on hold for a second?" Mavlyn interrupted, her voice tinged with exasperation. "I don't know about you all, but I have questions. Specifically about this Nox being that's taken over Gelsyne's body. Who exactly is she? And what does she want?"

"Right." Kiryan cleared his throat, somewhat awkwardly. "Nox is a powerful Shadow, one of the oldest of her kind, hence why she is known as the 'Mother of Shadows' even though it's unclear whether she truly did birth the rest of her race. The Shadows are to the darkness what Radiants are to the light, but unlike Radiants, who are givers by nature, Shadows can only take. They thrive on chaos and destruction, and while they can use their influence in small ways in your world, just as we do, it is not enough for them. Nox has long been searching for an opportunity to tear a hole between our worlds, so she and her legion can devour Ediria. There is powerful magic steeped in these lands, and if she succeeds, the balance of power between Radiants and Shadows—"

Kiryan gasped in pain and clutched at his head, the rest of his words lost in his obvious agony. Black veins pulsed at his temples, and he clenched his jaw as that same blackness began to bleed back into his eyes. Was the shadow soldier fighting back against his possession?

"Kiryan." I lunged forward, reaching for him—though I wasn't sure how to help—but he held up a hand to ward me off. "Are you okay?"

"I cannot remain in this body for much longer, so I'm afraid I will have to be brief," Kiryan gasped. He turned to Einar, his eyes glazed with pain. "Adara needs your help to defeat Nox, and it is in the best interest of the dragons that you aid her, Einar. If she fails, Nox and the shadow creatures will devour every living thing in the kingdom, including you."

The blood drained from Einar's face as realization dawned in his golden eyes. "My people would be next," he said in a hollow voice.

"Exactly so," Kiryan said. He grimaced as another wave of pain wracked him. "I must go before this body is further damaged."

"Why do you care if he's damaged?" I demanded. "He's a shadow soldier—he's already been corrupted."

"Exactly, which means he's even less viable than other hosts," Kiryan said. "The presence of shadow magic in this world has gotten to where I cannot remain long without compromising my own integrity—inhabiting a corrupted host only puts me at further risk. I will check on you again when I can, Adara, but in the meantime, complete the coming-of-age ritual as fast as you can. It's the only hope you have of defeating Nox."

He blinked, and when the soldier's eyes opened, they were pitch black, not a hint of green or gold to be seen. He opened his mouth, confusion settling into the lines of his face, but Einar moved in a blur. Before the fae could utter a single word, the dragon warrior snapped his neck.

A deathly silence settled over the forest, punctuated only by a crash as the fae's body hit the forest floor. Mavlyn and I stared at the fresh corpse, and even though I knew killing him was the right thing to do, the awful sense of finality felt like a premonition of things to come.

"All right, that's taken care of." Einar dusted off his hands, the way one might after taking out the trash. "Now, who's ready for dinner?"

3

Einar

After we disposed of the body, the three of us set off into the forest, looking for someplace secluded and safe to make camp.

The back of my head prickled from the heat of Adara's accusing stare as we marched through the forest, accusation searing the hairs on my nape. I wanted to kick myself for being so stupid, for not thinking before I opened my big mouth, but I hadn't been able to help myself.

I'd sacrificed everything so my people could escape, and to realize that Kiryan had broken his word, had ended the eternal slumber he'd promised me... I couldn't let that go unanswered. But of course, all I'd accomplished was making myself look like an asshole, and shoring up the wall I'd spent so much time trying to build between me and Adara.

A wall I desperately wanted to tear down.

But there was no time for that now, not when we were still so exposed. I was under no illusions that we were safe from Nox and General Slaugh, even if we were in water fae territory. Adara was the greatest threat to their plans; they couldn't afford to allow her to roam free. They would try to eliminate her as quickly as possible.

"I... I'm not feeling so well," Adara said. I glanced over my shoulder—we were walking single file, with Mavlyn bringing up the rear—to see her swaying on her feet, eyes glassy and face flushed. "I'm dizzy, and my leg hurts."

Cursing, I spun around and grabbed her by the shoulders, then pressed the back of my hand to her forehead.

"You're running a fever," I said gruffly. I glanced down at Adara's torn skirts, noting that she was favoring her left leg. "And you aren't healing, are you?"

"I guess not," Adara mumbled, her words slurring a little. She wobbled a little on her feet, and I had a feeling she would have toppled over if I wasn't gripping her shoulders.

"Her magic is depleted," Mavlyn said, coming up to stand by Adara's side. She crouched down and parted the torn fabric, then pursed her lips as she studied the gash. "The wound isn't healing, and worse, it looks like it's becoming infected."

"I-infected?" Adara asked, her eyes widening. "But—hey!" she protested as I swung her up into my arms. "What are you doing?"

"Taking you somewhere to lie down and rest," I said. "You're in no condition to be walking."

"I don't need you to carry me," Adara said stiffly, but I ignored her, cradling her body against my chest. She held herself rigid for a few moments, but exhaustion eventually forced her to relax, a soft moan of pain escaping her lips as her head lolled against me. Her skin was scalding against mine, and I quickened my pace.

Eventually we happened upon a small clearing, tucked a

ways away from the main path. It wasn't my first choice—I would have preferred a cave, something away from prying eyes and more defensible. But it was the best we could do for now, so I stalked through the small opening between the trees and prepared to lay Adara down.

"Hang on," Mavlyn said. She walked past me to a small patch of moss clustered at the roots of one of the trees, then knelt down and pressed her hand to it. Immediately, the moss began to multiply, thickening and spreading until it was roughly the same size as a single mattress. "There. You can lay her here."

"Clever," I murmured. I carefully set Adara down on the makeshift bed, then, out of sheer curiosity, pressed my hand against the moss to test it out. It was surprisingly plush, even a bit springy. Certainly more comfortable than any camp bed I'd ever made for myself.

Mavlyn pulled up Adara's skirt again, and I winced at the sight of the gash in her leg. It was an angry red and very swollen, clear fluid leaking from the cut and dribbling down her pale skin.

"This needs to be treated right away," Mavlyn said. She covered Adara's leg again, then twisted around to face me. "I don't have the herbs I need on hand, so I'm going to have to forage for them and find some water, too. Will you stay here and watch over her?"

"Of course." I fisted my hands at my sides as I looked at Adara. Her eyes were closed, lashes fanning against her flushed cheeks, her full, normally sassy mouth bracketed with lines of pain. "Is there anything else I can do? Anything that will ease her pain?"

Mavlyn shook her head. "Sadly, no. But you can cut strips of her skirt to use as bandages. Just make sure they're clean. I would ask you to make a fire, but we've no cookware to heat water in." Sighing, she raked a hand through her hair, looking as frustrated as I felt. "Just keep watch until I get back."

Mavlyn made herself scarce, and I sat down beside Adara, feeling utterly helpless. I wasn't used to sitting around and doing nothing—as a soldier, I was used to being in action, using brains or brawn to either solve my problems or slaughter them. We'd had medics in the dragon army, of course, but I hadn't been one of them. I knew nothing of the art of healing.

If the two of you were mated, you could have given her some of your life force.

I gritted my teeth against the snide voice in my head. Yes, if we were mated, it would solve many problems. But Adara was in no condition to complete the mating bond, and even if she were, I didn't want her to make that decision out of desperation. I'd heard tales of forced matings before—they never ended well, usually resulting in infertility or chronic illness in one or both members of the couple.

Adara moaned softly, distracting me from my thoughts. I looked over to see her face was flushed, beads of sweat gathering at her temples and upper lip. Biting back a curse, I brushed a lock of hair back from her damp brow, which was scalding. I half-expected to see steam rising from her pores, she was that hot.

Her lashes fluttered open at my touch, and she looked up at me through hazy, cornflower-blue eyes. "Why... Einar...?" she whispered.

I leaned closer, my brows furrowing in confusion. "Why what?"

"Why do you hate me?"

"Hate you?" I echoed, aghast. "I could never hate you, Adara."

"But you must," she said, struggling up into a half-sitting position. I tried to make her lie down again, but she knocked my hands away with what little strength she had left. "Because after everything we've been through, all the trials we've faced together, you still wish we'd never met." Tears shimmered in her lavender-blue eyes even as she scowled at me, and a spear of guilt stabbed straight through my heart at the pain I'd caused her. "And you know what? That's fine. You helped me kill King Aolis—you don't owe me anything else. You can go back to your tower, and once I've rescued my mother and turned her back to normal, I'll—"

I grabbed Adara, and she squealed as I hauled her into my lap. Ignoring her protests, I wrapped her up in a fierce hug, tucking her head beneath my chin and burying a kiss into the crown of her lavender hair. My arms banded around her, hands splaying across the curves of her back, and I simply breathed, willing the tension in her muscles to flow away, to open and receive the love I wanted to give her.

"I'm sorry," I mumbled into her hair.

"... for what?"

"For every nasty, barbed comment I've thrown at you. For every moment of grief I've given you. For the doubts I've planted in your mind." I sucked in a shuddering breath. "I've been pushing you away when I should have been pulling you closer, but it's not your fault, Adara. It's mine. I've been in denial about my feelings, blaming it on the ma—"

The sound of feet crashing through the underbrush drowned out the rest of my words, and Adara and I broke apart, my head whipping toward the intrusion. Leaping to my feet, I conjured a whip of fire and snapped it threateningly, ready to fight whoever was coming for us.

But my heart sank when a ribbon of water snaked its way through the air, colliding with my fire whip and dousing it in a cloud of steam.

"Water fae?" Adara asked, pushing herself to her feet behind me. I used my body to shield her as ten fae stalked into the clearing, clad in silver-blue scale armor molded to their slender bodies from wrist to ankle. I knew from experience how deceptively strong that armor was—it was crafted from diamond fish scales and was nearly impenetrable.

"Yes," I growled, as the squad of soldiers surrounded us. Even without that armor, their pale blue skin, webbed hands, and the gill flaps on the sides of their necks were a dead giveaway. The tallest among them, a male with silver hair pulled into a high tail and two hoops looped through the shell of his left ear, stepped forward and pressed the tip of his spear into my chest.

"State your name, and your business on our lands."

"Einar and Adara. We are two travelers passing through on our way to Wynth," I said calmly. My inner dragon was roaring, demanding that I slaughter these fae who posed a threat to my mate, but I knew that in our current condition, they outmatched us. "I wasn't aware it was illegal to travel through water fae lands, but we will happily change our course, if that is the case."

"It isn't illegal," the fae said, his eyes narrowing. "However, Lord Prentis, our master, has received word that traitors to the crown have passed through our border. He's ordered us to bring to him any travelers we find here."

"We're not traitors," Adara protested, coming to stand by my side. She was still flushed with fever, but she seemed to have found another reserve of strength, meeting the soldier's gaze without a hint of fear or weakness. "And I'm a water fae, just like you."

The soldier raised an eyebrow. "You may be a water fae, but you are clearly nothing like me," he said, taking in her torn dress and high-born features. "Even if you aren't traitors to the crown, two Greater Fae skulking through the forest sporting battle wounds is cause enough for suspicion. You can come with us peacefully, or with a fight, but come with us you must." He swung his spear away from my chest, pointing it in Adara's direction, and gave her a grim smile. "So tell me, my lady, which one will it be?"

4

Adara

We went with the water fae.

"You can't tie her up like this," Einar growled as the soldiers bound his hands behind his back with rope. "She's ill, can't you see that?"

The squad captain took a look at me, brushing my hair out of my eyes. His lips pursed as he took in my flushed face and glassy-eyed gaze. "You're a Greater Fae," he said, his tone almost accusatory. "What malady could possibly afflict you?"

"I'm not telling you anything until you stop treating me like a criminal," I said flatly. I was too exhausted to make up a convincing lie, and I knew I couldn't tell these soldiers the truth. Even if they believed me, there was a risk they might take us back to Kaipei, and that couldn't happen. I'd rather take my chances with this Lord Prentis, see if I could convince him to help us.

The captain's mouth flattened into a thin line. "Then we have no choice but to tie you up."

He bound my wrists himself, but at least he allowed me the

small mercy of tying them in front of my body instead of behind my back. That was the only leniency he gave, though, herding Einar and me at a punishing pace out of the forest and toward a canal waiting in the distance.

"Don't try anything funny," the captain warned as he ushered me into a rowboat. There were six boats beached along the bank of the river, large enough to seat four people each. I sat down on the bench, and out of impulse, skimmed my bound hands over the surface of the water. A rush of energy filled my limbs, and I sucked in a sharp breath as ice crystals formed along the surface of the water.

"None of that." The captain yanked my arms from the water as he took his seat next to me. I scowled, but the captain didn't notice, turning toward the dock and holding up a hand as Einar tried to clamber into the boat with us. "And not you. You go in the next one."

He pointed to two more soldiers, who climbed in and sat down on the bench across from us. Einar growled, his eyes flashing, but he kept his head down and allowed himself to be led to the boat behind us. My heart squeezed with sympathy for him— I knew how hard it was for him to subjugate himself to these soldiers, and that he was only doing it for my sake. He would rather die than surrender to the fae.

Except dying isn't an option for him, I thought to myself. *He has to stay alive to protect the location of his people.*

The captain made a shooing motion with his hand, and the boat lurched forward, seemingly of his own volition. It was then that I realized there were no oars in the rowboats—the water fae were using their own magic to propel the boats through the water. I glanced at the canal water as it rushed past us, wishing I could put my hands back in. That quick dip had given me a small burst of energy, enough to clear my head, and I couldn't help wondering if a longer soak would give me enough to heal my injuries. I'd never drawn energy from water in the past—was this another ability the amulet had stifled? I wanted to try it again, but the captain was watching me intently, so I didn't dare.

Instead, I glanced back at Einar to see how he was doing. He sat stiffly on the bench, his hands behind him, back straight as a pole as he stared out at the water. His expression softened a little when he noticed my stare, and he even managed a small smile. *I'm okay,* his gilded eyes seemed to say. *Don't worry about me.*

But how could I not, when he was trussed up like a prized fowl, ready to be taken home and feasted upon? He had to be absurdly uncomfortable, sitting like that with his arms bound behind him, and exhausted to boot. Unlike me, he couldn't draw energy from the water. He'd given everything he had to me, so I could defeat Aolis.

My gaze dropped to the cuff wrapped around my bicep, and I traced the edges of the ruby red primal stone set in the center with my eyes. There had been an enormous amount of energy in the stone when I'd tapped into it—I'd never felt anything like that in my life. How many years had it been since the stone had been used? Tiny foreign symbols I'd initially thought were meaningless patterns were etched into the edges—witchling spell marks, perhaps? It seemed like a priceless item, belonging to a noble house or even royalty. No doubt it had personal meaning to Einar, and yet he'd given it to me anyway.

I shook my head, not sure what to believe. I'd thought Einar was only with me because of our bargain, and his outburst at Kiryan had certainly seemed to support that. But the way he'd held me in the clearing, the kiss he'd brushed against my crown and the heartfelt words he'd spoken... I wish I knew what he'd been about to say before the soldiers had arrived. Wish I knew how he really felt about me.

I let my mind drift as we traveled along the canal, watching the ever-changing landscape. The terrain here was hilly, with many waterfalls and streams crisscrossing through the landscape. I remembered reading that the citizens of Lochanlee relied on a vast network of interconnecting canals to traverse the realm, and that seemed to be true. I hadn't seen a single horse, and very few fae traveled on foot here. We passed several villages, but not major cities, and I realized this was a fairly rural region of Lochanlee.

Lochanlee. I shook my head, hardly able to believe I was actually here. When I was a child, it had been a dream of mine to visit the homeland of my father—or at least, the fictional male I'd thought was my father. Had he been based on a real person, or had Mother fabricated him entirely?

But whether or not the male she'd told me about ever existed, there was no doubt I had family somewhere here in Lochanlee. My actual mother was the Princess Olette, who had been a powerful water fae in her own right. She and my grandfather, the former king, had been members of House Usciete, which meant I was, too.

But would the water fae truly accept me? After all, I could only use one aspect of water magic, which would make me a lesser fae in their eyes. I wondered if maybe with practice, I could tap into other forms of water magic. After all, I clearly favored my water fae heritage, at least in terms of looks. Surely that meant my water magic had the potential to be just as powerful as my fire magic?

These thoughts chased themselves around in my mind as we traveled, passing small villages here and there, until finally we found ourselves in one of the strangest cities I'd seen yet. Rather than streets, it was sectioned into a series of concentric circular canals surrounding a lake, with houses built on the strips of land in between. A floating palace rose from the center of the city, its pearly walls stained golden-red by the dying sun. Water poured from the mouths of stone fish placed on the corners of the hipped roofs, flowering vines twined around its slender spires, and as we passed through the canals and into the inner lake, I gawked at the massive piranhas swimming lazily through the water. I'd only seen illustrations of them in textbooks, but I recognized the shape of their fins, and I knew razor-sharp teeth hid behind those jutting lower lips.

The sight of them reminded me of the koi Lady Mossi had weaponized against me, and I shivered, leaning away from the edge of the boat.

"A greater water fae, afraid of piranha?" the captain raised an eyebrow at me. "Never seen that before."

I pressed my lips together, but said nothing. Even though my powers had been unlocked by taking off my protective "amulet", I still didn't exhibit the full range of abilities a greater water fae should have. I wasn't sure why that was—if I just needed practice, or if there was some other secret of my birth that was preventing me from being able to fully command the water. But I hoped I could figure that out during my time here in Lochanlee.

"Thank the Radiants," Einar muttered as we clambered out of the boats. The soldiers were forced to assist him since he didn't have the use of his hands, but the moment his feet were on dry land, he shrugged their grips off. As I stared at the sunset backlighting the palace, I realized then that it had been close to twenty-four hours since the last time either of us had gotten any sleep. While the water had briefly invigorated me earlier, exhaustion and dizziness began to drag at my mind once more.

But this was no time to let my guard down. We were about to meet Lord Prentis, and I needed to be on my toes.

The soldiers herded us up the wide steps to the palace. Einar was finally allowed to walk next to me, and I brushed my shoulder against his in support, trying my best to be subtle about it. He visibly relaxed at the contact, and a tightness I hadn't realized was in my chest loosened in response.

I still didn't understand how someone who infuriated me so often could also be such a profound source of comfort and peace, but I wasn't about to question it now.

The soldiers guarding the entrance stared curiously as we passed, their blue-eyed gazes lingering on Einar in particular. He kept his golden eyes downcast, but I knew it was only a matter of time until someone figured out what he was. My stomach clenched with dread—what would Prentis do once he found out Einar was a dragon? Would they try to kill him? My fists clenched—I couldn't allow that to happen. Einar and I were in this together, for better or for worse. I would defend him, even if that meant making enemies out of the very people I was supposed to be asking for help.

"Wait here," the captain said as he led us into a receiving hall. "I'll inform Lord Prentis of your arrival."

He left us there, along with six soldiers, and though I tried to take a moment to familiarize myself in these new, lavish surroundings, I found my mind drifting. From what little I remembered of House Usciete's nobility, Lord Prentis was Lady Axlya's nephew... did that make him my cousin? I wondered if telling him I was Princess Olette's daughter would ingratiate myself with him, or if he would see me as a threat. My brief encounter with Lady Mossi had taught me that Greater Fae considered their family ties paramount to all other concerns... but did that apply to all the houses, or just hers?

Footsteps ringing against the tile floors pulled me from my thoughts, and I looked up to see the captain returning with a Greater Fae in his wake. Dressed in a periwinkle-blue tunic and matching trousers embroidered with silver thread, he was tall and handsome, with long, peacock-blue hair that fell in waves around his broad shoulders, and a regal-yet-friendly face. I expected him to greet us with suspicion, but his crystal blue eyes twinkled as he approached us, and to my surprise, his mouth widened into a welcoming smile.

"Cousin Adara!" He sailed over to me, and to my shock, took my shackled hand in his and pressed a kiss to it. "I'm Lord Prentis. Welcome to Thurston. It's wonderful to finally meet you."

I opened my mouth, not entirely sure how to respond to Prentis's audacity. Was he really going to pretend his soldiers hadn't just dragged me into the hall in chains? But the room chose that moment to swim, coalescing into a swirling kaleidoscope of colors. I sank to the ground, shouts echoing in my ears, and before I lost consciousness, my only thought was that after all the trials I'd faced, after killing the Shadows-damned king, I was brought low by the simple act of a male brushing his lips against my knuckles.

5

Lord Prentis

Prentis swooped in as Adara crumpled to the floor with all the aplomb of a discarded garment. He caught her before her head hit the ground, flinching a little as her coal-hot skin brushed against his forearm. A few feet away, her dragon companion struggled against the guards, but Prentis ignored him, brushing his hand against Adara's forehead and taking in her flushed complexion with a scowl.

"She's burning up," Prentis said, leveling a glare at the captain of the squad that had retrieved her. "Did you know she was ill when you captured her?"

"Yes," the captain admitted, looking more than a little uncomfortable. "But it didn't seem to be life-threatening, and you told us to bring anyone we found post-haste."

"Imbecile." Prentis wanted to roll his eyes, but that wasn't becoming of a man of his station. "She is of no use to me if she is dead! Fetch the healers at once."

The captain paled, then spun on his heel and strode from the room, two of his soldiers peeling away from the group to follow him. Sighing, Prentis untied Adara's wrists, which the captain had left bound, then carried her to a nearby settee. Gently, he set her down, then turned to face Einar, who had finally stopped struggling.

"Calm yourself, dragon. Adara will come to no harm while she is in my care."

Einar's eyes narrowed. "You know what I am."

Prentis scoffed. "Of course I know. I've been killing your kind for decades. And I was at Daryan and Olette's wedding, so I recognize you. You're Einar, the late dragon prince's closest confidante, and the former general of the dragon army."

"You, with your lily-white hands?" Einar sneered, his gold eyes flashing. "If I was at full strength, I don't think you'd be speaking so flippantly about killing dragons, you slimy water snake."

Prentis casually closed the distance between him and Einar, strolling up to the bound dragon as though he were a mildly interesting statue he was admiring on a garden stroll.

"Funny that you would call me a snake, when you're the one with scales and fangs, dragon."

The two males stared at each other for a long moment, stone-faced. Prentis could sense that Einar was severely exhausted, yet he still radiated the kind of feral energy a male only exhibits when his loved ones were in danger.

What sort of relationship did this dragon have with his cousin? Were they lovers, as Olette and Daryan had been? His jaw clenched at the thought—he remembered all too well how that had ended, and though he didn't know Adara, he did not wish Olette's fate upon any of his kin. If there was any connection between the two, he would have to do his best to break it.

"My aunt has spies in Kaipei Castle, dragon," Prentis said, close enough for his breath to whisper against Einar's cheek. "We've already heard about what happened between you and the former king. But I wonder, what is your agenda here? Why put your life at risk to help my cousin? And why has the fearsome dragon general chosen to appear now, when you've been cowering for the last two decades, hidden so well, in fact, that we all thought you were dead?"

Einar gave Prentis a slow smile. "You'd like for me to lose my temper and spill all my secrets, wouldn't you? To tell you how I survived, if there are other living dragons, and any other juicy tidbits that will ingratiate you to your dear Aunt Axlya?" The dragon general gave Prentis a slow once over. "How does it feel to be languishing in this backwater post, instead of lounging on the Edirian throne? Or did you think I'd forgotten that you were next in line before the people ousted you in favor of Aolis? That even your dear Auntie Axlya didn't back your claim?"

A tic started in Prentis's jaw, and Einar's smile widened. Prentis was tempted to throw the scaly bastard in the dungeons for the night, if only to teach him some manners. But he knew that if he did, he would have a hard time winning Adara's favor.

He would have to control his temper around the dragon, regardless of the fact that they were mortal enemies.

"Take our guest to his quarters, and remove the chains on his shackles," Prentis said, just as the healers entered the room. He broke Einar's gaze to watch them load Adara's unconscious form onto a stretcher. "Bring him a meal, and make sure he remains there until I send for him."

"I should be the one to go with her to the infirmary," Einar growled as Prentis made to follow Adara and the healers. "Not you."

Prentis glanced over his shoulder, briefly holding the dragon's golden gaze. "And yet, here you are."

He strode from the room, leaving his soldiers to deal with Einar. But Prentis didn't follow Adara and the healers to the infirmary. Instead, he took a left turn, then a right, and followed the main hallway to the courtyard at the heart of the palace.

The courtyard was circular, the walls carved with reliefs of the five water spirits—Rusa, Fonta, Nedis, Tiber, and Salaca. A small temple stood in the center, and Prentis ducked inside. He knelt in front of the stone altar, lit the five candles surrounding the prayer basin, then drew the curtain behind him for privacy.

With only the candlelight to guide him, Prentis withdrew a silver knife from his belt and made a small incision in his thumb. He held the wounded digit over the basin and allowed five drops of blood to fall into the basin, then sat back and waited.

Ten seconds later, Lady Axlya's oval face swam into view.

"Well?" she demanded. "Do you have the girl?"

"Yes, and her dragon companion," Prentis said.

Lady Axlya frowned as she leaned back in what Prentis suspected was a lounge chair. Her pale, bluish-white face was bare of any adornment, her cerulean hair cascading freely around her shoulders—a relaxed picture that differed greatly from the one she presented to the rest of the world. "You didn't find a way to get rid of him?"

"No," Prentis admitted, "and I don't think it would be wise to do so. I'm uncertain of the nature of Adara and Einar's relationship, but I sense they are close."

Axlya snorted. "Sounds like the girl has the same poor taste in males that her mother did," she said. She waved a jeweled hand. "No matter—you may bring the dragon with you if it ensures Adara's compliance, but only if he agrees to be shackled. I won't have an unbound dragon running free in my realm."

"Of course." Prentis inclined his head. He hesitated, then asked, "How is Cousin Cascada doing?"

Axlya smiled, her crystalline eyes lighting up in the way only a mother's did when speaking about a beloved child. "Recovering beautifully. She was riddled with shadow sickness when she arrived, but the healers were able to beat it back with copious amounts of everbright potion. She may have to take it for the rest of her life... but she is with us, and that's all that matters."

"I'm pleased to hear that." Cascada was the reason they knew the details of what happened at Kaipei Castle—she'd been in the room when Adara and Einar had combined their magic to defeat King Aolis and had told Axlya everything. Apparently she'd fled the castle with shadow soldiers on her heels, and followed a trail of aural lights to a grotto with an underwater tunnel. She'd gone in expecting only to travel a few yards, and had somehow ended up on the outskirts of Usciete. "The Radiants have been watching over our family."

"Indeed." Axlya inclined her head. "But we must remain vigilant if House Usciete is to remain in control of the throne. You will depart for Usciete tomorrow?"

"Yes."

"Good."

Axlya vanished from the water bowl, and Prentis knelt there for a moment longer, staring into his own reflection. His mouth was a grim line, his eyes glittering with a hope and determination he hadn't felt in a very long time.

He'd allowed the throne to slip through his fingers before, but the Radiants had given him another chance to claim it. And he would not let it slip through his fingers.

6

Einar

I waited until night had fully set in before I made my escape.

True to his word, Prentis made sure I was fed—a surprisingly decent meal of trout and vegetables—and had also posted a guard outside my door to make sure I didn't leave my quarters.

The room he'd given me was decent enough, with a view of the south side of the lake surrounding the palace. There was even a tub with three spouts, one emitting hot water, another cold, and another, bubbles. I wasted no time in using it, cleaning off the blood and grime and horror of the last few days. I washed my clothes as well, then used my fire magic to heat them until they were dry enough to put on again.

By the time I finished, the night was full of frosted starlight, the crescent moon winking at me from her perch in the sky. I stared up at her through the glass window for a moment, then carefully undid the latch and swung it inward. The poorly oiled hinges squealed, and I froze, heart pounding as I listened at the door. But if the guard stationed outside had heard anything, he'd clearly decided it wasn't worth investigating.

What a fool.

I shifted into my half-dragon form, wings sprouting from my back, claws extending from my fingers and toes, scales rippling up my calves and forearms, then hopped up onto the window ledge. Leaning out of the opening, I did a visual scan of the area, picking out the guards stationed on the walls and in the patrol boats cruising the lake. The guards on board would spot me if I flew, so instead I gripped the window ledge, then swung myself down and began climbing sideways.

Dragon claws are harder than stone, so I had no trouble scaling the wall, my clawed hands and toes puncturing the rock wherever I couldn't find a hand or foothold. Following the mating bond, I climbed around the palace until I found the infirmary in the east tower. Peering through the window, I saw Adara's supine form in one of the beds, chest rising and falling slowly. And while I imagined Prentis had posted a guard outside the infirmary door to ensure no one tried to get in, there was no one in the room watching over her.

I shook my head again, then summoned heat to my fingertip and pressed it against the window frame. The metal warped and bent, the latch on the inside bending just enough to allow me to ease the window open. Shifting back into bipedal form, I climbed in and shut the window as best I could, then quietly drew up a stool to Adara's bedside.

Adara didn't stir at my presence at all—not so much as a wrinkle in her brow, or a twitch of her pointed ears. The healers had likely put her into a deep, healing sleep so she could fight the infection and recover her magic faster. I sat and watched her for a long moment, debating the merits of slinging her over my shoulder, stealing back through the window, and making a run for it.

Eventually, I discarded the idea. I hadn't slept in nearly two days, and while the meal I'd eaten had given me enough energy to shift into my half-dragon form, I didn't have the energy to protect Adara if we left now.

If I was truthful with myself, I hadn't snuck out of my quarters so I could steal Adara away from Prentis's clutches.

I snuck out because I couldn't bear to be separated from her, even if just by a few walls. Not after I'd nearly lost her to Aolis.

Unable to help myself, I reached out and brushed the backs of my knuckles against Adara's cheek. She mumbled a little, turning into my touch, and though she didn't wake, her fingers reached up to curl around mine.

My heart skipped a beat at her feather-light touch, and it took all my willpower not to crawl into that criminally tiny bed and wrap myself around her. Every fiber of my being wanted to be as close to her as possible, to bury my nose in her hair, to feel her skin against mine and her long leg slung around my hip. To feel the heat of her core against my...

I growled as my cock began to stir, and ordered the blasted thing to stand down. Pulling in a deep breath through my nose, I gently extricated my fingers from Adara's and focused on my breathing until my blood calmed and the lust receded.

Well, somewhat, anyway.

Shaking my head, I slipped off the stool, then rummaged through the healer's supplies until I found a piece of twine. I tied one end to the doorknob, the other around my ankle, then made myself comfortable on the bed between Adara and the door. The healer was going to piss herself when she walked in tomorrow morning and found me here, and Prentis would throw a fit. But at least the bastard would know exactly who he was dealing with.

Smiling at the thought, I turned to look at Adara one last time, then slipped into a peaceful sleep.

7

Adara

An ear-splitting shriek woke me from the deepest sleep I'd ever had in my life.

"What is the meaning of this!" a voice roared, and I bolted upright in bed, heart hammering. I whipped my head around, looking for the source of the commotion, then blinked at the scene unfolding in front of me. A fae dressed in white healer's robes stood in the doorway, wringing her hands, her eyes wide with shock. Next to her was Prentis, his face livid with rage, a glowing water whip snaking from his outstretched hand.

And dangling upside down from it, by the ankle, was Einar.

"Put me down!" Einar snarled, or at least he tried to. His tunic was hanging around his face, muffling his words, his legs kicking as he tried to get free from the whip's grasp.

I stared at the ridiculous scene, my brain fogging with confusion as a jumble of memories crashed into my mind's eye from the last twenty-four hours. I knew I should get up and help him. That I should be questioning where I was, and probably be more concerned for both Einar's safety and mine.

But a small giggle escaped from my lips. Then another. And before I knew it, I was roaring with laughter.

Einar craned his neck to face me, and Prentis pursed his lips, his gaze flickering my way. "Do you find this amusing?" they asked simultaneously, then scowled at each other, which only made me laugh harder.

"I'm sorry." I clutched my aching sides and ballooned my cheeks, trying to get my mirth under control. "I know I shouldn't be laughing, but..." I gestured helplessly at the pair of them. "I can't help it. This is just so absurd. Please, Lord Prentis, put Einar down." Some of the laughter died from my expression when Prentis didn't immediately move to do so. "He's my protector. I'm sure that whatever he was doing here, it was for my safety."

Prentis huffed, and with a snap of his fingers, made the whip vanish. Einar crashed unceremoniously to the ground, but he was on his feet in a flash, fangs bared, golden eyes sparking with fire.

"You did that on purpose!"

"It's the least you deserve," Prentis retorted, stepping forward so the two males were nose to nose. "Shadows take it, how did you even get in here in the first place? I had guards posted outside both your doors!"

Einar smirked. "A dragon doesn't kiss and tell."

Prentis raised an eyebrow, his gaze turning to me. "Is that what was happening in here last night?"

I shrugged, trying to ignore the blush rising to my cheeks. "If any kissing occurred, it was without my knowledge. I was dead asleep."

Prentis's other eyebrow winged up as he looked back at Einar. "I didn't know dragons preferred their females unconscious."

I expected Einar to lose his temper at that, but he only

smirked. "Believe me, Lord Prentis, if I'd bedded Adara last night, you would have heard. As well as every servant and soldier within these palace walls."

The sensual confidence in Einar's voice slid down my spine like a lover's caress, and I clenched my legs together at the sudden rush of heat between them. "That's enough of that," I said hotly, swinging said legs over the side of the bed before Einar and Prentis could come to blows. "I'm guessing that Einar snuck into the infirmary last night to watch over me, and that you're pissed about it because he didn't stay quietly wherever you put him. But it's his *job to protect me,* Lord Prentis. Did you truly expect anything less of him?"

Prentis seemed taken aback as I approached him, not caring in the least that I was barefoot and clad in only a thin, white nightgown. "Protection from what, Cousin Adara? You are with your people now—"

"We were brought to your palace as prisoners," I interrupted, the memories falling into place now that I was properly awake. "I fainted from sickness and exhaustion moments after arriving on your doorstep. And while I thank you and your healer for treating me, I can't help wondering why you're so adamant about keeping away the one person in all of Ediria who has made it his mission to make sure I stay alive and safe. The only reason I can think for you to do that is that you have ill intentions, Lord Prentis. Is that the case?"

Prentis's lips thinned, and the room grew so quiet, you could have heard a pin drop. I could feel Einar's stare boring into me, but I didn't dare turn to look at him. Even so, the heat of his gaze sent a flush up the back of my neck, and I had to clench my hands at my sides to keep myself from shivering.

"I realize that we've gotten off to a rough start," Prentis said after a long moment. Einar scoffed loudly at this, but Prentis ignored him, his face softening into an earnest expression. He clasped my hand in both of his. "But you are family, Adara, and I would never want any harm to come to you. You have to know that."

I bit back a sigh, not entirely certain I believed Prentis's pretty words. But the fact remained that I needed allies in the water realm, and Prentis was as good a place to start as any. I didn't know what kind of game he was playing, but that didn't mean I couldn't play my own while I figured it out. If I wanted him to help me, I was going to have to pretend like his charms were working on me.

"I appreciate that, Lord Prentis," I demurred, lowering my lashes. "I admit, I have always been curious about my water fae heritage. I was raised in earth fae lands all my life, and had very little contact with water fae. I've never been very good at using my water magic, and I'm hoping I might fix that now that I'm here with you."

Prentis nodded gravely. "A genuine tragedy, to have been kept from your birthright for so long." He squeezed my hands once, then released them. "Lady Axlya will test your abilities in Usciete. I spoke to her last night, and she is expecting us tomorrow."

"So soon?" I asked, surprised. "But doesn't that mean we'll have to leave today?"

"Yes." He glanced sideways at Einar. "And unfortunately, Axlya has given express instructions that your dragon wear shackles while he is on water fae land."

"Shackles?" I repeated, outraged. "I thought I made myself clear—"

Prentis held up a hand. "I understand your position completely," he said, "and if there was anything I could do about it, I would. But I cannot gainsay the head of my house, Cousin Adara. Axlya's word is law in these lands. You should be lucky she's allowing Einar to accompany you to the capital at all."

I glanced at Einar, expecting him to be as furious as I was. But to my surprise, he only shrugged.

"Doesn't bother me," he said, holding his hands out to Prentis. "If putting irons on me will help Lord Prentis maintain the illusion that he's the superior male, I'm all for it."

He winked at me, and I nearly choked.

"That's clever, dragon," Prentis said. His tone was mild, but there was a tic fluttering in his jaw, betraying his anger. "But playing mind games with me won't change anything."

"I'm not playing any mind games." Einar smirked. "Just pointing out the obvious. I'm happy to agree to any demands Lady Axlya makes if it will ensure that I stay by Adara's side. But make no mistake, Lord Prentis," he said, a dangerous glint entering his golden eyes. "If you harm even a single hair on Adara's head, there are no shackles in this world strong enough to stop me from ripping out your heart, shoving it down your throat, and watching you choke on it with your dying breath."

"Charming." Prentis drawled. "But I've no wish to hurt Adara. In fact, if any harm comes to her while she's in my care, I'll gladly tear my heart out and offer it to you myself." He turned to me with a smile. "Now, why don't we let the healer have a look at you so we can pack up and be on our way?"

8

Mavlyn

"Is this really how you three snuck into Wynth last time?" Mavlyn hissed as she and Leap emerged through a manhole cover into an alley behind a grocery shop. She stomped her boots on the cobblestones, trying to shake off the muck from the sewer, still breathing shallowly through her mouth to minimize the stench.

"No," Leap said as he clambered out after her. He scrubbed a hand through his spiky white hair, and Mavlyn shook her head, unable to understand how he'd managed to remain spotless after they'd trekked three miles in an underground maze filled with rat dung, sewer water, and other unpleasant things. "We took the surface streets last time, but I didn't want to risk running into Storm or his cronies this time around."

"Fair enough." Mavlyn followed Leap out of the alleyway and into a charming section of the city filled with boutique shops and restaurants. Their doors and shutters were closed against the frigid wind, the tiny cobblestone streets empty save for the gently falling snowflakes collecting on their surfaces. But

Mavlyn wasn't surprised—it was well after midnight, as it had taken a full day for them to fly back to Wynth from Lochanlee.

She hadn't thought to find herself here again so soon, and especially not without Adara and Einar. But when she and Leap had attempted to follow their friends' trail, they'd run straight into a rainstorm. The downpour had been so heavy and vicious, Leap couldn't use his wind magic to cut a path through the rain clouds.

It was clear someone was using water fae magic to stop anyone from pursuing Adara, so they'd attempted to circumvent it by flying to Usciete—where, Leap reasoned, Adara would eventually end up—rather than following Adara directly. That had worked better, but the moment Leap and Mavlyn had gone to the ground, patrolling water fae soldiers had set upon them with orders to bring "any foreign fae without proper documentation" to the capital for questioning. They'd barely escaped, and had nearly been caught in another magical storm before they'd made it across the Lochanlee border and back into neutral fae territory.

With no way to get to Adara, they'd decided to go and find the only person who they could trust to help them.

The Oracle.

Looking past the building rooflines, Mavlyn gazed at the air temple looming above the city, the brilliant arcs of electricity emanating from the tips of its spires blazing like stars falling to the earth. Her heart skipped a beat at the thought of coming face to face with Quye again—their first encounter had been brief, but the Oracle's mischievous smile and electric blue eyes had haunted Mavlyn's dreams ever since. She wondered if Quye was watching them even now, perhaps from a balcony high atop one of the spires, her wild mane of snow-white curls whipping in the wind as she waited for their arrival.

She would have foreseen Leap and Mavlyn's arrival. Of that,

Mavlyn was certain. But the real question was, would Quye help them?

"Come on," Leap said, shaking Mavlyn from her reverie. "This way."

He led Mavlyn up the winding city streets, switchbacking up the mountain toward the base of the temple. But instead of taking the main road that led to the front entrance, they cut through a neighborhood tucked right against the edge of a small forest.

The moment they entered the wooded area, Mavlyn relaxed. The scents of pine and loamy earth wrapped around her senses like a mother's welcoming arms, the soft warbling of nocturnal birds a soothing lullaby. For half a second, she could almost imagine she was back in Domhain. That in just a few more steps, she would emerge in her backyard to the sound of her father hammering away in the forge, or her mother humming one of her folksongs as she prepared the venison stew she loved to make on cold winter nights such as this.

A twinge of guilt pinched at Mavlyn's chest at the thought of her parents, who had to be worried sick. Her father had returned home from his travels shortly after Adara and Einar had fled Fenwood, and he and Mavlyn had fought bitterly when she told him she was going after Adara. Mavlyn understood why he hadn't wanted her to go—he was no stranger to the dangers shadow creatures posed along the roads, and Mavlyn *was* his only child. Not to mention she'd been set to start at Talamh University in just a few days.

But Mavlyn knew it would be impossible to focus on her studies while her best friend was in mortal peril. And so, with the promise that she would travel with Mrs. Aeolan, her parents had reluctantly allowed Mavlyn to go.

Mavlyn wished she could hug them and tell them not to worry about her. Or at least tell them she was all right. Maybe

Quye could help her send a message to them so they would know she was still alive.

But first, they had to get inside the temple without getting caught by the guards.

Mavlyn and Leap crept silently through the woods, which were tucked below a service road that wound around the back of the temple. Another fae might have climbed the cliff wall up to that road, taken it to the service entrance, and tried to sneak past the guards by posing as deliverymen.

But Leap wasn't just any fae. He was a member of the air fae nobility, cousin to the Oracle herself. And as such, he had a few tricks up his sleeve.

"Here we go," Leap murmured after searching along the cliff wall for several minutes. He pressed his thumb against a small green stone jutting out of the wall, barely larger than a coat button. A deep groan reverberated from the earth, and a rectangular section of the wall swung inward to reveal a stone staircase.

"Well, I'll be damned." Mavlyn clapped Leap on the shoulder. "You were right."

"Of course I'm right," Leap huffed. "Quye used to sneak out of the temple all the time when we were kids. I would meet her here once a week and take her to play knucklebones with my friends." A wistful look entered his eyes, and Mavlyn imagined he was remembering happier times, when his parents had still been alive and he'd been a carefree boy. "Judging by the look of these footprints, I'd say she still uses the entrance."

Mavlyn cast a look at the boot outlines on the base of the dusty steps. "Yeah, but it looks like it's been at least a week since she's tried." Opening one of the pouches at her belt, she pulled out a dried flower bud and placed it in the center of her palm. She held it up to the moonlight and allowed a tiny bit of magic to flow from her hand into the plant. The bud came to life at once, color flooding into the petals as they opened. For a moment, nothing happened, but then the bluish-white petals began to glow, absorbing the moonlight from the trees and reflecting it back into Leap's shining eyes.

"A moon blossom," he said in a hushed voice, reaching out to touch it. "Where'd you get it? They're supposed to be rare."

Mavlyn smacked his hand away. "I got this from Talamh University's gardens when I visited for my exam last summer. It's one of the rarest specimens I own, and it's quite fragile, so keep your hands to yourself."

"Fine." Pouting, Leap stepped aside and swept an arm toward the staircase. "Guess you'll have to lead the way, then."

She grinned. "That was the idea."

Balancing the moon blossom carefully in her hand, Mavlyn started up the staircase, Leap following close behind. The earthen door closed behind them with a groan, leaving them in total darkness save for the moonlight emanating from the flower in Mavlyn's palm. Up and up and up they climbed, the staircase zig zagging through the mountain, until her breath came in pants and her legs trembled from the exertion.

"Finally," she gasped as they reached a landing with a single door. While Leap pressed his ear against it to listen for guards, Mavlyn gently closed her fists around the moon blossom and focused her power again, this time drawing its essence into her body. The flower shriveled back into a bud, and she gently replaced it in its pouch.

"All clear," Leap murmured. He pushed the door open, and they emerged into an empty salon. Mavlyn's heart leapt in her chest at the sight of Quye sitting on a settee facing the fireplace, her white hair a curly halo around her head as she bent over a thick tome.

She waited for the Oracle to turn around, to tell them she'd been expecting them, to ask what had taken them so long, but the female on the couch didn't move. Didn't even seem to have noticed their arrival.

"Oi," Leap said, his voice as loud as a whip-crack in the silent room. "No pithy comments for us today, Quye?"

Quye jumped like a rat whose tail had been caught in a trap, the book falling from her hands as she spun around to face them. Mavlyn's mouth dropped open, mirroring the same shock on her face, but for entirely different reasons because —

"You're not Quye."

Leap was between me and the imposter in an instant, lightning crackling at his hands, an accusatory finger jabbed in the woman's direction. "Who in the Shadows are you, and where's Quye?"

"Guards!" the woman shrieked. She was a close copy, her slender, willowy figure and curly, snow-white hair almost identical to the Oracle's. But her eyes were heavy-lidded, her mouth too wide, and her high-pitched voice was absolutely nothing like the Oracle's playfully sultry tones. "Guards, *there are intruders in my room!*"

The door crashed open, and four temple guards rushed into the room, swords drawn. They looked ready to lop the intruders' heads off, but the one in the lead's eyes widened in recognition as he stared at Leap.

"You!" He jabbed his sword in Leap's direction. "You're Lord Oren's nephew!"

"Who, me?" Leap's hands were suddenly behind his back, the lightning vanishing from his fingertips as though it had never been there. "No, no, I'm just a commoner. I came to ask the Oracle if she'd tell me my future."

Six more guards filed into the room. "Nice try," the lead guard said as the others surrounded Mavlyn and Leap on all sides. "But I saw the lightning in your hands, and the family resemblance is unmistakable." He smiled. "Lord Oren is going to be *thrilled* when I tell him we've found you."

"*No.*"

Leap whipped his hands out from behind his back, balls of lightning sizzling in the palms of his hands. "I don't care what orders you have," he snarled. "You're not taking me to him!"

But before Leap could attack, one of the guards threw an iron net on him. The lightning magic in Leap's hands fizzled in an instant, and he cried out as four of the guards jumped him to keep him from throwing off the net.

"Leap!" Mavlyn pulled a handful of seeds from her pouch and tossed them to the ground. The seeds exploded on contact, filling the room with noxious purple smoke, and she held her breath, waiting for the paralytic effect to take hold. But before the smoke could spread further, a gust of wind swept through the room and whisked it up into a vent.

Something heavy struck the back of Mavlyn's head, and stars exploded in her vision. "Clever bitch," the lead guard said as she dropped to her knees, head spinning. She felt him yank her arms behind her back, sobbed as he clasped manacles around her wrists and the magic drained right out of her. "But I wouldn't expect anything less from an earth fae assassin."

"I'm not an assassin—" she tried to say, but someone shoved a gag in her mouth, choking off the rest of her words.

"Save your breath for Lord Oren, not me," the guard said as they hauled her to her feet. "You'll be taken to him tomorrow, and you can explain how you bewitched his nephew and convinced him to help you sneak into the temple to get to his niece." He gave her a wide smile that sent chills down her spine. "I'm sure he'll be *very* understanding."

9

Adara

S alt spray stung my nose as I stood at the prow of Prentis's
ship, watching the coastline shrink into the distance. Once
the healer had determined I was healthy, Prentis had wasted no
time in getting us underway, the supplies for the journey already
loaded onto the ship and ready to go. Tomorrow evening, we
would be in Usciete, and I would present myself to Lady Axlya,
ruler of the water fae.

The thought sent a frisson of nerves skittering down my
spine, and I gripped the railing hard, nails digging into the time-
worn wood. Though honestly, I wasn't sure why I should be
nervous at the idea of meeting House Usciete's matriarch. I'd
faced so many of Ediria's power players already—Lady Mossi,
the Harpy Queen, the Oracle, General Slaugh, and King Aolis—
and had more or less come away unscathed from each
encounter.

Then again, Lady Axlya wasn't just another noble. She was
my maternal great-grandmother, the head of the house my
mother had grown up in. In another life, she might have doted

on me as a child, given me the benefit of her wisdom, perhaps even cheered me on as I pursued dreams and exploits. And I would have had cousins, aunts, uncles, people who would have embraced me and taught me how to use my magic.

Your water *magic, you mean.*

The voice in my head brought me up short, shattering the quaint little fantasy I'd been building in my head. Because of course, I wasn't just my mother's daughter. I was a child of dragons, my late father the dragon prince himself. Fire magic coursed through my veins, magic that had been so dangerous, my mother had an amulet fashioned for me to make sure it stayed hidden away.

If my parents hadn't been killed, if they'd become the king and queen of our newly joined realms, perhaps my magic would have been accepted, even revered as a symbol of the union.

But I knew all too well from my experience in Fenwood how people felt about outsiders. My neighbors had ostracized me not just for my water fae features, but for being a magical cripple. If Lady Axlya had taken me in instead of Gelsyne, and if my fire magic hadn't been suppressed, who knows how I would have been treated?

And who knew how I would be treated now, after using said magic to kill King Aolis, who, for all his flaws, had been one of Lady Axlya's nephews? I knew nothing about Axlya, what her relationship to her kin was like, but I remembered how attached Lady Mossi had been to hers. So much so that she'd been willing to trade me to King Aolis to get her great-granddaughter back. And that was after *knowing* that Gelsyne, another of her granddaughters, had spent her life raising me and keeping me out of his clutches.

I'd made the mistake of putting my trust in the wrong people before. And while I wanted—no, *needed*—Lady Axlya to help me, I couldn't walk into this as naively as I had with

Lady Mossi. I had to hope for the best, but be prepared for anything.

A tingling sensation running down the back of my neck distracted me from my thoughts, and I turned my head, gaze trailing up the middle mast until I found Einar perched on the crossbeam, legs dangling in the open air. He'd flown up there not long after we set sail, claiming he suffered terrible seasickness unless he was close to the sky, so I hadn't had a chance to speak to him alone yet.

Our gazes met, gold on blue, and my heart surged into my throat. Even at this distance, I could see the swirling storm of emotions behind his eyes, and I could tell there was so much he wanted to say to me. The unfinished conversation from before seemed to swell between us, and the pressure of words unsaid made my chest ache.

I wanted to climb up that mast, pin him to the beam, and demand an explanation. I wanted to know why he seemed like he could barely stand me, and yet couldn't seem to stay away. Why he'd gone from being a reluctant ally to a staunch protector. Why he'd held me with such tenderness earlier, when just a few days ago, he'd barely been able to stomach touching me.

Because that was the truth, wasn't it? That even though we'd been through so much together, we'd really only known each other for a few weeks. That wasn't nearly enough time for such a drastic change of heart, for two people to go from loathing each other to... to...

"Adara." I jerked my gaze away from Einar's at the sound of Prentis's voice and turned to see him walking across the deck toward me. "I was hoping I would find you here."

"Lord Prentis." Clearing my throat, I turned toward him properly, putting my back to Einar. I could still feel his gaze on me, but I did my best to ignore it, focusing on the male in front of me instead.

"Please, there's no need to be formal." Prentis stopped in front of me, a lopsided smile on his face. He stood there awkwardly for a moment, seeming not to know what to do with his hands, before finally deciding to shove them into his trouser pockets. "You can just call me Prentis."

"All right." I forced a smile. "Prentis."

He sighed, his face falling. "You're still angry with me, aren't you." It wasn't a question.

"I'm trying not to be," I admitted, my gaze flicking up at Einar. He was no longer looking at me, his gaze trained on the horizon, but I had no doubt he was listening to every word. "You put my protector in shackles after I deliberately told you not to. But," I added, holding up a hand before Prentis could protest, "I recognize that in these lands, my words hold little weight. I can't gainsay Lady Axlya's orders, no matter how much I wish otherwise."

"I'm glad you understand," Prentis said, sounding genuinely grateful. He glanced up at Einar as well, then back to me. "I may not be comfortable having a dragon in my territory any more than any fae would, but for all his flaws, I can see Einar is deeply loyal to you. If it was in my power, he would walk freely by your side so he can protect you when I cannot."

"I didn't realize my protection was your responsibility, Prentis."

I expected Prentis to bristle at my tone, but instead he laughed, his crystal-blue eyes sparkling. I had to admit he cut a fine figure in his navy peacoat and leather boots—if they weren't so polished and fancy, I might have mistaken him for a sailor. "Olette used to use the same haughty voice whenever she would put someone in their place," he said. "You remind me a lot of her."

"I do?" My defensiveness crumbled away, and I leaned closer, eager to hear more about my mother. "Did the two of you spend much time together?"

"Oh, yes." Prentis smiled. "We grew up together in Usciete, only a few years apart in age. Olette was very competitive, and we did our magical training together, so we were always trying to best each other—seeing who could make the biggest rain clouds, the longest water whips, the sharpest ice blades." His expression softened. "She was a fierce fighter when she had to be, but her greatest talent lay in healing."

I blinked. "Water magic can be used for healing?"

"Of course. There are a great many things that one can do with water magic." He twirled his fingers, and a ribbon of water began to wind its way through them, back and forth, back and forth, slowly transforming into a tiny sea serpent, complete with fangs and scales. It raised its glittering head above Prentis's knuckles, tongue flickering, and I swore it winked at me. "I'd love to show you, if you'll let me."

My heart leapt at the prospect, but my gaze dropped to my boots as shame crept across my cheeks. "My water magic doesn't work properly," I confessed. "It never has, really."

He frowned. "What do you mean?"

I bit my lip, thinking of the amulet. Of the secrets kept from me all my life that had all unraveled in a matter of days. "It's a long story."

He leaned against the railing, his gaze intent upon my face. "I'm a good listener."

I opened my mouth, ready to come up with an excuse, a refusal, but something about the way Prentis was looking at me made me stop and reconsider. It was true Lady Axlya was the one I needed to win over, but Prentis was a member of her court, which meant he had influence over her. The more allies I could make in House Usciete, the better.

And so, I told Prentis about the struggle with my magic. Told him about the amulet my mother had ordered Gelsyne to make me wear, and how I'd always struggled to make my power manifest until that fateful day at the army trials when Dune had ripped it from my chest and I'd nearly burned everyone alive. How even though my fire magic raged wild and fierce like a storm, my water magic was more like a sluggish river, and that aside from ice, I didn't seem to be able to manipulate it at all.

"Do you think I'll only ever be able to wield ice magic?" I asked, worry gnawing at my gut. "And will Lady Axlya think me weak because of it?"

Prentis chewed on his lower lip as he considered my questions, his crystal blue gaze scanning the horizon. The coastline was a distant memory now, the ocean stretching endlessly around us in all directions.

"It's hard to say whether you're only able to control ice magic because that's the only water magic you inherited from your mother, or because you haven't unlocked your inner beast with your coming-of-age ceremony," he finally said. "But it would be quite strange to me if your water fae magic was recessive, considering how strongly your features favor your water fae heritage."

He reached out and brushed a lock of my lavender-blue hair away from my face, briefly letting it curl around his index finger before it fell away. We stared at each other for a long moment, and I wondered if I should balk against the intimate touch, or let it slide in favor of continuing the conversation.

A rustle of wings interrupted my train of thought, and I turned to see Einar land a few feet away from us, his boots thumping heavily on the deck. His expression was placid as he surveyed us, but I didn't miss the glint in his golden eyes as he looked between me and Prentis.

"Something I can help you with, dragon?" Prentis asked, raising an eyebrow.

"Not at all," Einar smiled right back. He tucked his wings

behind his back as he leaned against the mast behind him, looking at ease despite the shackles he wore. Prentis had added more length to the chains so Einar could move his hands freely, and had allowed Einar to shift into his half-dragon form so he wasn't completely defenseless. I knew he'd made the concessions for my sake, not Einar's, but I couldn't help appreciating them nonetheless. "I got tired of staring at the ocean, so I thought I'd come down here for a change of scenery."

A massive wave smacked the side of the ship just then, and I gripped the railing to keep from pitching forward. Einar's face went green as he stumbled across the deck, and he grabbed the railing on the opposite side before turning around to pin Prentis with a glare.

"You did that on purpose, didn't you?"

Prentis chuckled. "I assure you, I would not waste my magic on something so petty. The sea is doing a fine job tormenting you without my assistance."

Einar huffed. "This is—" he started, but a startled yelp choked the rest of his sentence off as a massive eggplant-colored tentacle rose from beyond the hull and twined around his waist.

"Einar!" I shrieked as the creature yanked him overboard. I raced across the deck just in time to see him disappear beneath the churning waves of the ocean, and though I had no idea what manner of monster had taken him, I leapt the railing and dove right after him.

"Adara, wait!" Prentis cried as I sliced through the water, arms pointed straight in front of me. The world went quiet around me as water replaced air, and it took my eyes a minute to adjust, the ocean blurring everything around me. But once my vision cleared, I froze at the impossible sight twenty feet below me.

The tentacle that had swiped Einar from the deck of Prentis's ship belonged to a giant sea creature. It looked something like an octopus, with a round head and bulging eyes with yellow sclera. That is, if octupuses had sixteen tentacles instead of eight, and were roughly half the size of Prentis's ship.

There was only one creature it could be, and my heart sank straight into my shoes as I remembered the stories and illustrations from my childhood.

A kraken.

Einar fought valiantly against the thing's hold, using his claws to tear at the monster's appendages, but the chains around his wrist limited his range, so his strikes weren't very effective. The monster roared, baring rows of golden teeth as sharp as daggers, and he used another tentacle to bind Einar's arms to his sides, then lifted him toward his mouth.

I raised my hands as I called to my power, a half-cocked plan forming in my mind. But a flicker of movement out of the corner of my eye caught my attention, and on instinct, I turned to look. My mouth dropped open at the sight of a massive ice blue orca with mother-of-pearl fins hurtling through the water. I'd never seen one before, but judging by the descriptions I'd read, this orca was twice the size of a normal one. My bowels went watery when its maw opened wide, revealing rows of ivory teeth as long as my arms that could easily spear me in two.

But as its crystal-blue eyes locked on me, the fear that caught me by the throat evaporated instantly, replaced by a sense of recognition.

Prentis.

The orca barreled past me, and I whipped around to see him dive for the kraken. I expected the sea monster to drop Einar, but he merely held his prize out of reach as he avoided the orca's first strike. Purple ink oozed out of the kraken's tentacles, but an invisible force whipped the fluid away before it could coalesce around us. Prentis turned around and attacked again, this time closing its maw around one of the tentacles. The kraken let out a warbling shriek of pain, its cries muffled by the ocean as its appendage was severed, and golden blood clouded the water, creating a shimmering haze.

Furious, the kraken lashed out with two of its tentacles, slapping the side of the orca's face. Huge angry welts bubbled on the side of Prentis's face, and I winced, wondering if there was some kind of poison in them. But I also noticed that the kraken had finally dropped Einar... and that my dragon protector was unconscious, and slowly sinking toward the ocean floor.

Panic flooded my veins, and I began swimming frantically toward him, trying to reach Einar before the sea could claim him. As I dove deeper, the darkness seemed to rise around me, threatening to swallow us whole. Only a hint of light remained, illuminating Einar's normally swarthy complexion with a pale, bluish tint. His golden eyes were hazy as they met mine, the life fading away from them, his wings fluttering uselessly behind him.

"Damn you!" I shouted, a froth of livid bubbles escaping my mouth along with the words. "You're stronger than this, Einar. For Radiant's sake, *fight!*"

Something in my words must have reached him, because his legs twitched a little, and his eyes flashed open. His wings, which had been hanging limp, flared wide, and they flapped hard against the water, propelling him upward toward me.

Yes, I crowed silently as he finally came within reach. Above me, the battle between the orca and the kraken continued to rage, but I only had eyes for Einar. Hope flared in my chest as I finally closed my hand around his wrist, heedless of the scales scraping against my palm. But it dimmed when I noticed the life was fading away from him, strength leaving his limbs as the water in his lungs choked off his remaining oxygen.

No. I won't lose him like this.

Power surged in me, and searing pain sliced through the side of my neck. On pure instinct, I placed my hand against his chest, pushing my power into him as I demanded that the water vacate his lungs.

His mouth opened wide, and a torrent of bubbles rushed out as the water spewed from his body, clearing his lungs and esophagus. Before he could suck in more, I yanked him into me and pressed my mouth against his, breathing oxygen from my body into his.

His body stiffened, and then he gripped me tight, his claws tearing through my clothing and into my flesh as he sucked more air from me. At first I thought there was no air left to give, but as he flapped his wings, propelling us toward the surface, I felt something ripple through the sides of my neck. My eyes opened wide as my lungs expanded, and my hands flew to my neck to feel fresh, ragged slices rippling along the skin.

Gills. Giant's teeth, those are gills!

Einar pulled his mouth away from mine, some of the life returning to his eyes, his lungs clear of water and filled with oxygen once more. But he was still weak, his brain still waterlogged from the near-drowning, so I grabbed him by the underarms and kicked upward, fighting against the ocean pressure to push us to the surface.

Above us, the battle continued to rage, Prentis snapping at the kraken's tentacles while doing his best to avoid the sea monster's poisonous blows. I tried to angle us away from the kraken, but the beast chose that moment to swivel one bulbous yellow eye toward us. Rage flashed in the depths of its iris, and it speared a massive tentacle toward us, so fast I knew there was no way my leaden legs could clear it in time.

The danger finally snapped Einar out of his fugue state, and he yanked me against him, arms banding tight as his wings flapped mightily, shoving us upward through the water and away from the kraken. A mighty force swelled beneath us, and we shot to the surface so fast, I was instantly light-headed. Dizziness swamped me, and I leaned away from Einar and vomited my breakfast out into the open air.

"I've got you," Einar said roughly, refusing to let go of me even though I'd probably splattered kippers and porridge all over his trousers. He flapped his wings hard again, shaking the water off them, then glided down to the deck of the ship waiting just a few yards off. My head was still spinning as we collapsed on the deck of the ship, Einar angling his body to shield me from the impact. As the cacophony of rushing footsteps echoed in my ears, I realized why I was still dizzy, why the edges of my vision were blackening, why I couldn't focus.

"She's not breathing!" Einar shouted, his voice stretched taut with panic. He gripped my shoulders hard as he pulled me up into a sitting position, his panic-stricken face moving in and out of focus. "Adara, you need to breathe! *Please!*"

I opened my mouth, trying to suck in air, but I couldn't get my throat to open. My gills flapped uselessly against the sides of my neck, trying to pull air in through the water, but of course there was no water, just air, and why couldn't I breathe in the air—

"Adara. Look at me."

I blinked at the sight of Prentis crouching in front of me, not sure how he got there. Icy fingers gripped my chin gently, forcing me to meet his crystal-blue gaze, and my vision narrowed until he was all I could see.

"Relax," he said, his voice low and hypnotic. "You're safe now. Einar is safe now, and he doesn't need your oxygen anymore. You can let go of your power now."

I blinked, realizing that I was still using my magic, that it was pulsing in my veins, sizzling along my skin. There was a strange sensation between my fingers and toes, and I lifted one hand to see webbing had formed between my digits, and patches of blue scales shimmered along the back of my hand.

Somehow, I'd forced some kind of transformation with my magic, a transformation that had allowed me to breathe oxygen from the water and give it to Einar, and to swim faster so I could get him to the surface.

But we were safe now. I didn't need these gills, this webbing anymore. It was okay. I could let go.

"That's it," Prentis murmured as I released the vise grip on my magic. It slowly receded from my veins, the gills and webbing along with it, and I sucked in a gulp of air as my throat finally relaxed. "You're okay, Adara. You're okay."

"Thank you," I gasped, still trying to get my bearings. I was a little woozy, but my head was clearing with each breath, my surroundings coming into focus. I realized that most of the crew had gathered around us, gawking openly. Self-consciousness prickled across my skin, but I tried to ignore it, instead turning to Einar, who was kneeling two feet to my right, his golden gaze fixed on mine. I reached for him, and he gripped my hand with his clawed one, chains clanking with the movement.

"That," he said in a rasping voice, his throat likely raw from all the water he'd inhaled, "was the most foolish thing you've ever done."

I snatched my hand back, the tips of my ears burning. "Just what is that supposed to mean?" I demanded.

"It means that *I* am supposed to protect *you*, not the other way around!" Einar snarled, his golden eyes sparking with ire. "You barely know how to use your water magic, and yet you dove after me and that shadows-damned *kraken* instead of letting Prentis or any of the other water fae handle it!"

He grabbed my shoulders, clawed fingers scraping against the wounds he'd already made, looking as though he was a hairsbreadth away from shaking me like a rag doll. "You're the only person in the entire world who can defeat Nox and purge the shadow magic from the realm! You can't afford to risk yourself for anyone, even me!"

Furious, I shoved Einar away from me and surged to my feet, ignoring our rapt audience. "Well, if you don't want me rescuing your sorry ass, maybe try not getting so distracted by petty arguments that you don't notice when a giant sea creature rises out of the water and attacks you!"

I turned to Prentis, who was staring at us both, a dozen questions swirling in his crystalline gaze. "Thank you for fighting so valiantly for us today," I said, giving him the sunniest smile I could muster even though I was fuming. "And for keeping me from suffocating myself."

I planted a sound kiss on his cheek, just to piss Einar off, then spun on my heel and stomped toward the stairs, heading for my cabin belowdecks.

"Very impressive, the way you shoved your foot into your mouth like that," I heard Prentis say smugly as I headed down the staircase. "You've managed to to insert it so far, I think I can see your toes wiggling out of your ass."

"Shut up, or I'll shove my toes up *your* ass."

I rolled my eyes, but as their voices faded away, the exhaustion rushed back into me, making my limbs so leaden I could barely lift one foot in front of the other. Somehow, I managed to make it to my cabin and drag off my wet clothes.

Questions crowded in my brain as I wondered how I'd transformed, what facet of my power I'd accessed, but the moment my back hit the mattress, darkness crashed in on me. I could ask my questions tomorrow, when I had the energy to deal with Prentis and Einar and their annoying rivalry.

But right now, all I wanted was sleep.

Lady Mossi

So, it's true.

Lady Mossi stared at Kaipei Castle as she clung to the back of her griffin, her neck pressed against its feathered neck to shield her from the worst of the cold. It had been years since she'd last come to the capital—in fact, she had not set foot in the place since King Aolis had the Edirian crown placed on his accursed head.

But she'd seen it plenty of times from afar, seen the noxious cloud of shadow magic that had hung over it. That cloud was a clear sign of the infestation that all had known about, but had desperately turned a blind eye to for years.

But now, just like that fateful day nearly two decades ago, that shadow was nowhere to be seen. The clouds that clustered over Kaipei now were fat, fluffy, and pearly-grey, heavy with the impending winter snowstorm.

The other house heads—Lord Oren and Lady Axlya— would have noticed as well. Oren would have heard whispers on the wind from his precious Oracle, and Axlya would have seen glimpses using that annoying water scrying ability of hers.

But it was Mossi who would see the truth of things with her own eyes.

Flanked by the remaining griffin riders in her cadre, Lady Mossi landed in the outer bailey of the castle. The courtyard and much of the walls were in ruins, badly damaged by what appeared to be lightning strikes, and many of the flagstones were now missing.

"Lady Mossi." An earth fae dressed in a stable master's uniform came rushing up to help her dismount. "May I take your griffins to the stables to be fed and watered?"

Mossi shook her head. "You may feed and water them, but they will remain here in the courtyard." She gestured to one of her riders, who stepped forward. "Monty will remain with you and give you instructions for their care."

Her lips thinned as she looked around at her cadre—only six griffins left, out of the fourteen she'd had but a few days ago. That bitch Adara and her bloodthirsty dragon had taken out nearly all of them when they'd fled. She should have pursued them herself, but she had forgotten exactly how devastating a single dragon could be.

That was one mistake she'd never make again.

The front doors of the castle opened, and General Slaugh walked out. "My Lady Aunt," he said, his mutilated face pulling into a grotesque smile. "Thank you for coming so quickly."

Lady Mossi snorted. "I had my griffins saddled as soon as I received your message." She rushed up the steps and took his hand in hers as she scanned his face. "So, it's true then? King Aolis is dead? Killed by that upstart brat, Adara?"

"It is true," a feminine voice said, stepping out from behind the doors. She smiled, and Lady Mossi's jaw dropped. "Did you miss me, Grandmother?"

"Gelsyne!" Lady Mossi dropped Slaugh's hand. "Is it really you?" She looked her granddaughter up and down, noting the paler skin, the dark hair and sinister black eyes, the hip-hugging dress that was very much not Gelsyne's style. And yet the curve of her cheek, the shape of her mouth and nose, the willowy figure, were very much hers. "What happened to—"

Gelsyne stepped forward and flung her arms around Lady Mossi, enveloping her in a fierce hug. "It's been so long," she whispered, and her voice seemed to *slither* into Lady Mossi's ear, dulling her thoughts. Her suspicions dwindled away, eclipsed by the relief and happiness she felt at seeing her long-lost granddaughter alive again. "I wish I could have visited you. Wish I could have sat in the atrium and tended the flowers with you like we always did."

"I wish that too." Anguish tightened Lady Mossi's throat even as joy swelled in her chest. She pulled back so she could look at Gelsyne properly. "I still don't understand why you didn't."

"I should have." Guilt crossed Gelsyne's face, and she looked away, as though ashamed. "There were so many times when I could have used your guidance. But Olette made me promise to keep Adara a secret from everyone, including you. It was her dying wish, and I swore to uphold it."

"So Adara truly is Olette and Daryan's daughter," Lady Mossi said. She shook her head—it made sense, of course, but it was one thing to suspect, and another for it to be confirmed aloud. "She told me you raised her when she came to visit me."

Gelsyne's eyes flickered, turning emerald for just a moment, and Lady Mossi could have sworn she saw stark fear, a cry for help. But in the next second they were pure black again, the flash of emotion gone.

"Yes, she came to you and asked for help, didn't she? And your plan was to trade her to Aolis for me and Avani."

"Yes, well, King Aolis would have demanded I hand her over once he found out I had her," Lady Mossi said, a little defensively. "I wasn't about to risk the safety of my family or my realm for her."

"Oh grandmother, I'm not blaming you." Gelsyne placed a comforting hand against Lady Mossi's cheek. "You did what you felt you had to under the circumstances."

Slaugh cleared his throat, and they both turned to look at him. "If we could take this inside?" he asked politely. "There is much to discuss, and I'm sure you are hungry."

"Yes, of course."

Slaugh led Lady Mossi and her cadre into the castle, where they were shown to their quarters. Mossi took some time to freshen up and change into a dress before she met Slaugh and Gelsyne in the dining room, along with her general and advisor. Several members of the kingsguard stood along the walls of the room, but Lady Mossi hardly paid them any mind as she dug into the feast laid out on the table. She'd traveled a full day and night to get here, and was positively famished.

"So Adara has killed King Aolis and run off with her dragon lover," Lady Mossi said once she'd assuaged the worst of her hunger. "Which has left you in charge of Kaipei Castle."

"That's correct." Slaugh took a sip from the wine goblet in his hand. "No one has challenged me so far, but we all know that is because the other houses haven't gathered their wits yet. My spies tell me that Adara is on her way to the water capital, where I gather she will seek Lady Axlya's backing so she can assume the throne. Axlya will be only too happy to take advantage of the situation."

"Of course she will," Lady Mossi sneered. She sat back in her chair and assessed the situation for a moment. Axlya would no doubt spin Adara as the savior of the realm, since shadow magic vanished the moment she killed Aolis. It wasn't just the cloud that had disappeared from above Kaipei Castle—reports had been coming in across Domhain that the pockets of shadow infestation that had been plaguing their lands had mysteriously vanished.

It appeared Aolis had been right about the prophecy, and the girl's role in it.

But the bastard probably hadn't counted on his own death being part of the solution.

"I think we all agree that the realm owes Adara a great debt," Gelsyne said. "But though I love Adara and have raised her as my own all these years, I don't think she should take the throne. She doesn't have the experience or knowledge necessary to rule, and her half-dragon lineage will make the people very reluctant to follow her."

She reached for Slaugh's hand, twined her delicate fingers with his big, rough hand.

"I think the water fae need to relinquish their control over the Edirian throne," she said. "It's time for the earth fae to rule again."

Lady Mossi's eyebrows rose as she took in their joined hands, the cunning glint in Slaugh's eyes and the smile on Gelsyne's face. "You want to claim the Edirian throne? As king and queen?"

"Yes," Slaugh said. He leaned across the table, his burned face stretching into a macabre grin as he grabbed Lady Mossi's hand with his free one. "Think of it, Auntie. You'll finally get what you've always wanted."

Lady Mossi's breath caught in her throat, hope unfurling before her for the first time in centuries. Ever since their family had lost the throne to House Usciete nearly twelve hundred years ago, she'd been fighting for a way to get it back. This could be the chance she'd been waiting for.

"Very well," she said. "What do you need from me?"

Adara

"S o, are you ready to talk about what happened yesterday?" Einar asked.

I snapped my gaze up from my breakfast platter to glare at Einar, who was sitting across from me in the galley. We'd come down to the galley for breakfast, along with Prentis. But unlike Prentis and I, who'd piled our plates high with kippers and other goodies, Einar's own plate was empty save for a hunk of bread and a cup of tea.

I supposed if I suffered from seasickness, I would do the same.

"What exactly did you want to talk about, regarding yesterday?" I asked with forced politeness as I speared one of my kippers with a fork. The fish seemed determined to thwart me—it split neatly in two, then slipped off my fork when I tried to scoop it up instead. Annoyed, I plucked it off the plate with my fingers and shoved it into my mouth. "How Prentis turned into a giant orca and fought a kraken to save your sorry hide? Or about how you didn't thank either of us, but wasted no time scolding me for coming after you instead of waiting on the deck like some useless damsel?"

Einar rolled his eyes. "First of all, Prentis didn't fight the kraken for my sake only. He had to destroy it for the safety of the ship and everyone on board—"

Prentis snorted. "Such gratitude."

"—including you," Einar continued. "But no, I wasn't talking about any of that. I was referring to what *you* did." He pointed to my neck. "To the new facet of power you displayed."

Unconsciously, my hand drifted to the side of my neck, where I could almost feel the gills again. I'd intended to ask Prentis about it yesterday, but the truth was I'd been so exhausted that I'd slept the rest of the day away. In fact, I'm not sure I would have even come out for breakfast if one of the crew hadn't roused me.

I glanced sideways at Prentis, who was staring at me. "Is what happened to me yesterday normal?" I asked, a little hesitant to hear the answer. "The gills, the webbing between my fingers and toes... are you able to transform like that as well?"

"I am," Prentis said with a smile. "And this is good news for you, Adara. Half-transformations like those are a Greater Fae trait. It means that once you complete the coming-of-age ritual, you should be able to unlock all of your water fae abilities."

I glanced down at my hands, rubbed the spaces between the fingers on my left hand with my right thumb. It had been so strange to feel the webbing there, and a part of me wanted to transform again so I could try swimming again, this time with my webbed feet free of shoes as well. But I'd tried this morning before I'd come to breakfast, and nothing had happened.

I wondered if I had to be in the water to trigger the transformation. That would make sense. After all, if I did it on land, I wouldn't be able to breathe, and I'd panic like I did yesterday.

"I'm happy to hear that," I said slowly, "but why was I able to transform like that, since I haven't unlocked my magic yet? And is this something I'll be able to do again?"

Prentis hesitated. "Sometimes when we are under great stress, or feeling some particularly strong emotion, we can temporarily access abilities we wouldn't normally be able to wield." His gaze flickered to Einar briefly. "Your attachment to your dragon protector seems to be strong enough to allow you to draw from that hidden magic."

I looked at Einar, who was staring back at me, his golden eyes glittering. I wish I could tell what he was thinking, but for once, his expression was completely undecipherable.

"So it's a good thing, then, that I came after you," I said, a little smugly.

"It's a good thing you didn't become dinner," he countered. I opened my mouth, ready to argue, but then he reached across the table and squeezed my hand. "But I'm glad you rescued me, all the same."

The retort dried on my lips, my mind going blank. I stared at our twined fingers as heat tingled up my arm, and suddenly, my mind whisked me back to that night in the air temple when Einar and I had danced. I could still remember the feel of his hands on my body, the way he'd expertly twirled me across the dance floor while secretly searching for the Oracle.

And I could tell from the look in his eyes that he was reliving that moment, too.

Einar winked at me, then took his plate and sauntered out of the galley, leaving me and Prentis alone. There was something smug about the way he walked, as if he'd won some kind of argument or contest. Curious, I glanced at Prentis, who wore a black look on his face as he watched Einar leave the room.

"What?" I asked, a little annoyed. "Is there something I missed?"

"Nothing." Prentis stabbed a halved tomato with his fork and shoved the whole thing into his mouth. "Nothing at all."

After breakfast, I went to the upper deck to find Einar. Aside from the brief, half-delirious conversation I'd had with him before Prentis's soldiers had captured us, I hadn't spoken with him privately since the fight against King Aolis.

But the moment I set eyes on the horizon, all thoughts of Einar fled from my head.

Spread out on the coastline like a bed of glittering jewels, the city of Usciete was a sight for sore eyes. Colorful houses and buildings clustered near the beaches, while manor houses perched on cliffs and hillsides farther inland. Usciete Palace loomed above it all, built at the top of the tallest cliff, its sea-foam-green domes and eggshell walls gleaming softly in the morning light. A tunnel had been carved into the base of the cliff—the only means of accessing the palace from the coast, unless one felt like scaling the cliff's rocky face.

We would be traveling through that tunnel all too soon.

I grabbed the sleeve of a passing sailor, pulling him to a stop. "How long until we reach the docks?" I asked, my voice tight with nerves.

He glanced at the coastline, which was approaching far too rapidly for my tastes, and then back at me. "Within the hour, my lady."

I nodded, then let him go. Anxiety reared its ugly head as I looked at the shoreline, at the dockworkers and sailors already anchored in the bay, at the bustling port city and the magnificent castle beyond. I was about to meet my maternal great-grandmother, and I looked like something the cat had dragged in. I needed to wash up, comb my hair, find something to wear. Did Prentis bring anything suitable for me, or was I expected to present myself to Axlya wearing the clothes I—

"Adara." Einar's voice rumbled from behind me, and I jumped. Frazzled, I spun around on my heel, ready to scold him for sneaking up on me, but the words died on my lips when I looked up at him. His normally stoic face was soft with concern as he looked me up and down, and when he brushed a stray hair away from my cheek, all the pent-up emotion inside me welled straight to the surface and into my eyes.

"Is everything all right?" he asked, clawed hands coming to cup my shoulders. His touch was gentle, and yet it felt like he was holding me together. As though he could sense the storm of anxiety churning in my gut, threatening to rip me open at the seams.

"I just..." a tear escaped the corner of my eye, and I swiped at it angrily. "I just feel so lost right now, Einar. I should be happy that we made it here, excited to meet Lady Axlya and get the ritual underway, but I'm afraid. Maybe even terrified." More tears leaked out, and I let out a bitter laugh. "I'm so pathetic."

Einar's grip tightened on my shoulders. "You are *not* pathetic, Adara," he said sternly, pinning me with his fierce golden eyes. "You're one of the strongest females I've ever met, and I've had the privilege of fighting alongside some of the fiercest dragon females in my army. Your adoptive mother was kidnapped, you've been forced to learn how to wield new magic your people thought lost forever, you found out that you're actually a princess of the realm, you vanquished the false king that stole your throne, watched as an evil entity took possession of your mother's body, fled the capital, were taken captive, and now you're on your way to meet one of the most powerful fae in the realm. Yet you have risen to every challenge thrown your way with dogged determination, refusing to give up no matter how heavily the odds have been stacked against you."

"You are many things, Adara. Smart, strong, beautiful, brave, loyal, and stubborn, sometimes even to a fault. But you are not pathetic. You are a miracle, a daughter of fae and dragons, a child of ice and fire, and I refuse to hear you put yourself down like this, not even for one second."

He dropped his hands from my shoulders, and for a second, I thought he was going to pull away. Instead, he wrapped his arms around me and pulled me into a crushing embrace. The heady, masculine scent of him filled my head, and a sense of security filled my heart as he held me tight to him, saying nothing, demanding nothing.

Simply holding me, so I could fall apart.

Burying my face in his chest, I sobbed silently, but violently, letting out all the grief, all the frustration, all the rage from the last few days. My tears soaked the front of his shirt, my fingernails tore through the back, but still he held me as I quaked. I felt like a lone sapling in the middle of a storm-torn vale, holding on for dear life as the winds threatened to rip me out by the roots and send me sailing into the abyss.

But the storm didn't take me, of course. It simply passed through me, until I was empty and drained, until I slumped against Einar, my nose clogged, my eyelids heavy. I wanted to drag myself back to my cabin and sleep the rest of the world away.

Someone cleared their throat, and I lifted my splotchy face to see Prentis standing a few feet away. He shuffled from one foot to the other, looking horribly awkward, as if he wasn't sure how to approach us.

I knew I should feel embarrassed to let him see me like this, especially in such an intimate embrace. But the truth was, I was too emotionally drained to care.

"What do you want?" Einar growled, his arms tightening around me. It was impossible to mistake the jealousy in his tone for anything else, yet his embrace felt protective rather than possessive. And I realized I liked it, far more than I should.

Prentis lifted an arm, drawing my gaze to a glittering dress draped over his forearm. "I came to give this to Adara. She needs to be presentable for her court appearance." A female servant dressed in Prentis's livery appeared at his elbow, holding an armful of toiletry items. "I've asked Misha here to help her freshen up and change."

Sniffing, I gently extricated myself from Einar's hold and gave Prentis a watery smile. "Yes, that would be lovely. I was just wondering if you'd packed anything for me to wear." I took the dress from him, running my hand over the silky, lightweight fabric. The colors shifted beneath my fingers, revealing strands of iridescence beneath the gown's eggshell-blue hue. "It's gorgeous."

"Of course." Prentis smiled, looking pleased. "I would never allow you to walk into court looking anything less than your best." He stepped back and gestured to Misha. "Follow Misha. She'll take care of everything."

Misha led me below decks to an empty salon, where a large bucket of steaming water and several towels waited. Over the next hour, she scrubbed me down, washed and brushed my hair, cleaned and trimmed my nails, and exfoliated my skin. Only when I was pink and soft and shiny and free of dirt did she help me into the dress and its accompanying undergarments, then plait and style my hair before finishing the look with a string of sapphires around my neck.

"There you are, my lady." She stepped back, then turned me

toward a full-length mirror bolted to the wall. "What do you think?"

"I... it's incredible," I said honestly, because it was true. I didn't think I'd ever worn anything so fine in my life, not during the masquerade ball, or even during my brief time as King Aolis's captive, when I'd had an entire wardrobe of fashionable dresses fit for nobility to choose from. The dress was a near perfect fit, nipping in at my waist and flaring out in a waterfall of skirts that swished around my ankles. The neckline was low enough to hint at cleavage while still being modest, and the jewels clustered at my neck elevated the look further. "I don't think I've ever looked so regal in my life."

But as amazing as the dress looked, I felt like an imposter in it. Regardless of the discovery that I was the daughter of Prince Daryan and Princess Olette, that I had the blood of dragons and fae running through my veins, the powers of water and fire blazing in my soul... in my heart, I was still Adara Greenwood. A simple fae girl who'd grown up in a small village with no concept of her powers or destiny, with none of the training or the wiles necessary to navigate political machinations or court intrigue.

Which was ironic, considering that the fae who'd raised me had been my mother's lady-in-waiting, and likely knew everything there was to know about court life. If things had been different, if she'd told me the truth about my origins, she could have prepared me for all of this.

But there was no sense in going down that path. The past was stone, the future an ever-shifting landscape. The only thing I had any control over was the present.

Fake it till you make it, right?

Steeling myself, I followed Misha out of the room and into the captain's office, where Prentis and Einar waited. The two men turned as I entered the room, and I stopped where I was, letting them get a good look at me.

"You look stunning," Prentis said. There was an appreciative glint in his crystal blue eyes as he appraised me, and he gave me a pleased smile. "Misha did her job very well. You look like a princess who has stepped from the pages of a prophecy, just like you should."

I blushed, then glanced at Einar. My breath caught at the molten look in his eyes as they traveled up and down my body, and I tensed, suddenly nervous. Though honestly, I didn't know why I should care whether Einar liked the dress, or my hair, or the jewels. It was Lady Axlya's opinion that counted, not—

"She doesn't look like a princess," Einar said to Prentis, a smirk kicking up the corners of his mouth. "She looks like a fucking *queen*."

He practically purred the word *queen*, and if I was blushing before, it was nothing compared to what I felt now. My body went hot all over, a tingle rushing from the tips of my ears all the way down to my toes, and I barely stopped myself from taking a step toward Einar. There was no denying the desire pulsing through my veins—it was as if an invisible hook had sunk into my chest and was pulling me toward him, demanding that I do something about the sudden throb slowly spreading from my core and through the rest of my body.

Einar's nostrils flared, and his gaze grew heavy lidded, his smirk sensual, as though he could sense my need. I blushed even harder, and I had a feeling that if Prentis wasn't standing there, my dress would be in grave danger, my virtue even more so.

Prentis cleared his throat, breaking the spell between us. "She does," he agreed, though there was a hint of reluctance in his voice. I wondered if it was because he didn't like the idea of me being queen, or if it was that Einar had one-upped him with the compliment. The two of them definitely seemed to have some sort of rivalry going between them when it came to me, and I had no idea what to make of it.

We docked shortly after that, and Prentis led me down the gangplank to a carriage waiting at the docks. Einar was forced to ride with the soldiers, since his wings were too big to fit in the carriage with him and he refused to transform back. Which left Prentis and me alone together in the confined space.

"I must admit," Prentis said with a sigh as we rumbled through the port and into the upper city. "I am glad to have a break from your dragon protector's overbearing presence."

I raised an eyebrow. "Einar is just doing his job, you know," I said. "It's only natural that he doesn't trust you, or any other fae, for that matter."

"But that's just the thing," Prentis said, his crystal-blue eyes glittering as he appraised me. "He doesn't trust the fae, and yet he continues to stand by you, a water fae. Why do you think that is?"

"Well, I'm not *just* a fae," I said, feeling suddenly defensive of Einar. "I'm also half-dragon. And Einar was my father's best friend. It's only natural for him to want to protect me."

"So he knew that, did he?" Prentis asked. "Knew that you were half-dragon when you met? Is that why you moved on King Aolis so quickly? Because the dragon taught you how to use your power?"

Prentis's questions sounded casual, but I didn't miss the glitter in his eyes. He was mining me for information, and I pressed my lips together, defenses coming up.

"Einar did help me learn how to control my power," I said after a few seconds. "But he didn't know about my heritage. And I didn't come to Kaipei to kill the king or fulfill the prophecy or any of that. I just came to get my mother back."

"Your mother?" Prentis leaned forward, a frown marring his perfect brow. "But your mother is dead."

I shook my head. "I'm not talking about Olette. I'm talking about the woman who raised me."

"And that is?" Prentis prodded.

I opened my mouth, then closed it again.

He sighed. "You're going to have to tell Lady Axlya about all this anyway, if you want her to help. You might as well tell me first. In fact, I wish you had earlier, while we had more time. I could have given you advice, although I don't know what I'd be giving you advice about. You haven't even told me what you want her help with."

My fingers itched with the urge to rake my hands through my hair, but I couldn't muss it up, so I buried them in the layers of my skirt instead. "And you haven't told me why you want to help me. In fact, you didn't tell me you wanted to help me at all. You're only taking me to Lady Axlya because she ordered you to."

"Yes, but I'm not an idiot, Adara." Prentis's voice tightened with impatience. "You've killed the king of Ediria, and while your only ally is formidable in his own right—" he glanced out the window at Einar, who was riding alongside, wings tucked in against his back and hidden beneath a cloak, "—he's not enough to protect you against the entire realm. You need the support of my house, of my aunt, if you want to take the throne."

I laughed. "Who said I wanted the throne?"

Prentis gave me an incredulous look. "Are you saying that you don't?"

We entered the tunnel then, briefly plunging the carriage into darkness. Grateful for the distraction, I turned to look out the window, not sure how to answer that. Light from the torches set in intervals along the tunnel walls streaked across my vision as I thought about how to answer Prentis's question. The throne was obviously my birthright, and with Nox in possession of Kaipei and General Slaugh by her side, I knew taking it was my best chance to make sure it stayed out of the wrong hands. But at the same time, I knew I wasn't qualified to rule a kingdom.

"It's complicated," I finally said, because that was the truth. What had started out as a mission to rescue my mother had turned into a quest to save the kingdom. I hadn't counted on being embroiled in political machinations, or having to master new powers, or even fighting the king, never mind the shadow entity who had taken his place and stolen my mother's body.

To my horror, tears began to sting at the corners of my eyes. I blinked hard, swallowing against my tightening throat, and Prentis's gaze softened.

"I know it's complicated," he said gently. "And I know you must have been through a lot. Were you able to rescue your mother, at least? Was she still alive when you killed King Aolis? Who is she?"

"Her name is Gelsyne, and she is still alive, but I wasn't able to help her." I hung my head, the shame and horror of it all washing over me again. "And if Lady Axlya doesn't help me, I will lose her forever."

"Gelsyne?" Prentis echoed, sounding shocked. "Not the same Gelsyne who served as Olette's lady-in-waiting?"

"The very same." I gave him a shaky smile.

Prentis opened his mouth to ask more questions, but we emerged from the tunnel, light bursting in through the carriage windows once more. My heart beat faster as I pressed my face to the window, as close as I dared without ruining my makeup so I could watch as we rumbled through the castle gates. The gates were adorned with House Usciete's crest—a waxing crescent moon with a wave drawn inside of it, and water droplets splashing out from its center. That same symbol was prevalent everywhere as we pulled into the bailey, including on the uniform of the footman who helped us out of the carriage.

"Welcome back, Lord Prentis," a tall fae dressed in a household uniform greeted us. "Lady Axlya is pleased at your timely arrival." His gaze flickered to me. "I take it this is the Lady Adara?"

"Yes," Prentis said. "And her protector, Einar," he added as Einar appeared at my elbow. "Adara, Einar, this is Roch, Castle Usciete's steward. He will take care of your needs while you are here."

"A pleasure." The steward's lips thinned as he glanced at Einar, taking in his golden eyes and clawed hands, but they curved into a solicitous smile when he turned to me. "Since you're already dressed and ready, I'll take the three of you to the audience chamber while the castle staff deliver your bags. Lady Axlya and the court are waiting for you."

Dune

"Do you know why you've been summoned, cadet?"

Dune blinked, caught off guard by the question. He stood in the throne room at Kaipei Castle, hands clasped behind his back, trying not to shuffle his boots or show other signs of awkwardness as General Slaugh scrutinized him.

"I was only told I was needed for a sensitive mission, Sir," he said honestly. His commander had received a missive at the training camp two nights ago, and the two of them had ridden hard, arriving at Kaipei only this morning. They'd barely handed off their horses before a guard had ushered Dune to the throne room, leaving his commander to cool his heels in the great hall.

Dune had to hide a smirk at that. The commander was already annoyed that he, a cadet who had been in the army for less than a week, had already been selected for an important mission. He had to be fuming out there at being kept completely out of the loop as to what the mission even entailed after riding at a breakneck pace to escort Dune here.

"Good," the fae standing next to Dune murmured. "So no one knows about the nature of the mission, then."

Dune startled as he got a good look at the fae. "Gelsyne?" he asked, voice pitched high in shock. Her coloring was different, and the outfit she wore was far more seductive than what he was used to seeing on her.

But there was no mistaking the fae who'd served as Fenwood's healer for as long as he could remember. The last time he'd seen her, she'd been unconscious and in chains, in the custody of General Slaugh's men.

"What—" he began to ask.

"Gelsyne has seen the error of her ways," General Slaugh interrupted. "She thought she was doing the right thing by keeping Adara hidden, but now that Adara has murdered King Aolis in cold blood and thrown the kingdom into chaos, Gelsyne is committed to bringing her foster daughter to justice."

"Too right," Gelsyne said. She bowed her head, folding her hands against her thighs. "General Slaugh could have had me executed, and that would have been just and right. But he's allowed me to serve the throne instead. I can only hope that I can make up for what Adara has done."

"How merciful," Dune said, hiding his confusion behind a polite mask. There had to be some underlying reason for General Slaugh keeping Gelsyne at his side rather than executing her or letting her rot in the dungeons. But what value could she bring, and how could she be trusted?

"What is your relationship with Adara Greenwood?" General Slaugh asked.

"Adara?" Dune was taken aback by the question. "She... we grew up together." He glanced at Gelsyne, wondering just how much she knew, and what she'd told Slaugh, but her expression revealed nothing as she stared back at him.

Had Gelsyne's eyes always been so black, so unfathomable?

What exactly had happened to her since she'd been taken prisoner?

"Is that all?" General Slaugh raised an eyebrow. "I watched the two of you at the trials. There seemed to be some sort of rivalry between you."

Dune pressed his lips together. "We were rivals, of a sort," he admitted reluctantly. "At one point, we'd nearly become lovers. But I knew my father would never allow me to marry a fae with no magic, so I rejected her. You could say she took that personally."

"Interesting." General Slaugh tapped a finger on his chin. "Would you say you know her well, then?"

"Better than most... although I don't think that's saying much," Dune said dryly. "None of us knew about her fire magic." Ironic, that the one fae everyone in the village had deemed useless actually turned out to have a powerful magic that everyone in Ediria had assumed was extinct. There was no way Adara hadn't known about it—he wondered if she'd secretly been plotting to kill the king this entire time, and that's why she'd trained to become a warrior. He'd always sensed that she had secrets about her—that was one of the reasons he'd been drawn to her, despite his father's insistence that she was trash and that he shouldn't concern himself with her.

Perhaps his father knew about those secrets. Maybe that was why he'd wanted Dune to stay away from her.

"That may be so," Gelsyne said. "But there's a connection between you two, and there always has been. That's why you'll be a good fit for this mission."

Her lips curved into a smile that sent a shiver skating down Dune's spine. "And what is this mission, exactly?"

"It's a simple one," Slaugh said. "We want you to kill Adara."

Dune froze. "Kill her?" he echoed, not quite sure he'd heard right. "As in... end her life?"

"I believe that is what the word 'kill' means," Slaugh said dryly. "Is that going to be a problem, cadet? Bringing a known murderer, a king slayer, to justice?"

"No, of course not," Dune said quickly. His resolve hardened as he recalled how Adara had set fire to the field, badly injuring many of the cadets. She was clearly a threat, and if she was powerful enough to kill King Aolis, that meant she was a danger to everyone in Ediria.

... but that was the problem, wasn't it?

"I'm very flattered that you've considered me for this mission," Dune said carefully, "but while I consider myself a competent fighter and earth magic wielder, I am still a lesser fae. What hope do I have of killing Adara, when she killed the king of Ediria himself?"

That he had to say that aloud, had to admit Adara was more powerful than him, chagrined him. But Dune wasn't a fool. He couldn't rush headlong into this mission. He had to know if there was a way to succeed first.

"That's an excellent point." General Slaugh smiled, or at least the unburnt half of his face did. The left side of his twisted mouth pulled into what could only be referred to as a polite grimace. "Should you choose to accept this mission, we will grant you access to a rare magic, one traditionally wielded only by the king and his personal guard."

"Really?" Excitement leapt in Dune's chest, and his blood pumped faster. "What kind of magic is this?"

"Do you accept the mission?" Slaugh asked.

A warning bell went off in the back of Dune's head, but he ignored it. This was the chance he'd been waiting for, to prove to his father that he was more than just a second son. That he would be granted special abilities, and given the chance to bring a king killer to justice, meant he could finally make a name for *himself.*

"Yes," he said decisively. "I do."

"Excellent." Gelsyne purred. She stepped closer to him, and Dune had to stop himself from taking a step back. He still couldn't put his finger on what was different about her, and he wasn't referring to her appearance. There was a darkness in her, a fathomless, yawning pit in her black eyes that made the hairs on his arms and the back of his neck prickle with warning.

But when he glanced at General Slaugh, questions in his eyes, the general merely dipped his head in approval.

So Dune forced himself to stand still as Gelsyne put her hands on his chest, forced himself not to shiver even though his skin crawled beneath her touch.

But he couldn't hold in a gasp when she leaned up and pressed her icy cold mouth to his.

He tried to pull away, but his body went rigid as an invisible force rushed from her open mouth and into his. It felt like he was swallowing clouds of thick, viscid smoke, the noxious vapor permeating his lungs and spreading through his veins like poison. His body shook, trying to reject the toxic invasion as black liquid streamed from his pores.

But then a voice spoke in his head. A voice born of the darkest dreams, raised from the depths of madness, the deepest depravities.

"Dune Terran," it purred, wrapping around his thoughts the way a cat winds around its owner's legs. "By accepting my power into your blood, you relinquish your ties to the kingdom of Ediria, and your birthright as a son of Domhain. From this day forth, you are a child of darkness. The power of Shadows now runs in your veins. And you are, and shall ever be, my servant."

Dune screamed as the magic exploded inside him, transforming his entire body. His skin became the pitch-black space between stars, his eyes the bottomless pits of the abyss, his hair the inky black of despair. Long claws and fangs sprouted from his fingertips and mouth, and the shadow his form cast began to bleed, spreading across the floor and creeping up the walls until the entire room plunged into darkness.

"Mother of Shadows," Dune rasped, his voice a little thick behind his newly grown fangs. He dropped to one knee before the shadow demon and bowed his head. "I live to serve."

"You've given him a lot of shadow magic," Slaugh said, the barest hint of disapproval in his voice.

"Yes." Nox stroked the top of Dune's head, her nails scraping his scalp and sending pleasurable tingles through his body. "He'll need it if he's going to take on Adara and that pesky dragon sidekick of hers." She slid a finger under Dune's chin and tilted his head up to look at her, and his body thrilled at the smile she gave him. "You magnificent creature. You'll follow my instructions to the letter, won't you?"

"Yes, Mother," Dune said eagerly. He no longer cared about General Slaugh's approval, or anyone else's. The Mother of Shadows was the only one that mattered, the one who had given him this glorious power and purpose. He would do whatever it took to please her, vanquish any enemy who stood in her way.

And if that enemy was Adara, the girl who had humiliated and bested him, well, that was merely icing on the cake.

13

Adara

"There she is."

"... girl from the prophecy..."

"... dragon-born abomination..."

"... *king slayer*..."

I nearly flinched at that last whispered accusation, but kept my eyes straight ahead as I stepped into the audience chamber, trying not to look at the assembled courtiers gathered in the gallery. Their dozens of eyes followed me as I walked down the aisle toward the dais, their whispers snapping at my heels, and I knew it wasn't just me they were talking about. Their sharp eyes were also glued to Einar's wings, which were now on full display. The guards had searched us for weapons and required us to remove all outer garments before entering the room, so he could no longer hide them, nor the shackles at his wrists.

"Ignore them," Prentis murmured in my ear as we approached. "Lady Axlya's opinion is the only one that matters."

I nodded, my attention on the seven figures assembled on the dais. The female seated on the throne, dressed in a diaphanous gown made up of nearly every shade of blue I could think of, was obviously Lady Axlya. She studied me out of crystalline blue eyes the exact same shade as Prentis's, her youthful, elegant features arranged into an expression of pure serenity that revealed nothing. I had no more chance of divining her thoughts than I did a goldfish staring at me through a glass bowl.

Seated on both sides of Lady Axlya's throne were four males and two females, all dressed in Usciete's colors—blue and silver. They viewed me with varying shades of curiosity, with smidges of amusement, hostility, and boredom mixed in. I couldn't tell if these were family members or advisors, but they must have been very important to be sitting up here with the matriarch.

"My Lady Aunt." Prentis stopped at the foot of the dais and swept into a low bow. "May I present Adara, daughter of the late Princess Olette and Prince Daryan, and the lost heir to the Edirian throne?"

More whispers broke out in the gallery behind us, but I forced myself to tune them out.

"It's an honor to meet you, Great-Grandmother."

The whispers stilled, and Lady Axlya's blue-painted lips curved into a shimmering smile.

"Great-Grandmother," she said, her crystalline eyes twinkling. "I must say, the Radiants have answered my prayers for another grandchild in a rather unexpected manner." She tilted her head as she studied me, and I tried not to fidget under the weight of her regard. "Your hair, your nose, even the shape of your jaw... you bear a striking resemblance to your grandfather, the late King Ciryan. But the tilt and color of your eyes, those most definitely came from Olette."

"I hope that's a good thing," I said.

"Of course it is. It's clear you strongly favor your water fae ancestry." Her smile dimmed as she turned her gaze toward

Einar, taking in his wings, which were on proud display. "Though I must say, I am not incredibly fond of the company you keep."

"That's unfortunate," I said before Einar could open his mouth and get us in trouble, "because he's saved my life several times. Without him, I don't think I ever would have made it to your halls."

There was a long pause at that, so long that I began to wonder if I'd misspoken. "I would say that we are in your debt, Einar," Axlya said. "But as you have killed many of my subjects, I suppose we shall call this a wash."

Axlya's smile remained serene, but her crystalline eyes turned diamond-sharp. I held my breath as I awaited Einar's response, but instead of snapping at her, he merely shrugged.

"I'm not concerned with past feuds between your family and mine," he said. "My only desire is to make sure Adara is safe and protected."

"And you do not consider that she is safe and protected?" Lady Axlya rose an eyebrow. "Now that she is here in the heart of my realm, back in the bosom of her family where she belongs?"

"She is safer here than anywhere else," Einar agreed. "But she will never be safe until she has mastered her powers and eradicated all shadow magic from the kingdom." He took a small step forward, positioning himself ever so slightly between me and Axlya. "And until that day comes, I will remain at her side."

Einar's impassioned declaration of loyalty filled my heart, warmth spilling over to flow through my veins until I felt like I was glowing from the inside. But Lady Axlya seemed less than impressed.

"Eradicate shadow magic?" she said archly. "But according to my sources, shadow magic has *already* been eradicated." Her gaze returned to me. "That is why you traveled all the way to Kaipei and killed King Aolis, wasn't it?"

Her pointed question sliced through the tension in the room, causing the gallery to break out in whispers again. "That was one of the reasons," I said, raising my voice to be heard, "but although I did kill the king, I didn't rid the realm of shadow magic. General Slaugh and his men still wield the shadow magic Aolis gave them, and they are holding Kaipei with the help of a powerful shadow demon. That's why I've come to you, Grandmother. I need your help."

"A shadow demon?" one of the males sitting to Lady Axlya's right spoke up. "This is the first we've heard of this. Cascada didn't mention a shadow demon."

"Cascada?" Einar asked, his voice sharpening. "Who is Cascada?"

"Me," a familiar voice spoke from the gallery, and the hairs on the back of my neck rose. I turned to see a turquoise-haired fae rise from her seat and walk toward the dais, and my mouth dropped open. It was Cascada, one of the three hostages King Aolis had been keeping in his castle as security to keep the nobles from the other houses from trying to usurp him. She smirked a little as she met my shocked gaze and paused in front of me. "Surprised to see me here, are you?"

I picked up my jaw off the floor and straightened, trying not to bristle at her snarky attitude. "I just... I'm surprised you made it out of the castle alive," I said honestly. "I thought General Slaugh and his men would have slaughtered you."

"Oh they tried," Cascada said sweetly. "But Slaugh and his cronies lost their shadow magic once we killed that shadow bitch, and after that, it was easy to escape."

She flicked some imaginary dust off her shoulder, and my world screeched to a sudden halt. "Y-you *killed* her?" I said faintly, my heart hammering so hard in my chest that I thought I was going to pass out. "You killed Gelsyne?"

Einar caught me as I stumbled back a step, reeling from the news. "What's happening?" Prentis demanded as the nobles rose from their chairs, their murmurs filling the chamber. "What's wrong, Adara?"

"Gelsyne was her mother," Einar growled. "Or at least, she became her mother after Olette died. The entire reason she traveled to Kaipei Castle was to rescue her, but all that went to shit once the shadow demon left King Aolis's body and inhabited hers instead." He gave Cascada a sharp look. "You say that you killed her, and the shadow magic just disappeared? You didn't see it enter anyone else's body?"

Cascada shook her head, her eyes wide and innocent as a newborn babe as she stared at me. "It vanished completely," she insisted.

I shook my head slowly, brushing Einar's hands aside. "That can't be true. You're lying."

Gasps rang out from the gallery, and Lady Axlya cleared her throat. "Excuse me," she said in an icy tone, her serenity cracking for the first time, "but did you just accuse my daughter of lying?"

I spun around to face the throne. "I'm your family too," I snapped, nails digging into my palms as I spoke, "And I'm the one who fought King Aolis, not Cascada. I saw that shadow demon leave King Aolis's body and take possession of my mother's, and I'm telling you right now, there is no way it would have easily left. It took every ounce of power I had to drive it out of King Aolis, *plus* the decades of fire magic stored in the primal stone Einar gave me." I held up my wrist to show the room the golden cuff glinting there, the deep red stone glittering in the morning light. "There is no way that Cascada and the other two could have killed her."

Cascada huffed. "That's because you're a whelp," she said. "Tempest, Avani, and I have at least eight-hundred years on you, collectively. Is it so hard to imagine that the three of us could have taken down the shadow demon together?"

"I..." I hesitated, glancing at Einar and Prentis. Einar's brows bunched together in a suspicious glower, but Prentis was looking at me with something akin to pity, and my insides squirmed. Was it possible that I was just overreacting? Could it be that they really did kill Gelsyne, and the shadow demon, for whatever reason, was forced back into its own world?

"Lady Axlya," Prentis said, breaking the awkward silence. "Please, forgive Cousin Adara. She's had quite an ordeal over the last few days, and as Einar said, Gelsyne was basically her mother. It's only natural that she would take the loss hard." He put a comforting hand on my shoulder. "I think Adara should take some time to recover from the journey. We can talk more later and sort this all out, perhaps as a family."

He gave a pointed glance to the gallery, and Lady Axlya gave a regal nod. "Of course," she said, her anger melting into an understanding smile. "Please, rest, Adara, and we'll discuss how I can help you over dinner. I've had the steward prepare Olette's old rooms for you. I think you'll find them quite comfortable."

"Thank you, Great-Grandmother." I curtseyed again, hoping Axlya wouldn't notice the shameful flush creeping up the back of my neck. "I'm humbled by your generosity."

"Nonsense," she insisted. "My home is your home."

She glanced at Prentis, and he nodded, then led me and Einar out of the chamber. I tried to ignore the stares as we walked past the gallery, but I couldn't help glancing back one last time as the doors opened, meeting Cascada's gaze one more time.

I could have sworn I saw a flicker of shadow in her gaze right before the doors closed behind me.

14

Leap

The guards didn't take any chances with Leap. They searched him thoroughly, confiscating his boots, his lock picks, and anything else they thought might be useful, before fastening magic-dampening manacles around his wrists and tossing him into a cell to spend the night.

"This is just fantastic," Mavlyn growled from the cell across from him. She paced behind the bars, heedless of the icy stone beneath her bare feet. "They've taken my pouches and put magical bindings on us, Leap. How in the Shadows are we supposed to get out of here?"

"We can't," Leap said dully. He flopped onto his cot and gazed up at the ceiling. "We're stuck here until morning."

Mavlyn stopped pacing so she could shoot a death glare at Leap through the bars. "So, you're giving up then?" she accused.

"Of course we're not giving up," Leap snapped, sitting up on his elbows so he could glare right back at her. "I said we're stuck here until morning, not that we're stuck here *forever*. The guards will have to come back tomorrow to escort us to Angtun. We'll find an opportunity to escape then."

"And then what?" Mavlyn asked. She'd curled her fingers around the bars now, her grip so tight her knuckles were turning white. "Even if we can escape, we have no idea where Quye is. Why wasn't she in her rooms? Who was that imposter? And if we can't escape, then what is Lord Oren going to do with us?"

Her voice pitched higher and higher with each word, and Leap realized Mavlyn was terrified. Guilt swamped him as he took a good look at her—her eyes were like saucers, her face pale beneath her dark complexion, and her chest was rising and falling so rapidly he worried she was going to hyperventilate.

Of course she's terrified, you idiot. She's an earth fae who got caught committing a crime in air fae territory. Even you don't know what's going to happen to her, especially now that the kingdom is about to be thrown into an upheaval.

But of course, he couldn't say that. Not when Mavlyn looked like she was about to have a panic attack.

"I don't know exactly what's happened to Quye," Leap said in a soothing tone. "But if I had to guess, I'd say that my uncle has hidden her somewhere to ensure she's protected during the coming political unrest. She's his own daughter, and most precious commodity, or at least she is after his own heir." He snorted. "Uncle Oren would never let anything happen to her."

"Oh." Mavlyn's grip on the bars loosened, and her shoulders relaxed. "Well, if that's the case, then at least she's safe."

Leap frowned. "You were that worried about her?"

"Of course I was." Mavlyn's cheeks pinkened, and she glanced away. "I thought something terrible had happened to her, that maybe General Slaugh's shadow soldiers had gotten to her, and Lord Oren had installed a stand-in so no one would know." She chewed her bottom lip, her brow furrowing with worry as she met his gaze. "Are you sure that isn't a possibility?"

"It's extremely unlikely." Leap sat up and crossed his arms, studying Mavlyn closely. "Are you sure there isn't something else going on?"

"I think you're the one who should be answering that question," Mavlyn pointed out. "I understand why *I'm* locked up in chains, but why are you? You're Lord Oren's *nephew*. Shouldn't they at least give you a proper bed to sleep on?"

Leap snorted. "They know if they put me in a regular room I'll escape the moment they lock the door. Besides, Uncle Oren isn't exactly happy I've spent the last couple of years hiding from him. Not only would he not bat an eye if I told him I'd spent the night in a jail cell, he'd probably say it was good character-building."

"Giant's Teeth." Mavlyn shook her head. "You've got a pretty messed up family dynamic, Leap."

"Ha." Leap flopped back onto the cot. "You don't know the half of it."

"It's too bad you're not on good terms with your uncle," she mused. "If you were, we might be able to convince him to help Adara."

Leap scowled. "That would require actually going back to Angtun. Which I have no intention of doing."

Leap rolled over on his cot to face the wall, but he could still feel Mavlyn's gaze boring into the space between his shoulder blades. His body tensed, and he braced himself for more arguments and questions. But to Leap's surprise, Mavlyn didn't ask him anything more. She merely settled down on her own cot, and within no time, the soft sound of her snores filled the air.

It took a lot longer for sleep to find Leap. Thoughts of his family and the life he'd left behind swirled behind his eyelids, most notably a pair of taunting yellow eyes and a mocking sneer. His gut clenched, and he rolled over in his bed, praying that the nightmare he'd run away from wouldn't be waiting for him in Angtun when he returned.

But he knew better than to expect the Radiants to answer. A reckoning was coming, and his time had finally run out.

15

Einar

After Lady Axlya dismissed Adara, Prentis escorted us out of the audience chamber and handed us off to the steward so we could be shown to our rooms. I half-expected the steward to give us rooms in opposite wings, but to my surprise and relief, he placed us in the same hall, only a few doors apart. A change of clothes awaited me on the bed, and as I looked at the feather mattress with its plumped-up pillows, exhaustion began to drag at my limbs.

Before I could even think of collapsing on my bed and passing out for a few hours, the door behind me flew open. I spun on my heel, wings flaring out behind me as I prepared to confront the intruder. But instead of a guard or assassin or some other enemy, it was Adara who stalked into the room.

"Can you believe this?" she slammed the door behind her hard enough to shake the walls, her cornflower blue eyes blazing with righteous fury. The skirts and trailing sleeves of her gown flared out behind her as she stalked across the room toward me, wisps of lavender blue hair escaping from her braids to frame her flushed cheeks. "Cascada stood up in front of a roomful of nobles and claimed she and her friends killed my mother and defeated Nox. And we're expected to just *believe* that?"

"It does seem a little far-fetched," I admitted, leaning against the mantle to watch Adara pace around the room. "But it's not impossible. Nox might have realized that using Gelsyne as a host was not in her best interest after allowing you to leave the castle alive. She might have cast your mother aside in favor of choosing a better host."

"Like who?"

"I don't know." Adara tore at her hair, and the tresses tumbled free, pins scattering across the floor, as haphazard as her emotions seemed to be. She turned to face me, her bottom lip trembling, eyes shining with unshed tears. "I just know Cascada has to be lying about killing my mother. Because if she isn't, all of this has been for nothing. And I don't know how to deal with that."

"Oh, Adara." My chest ached at the heartbreak on her face, and I reached out to pull her into my arms. But she dodged my attempt at an embrace, shaking her head.

"I can't keep using you as a shoulder to cry on, Einar." She swiped at her eyes. "I need to be able to stand on my own two feet. To stop crumbling every time I get hit with another bit of bad news. This is my life now." She sucked in a shuddering breath and squared her shoulders. "I can't afford to be weak."

Adara started to pace again, but I reached out and snagged her by the waist, dragging her against me. "First of all," I said, using a clawed hand to brush one of her tresses away from her face, "there's nothing weak about you, so stop saying stupid things like that. And second of all—" I grabbed her hand and placed it right over my heart—"You can use me for anything you damn well want."

The air thickened between us, and Adara slowly curled her hand around the fabric of my shirt. Her nails scraped against my skin, sending a tremor of need through me, and I silently cursed the shackles around my wrists that prevented me from touching her the way I wanted to.

"Anything?" she asked, a husky note in her voice. There was something in the depths of her cornflower-blue eyes I hadn't seen before—a hunger that stirred the fiery beast in my chest.

"Anything," I repeated, my voice a dry rasp.

Adara pulled me closer until our chests were nearly touching, and then lifted her chin, bringing her lush mouth within a hairsbreadth of mine. I could almost taste her on my tongue, and part of me wanted to close the gap between us. To claim her mouth fully, *consciously* this time, and show her what it would be like to be *mine*.

But I wanted the choice to be hers, so I held still. And I waited.

The first brush of her lips against mine was tentative. Feather light. Like she was testing the surface of an icy river, seeing if it was solid enough to bear her weight. An unconscious purr of approval rumbled up my throat, and that seemed to embolden her, encouraging her to slide her other hand up to my shoulder, to press her lips more firmly against mine.

My own fingers itched to grab Adara's ass, to pull her against me so she could feel my growing need for her. But this moment was too precious for that. It was the first time the two of us had willingly gone to the other's arms, the first time we'd set aside our pride and differences and acknowledged the growing feelings between us.

So I didn't give into the urge. Instead, I closed my eyes and kissed her back, using my mouth and tongue to slowly stoke the fire within her. My free hand hung loosely between us as I explored the contours of her mouth, teasing her with little flicks of my tongue. She opened her mouth to catch my tongue, but I retreated, chuckling a little when she growled.

"You're holding back," she accused, her eyes sparking with ire.

"I'm just waiting for you to tell me what you want." I leaned my hip against the edge of the bed, a taunting grin on my lips. "Or to take it, if that's the mood you're in."

Adara stalked toward me, her hips bumping into mine and forcing me onto the bed. She stepped in between my legs and grabbed my face between hers, then leaned in and caught my mouth in a savage kiss. Instantly, my inner beast reared up, roaring its approval, and I matched her ferocity with my own, yanking her hips into mine as I plundered her mouth with a single-minded intensity.

The kiss was a battle of wills as much as it was a battle of tongues, both of us seeking the upper hand, neither of us giving in. Somehow my hand found its way into her hair, hers beneath my shirt, seeking out secrets between each pounding heartbeat. Her touch was electrifying, the taste of her all-consuming—I wanted to drown myself in her, wanted to mark every inch of her with my scent until I imprinted myself into the very marrow of her bones.

My fingers tightened on the hair at the base of her skull, tugging her head back so I could trail kisses across her jawline and down the side of her neck. A gasp flew from her swollen lips as I nipped at her collarbone, and I grinned against her skin as I felt a shudder race through her spine.

"Einar..." her nails dug into my shoulders as I licked the spot where I'd just bitten her.

"Mmm?" I continued along the neckline of her gown, careful not to stray beneath the fabric. "Is there something you need, Adara?"

"I..." she sucked in another sharp breath as my teeth closed around a particularly juicy spot on her neck, and the scent of her desire thickened in the air, so potent that my fangs lengthened. She cried out as they punctured her skin, sinking into flesh, and the sweet, coppery taste of her blood gushed into my mouth.

Fuck! A rush of images flooded my head from Adara's past—running through the fields with Mavlyn as a toddler, struggling to use her water magic in front of her jeering classmates, kicking Dune in the chest and sending him flying into what looked like a picnic spread. Touching my stone hide and watching me come to life, dancing with me in the air temple, opening her mouth to my kiss—

Adara moaned, the lustful sound echoing through the room and snapping me free from the reverie. I wrenched my mouth free of her neck, horrified at what I'd done, swiping at the hot blood on my lips as though I could erase the stain of the sin I'd just committed.

"What..." Adara stared at me, eyes glassy with shock and desire as her fingers slowly came up to graze the bite marks on her neck. But before I could say anything more, the door banged open, and Adara leaped back as Prentis barged into the room, his eyes wild, a swirling ball of water magic in his hand.

"What's going on in here?" Prentis demanded. "I heard you scream..."

The words died in Prentis's throat as his gaze zeroed in on Adara's bleeding neck. She clutched at the wound, angling her body away as though she could hide it, but he was there in an instant, pulling her hand away so he could study the bloody bite marks. Guilt clawed at the inside of my chest like a living thing, and when Prentis rounded on me, his expression livid, I didn't even bother defending myself.

"You bastard!" He flung out his hand toward me, and the sphere of water spun across the room, unraveling into a glowing blue rope that wrapped around my ankle. I cursed as Prentis yanked my feet out from under me, and my world went spinning as he whipped me through the air and slammed me onto the floor. Wood splintered beneath me, and I roared in pain as the bones in my wings snapped from the force of the blow.

"Prentis, no!" Adara screamed. She grabbed Prentis's arm and yanked him back, but he shrugged her off as he continued to stalk toward me. I tried to struggle to my feet, but he yanked on the whip again, and I went right back down.

"You sick, depraved, rot-brained fire worm," Prentis snarled. He planted his boot in the center of my chest, his lip curling into a sneer as I bared my blood-stained fangs at him. "You claim to be Adara's protector, and yet the moment the two of you are alone, you attack her?"

"I didn't mean—" I began, but the words ended in a gargle as Prentis pressed his boot against my throat. I would have been impressed by how intensely he defended Adara's honor if he weren't trying to kill me, and once more, I cursed the shackles that still bound my magic.

But just because I didn't have my powers, didn't mean I was powerless.

Righteous rage flooded me with renewed strength, and I grabbed Prentis's leg with both my clawed hands and bucked my hips at the same time. My wings shrieked in pain as I put all my weight onto my upper back and flung my legs high, hooking my heels around Prentis's hipbones. The water fae lord's eyes widened as I flexed my legs again, jumping up to my feet and taking him down in one motion. His water whip snaked around my legs even as he crashed into the floor, trying to trip me up. But instead of trying to stay upright, I dropped all my weight on top of him so I was straddling him.

"I would never dream of attacking Adara," I snarled, pulling my fist back. "But I have no qualms about attacking *you*."

I punched him square in the face, baring my fangs in a savage grin as Prentis's nose crunched beneath my fist. He swore loudly as blood gushed from his nose, and I reared back to punch him again, already feeling his water rope snaking up my back to try and tie my arms up. If I could just knock him out before he could use his magic on me again—

"That. Is. Enough!"

A firm hand curled around the back of my collar, and I went sailing through the air once again. Mercifully, I crash-landed on the bed instead of the floor, but my broken wings still shrieked in pain from the impact, stars exploding behind my eyes. The sounds in the room faded into a faint buzz, and it took a supreme effort of will for me to force myself upright and try to see what was happening.

The room was a pain-filled blur at first, but my vision sharpened just in time to see Adara shove Prentis against the wall. A surge of emotion filled me at the sight of her. Sparks danced all along her skin and hair, her cornflower-blue gaze blazing with unbridled fury, and she looked like she was on the verge of combusting into a flaming supernova.

But Prentis was hardly cowed by the display of power, filled with his own righteous anger. "Why are you doing this?" he snarled, his fingers wrapping around the wrist of the hand that was pinning him to the wall. "How can you defend him when he mauled you like a savage anim—"

"He didn't maul me," Adara interrupted, her voice so frigid that it sent an icy shiver from my spine to my toes. "He bit me on the neck, because I *asked him to.*"

I froze as the bald-faced lie dropped from Adara's lips, shattering the tension in the air. "You did *what?*" Prentis asked, his face going slack.

"You heard what I said." Adara's cheeks were bright pink

now, but she didn't back down. "I told him to bite me. I *wanted it.*"

Prentis stared at Adara for a long moment, his face frozen in an almost comical expression of confused horror. When he finally turned his head to look at me, I'd schooled my own features into a stoic mask. But privately, I was just as blown away by Adara's statement as he was.

I'd expected Adara to condemn me for what I'd done, even if she didn't yet understand the full extent of it. The violation I'd committed on her body was unforgivable, even under the laws of my own people, and if Prentis fully understood what I'd just done, he would have had me executed.

Yet not only did she not lash out at me, she'd put herself between me and Prentis and defended me. Had outright *lied* for me.

Shame burned at the corners of my eyes, and I had to resist the urge to hang my head.

Finally, Prentis shook his head and pushed Adara's hand off him. He walked to the still-open door, then paused at the threshold, hand digging into one of his pockets.

"I came here to unlock your shackles," he said. Something flashed through the air, and I instinctively reached out and caught it. "Lady Axlya said that since you've done the water realm such a tremendous service by fighting at Adara's side, it would be remiss of us to keep you trussed up like a prisoner." His jaw hardened as he met my gaze, his crystalline eyes sharp as fresh-cut glass. "I hope her faith in you is not misplaced."

He strode out the door, leaving the keys to my shackles burning a hole in my palm.

16

Adara

"How are you feeling, my dear? All rested up from your travels?"

I sipped from my cup of tea as I pretended to consider Lady Axlya's question. We were having tea in her sunroom, my legs tucked under me as I sat on one of the many large, plush pillows clustered around a low table. A spread of assorted cakes and sandwiches had been set out atop it, along with a crystal-blue tea service that had to cost more than my mother's house.

"I'm feeling much better, Great-Grandmother," I said, setting my cup of tea on the matching saucer. My neck tingled where Einar had bitten me yesterday, and I had to resist the urge to brush my fingers against the spot. It had healed in less than an hour, just like most of my injuries did when I wasn't magically exhausted. Yet I could still feel the phantom puncture of his fangs in my flesh. It was if he were still inside me, as though he'd left a piece of himself within me, and while it didn't hurt, I didn't quite know what to make of it. "A good night's rest was exactly what I needed after yesterday's events."

"I would imagine so," she said archly. "You've been through quite a lot over the past week, not just yesterday."

"It's only natural that she would have been out of sorts," Kalis, the fae male sitting on Axlya's right, said. He reached over and plucked a sandwich from one of the trays, offering it to Axlya. I watched, slightly uncomfortable--and more than slightly fascinated--as she allowed him to feed it to her, licking the crumbs off his fingers before sitting back with a satisfied smile on her face. He'd been one of the fae sitting on the dais next to Axlya yesterday, and it had shocked me to learn that two of those fae hadn't just been Lady Axlya's advisors.

They were also her *consorts*.

The consorts were with us this morning—Kalis, and also Ilsa, a female with short, wavy teal hair who sat on Axlya's left. Axlya had introduced them when I'd walked in, and I'd had to clench my jaw to keep it from dropping off the floor when she'd told me about the nature of their relationship.

"We heard about the... incident, involving you, Einar, and Lord Prentis," Ilsa spoke up. She picked up the teapot and refilled my cup, her lips curving with faint amusement. "It appears you've inherited your mother's talent for fostering romantic drama."

I stiffened at the implied insult. "I beg your pardon?"

"Don't mind Ilsa," Lady Axlya said. She gave her consort a mild look of disapproval, but Ilsa merely lifted a shoulder, looking unrepentant. It seemed that Lady Axlya's consorts weren't especially subservient to her. "She lets her tongue run away with her sometimes, and she has a quite a taste for juicy gossip and rumors." Her gaze flickered to my neck, and I had to fight against the blush threatening to creep up my face. "You haven't actually engaged in relations with the dragon, have you?"

"No!" Heat exploded across my face, and the spot on my neck throbbed in response, sending a pulse of need straight into my core. It took everything I had not to bury myself in the pillows out of sheer embarrassment. "I haven't engaged in relations with anyone."

"Really? You're a virgin? At your age?" Axlya clucked her tongue.

"I... is that a bad thing?"

"It's uncommon amongst water fae for a female to remain chaste once she reaches puberty," Axlya said in a matter-of-fact tone. She gave Kalis a sly smile, threading her fingers through his. "When I took Kalis to my bed, I was sixteen years old, fresh from my coming-of-age ceremony." Her voice lowered into a sensual purr that made me want to squirm. "The chemistry between us was positively explosive."

Kalis gave Axlya a wicked grin. "It was even more explosive once Ilsa entered our lives." He met the other fae's gaze over Axlya's shoulder, the thoughts dancing behind his eyes so obviously carnal, I wondered if I should leave the room.

"I didn't realize water fae were so openly sensual... or in the habit of taking multiple partners.," I said, trying to draw their attention away from each other. I had no desire to witness my great-grandmother tango with her two closest lovers.

Lady Axlya laughed. "Of course you didn't realize," she said, picking up her tea cup again. She took a long sip as she studied me from over the rim. "The earth fae may be more fertile than us, but they are also far more prudish. It seems you've inherited that trait from them."

"I'm not prudish," I said, a little defensively. "I'm just waiting for the right male to give myself to."

"And you've decided Einar is the right male, then?" Ilsa asked pointedly.

Embarrassed heat crept up the back of my neck, and I wished that the coffee table was higher so I could crawl underneath it. "That was... an impulsive decision," I said, trying not to sound as flustered as I felt. "I was emotional and stressed, and I needed someone to take it out on."

"And there's nothing wrong with that," Lady Axlya declared. "Having sex with someone merely means you are sharing your body with them, and taking pleasure from them in return. It doesn't have to mean you are giving your *soul* to him, Adara."

I blinked, surprised at Lady Axlya's matter-of-fact views on the matter. She clearly didn't view sex with the same gravity as the fae I'd grown up with. "Are you saying that you wouldn't care if I slept with Einar?" I asked carefully, trying to figure out where she was going with this.

"Oh, I certainly don't approve," Axlya said. "But I can see the two of you have an attraction, and my centuries of sitting on the throne have taught me that forbidding two people from sleeping with each other will only ensure they do exactly that. Get him out of your system if you must, Adara, but if you intend to take the throne, you must move on from him. It's already bad enough that you are half-dragon. Taking a dragon for a husband will spell a death-sentence for your legitimacy."

An angry retort sprang to my lips, and I had to clench my jaw to keep from blurting it out. I knew Lady Axlya was right, that the fae hated the dragons and I needed to lean into my fae heritage as hard as possible if I wanted their favor. And yet, it was my half-dragon blood that allowed me to defeat King Aolis in the first place, along with the primal stone full of dragon fire magic Einar had given me.

How could I pretend none of that mattered?

Kalis saved me from having to respond. "While you are right to caution Adara against consorting with dragons," he said, leaning forward with a gleam in his eye, "I, for one, have been looking forward to seeing a display of fire magic from Adara. It's been at least four hundred years since we've last seen a fae who could wield fire."

"True, and no one in our court has actually seen Adara use her magic. Not even Cascada," Ilsa pointed out. "How do we know she can do what she says?"

I lifted my palm before Lady Axlya could respond, calling to the ever-burning spark inside me. It answered eagerly, as if it were waiting for this moment, and my small audience gasped as a ball of flame sprang to life in my hand. Even the servants in the room stopped what they were doing to turn and watch, and I smiled as I made small tugging motions with my other hand, pulling strands of flame from the ball and coaxing them into a sinuous shape. The flames flickered in Lady Axlya's gaze as I fashioned them into the rough, but unmistakable form of a fire serpent.

"You may disapprove of my dragon heritage," I said quietly, "but it's an undeniable part of me."

I let the flaming dragon twine sinuously through the air for a few more seconds, then vanished it with a snap of my fingers. A faint plume of smoke drifted toward the ceiling, the only sign that it had been there, and I sat back, satisfied.

"Impressive," Lady Axlya said. Her face was the surface of a lake in the stillness of dawn, and just as impossible to read. "But can you do the same with your water magic?"

My face fell at that. "No," I admitted. "My ice magic is the only thing I can control."

I pointed a finger at my half-filled cup of tea, and the dark liquid rose from the cup, already crystalizing. I focused my attention on it, first willing it into the shape of a ball, then forming the layers. Icy petals unfurled, revealing the shape of a rose, and I gently coaxed it to land in the center of the table, right in front of Lady Axlya.

Ilsa's eyebrows rose. "It seems you have a talent for sculpting," she said, tracing one of the petals with her forefinger.

"Yes," Axlya agreed. She waved her hand, and the ice instantly melted back into tea, arcing through the air before splashing back into my cup. "Pity your tea has gone cold, though."

She smirked, and a surprised laugh burst out of me. "Yes, I guess that might have been a waste of perfectly good tea," I admitted, then dutifully brought the cup to my lips and took a sip. My eyebrows shot up as scalding liquid flowed over my tongue, and I nearly dropped the cup. "It's hot!"

Lady Axlya laughed. "You didn't think I would force you to drink lukewarm tea, did you?" she asked, her eyes twinkling.

"I didn't realize you could make the water hot," I admitted, staring at the cup in wonder.

"Of course I can," Axlya said. "You are able to make the water cold—that's how you're turning it into ice in the first place. I have full mastery over all aspects of water magic—making cold water hot is the least of my abilities." She tilted her head as she studied me. "It seems this is another way in which you favor Olette."

"Oh?" My heartbeat picked up at the mention of my mother.

"She, too, had a strong preference for ice magic," Kalis explained. "Once she had her coming-of-age ceremony and unlocked her fae beast, she was able to use the other aspects, but ice was her favorite."

The affection sparkling in his eyes made my heart ache for the father I'd never known. I wondered what it would have been like to have been raised the way my mother had. It seemed strange, the idea of having multiple parental figures, but perhaps that was because I'd only ever had one. I couldn't even imagine what it would be like to have that many adults watching over me and giving me love and guidance as a child.

"I have to say, learning that my mother's magic might be similar to mine gives me hope," I said, steering the subject back to less emotional matters. "Prentis told me that once I complete the ceremony, I should be able to use the other aspects of my water magic that I'm struggling with now. In fact, I was on my way to ask you for help when Prentis's men found me. I need to complete the ritual so I can rid the kingdom of shadow magic once and for all."

"But didn't you already accomplish that when you killed the king?" Kalis asked. "According to Cascada, Slaugh and the others have lost their powers."

Ilsa scoffed. "Yes, but Adara thinks Cascada is lying about that." She raised her eyebrows at me. "Or so you said during your court presentation."

I hesitated, wanting to approach this as tactfully as possible. "I'm not saying Cascada is being deliberately untruthful. But General Slaugh and his shadow soldiers could have deceived her. They pretended to give up when Einar and my friends attacked the castle and came to my rescue, but in reality, they were paving the way for me to kill the king."

Lady Axlya sat up straighter. "You're suggesting that General Slaugh was plotting against the king?" she asked sharply.

"I know he was. He admitted it to me himself."

The three fae began to speak all at once, but an urgent knock cut them off. "Enter," Lady Axlya said, throwing an annoyed glance at the door.

The door opened, and a messenger rushed into the room. "An urgent missive for you, Lady Axlya," he said, executing a hasty bow. He held a scroll out for her, and she took it from him.

"What is it?" Kalis asked as Lady Axlya read the message.

"It's a letter from General Slaugh." Lady Axlya lowered the

vellum to look at me. "He's announced his intentions to claim the throne, and he's demanded you be brought back to Kaipei to face trial."

"Trial?" I repeated, incensed. "Trial for what?"

"For the murder of King Aolis."

17

Mavlyn

The next morning, Leap and Mavlyn were loaded onto an airship bound for Angtun.

"Well, this isn't so bad," Mavlyn said as the ship took flight. The chains on her wrists clanked as she reached up to comb her windblown hair back. "I thought they were going to throw us into the brig."

Leap only nodded in answer, his gaze fixated on the city of Wynth as it shrank into the distance, much like their combined hopes of escape. A dark cloud seemed to hover over him, one that Mavlyn completely understood. She knew he'd planned to stage an escape using Cirra, who was faithfully following them, doing her best to blend in with the cloud cover. But Lord Oren had tasked not one, but *three* lightning riders to escort him, and though they were patrolling the ship rather than riding on their own cloud familiars, Mavlyn had no doubt they were waiting in the clouds nearby, just like Cirra. There was no way they could outrun all three of them.

One of the lightning riders sat on a bench a few feet away from them, a giant male with long silver braids tied in a low tail at the nape of his neck. Swirling blue tattoos peaked out from beneath his armor, gold beads glinting from a thick, silver beard. He seemed intent on oiling his blade, but when Mavlyn glanced over at him, he looked up to meet her stare.

"The captain wanted to throw you both in the brig," the lightning rider said. "But Leap's parents were lightning riders, and riders do not forget our own. They were brave, honorable warriors, and we would not do them the disservice of treating their son like a common criminal while you are in our custody. Even if he has been behaving like one."

He raised a bushy white eyebrow, and Leap's cheeks colored with shame. For a second, it appeared he might drop the other male's gaze, but he dug his heels in, fisting his hands at his sides.

"You don't know what I've been through," he said. "You don't get to judge me."

The rider shrugged. "I'm not here to judge you. Your fate is for Lord Oren to decide."

He returned to oiling his blade, and silence fell between them, thick and heavy as the approaching winter snows. Leap stared at the manacles on his hands, refusing to meet Mavlyn's gaze. He was clearly trying to avoid answering questions about his past, and Mavlyn bit her lip, fighting against the frustration bubbling inside her. She hated being kept in the dark, especially since she was probably going to find out whatever he was hiding once they arrived at Castle Angtun. If he would just tell her, at least they could be prepared. Frogs, maybe she could even help.

Mavlyn was just about to go belowdecks to get out of the wind when Leap spoke again. "It's nice to meet someone who still remembers my parents," he said to the rider. "What's your name? And did you know them well?"

The rider smiled. "My name is Gale," he said. "Your mother and I weren't close, but your father and I were training partners in the academy."

Leap seemed to brighten up a little at that. "I think I remember you," he said, his storm-grey eyes sparkling with a fond memory. "You used to play wind games with me when I was little."

Gale grinned. "Yes I did. You were a feisty little tyke, always chasing people and shocking them with lightning sparks from your fingertips." His smile faded a little as he studied Leap. "Your parents were so proud that you'd manifested your powers so early. They were certain you would follow in their footsteps one day. I wonder what they would say if they knew what path you'd chosen."

"If they could say anything about it, they'd still be alive," Leap pointed out. "And if they were alive, I wouldn't have chosen the path that I did."

He glanced away from Gale, a stubborn tilt to his jaw. The rider looked like he wanted to argue, but he merely sighed and returned to cleaning his blade.

Mavlyn bit her lip as she watched him work, questions burning on the tip of her tongue. "What happened to the Oracle?" she asked, though she knew he probably wouldn't answer. "Why was she removed from Wynth?"

The rider did not disappoint. "Who said she was removed?" he asked, not even bothering to look up from his task.

Leap rolled his eyes, turning back to glare at Gale. "We all know that she's not at the air temple," he said. "Unless the monks suddenly decided to give Quye free rein of the city, Uncle Oren either moved her, or she's been taken. Which one is it?"

"I can't divulge any details to you," Gale said. "But you don't need to worry about the Oracle. She's being kept in a safe place."

"So Uncle *did* have her moved." Leap frowned. "She won't be happy about that."

"Why?" Mavlyn asked. "I thought she'd jump at the chance to leave the temple, since she's locked in there all the time."

Leap shook his head. "Quye likes to complain about being locked up like a princess in an ivory tower, but the truth is that even though she enjoys sneaking out every once in a while to give her caretakers a hard time and make mischief in the city, she loves the air temple. It's her haven, and it's also where the winds come to whisper their secrets to her. She's most powerful there."

Mavlyn frowned. "If the air temple is where the Oracle is most powerful, then wouldn't Lord Oren want her to stay there? Her predictions won't be as accurate if the winds can't speak to her."

"Taking her from the temple was the right decision," the rider said. "King Aolis's death has thrown the entire country into a political upheaval. With no clear contender for the throne, all three houses are vying for position. The only good thing that's come of all this is that the shadow creatures have disappeared."

"What?" Mavlyn stared, sure that she'd misheard him. "What do you mean, the shadow creatures have disappeared?" That was impossible. She'd seen the shadow demon take over Gelsyne's body, turning Adara's poor mother into her very own avatar. There was no way that shadow magic had disappeared from Ediria, not while that monstrous creature was still in their world.

"I mean exactly that," Gale said. "The shadow creatures that have been plaguing the Deadlands border have vanished. We haven't had a single one try to cross over into air fae territory in nearly a week now. And we've gotten reports from the other realms that their pockets of infestation have also disappeared. It seems the girl from the prophecy did her job."

Mavlyn glanced at Leap to gauge his reaction. She could see that this news was just as unsettling to him as it was to her, yet he didn't question the rider about it. "It must be a relief for the rest of the lightning riders to be able to take a break from guarding the border," he said instead, the question a little too casual.

Gale blew out a breath. "Well, I can't say that we've done that yet," he said, sheathing his blade. "We're still guarding the border vigilantly, in case this is some kind of fluke or trick. But I have a feeling that if we continue to see no activity, Lord Oren will order us to pull back so we can deal with any potential threats from the other fae territories."

Leap looked at Mavlyn then, and the dread in his eyes made her stomach lurch. She sensed he was thinking the same thing —that if this was some kind of trick, then the border would be unguarded when the shadow demon was ready to make her move. She'd done her best to fill Leap in on what had transpired in the castle, knew that he'd seen Nox himself when he'd gone looking for them.

It was more important than ever that they find Quye, so she could advise them on how to best help Adara. But how could they do that when Lord Oren was keeping her under lock and key?

Sighing, Mavlyn turned and walked away, suddenly tired of this conversation. Everything seemed so hopeless, and as she looked around at the billowing sails and the fluffy clouds whipping by, an almost crippling wave of homesickness struck her. She wished she could talk to her mother, or even Mrs. Aeolan, and ask them for advice. She'd never been away from home before, and although she tried her best to keep a brave face for the others, she felt out of place here. Adara was a lost princess and a child of prophecy, Einar a dragon general, Leap the son of two famous lightning riders and nephew to one of the most powerful fae in Ediria. Who was Mavlyn compared to all of that?

These thoughts gnawed at Mavlyn for the rest of the journey, and when Angtun finally came into view, she was almost glad for the distraction. Like Wynth, the city of Angtun was built on the peak of a mountain, protected on all sides by an electric energy field.

But that was where the similarities ended.

"It's ugly, isn't it?" Leap said, sidling up to her. His lip curled in disgust as he looked down at the city. "Like a mouthful of teeth from some giant monstrosity, waiting to devour the world."

Mavlyn raised an eyebrow. "That's one way to describe it," she said, studying the city skyline. The buildings rose from the mountaintop like a bristling pyramid of spines, each one gilded orange by the dying sunlight. The spire-like buildings were all constructed from smooth white stone, save for Angtun Castle, whose spires were painted gold. Like the air temple, it perched at the tip of the mountain's peak, six of its twelve spires tipped with rods that fed into the city's electrical field.

The captain steered the airship toward the city gate, a circular metal portal that appeared to be floating in the air. Two lightning riders manned the portal, and Gale went to confer with them while the other three lightning riders on board the airship guarded Leap and Mavlyn, their narrowed eyes glued to them like a hawk's to his prey. The riders manning the portal gave Mavlyn suspicious looks, but their expressions seemed to soften when they looked at Leap, and they gave Gale a nod of approval, allowing the group to pass.

"I think you have more allies here than you may realize," Mavlyn murmured to Leap as the airship sailed through the portal, aiming for the docks waiting several thousand feet below.

Leap shrugged, but Mavlyn could tell by the uncertain look

on his face that he hadn't expected to find so much sympathy amongst the lightning riders. It was clear there was more to the story of why Leap had fled Angtun, and Mavlyn wondered if he'd tried turning to the lightning riders for help. Perhaps he'd thought they wouldn't be able to assist him—they did answer to Lord Oren, after all. But she suspected that even though the riders were servants of Oren, they held power in their own right. After all, they were an elite force, and they wielded an ability that was rare amongst even air fae.

Night descended on Angtun as they docked in the harbor, and the guards ushered them off the ship and through the city. Mavlyn craned her neck to study the buildings, which rose around them like a cluster of stalagmites, tall and narrow, with points that tapered off into the sky. Even the shortest ones were ten stories tall, with windows spiraling along the outsides. The narrow, winding streets were nearly empty, and it wasn't difficult to see why. Almost everyone in the city used some kind of air transportation, from the wind tunnels that snaked between the buildings, to small flying contraptions powered by electricity.

"Why aren't we using the wind tunnels, like everyone else?" Mavlyn wondered aloud. "It's obviously much faster that way."

"It's easier for the guards to keep an eye on us," Leap muttered back. "Even without access to my powers, I can still catch a ride on any of these wind tunnels, jump through a window, and be ten streets away before they can blink. Here on the ground, it's much harder."

"Hmm." Mavlyn looked at the surface streets again. Aside from a few threadbare beggars and children, there were hardly any fae down here. And there also weren't any doors on the ground levels of the buildings, or at least none facing the street. The entrances were at least two stories up, which meant that just like with the air temple, you had to be an air fae, or with an air fae, in order to enter.

It took them a good forty minutes to arrive at the castle, and by the time they did, Mavlyn's eyes were burning with exhaustion. She hadn't slept much last night, plagued by worries for Quye and also the uncertainty of her own fate. And even though their audience with Lord Oren was imminent, Mavlyn wanted nothing more than to curl into a ball in a corner and sleep.

As they entered the palace gates, Mavlyn noticed an immediate change come over Leap. He straightened his posture and held his head high, marching through the bailey as though he wasn't shackled and clad in filthy, torn clothes. The stable staff and guards seemed to recognize him, their stares and whispers following them as they were marched up the steps and into the foyer.

It was only when the guards started leading them to a hall off the right that Leap began to show signs of resistance. "You're not taking us to the dungeons?" he asked, coming to a stop.

Gale turned to look at us, his eyebrows arched. "Would you prefer that?"

Leap shrugged. "I don't want to be here at all. But since you've brought me back to Angtun in chains, dirty and starving, I figured my uncle was going to keep me in a cell, not give me an actual bed."

Gale snorted. "Regardless of your crimes, you are still air fae nobility. The guards might have had a little fun with you by sticking you in a jail cell last night, but Lord Oren won't be pleased if you're brought before him looking like a gutter rat. He'll see you tomorrow, once you're clean, fed, and rested."

"And what about me?" Mavlyn asked. "I thought I was a filthy earth fae spy, not to be trusted?"

Gale shrugged. "It's easier to keep watch over the two of you if you're together."

Mavlyn frowned, not sure if she bought that explanation. But she wasn't about to argue her way into spending another night in a jail cell, so she allowed the guards to lead her and Leap into a guest chamber. Fresh bedclothes, towels, and a bath with a privacy screen awaited, and Mavlyn's entire body cried out at the sight of the two soft feather beds. She barely noticed the rest of her surroundings, nor when the guards shut and bolted the door behind them.

"Hey." Leap waved a hand in front of Mavlyn's face, and she blinked, realizing that she'd dozed off while standing. She turned to see him frowning at her, a concerned look on his face. "I was asking if you wanted to use the bath first."

"Oh. Right. Yeah, if you don't mind." Mavlyn glanced down at herself, and her skin crawled as she realized how dirty she was. She couldn't lie down on those pristine bedsheets without bathing first.

Grabbing a set of towels and bed clothes from the edge of the nearest bed, she hung them across the top of the privacy screen, then ducked behind it and stripped off her clothes. An involuntary moan slipped from between her lips as she sank into the bathtub, muscles she hadn't even realized were tense relaxing as the hot water soaked into them.

"Hey," Leap warned, though there was a note of amusement in his voice. "Don't enjoy yourself *too* much. There are children present."

"Oh, shut up." Mavlyn said, but the words came out more like a chuckle than a true admonishment. "I'll be out in a minute."

Grabbing a bar of soap, she lathered it up and scrubbed herself down, washing off the travel dust and grime until her skin was soft and shiny. She knew she should get out now, let Leap have his turn, but the water was so warm and inviting, her limbs so lethargic, that she couldn't bring herself to leave it yet.

Just one more minute, she told herself, leaning the back of her head against the rim of the tub.

Her thoughts drifted, and soon Mavlyn found herself floating in darkness. She felt weightless, as though she had become a formless entity with no physical body, and she let herself drift there for a while, enjoying the sensation of being free of all burdens. But all too soon, the darkness faded away, revealing a windowless room with grey walls. Mavlyn frowned as she stared around at the space—it was lavishly furnished, with all the creature comforts, and yet the stone walls felt oppressive, almost like a prison. Was she in some kind of underground bunker? How did she get here?

"Mavlyn?" a familiar voice said from behind her, bubbling with delight. "Is that really you?"

Mavlyn spun toward the voice, and would have toppled over if she'd had a body. Quye sat just a few feet away on a massive, overstuffed couch, her feet propped up on a matching stool, an open book on her lap. Her cloud of white curls were tied into a long braid that hung over her shoulder. Her heart-shaped face beamed with delight as she looked at Mavlyn, blue-grey eyes sparkling, cheeks flushed. Mavlyn could only stare, stunned speechless at the sight.

She'd forgotten just how stunning the Oracle was.

"Oh, I'm so happy you're here!" Quye leaped off the couch, book forgotten, and rushed over to Mavlyn with outstretched hands. Mavlyn tried to grasp them, but with no corporeal form, she passed straight through Quye's body. Still, the phantom touch sent an electric thrill through her.

"Where are we?" she asked, looking around the room. "Is this real?"

"Yes, and also no," Quye admitted. She tucked a stray curl of hair behind her ear, and Mavlyn wasn't sure why, but she found the gesture ridiculously adorable. "We're on a different plane of existence, somewhere between the dream realm and the spirit realm. As the Oracle, I've always had a strong connection to both, and I've been using it to try and reach you for the last few days. I'm so glad it finally worked," she added, looking around the room with a hopeless sigh. "Uncle Oren tried to make this place feel like home, but his decorator has awful taste. I need you to come rescue me before I perish from boredom."

Despite the bizarreness of the situation, Mavlyn sorted. "Is that all?" she asked, a little dryly. "Just boredom?"

"Well, no." Quye flipped her braid over her shoulder. "There is the fate of the world and all that, too. Uncle Oren means well and all, but my life is not the one at stake here. If you don't get me out of here in the next few days, and we don't do what needs to be done, Adara will die."

Mavlyn's mood plummeted like the temperature of a frozen wasteland. "What do you mean, Adara will die?" she asked, her voice rising along with her panic. "And how are we supposed to find you? Where is this place?"

"I—"

Someone shook Mavlyn by the shoulders, and she reared up from the bathtub, water sloshing all over the floor. "Mavlyn, wake up!" Leap shouted in her face. His nose was mere inches from hers, eyes wide with panic, and she realized it was his fingers curled around her shoulders, his nails digging into her bare skin.

"Giant's teeth!" Mavlyn shoved him back, heart-pounding, then immediately regretted it when he went skidding across the sopping wet floor, nearly falling on his ass. She started to rise from the tub, then dropped back into the water when she remembered she was stark naked. "What was that for?" she demanded.

"You were out cold!" Leap snapped, placing a hand on the windowsill to steady himself. He glared at Mavlyn, his storm-grey eyes not quite meeting her own, and Mavlyn suspected the pink flush in his cheeks had more to do with embarrassment than anger. "You were in that tub for over thirty minutes and didn't answer when I called your name, so I came over here to check on you and found you passed out. I thought you were dead!"

"Thirty minutes?" Mavlyn raked a hand through her auburn hair, still trying to orient herself. "Giant's Teeth. I'm so sorry, Leap. I had no idea." Guilt stung at her as she realized the bathwater was now tepid, half of it spilled onto the marble floor. But the emotion faded as the dream began to come back to her, and she sat up straight in the tub. "That's right! I had a dream—"

"Squalls!" Leap grabbed the towel hanging over the privacy screen and tossed it in Mavlyn's direction, averting his now tomato-red face. "Will you get out of the tub and put something on first?"

Shaking her head, Mavlyn did as he asked, using the towel to dry her skin. Like most earth fae, she wasn't particularly self-conscious about her body, but perhaps the air fae were more prudish, and besides, Leap *was* just a teenage boy. He kept his back to her while she wrapped the towel around her hair and put on the pajamas that had been left for them, working as fast as she could.

"You can turn around now." When he made no move to do so, Mavlyn sighed. "Quye visited me in a dream. She was about to tell me her location when you shook me awake."

Leap whirled around, and Mavlyn blinked at the scowl on his face. She'd expected him to be excited about this news, not mutinous. "She visited *you* in your dreams, but not me?" he demanded.

The back of Mavlyn's neck prickled. "I don't think it's personal," she said gently. "Quye might have tried to reach you first but found it easier to get to me. We have some kind of... connection."

Leap's eyebrows rose. "Quye is the Oracle. She's got a connection to everyone."

Mavlyn shook her head. "It's different," she insisted, though she wasn't so sure if that was true. She'd definitely felt an instant pull when she'd met Quye, and had thought it was reciprocal, but maybe everyone who met the Oracle experienced the same thing. She *was* different from the rest of the fae, with a direct connection to the spirit realm, able to see the threads of fate that connected all fae. Maybe everyone in her presence felt that connection.

That thought made her heart sink a little, but she tried to push it out of her mind. She hadn't come searching for the Oracle for her own selfish feelings. She was doing it to help Adara, and to save their kingdom.

"If you say so." Leap crossed his arms as he leaned against the window, the annoyance on his face giving way to a more thoughtful expression. "Were you able to get a sense of where she was, at least? Or were you two frolicking through some fanciful dreamscape?"

"No, I think the place in the dream is a facsimile of the place she's being kept." Mavlyn did her best to describe the room, specifically mentioning the grey stone walls and lack of windows that all the fancy white furniture hadn't failed to cover up.

"Hmm. It felt like an underground bunker?" Leap tapped his chin as he considered what Mavlyn had said. "Sounds like she's being held at Windhelm." At Mavlyn's blank look, he added, "It's a fortress built into the heart of one of the Gaoth Aire mountains, about a two-hour ride from here on Cirra. It's an ancient stronghold that predates the Dragon-Fae war, back when the clans were still warring for dominance over the Gaoth Aire. Once House Seifir had established itself as the ruling clan, they established Angtun as their official seat of power. But Windhelm still exists, and our military still uses it as an operations base."

"Great," Mavlyn grumbled. "That means it's going to be heavily defended."

"I'm sure we can figure out a way to break in." Leap sighed, turning to look out the window at the glittering spires below. "The real challenge is going to be figuring out how to get out of *here* first."

18

Adara

L ady Axlya wasted no time after General Slaugh's calamitous declaration. She called an emergency council meeting with the leaders of each of the water clans—lake, marsh, ocean, and ice—and ordered all family members residing in the castle to attend.

"How is she going to get the clan leaders here on short notice?" I asked as Prentis and I hurried toward the meeting place. "She's given us all mere hours to appear."

"The clan leaders won't be attending in person," Prentis explained. His stride ate up the ground, and I had to take two steps for every one of his just to keep pace. His expression revealed nothing, but there was a determined set to his jaw as we walked, lines of tension running from his shoulders and into the soles of his boots as they echoed across the tiled floors. "They'll be appearing via ice mirror."

"Ice mirror?" I echoed, not sure if I'd heard him right. "What do you mean, ice mirror?"

Prentis's mouth twisted into a smirk. "You're about to find

out."

We rounded the corner, where a set of double doors awaited us at the end of a long corridor. The doors were thrown wide open and flanked by two guards, who inclined their heads respectfully to Prentis as we passed into a large tower room. The ceiling stretched impossibly high above, light filtering in through a series of rectangular windows that trailed up the sides of the tower in a spiral pattern. Below the windows, a set of twelve mirrors ringed the circumference of the room, each one ten feet tall and set in silver frames. At first, I thought they were made of frosted glass, but upon closer inspection, I realized that the glass panes were actually sheets of *ice.*

Ice mirrors indeed.

"Adara, Prentis, you're here." Lady Axlya's voice ripped my attention from the mirrors, and I turned to the assembled nobles. A semi-circle of chairs had been placed on the left side of the room, where Axlya sat in the center, her consorts and advisors seated on her right. An unpleasant feeling rippled through me as I spied Cascada seated in a chair to Axlya's left, but I barely spared her a thought as I noticed the male sitting right next to her.

Einar.

Though Axlya's presence dominated the room, I found my gaze riveted to the dragon male who infuriated and inspired me in equal parts. His golden gaze ensnared mine, and the phantom puncture marks he'd left *throbbed,* shooting straight from my neck into my groin. Heat pooled between my thighs, and his nostrils flared as though he could sense my sudden rush of desire.

Damn him. I resisted the urge to clench my fists. Einar had done something to me when he'd bitten me, and judging by the glint in his eyes, he knew exactly what was happening to me. I'd always been drawn to him, I could admit that now, but I'd never felt the pull with such intensity. It was as though no one else in the room existed, only the two of us. My legs trembled beneath my dress as I fought against the desire to take a running leap straight into his lap and finish what we'd started yesterday. *This* was why I'd been avoiding him since Prentis had found us yesterday.

And why, I suspected, he'd been avoiding me as well.

"Adara?" Prentis's fingers were at my elbow, pulling me back to the present. I was suddenly aware of everyone else's eyes on me, and my skin prickled with embarrassment as I realized they'd all watched me salivate over Einar like a lust-ridden nymph. Prentis himself didn't seem pleased. His mouth flattened into a thin line, and he looked at Einar as if he'd enjoy nothing more than to use his water whip to throw him bodily from the room. The smirk curling at the corner of Einar's lips told me he, too, was aware of that. I fought the urge to roll my eyes as I took my seat next to him, sandwiched between him and Prentis, who was seated directly to Axlya's left.

"How did you convince Lady Axlya to let you in?" I muttered out of the corner of my lips, leaning toward him so the others wouldn't hear.

He only winked at me. "A gentleman doesn't kiss and tell."

I *did* roll my eyes at him then, leaning away from Einar and cutting off the conversation. I glanced at the mirrors across the room and immediately wished I hadn't—three of them flashed a brilliant gold, so bright they scorched my eyes. As I blinked rapidly, trying to get rid of the spots that appeared in my vision, shadowy forms took shape on the icy surfaces, revealing three Greater Fae.

"Thank you for coming on short notice," Lady Axlya said, her voice echoing in the chamber. She sat straight backed in her chair, no longer the languorous noble playing games of cat and mouse, but an iron-fisted leader, prepared to do whatever it took to protect her realm. "I've summoned you here today because I've received some shocking news."

As Lady Axlya informed them about General Slaugh's missive, Prentis filled me in on the clan leaders. The fae on the left was Lady Ria of the Marsh Fae. She wore her heather colored braid in loose waves down her back, her willowy form draped in a daffodil colored gown with a square neckline. The fae in the middle was Lord Aigean of the Ocean Fae. He wore a skin-tight suit that molded to every inch of his swimmer's body, and perched on a throne that seemed crafted from seashells. In the mirror on the right, wearing ice blue leathers trimmed with fur, was Lady Tamil, representative of the Ice Fae. Her father, Lord Tor, was the ice clan's patriarch, but a terrible illness had afflicted him, leaving her to rule in his stead while he recovered.

"And what about the lake fae clan leader?" I whispered to Prentis.

His voice was entirely too smug as he answered, "You're sitting right next to him."

My cheeks burned as I sat back in my chair. I felt woefully out of my depth in this room—I might be water fae, might be a descendent of House Usciete and the rightful heir to Ediria's throne. But this was yet another subtle reminder that I knew nothing, that I wasn't qualified to even be in this room, never mind sit on the throne.

What had I been thinking, coming here?

Einar's leg brushed against mine, offering me comfort. Warmth spread through my limbs as the anxious thoughts in my head receded, and a rush of gratitude filled me. I didn't know how he'd convinced Axlya to let him into the room when she barely tolerated him, but I was so thankful. Einar might drive me crazy, but he also grounded me in a way that no one else seemed to be able.

As Lady Axlya continued speaking, I found my gaze drawn

to Tamil more than the others, though I wasn't sure why. Her snow-white hair was cut into a short and choppy windswept style, her wintry eyes as piercing as a falcon's, her angular cheekbones sharper than ice picks. Yet I sensed a nobility of spirit in her that the others seemed to lack. She was simply... more.

Either that, or it was her ice fae nature that drew me to her.

"So the rumors are true, then?" Lord Aigean demanded when Axlya had finished. "King Aolis is dead?"

"Yes," Lady Axlya said. She turned to me, and I had to fight the sudden urge to squirm in my seat like a child who had been caught doing wrong. "Adara here is the one who killed him. She is the child from the prophecy that foretold of a fae with the power to banish shadow magic from our kingdom. And I believe she has succeeded."

Murmuring broke out from all three mirrors as the three leaders spoke with their advisors, who were partially out of frame. Finally, Lady Ria spoke. "We would like to hear Adara's testimony regarding this matter. King Aolis might have been corrupt, but he was one of us. And prophecy or not, regicide is a serious crime.

I glanced at Lady Axlya, who inclined her head. My intestines knotted themselves into a ball as I stood, and with my hands clasped behind my back to keep from wringing them, I told the water fae court the entire story. Of how I was the long-lost daughter of Daryan and Olette, hidden away in the earth fae realm and raised by Gelsyne, my mother's closest confidante. Of how I'd had no knowledge that Gelsyne wasn't my true mother until after I'd manifested my powers, Slaugh had stolen her away, and I'd traveled across half the kingdom to rescue her from his clutches. And of how, with the dragon the Radiants had chosen as my protector at my side, I'd confronted Aolis, learned the truth about his involvement with shadow magic, and used our combined powers to defeat the king once and for all.

"But," I went on, after being interrupted for the umpteenth time, "Lady Axlya is incorrect about one thing. I haven't succeeded. Nox, the shadow demon who has been controlling King Aolis and through him, General Slaugh, now lives inside my foster mother, Gelsyne. She is using the general as a puppet, and if we allow Slaugh to take the throne, *she* will become the ruler of Ediria by proxy. If that happens, King Aolis's death will have been for nothing!"

"I have to say that this story sounds highly convenient," Lord Aigean said after a long, fraught pause. He gave me a supercilious look as he raked his eyes down my body, as if I was a piece of riffraff that had been dragged into the hall, and he wasn't sure why I'd been allowed to remain. "An unknown girl claiming to be the long-lost heir shows up at the same time all the shadow creatures vanish, kills King Aolis, takes the credit, and makes a play for his throne."

"Wait a minute." Einar's deep voice snapped through the chamber. "What do you mean, the shadow creatures have disappeared?"

"He means exactly that, *dragon*." It was Lady Ria who spoke this time. "News has been spreading across the lands that the forests and lakes previously claimed by shadow creatures have all but been restored."

"My lords and ladies," Lady Axlya intervened in a deceptively pleasant voice. "I may be mistaken, but it seems you are suggesting that, in my advanced age, I am so far gone as to be incapable of recognizing my own kin. That I would not be able to tell if Adara was an imposter, rather than the child of my late granddaughter, who was beloved by us *all*."

Her gaze sharpened as she met the eyes of the clan leaders, and an uncomfortable silence filled the room. "We do not mean any disrespect," Lord Aigean said, choosing his words with care. "We are merely exercising caution. After all, we already made a grave mistake when we chose Aolis as our next king. We cannot afford such a grievous error again."

"I know that better than anyone else," Lady Axlya said. "It was *my* child who was taken and held hostage by Aolis when he came to power, not yours."

"Speaking of Lady Cascada," Tamil interrupted, her gaze landing on the fae in question. "You were there at the castle, weren't you? Perhaps you could shed some light on this matter of the shadow creatures disappearing."

Cascada nodded. "The account Adara gave the court today is correct," she said in a serene tone absolutely nothing like her usual acerbic personality. "King Aolis was corrupted by the shadow magic he and his guards wielded. They used that magic to weaken me and the other hostages so we would be pliant to his demands." Her voice trembled, and the emotion was so real I almost forgot she was a lying bitch. "I was so grateful when Adara finally slayed Aolis that I was happy to join my fellow hostages in holding off Slaugh and his cronies so she and her friends could escape."

She flicked her gaze toward Einar for a split second, and I could have sworn her eyes were black as pitch at that moment. But they were cornflower blue once more as they turned back to the court, eyes wide with emotion.

"But Adara wasn't there when the shadow magic vanished. I saw it leave from Slaugh and Gelsyne's bodies like noxious clouds being purged from their pores. Adara may not believe me, but..." she shrugged, splaying her hands wide in a what-can-you-do manner. "If that wasn't the case, how did I get here? Why would General Slaugh have let me go when keeping me and the other hostages would have given him the leverage he needed to keep the other house rulers in line?"

Cascada glanced at me then, and my anger for her faltered like a guttering candle. The hurt look in her eyes was so profound I began to second-guess myself. Was there even a remote possibility that Cascada could be right? That Nox and the shadow magic really *had* vanished from Ediria, and my work here was done?

I desperately wanted to believe that was true. But I didn't dare. Not until I could verify it with my own eyes.

"See?" Lady Ria's scathing tone snapped my attention back to the nobles. She and Aegian were looking at me like two cats who had found the hidden stash of cream, while Tamil was more reserved, a troubled look in her eyes. "You were right, Lord Aegian—Adara's story was entirely too convenient to be believable." She raised an eyebrow at me. "If you weren't so insistent that claiming the throne before General Slaugh does is the only way to save the kingdom from shadow magic, then perhaps your claims would be easier to believe. But as it stands, you sound more like an opportunist than anything else."

The mocking smile Lady Ria gave me sparked an impotent rage in me, and an intense urge to reach through the glass and throttle her seized me. The flames in my chest roared to life, sparks kindling in the palms of my hands, and before I could stop myself, I raised my hands, letting the sparks ignite into full-fledged gouts of flame.

"You want convenient?" I sneered. "I'll show you convenient."

Their eyes widened as I let the flames fly, shooting balls of fire at each of their faces. Even Tamil, though she was the only one who hadn't mocked me. The clan leaders' eyes widened as the flames struck true, and the ice sheets evaporated in an instant, clouds of mist swirling upward.

Lady Axlya raised a hand, twirling her fingers through the air. The mist responded to her magic, coalesced into a trio of clouds that burst above the mirrors. The frames rapidly filled with water, and with a snap of Axlya's fingers, the water froze, coalescing into perfect sheets of ice once more.

But the fire had done its job. The clan leaders were gone, the frozen surfaces reflecting only my own heaving chest and flushed cheeks. My eyes were wild, the flames still raging from my hands, and I hastily put them out, realizing that I must look like a deranged lunatic to the remaining court members.

"Well," Kalis murmured, the first to break the tense silence. "I *have* always wondered what would happen if someone broke one of the mirrors."

I turned to see him staring at me with a bemused expression. Unfortunately, he seemed to be the only one. Lady Axlya's face was as still as the surface of a frozen lake, and with just as much emotion, while Ilsa looked nonplussed. Prentis and Cascada were both staring at me like they couldn't believe what I had done and were waiting for Lady Axlya to sever my head from my shoulders.

The only one who wasn't looking at me as though I'd lost my mind was Einar. I'd expected to see him smirking or even outright laughing at my blatant show of disrespect. Instead, his expression was stoic, the maelstrom of emotions swirling in his eyes the only sign that he was feeling anything. He was both impressed and proud that I'd had the balls to stand up to the water fae court... and judging by the heat in his gaze, more than a little turned on, too.

Heat flared between my legs, and I had to look away as the phantom mark on my neck throbbed once again.

"She didn't break the mirrors," Lady Axlya said. Her voice was a mere whisper, and yet it whipped through the chamber with the force of a blizzard. "She melted them." She turned to look at me now, and the expression in her eyes was almost... disturbed. "Do you have any idea the enormity of what you just did, child?"

Confusion and embarrassment crept up my spine, and I fought against the urge to shiver against the unwelcome tingles. "Umm, I was rude and disrespectful to my elders?" I ventured.

Ilsa rolled her eyes. "That's true, but it isn't just that. Those mirrors are ancient magic, crafted by powerful water fae over four thousand years ago. Not once have they suffered so much as a hairline crack, even through all the wars and sieges this castle has undergone. Not until you came along."

The gravity of her statement sent a shiver skating across my skin, and I stared down at my palms as if I were seeing them for the first time. I knew my fire magic was unusual, even by fae standards—unlike Einar's fire, it could kill shadow creatures and burn away shadow taint. But being able to destroy magic mirrors crafted by ancient fae, even temporarily? That seemed like a step beyond.

I met Einar's eyes to see that he was just as taken aback by this announcement as I was. I had a feeling he was wondering the same thing I was—if my fire magic could do this, what else was it capable of?

"I have already ordered the clan heads to travel to Usciete post-haste," Axlya said after a very pregnant pause. "As much as I would like to name you as our candidate for the throne, the clan leaders all must vote on the matter first. They will do so once you've completed your coming-of-age ritual and have come into your full power."

My heart leapt at Axlya's words, all of my troubled thoughts and questions evaporating. "Does that mean you're granting me permission to undergo the ritual?" I asked.

"Yes." Lady Axlya smiled for the first time, and hope burgeoned in my chest. But that hope deflated like a punctured balloon as the next words fell from her lips, heavy as stones. "One condition. You must marry Prentis."

19

Leap

Leap was almost grateful when the guards came to collect him for his audience with Lord Oren the next morning. He'd barely slept a wink, too consumed between his dread of the meeting to come and his thoughts about Quye.

He was, however, still mildly annoyed that Quye had come to Mavlyn instead of him. But he suspected the connection Mavlyn claimed she felt with Quye was more than mere friendship. He knew his cousin's romantic proclivities leaned toward female, just as he knew Quye's heart was as fickle as the very winds she relied upon for her visions. That was one of the reasons she snuck out of the air fae temple so often; she couldn't very well find romance amongst a gaggle of monks who had eschewed all mortal vices in their efforts to become one with the Divine Winds.

But none of that was Leap's problem. His only concern was getting out of this winds-forsaken place and finding his cousin.

Leap let these thoughts consume him as he trudged through the palace, surrounded by a bevy of guards on all sides, wrists still bound in iron. He didn't want to look at the tapestries hanging on the walls, the statues and portraits of various important air fae royals and heroes. He didn't want the terrible reminders of his time here that they would trigger.

But the closer they got to his uncle's study, the harder it was to ignore the memories. Leap's back and legs throbbed with the phantom pains from old beatings, and he gritted his teeth. He refused to let the other memories, memories that had long since ceased to torment him, crawl back to haunt him.

By the time they reached Uncle Oren's study, a sheen of cold sweat covered Leap's face, and his shirt was soaked through. He straightened his back as one of the guards knocked on the door, clenching his clammy hands to stop their trembling.

He would not show fear. No matter what he found on the other side of the door.

"Enter."

The door swung open, and the guards ushered Leap forward. He nearly collapsed in relief when he saw Uncle Oren was alone behind his desk save for his secretary, a diminutive fae perched inconspicuously on a chair in the corner. Leap peered around the room, checking the shadows and crevices just to be sure, but there was no sign of his tormentor.

He could be thankful for that small blessing, at least.

"Leap." His uncle's commanding voice boomed like a thunderclap, and he jerked to attention, his body reverting to years of training even as his mind wanted to rebel against it. A bead of sweat rolled down his spine as his uncle's thin lip curled, his yellow eyes flat with disappointment. "Even dragged back in chains, with an army of guards standing just over your shoulder, you refuse to show me proper respect."

Leap swallowed, unspoken retorts sliding down his throat like broken glass. "Why, Uncle Oren. How lovely to see you again," he said instead, sketching a courtly bow. He even managed to do it with a straight face.

Uncle Oren snorted. "Don't patronize me, boy." He flicked a lock of white hair over his broad shoulder as he leaned forward, his raptor eyes raking over Leap. "Seems like your years of running around Wynth as a street urchin haven't stunted your appetite, at least. You're at least two feet taller than when I last saw you."

Leap crossed his arms over his chest. "I was a thief, not a street urchin, and I was damn good at it." He smirked as a tic started in Oren's temple, but the expression faded from his face as his uncle's words set in. "You knew where I've been this whole time. Haven't you?"

"Of course I have." Uncle Oren gave Leap an impatient look. "You may be a brat, but you are still my sister's son. If I couldn't keep you in the castle, I at least had to make sure you were safe. I assigned a spy to keep tabs on you, and he paid off the authorities to keep you from getting into any real trouble."

Leap felt as though he'd been sucker-punched in the gut. "You're lying," he said through clenched teeth. He had to be.

Uncle Oren laughed, his white teeth flashing in the morning sunlight filtering in through the window on his left. "I assure you, I am telling the truth," he said, his shoulders shaking with mirth. "I know about every single one of your escapades, including that ridiculous heist you tried to pull on that silk merchant. That was especially foolish, you know."

A buzzing sound filled Leap's ears, an impotent rage building in his chest as he stared at his uncle. Electricity began humming along his fingertips, and he was so tempted to let the storm build up, to leap across the desk and strangle his uncle with lightning-clad fingers...

"You're a bastard," he said, his voice raw.

The mirth on Uncle Oren's face vanished, replaced by an

ugly look that filled Leap with dread. "Watch what you say to me, boy," he growled in a voice like thunder. "You may be kin, but I am still your lord and master. If you think your life was miserable before you left, it will be nothing compared to the hell I will create for you if you continue to defy me."

The air filled with static electricity as Oren spoke, his long hair lifting to float around his shoulders, and Leap felt the hair on his own arms stand on end. Leap might be powerful, especially for a fae of his age, but even unbound, he was no match for his uncle. Oren was centuries old, and he wore three primal stones practically bursting with power in the silver torque around his neck. He had more magic in his little finger than Leap had in his entire body.

And yet, he *still* wanted to punch the insufferable bastard in the face.

"If you know where I've been this entire time," Leap said, forcing each word out from behind his still-clenched teeth, "then why have you waited so long to bring me back here?"

Lord Oren sighed. "Because of your involvement with Adara, of course." His raptor gaze sharpened as he steepled his fingers beneath his chin, studying Leap with a critical eye. "My spies informed me you helped her break into the air temple, and also assisted her in King Aolis's assassination. But aside from that," he admitted, an uneasy expression flickering across his face, "I lost track of you when you fled Wynth and disappeared into the mountains. My spy feared the harpies had killed you. But when you resurfaced again in Wynth with Adara and her friends, I knew it was only a matter of time before you came back again. So, I put the guards on high alert for a fae matching your description, then sat back and waited." He raised an eyebrow. "I must admit that I didn't expect you to return so quickly. Why did you?"

"Just wanted to pay my cousin another visit," Leap said,

nonchalant. "Shame she wasn't there, though. The guards made it sound like something bad happened to her."

"Quye is perfectly safe," his uncle said. "I merely moved her as a precaution given recent events—and actually, it was your initial infiltration of the Air Temple that inspired that decision, so thank you."

Leap bit back a groan at that. He'd expected the temple to tighten security after his and Adara's shenanigans, but he hadn't imagined his uncle would actually *remove* Quye from her home. "It seems counter-intuitive for you to take her away from the winds," he pointed out. "Seems to me that with the political landscape shifting so much, you'd need her visions more than ever."

"True, but it's not as though Quye can't listen to the winds when she's outside the temple," Uncle Oren said. "It will take longer for the visions and whispers to reach her, but better that than for her to be killed, or worse, fall into enemy hands."

Leap rolled his eyes. Of course his uncle would list those two fates in that particular order. Radiants forbid that Quye use her talent for anyone else's benefit than his own. What little hope he had of asking his uncle to speak to Quye in person fizzled out. He knew he couldn't so much as hint that he was still trying to get to Quye. If he did, his uncle would move her again, and he would make sure that Quye remained in the dark about the location so she couldn't send Leap or Mavlyn any hints.

"All right, enough of all this," Uncle Oren said. "Tell me about Adara and her dragon, the events that transpired at Kaipei Castle, and the little earth fae spy you've thrown your lot in with."

"That 'little earth fae spy' 's name is Mavlyn, and she is Adara's best friend," Leap snapped. "She also knows more about the events at Kaipei than I do, since she was *inside* the castle—I was only involved in the attack from the outside."

Uncle Oren's lips thinned. "Very well." He ordered the guards outside the door to bring Mavlyn to him. "While we wait for her, you will fill me in on the events leading up to Kaipei."

Leap did so begrudgingly, delivering the details in a tone-less-but-professional voice, like a soldier might to a commander. The secretary took notes as he spoke, quill scratching away at an endless sheet of vellum. He might hate his uncle, but he needed to at least appear like he was cooperating if he wanted Oren to let his guard down enough for Leap and Mavlyn to escape.

As expected, Uncle Oren objected at certain points of the narrative, specifically the fact that Leap had joined forces with the harpies, had allowed Storm to blackmail him into stealing the fan, and that instead of coming to him for help, he'd sought out Quye instead.

"I am very impressed you took on the outer castle defenses on your own, though," Uncle Oren said. He shook his head, looking both amazed and flabbergasted. "You could have been well on your way to leading your own squadron by now, Leap. Why did you run away? I know life wasn't always pleasant for you here in the palace, but if you had waited one more year, you could have enrolled at the Lightning Rider Academy. Besides, it wasn't as if you had a terrible life here. Yes, I pushed you hard, and your studies were intensive, and you and Ryker had your fair share of scraps, but—"

"Wasn't pleasant?" Leap cut his uncle off, a ruthless laugh ripping from his throat. "Uncle, you have no idea—"

The door banged open, and Leap whirled around, heart hammering, palms sweating, his body already knowing who was there before his brain could catch up. A tall, broad-shouldered male with slender, elegant limbs and shoulder-length white hair sauntered into the room, a predatory gleam in his raptor-yellow eyes as they landed on Leap.

"Well, well, well," he said, his mouth widening into a vicious grin. "Look who the thunderbird dragged in."

Leap's knees threatened to buckle. He barely noticed Mavlyn filing into the room with two guards in tow, his entire field of vision tunneling to the fae standing in front of him. Shame and resentment filled the air between them, and every inch of Leap's body screamed for him to *get out* of that confined space, to throw himself out of the nearest window and run as far and fast as he could.

The way he'd done all those years ago, when he couldn't take it anymore.

His mouth was dry as desert sand as he stared back at his tormentor, who waited, arms crossed over his slender chest. Leap knew he was looking for a response. But he couldn't seem to make his mouth work.

"Ryker." Uncle Oren's voice snapped Leap out of his horrified trance. His tone was flat, lines of displeasure bracketing the sides of his mouth. "I don't remember inviting you to this meeting."

"You didn't," Ryker said airily, "but I couldn't help myself. It's been so long since I've seen my dear cousin." He slung an arm around Leap's shoulder. "I've missed him *so* much."

Leap's body went wooden as Ryker pulled him into his body. The moment their torsos made contact, dark memories of Ryker's punishing hands crashed into Leap's mind—slamming into his stomach, yanking his head back by the hair, smashing his face into the wall—

"Lord Oren." Mavlyn's rough velvet voice brought Leap back to reality like an icy bucket of water dumped atop his head. He'd completely forgotten his uncle had sent for her. "Under better circumstances, I'd say it's a pleasure to meet you, but..." she trailed off, holding up her manacled hands, and then shrugged. "You know how it is."

"I do indeed." Uncle Oren said. He sat back in his seat as he studied Mavlyn, and Leap sidled out from beneath Ryker's arm. His cousin smirked, seeing the escape attempt for what it was, but Leap ignored him as he went to go stand next to Mavlyn instead. His stomach was in knots, his heart palpitating, and he was thankful he hadn't eaten breakfast before he came, or he would have thrown up all over his uncle's carpet.

He'd known being near Ryker again would be difficult. But he hadn't expected it to be like *this*.

"My spies had very little to tell me about you, Mavlyn of Fenwood," Uncle Oren said after a moment. "I'm told you grew up in the same village as Adara did. And that you are also a distant relative of Lady Mossi, though not powerful enough to be a member of her house."

Mavlyn snorted. "I don't know that I'd want to be a member of House Ithir at this moment, considering where their loyalties lie right now." She folded her arms. "When Adara fled our village, I told her to go to Lady Mossi, mistakenly thinking she would help. Instead, Mossi tried to trade her to Aolis in exchange for one of her hostages. I could have stayed at home and minded my own business when I found that out. Instead, I left my family and traveled all the way to the Gaoth Aire to find her, then did everything in my power to help her get to King Aolis so she could rescue her mother and defeat the king." She swallowed, tears shining in her eyes for the briefest of moments before she blinked them away. "Maybe I'm a traitor to my realm. But I'm loyal to my friends. And I'm definitely no spy."

Lord Oren chuckled. "There's no need to defend yourself so. Quye spent copious amounts of time assuring me you were not a threat to my realm."

"What?" Leap practically shouted the words. "You mean to tell us you consulted Quye, and yet you're still treating us like criminals?"

"You *are* criminals," Uncle Oren snapped, his predatory eyes flashing. He bared his teeth at Leap, the fury in his gaze so intense that Leap took an involuntary step back. "Quye might have confirmed that you aren't spies, but that doesn't absolve you of your crimes against the realm, or the abandonment of your royal duties. Since Mavlyn is your friend, I have to assume that she shares your moral proclivities." He practically spat the last word before he turned back to Mavlyn. "Now. My nephew says that you were in the castle the night Adara killed King Aolis. Tell me what you saw."

The room went silent as Mavlyn recounted the events of that fateful night. Even Leap listened intently—he'd never gotten a full account of what transpired that night either, just the salient details, as he and Mavlyn had been preoccupied with finding Adara, and then Quye.

Goosebumps raced across his skin as Mavlyn described how Adara had combined forces with Einar to kill Aolis, consuming his entire body in her magical flames until there was nothing left but ash, and then how, from those ashes, the shadow demon had risen to take possession of Gelsyne's body.

"So General Slaugh admitted to being in cahoots with this shadow demon the entire time?" Uncle Oren demanded.

"Yes," Mavlyn said. "King Aolis was too resistant to the shadow demon's demands, so they set Adara up to kill him so she could find a more pliable host instead."

"Now I understand why Slaugh is making his move for the throne," Uncle Oren muttered, his gaze darkening. "With the shadow demon's backing, he probably thinks he's invincible." His upper lip curled in disgust. "How did you escape?"

"We almost didn't," Mavlyn admitted. "Nox ordered Slaugh and his guards to kill us, but the three hostages Aolis kept from the other kingdoms intervened. They attacked the shadow guard and kept them occupied so we could make our escape."

The blood drained from Uncle Oren's face, and he gripped the edges of his desk hard enough to make his knuckles turn white. "Tempest," he said hoarsely. "My daughter."

Leap flinched at the raw agony in his uncle's eyes. If his uncle had given even a tenth of a damn about him—

"What happened to the hostages?" Ryker's voice cracked through the room, his spade-like jaw clenched tight. "Do you know if my sister survived?"

Mavlyn's expression softened, pity in her eyes. "I don't know. I only know that she and the others made it possible for us to escape."

Uncle Oren and Ryker fell silent as they processed this news, the only sound in the room that of the secretary's quill scratching against her parchment. The two looked stricken, but Leap couldn't say he shared the sentiment. He'd never met Tempest, after all—she'd been sent to King Aolis as a hostage when Leap's parents had still been alive.

"She could still be alive," Ryker said after a long moment. "We don't know—"

"My spies tell me that Cascada showed up at Usciete yesterday, alive and unharmed," Uncle Oren snapped. "I assumed Tempest would follow suit, yet the only news I've received from General Slaugh is that obnoxious declaration of his intention to take the throne." Fury mottled Oren's pale skin, and cracks formed on the mahogany desk, spreading out from the tips of his fingers.

"I'm sorry," Mavlyn said. "I wish I knew more."

Uncle Oren shook his head, his expression a thundercloud of dark emotion. "You're dismissed. Both of you."

Mavlyn didn't need to be told twice. She turned on her heel almost immediately, and Leap made to follow her. But before he could, Ryker gripped his wrist, pulling him to a stop.

Slowly, he turned to meet his cousin's predatory gaze.

"You and I have much to catch up on, Leap," Ryker said in a soft tone. "You'll make some time for me this evening, won't you?"

Helpless rage ripped through Leap, so potent he nearly choked on it. He ripped his arm from Ryker's grasp and stormed through the door, oblivious to the concerned look Mavlyn sent him over her shoulder.

One foot in front of the other, he reminded himself, just as he had all those years ago during those long midnight walks back to his rooms. When his entire body had screamed in pain, his throat so raw he could barely speak, his eyes so waterlogged he had no tears left to spare.

One. Foot. In front. Of the other.

20

Einar

"No."

My growl echoed through the room, causing the water fae to swing their heads toward me in unison. Belatedly, I realized that I'd leapt to my feet, my hands bunched into fists, fangs puncturing my lower lip and making blood gush down my chin.

I probably looked like the crazed dragon monster these fae thought I was, but I didn't care.

Adara was *not* marrying Prentis.

"No?" Lady Axlya raised her eyebrows at me. Her expression was almost bored, but I wasn't fooled—there was a clear glint of amusement in her eyes, and I knew she took great pleasure in my rage. "As much as I appreciate your feelings on the matter, Einar, you are not the one who is being asked to marry my nephew." She glanced over at Adara. "My granddaughter is. And she's yet to give her answer."

Adara pressed her lips together. Her eyes darted about the

room, meeting everyone's gaze but mine, before landing on Lady Axlya. "I need time to think about it before I can decide."

Time? I barely stopped myself from shouting the word. What in the blazes did she mean, she needed *time?* Was she seriously considering marriage to Prentis as a viable option?

"There has to be another way," I said to Lady Axlya, the words coming out just shy of a growl. "Some other way Adara can prove her loyalty to you that doesn't involve a loveless marriage."

"Who said that it would be loveless?" Axlya gave Prentis a fond look. "My niece and nephew might not know each other very well yet, but there is no reason love couldn't grow between them eventually, providing there isn't a meddlesome figure around to break up their marriage."

She gave me a pointed look, and I stared right back, neither challenging nor denying the accusation. I couldn't promise that I wouldn't do everything in my power to stop Adara from marrying Prentis. She was my *mate*. As a dragon, I couldn't allow it.

Even if it was the quickest way to getting what she wanted

"Besides," Lady Axlya continued, "this marriage isn't a test of loyalty. Try as she might to deny it, the fact is that Adara's dragon heritage weakens her claim to the throne. Marriage to a prominent member of the water fae nobility will help strengthen that claim and discourage the other houses from questioning it."

I rolled my eyes. "Please. They will question the claim, regardless. You know that."

Axlya tilted her head at me. "If this is a matter of jealousy, there is no need, Einar. Adara can simply take you as one of her consorts, just as I have done with my own paramours." She gazed fondly at Kalis and Ilsa. "Prentis might be her husband, but there is no reason you can't remain a part of Adara's life... if she wants you to be, that is."

She looked at Adara, who was blushing furiously now. Prentis looked torn on the subject, which I suspected that had less to do with Adara having multiple consorts and more to do with the idea of having to share her with a dragon.

"Again," she said firmly, as though her face hadn't turned a brilliant shade of scarlet, "I need time to make my decision."

I spun on my heel and strode out of the room, the heels of my boots snapping against the marble tiles. Fury roared in my ears, so loud that I barely noticed my surroundings, and it was only until I was halfway back to my room when I realized Adara had followed me.

"Einar." Her small hand circled around my wrist, pulling me to a stop. "We need to talk."

I stilled beneath her touch and took in a deep breath, trying to control the maelstrom of emotions swirling inside me. "We can't talk about this right now," I said, the words coming out rougher than I intended. "I need to calm down." I could feel my skin rippling beneath my clothing, muscles straining against bones that wanted to elongate, fangs threatening to punch straight through my lower lip. My inner beast was raging against the potential loss of my mate, and I needed to get myself under control before I did something I would regret.

I might want to burn the entire castle down, but this was a water fae stronghold. Not only would my attempt be ineffective, but it would likely result in my death, regardless of my connection to Adara.

And I couldn't afford to die, not when my very life was tied to the safety and security of my people.

"Einar." The pain in Adara's voice cut me to the bone, and I fought against the urge to turn around. I knew that if I looked into her lavender-blue eyes now, I would lose what little resolve I had left. "Einar, you *bit* me. And we haven't had a chance to talk about it, but I can still feel your fangs in my skin, and whenever I see you it *throbs*, and I don't understand because it's not pain, but—"

I whirled around and grabbed Adara by the shoulders, shocking her into silence. The moment my hands touched her body, my beast reared its head and roared with the need to claim her. Scorching lust raced through my veins, and my fangs punched through my lower lip. Adara's eyes widened as blood gushed down my chin, and her pink tongue darted out to swipe across her own lips. The thought swirling in her lavender-blue eyes was clear as day—she wanted to lean in and lick the blood from my skin.

I couldn't let that happen.

Shaking my head, I backed away from Adara, then dove through the nearest window, heedless of the glass. The window shattered, shards scraping against my skin, but I hardly noticed, already caught up in the shift. I plummeted through the sky, wings unfurling, tail elongating as I took my dragon form for the first time since we'd fled the earth realm.

I'm sorry, I said through the bond. It tried to tug me back to her, and I closed my eyes against it, knowing that I couldn't give into the urge.

If I did, I would be taking the most important thing Adara had away from her.

Choice.

21

Adara

I wasn't sure how long I stood at the window, fingers gripping the sill hard enough to make my knuckles ache, eyes burning as I stared at the sprawling cityscape. Einar's form had long-since disappeared from the horizon—he'd shifted into dragon form as he'd fallen, then taken wing, flying somewhere my eyes couldn't follow.

When he'd vanished from my sight, the throbbing from his bite mark also disappeared. I should have felt relieved by that, but a hollow feeling had replaced the sensation in my chest, as though a piece of my heart had been scooped out.

He'll come back, I told myself. The last time he'd taken off like this, when we'd woken up after crash-landing in the Gaoth Aire mountains and I'd freaked out after kissing him, he'd returned within minutes. *He just needs to calm down. That's what he said, right?*

The shock began to fade, and I shook my head, pulling away from the window and walking the rest of the way back to my rooms. Of course Einar would come back. He'd promised to protect me, and he wasn't about to leave me in a castle full of fae he didn't trust. I still wasn't sure what was between us, exactly, but Einar obviously had feelings for me. He also loathed Prentis, so the idea that I might actually marry him had clearly pushed him over the edge.

I turned the corner and stopped short at the sight of Prentis leaning against my door. "You," I said, my tone flat.

Prentis raised an eyebrow. "That was a very accusatory 'you'," he said, straightening up. He took a step toward me, a wary look on his face. "Did I do something wrong?"

I closed the distance between us and jabbed a forefinger into his chest. "You knew Lady Axlya was going to spring this marriage proposal on me, didn't you?" I said, my voice crackling with ire. Something like guilt flashed in Prentis's eyes, and I shook my head, disappointment filling me. "That's why you've been so nice and tried to court my favor at every turn. So that when the time came, I would say yes and take you as my husband."

"What?" Prentis shook his head, looking genuinely shocked. He took the hand I was jabbing into his chest between both of his own, an imploring look in his eyes. "Adara, I pretended I was unaware of my aunt's plans. But even if marriage wasn't on the table, I would still treat you like family, because you *are*." His gaze darkened, grip on my hand tightening just a little. "I loved your mother, and you remind me so much of her. I would never shame her memory by trying to manipulate you like that."

I hesitated at Prentis's impassioned words, not entirely sure what to think. I believed that Prentis loved my mother, but that didn't mean he wasn't trying to manipulate me, even if he didn't view his intentions as malicious. He stood to gain quite a bit by marrying me, after all.

"What Lady Axlya said about taking consorts," I said, allowing the words to form slowly on my tongue. "Is that really so normal amongst the water fae? Do *you* have consorts?"

"I don't have consorts, so to speak, as I have never married." Prentis's eyes flickered away from me, then back again, as if he were debating telling me more. "But I do have several paramours, and it is normal amongst the water fae to do so, especially among our nobility."

My stomach dropped as Prentis confirmed my suspicions. "I don't know about this, Prentis." I pulled my hand from his grasp and took a step back. "Maybe if I'd been raised amongst water fae I'd be able to accept this, but earth fae don't have multiple partners." And I bet dragons didn't either. "If I married you, I'd expect you to be faithful to me."

"How silly," a familiar voice said, and I stiffened as Cascada appeared around the corner. Her eyes raked disapprovingly over me, and it was the most honest expression I'd seen on her face since I'd arrived here. "It's not in our nature as water fae to be faithful to one spouse, Adara. King Aolis himself had multiple partners in the early days of his rule, though he stopped taking paramours once he realized that his shadow taint was rendering them infertile." She smirked. "If you want the other water fae nobles to accept you as the heir, you need to adapt our ways. If you can't..." she trailed off with a shrug.

"Then what?" I crossed my arms and glared at Cascada. "Lady Axlya will choose someone else? Who would be a stronger candidate?"

Cascada scoffed. "Literally anyone else in House Usciete." She curled her lip at me. "You have no leadership experience, and no understanding of water fae customs and traditions. Why would any of us expect you to uphold our interests, especially when you're—"

"Cascada," Prentis snapped, his eyes flashing. "Enough." He stepped in front of Cascada, blocking her view of me. "Ignore my cousin," he said, his tone softening. "I would be faithful to you, and I already prepared to pledge myself to you. King Aolis aside—" he shot Cascada a venomous glare over his shoulder, "—Edirian monarchs don't have a history of taking multiple partners due to the confusion this would create in the line of succession. The king and queen have always been exclusively devoted to each other, as I would be with you." He took my hand in his, and my anger faded at the sincerity in his eyes. "I would be a good husband to you, Adara. I would help advise you on your royal duties, and fill in any gaps in your courtly knowledge. You need someone like me by your side if you intend to rule."

I sighed. I couldn't argue with Prentis—I didn't have the experience necessary to rule a country. None of the training I'd been given had prepared me for this. Having a husband versed in court politics and armed with ruling experience would be invaluable, and would assuage the water court's doubts about my suitability.

But did I *want* to rule Ediria? Being the only fae with the power to vanquish shadow magic was enough pressure as it was —why did I have to become queen, too? Couldn't I just perform the ritual, unlock my magic, vanquish Nox, and go home with my mother? Did I have to embroil myself in all these political machinations, too?

"Are you all right, Adara?" Prentis asked as I pinched the bridge of my nose.

I shook my head, fingers curling around my doorknob. "Today's events have been tiring," I said as I opened the door to my room. "I need some time to recover."

"Of course." Prentis stepped back, giving me space to walk through. "Come find me if you need anything. I'm here for you."

I shook my head as I closed the door in his face, then leaned my forehead against the door, eyes shutting.

There were only four people in this world who had truly been there for me. And all of them were gone.

Adara

"So, your dragon protector has run off, has he?"

I schooled my expression against Lady Axlya's barbed comment. She'd delivered it lightly, of course, but it struck home, the thorn lodging in the hollow spot that had formed in my chest yesterday.

I'd expected Einar to return last night, or at least this morning. But when I'd awoken after a fitful sleep, I'd found his room empty, his bedsheets smooth with only the faintest hint of his wood smoke and crisp night sky scent clinging to them.

Anxiety had gripped my stomach so tightly, I'd barely eaten anything at breakfast. Everyone had seemed to know what was wrong—Prentis kept shooting me worried looks, Cascada hiding her smirks behind spoonfuls of porridge. Only Lady Axlya had acted as though nothing were amiss, and I suspected she would have continued to do so if I hadn't asked to speak to her.

"He'll be back," I said, my words imbued with far more confidence than I felt. "He just needs to cool off. It's difficult for him to be here, in a city filled with water fae who loathe him."

Lady Axlya rolled her eyes. "Dragons are so dramatic," she said, clucking her tongue. "Their personalities are just like the fire magic they wield. Not that I should be surprised, considering that the fire fae were the same."

I blinked. "You were alive when the fire fae existed?"

"Radiants, no." Axlya laughed. "Even I am not that old. But the fire fae weren't completely extinct when I was born. Not all of them were in the Deadlands when the dragons arrived, and the remaining bloodlines endured for many centuries before they finally diluted to the point of extinction." A faraway look entered her eyes, some distant memory catching her attention, but she blinked it away. "In any case, dragons are far too volatile with their emotions. Water fae are more fluid—we don't allow the current of our emotions to sweep us away. We go with the flow when it suits us, and redirect it when it doesn't." She gave me a pointed look, coming to a stop in front of some hydrangea bushes. "You don't seem to have inherited that ability, based on your own emotional display yesterday."

Shame crept up the back of my neck, but I forced myself to meet Axlya's stare anyway. "I may have inherited more dragon traits than I realized," I admitted. "I apologize for my loss of control yesterday, Lady Axlya."

Axlya hummed low in her throat as she regarded me. Several guards trailed behind us, though they stopped a respectful distance away, giving us the illusion of privacy, but I knew they were listening to every word. For a moment, I wished Leap was here, so he could use his wind magic to create a sound barrier. Or Mavlyn.

"Do you truly think you are ready to rule, Adara?" Lady Axyla asked. Her gaze was piercing, and I shivered—it was as though she'd stripped me to the bone, baring all of my insecurities to her far-too perceptive eyes. "To take the throne and all the responsibility that comes with it?"

I hesitated, then decided to just tell her the truth. "I never came here seeking the throne, Lady Axlya. My only goal is to complete the ritual so I can unlock my full powers and eliminate the shadow magic threat. Becoming queen was never part of the plan."

Genuine surprise rippled across Axlya's face. "You don't desire the throne?"

"Not in the slightest." I laughed a little. "Until a week ago, I didn't even know I was royalty. If I didn't care so much about the safety of the realm, and if my mother wasn't being enslaved by a shadow demon, I wouldn't even be here right now."

Lady Axlya's mouth flattened. "I think your mother would be disappointed if she could hear those words. Your *real* mother," she added, a hint of derision in her tone. "Not the earth fae imposter who raised you in that backward village, cutting you off from your power and people." She shook her head. "No wonder you're so weak."

I reared back, her words sharper than a physical slap. "Weak?" I echoed, outraged. "How can you say that? After all I've been through—"

"All you've been through?" Lady Axlya laughed, the sound bright but sharp, like a knife's edge glinting in the sunlight. She leaned in, and the surrounding air thickened with moisture as her power rose to the surface. "You've walked this earth a mere nineteen years, child. I have been here for *centuries*. I've loved and lost countless people in my life—lovers, children, friends, family. The grief I've felt and the tears I've cried for them could fill an ocean all on their own." Her cerulean eyes were like a storm-tossed sea, the emotions frothing in their ancient depths so intense that for a moment, I could barely breathe. "Yet I continue to serve my people and safeguard my realm, because the Radiants gifted me with my power for a purpose. That purpose was not to hide away in a pocket of safety, where my abilities and my mind are of no use to anyone. And that is not your purpose either."

The challenge in her voice was clear, the impact of her words so profound that all I could do was stare, dumbstruck. Lady Axlya was only an inch or so taller than me, but at that moment, she seemed to tower over me, her power and presence swelling until it felt as if I stood before a giantess.

My thoughts must have been written on my face, because Lady Axlya's expression softened, her magic receding until she seemed her normal self once more. "I was born to rule, just as you were, but that does not mean I became a leader overnight. It will take time and training until you are big enough to truly fit the role, but that doesn't mean you refuse to step into the shoes. It merely means you have to work hard to grow into them."

She left me, then, to struggle with those heavy parting words, settling on shoulders far too slim to bear their weight.

I was still sitting in the garden hours later, staring at a statue of Tiber, one of the five water spirits, when a rustle of wings and a heavy thump sounded behind me. I didn't have to turn around to know Einar had returned. His smoke-and-sandalwood scent drifted to me on the wind, setting the mark on my shoulder throbbing once again.

"Adara." Einar's voice rumbled through the space between us. I kept my gaze fixed on the statue, its left side kissed by red and gold rays from the setting sun. But my dragon protector refused to be ignored. He stepped in front of me, blocking my view with his winged silhouette. My hands fisted into the folds of my skirts, and I nearly stood up, but he went down on his knee before I could.

I opened my mouth to tell him to move, but a gasp fell out instead as I looked down at the bowl he was holding. A water lily floated inside it, but not a common one. This one brimmed with magic, its silvery-white petals slicked with an otherworldly violet iridescence. The star-shaped center shimmered with an inner light, as if an actual star, albeit a tiny one, nestled in its depths.

It was the most beautiful flower I'd ever laid eyes on... one I'd thought only existed in myth and legend.

"This is a dream lily." I reached out to skim a reverent fingertip along one of the moonstone-colored petals. A tiny trail of shimmering dust rose from the petal where I'd touched it, and for a split second, a floating sensation overtook me. "Where did you find it?"

"On a tiny island some fifty miles northeast of here." Einar smiled, his eyes dancing as he took in my reaction. "Daryan used to bring these for your mother. They were her favorite flower, and they helped soothe her when she had restless nights." His smile faded. "I know you've been having nightmares since the battle with King Aolis. I thought this would help."

"I..." I wanted to thank him, but a knot of emotion swelled in my throat, cutting off my ability to speak. Tears spilled unbidden from my eyes as I took the bowl from Einar. The water rippled as a few drops hit the surface, and what little anger I had left dissipated.

How could I be angry when Einar had brought me a gift that didn't just touch my heart, but my very soul?

"Did you know her?" I whispered, not looking up at him. "My mother?"

"Not really." Regret tinged his voice as he wrapped his big hand around my forearm. His thumb stroked my bicep, sending warm tingles down my arm and into my core, and the bite mark throbbed again. "I was angry, as were most of us with Daryan, for falling in love with a fae, and spent more time trying to talk him out of the idea than getting to know his prospective bride." A soft chuckle escaped him, and he shook his head. "The spirits have a cruel sense of irony."

"What do you mean?"

I raised my eyes from the bowl to look at him, and he caught my gaze, his own more open and honest than I'd ever seen it. "I judged my best friend for his inability to resist the mating bond, and yet here I am, kneeling before a fae, head over heels in love with her."

My hands trembled as the sincerity of his words hit me, causing the water in the bowl to slosh over my skirt. I hardly noticed the cold liquid seeping into my skin, my mind still trying to process what he'd just said.

"You're... in love?" I finally said. "With... with *me*?"

Einar smirked. "You don't have to sound so horrified by the idea."

A startled laugh escaped me, and I set the bowl aside before I really did drop it. "I'm not horrified," I said, catching the hand resting on my bicep so I could lace his fingers with mine. "I just... don't understand. Last week you could barely stand the sight of me. How could you possibly be in love?"

"How could I not?" Einar countered. "You're the most incredible female I've ever met, Adara. You're strong and kind and brave and resourceful, and you don't give up no matter the obstacles thrown in your path." He lifted my hand to his mouth, golden eyes burning into me. "You might be fae on the outside, Adara, but the heart of a dragon beats within you. And I want that heart to be mine."

Einar's lips skimmed across my knuckles, shooting a bolt of need straight to my core. The bite mark on my neck flared with heat, and I could feel my own teeth aching in response. It was almost as if I wanted to bite him back...

"No." I shook my head, pulling my hand free of his. "You haven't told me everything, Einar. You haven't explained about this bite mark, or why my whole body aches every time I look at you. It's like a craving I can't shake, and I don't understand it." I massaged the spot on my neck, and Einar's eyes flared with heat as they tracked the movement. "And I don't buy the whole enemies-to-lovers thing either, Einar. Not after what happened with me and..."

I trailed off, but Einar wasn't going to let me off that easy. "You and who?" he growled, his tone murderous. He looked around as if Dune were hiding in a nearby shrub. "If some low-life fae hurt you, I'll rip out his—"

"Stop." Laughing, I clapped a hand across Einar's mouth. It wouldn't do to have him threatening to kill fae while we were enjoying Lady Axlya's hospitality. "It's no one here. Just an old flame from my past."

I told Einar about Dune, how we'd grown up as childhood enemies, constantly sniping and attacking each other until one fateful day when that hate had turned into one passionate make-out session, then two, until we were seeing each other weekly. How it had felt to have the attention of the most popular boy in the village, and how my dreams of joining the army together and fighting the shadow creatures side-by-side had come crashing down when Dune confessed his true feelings about me. I'd only been a temporary fling to him, one last short-term romance before his father shipped him off to the army, and he'd found the idea of me, a magically impotent fae joining him, laughable.

"I proved him wrong, obviously," I said, shrugging my shoulders. I fixed my gaze on the statue again—I couldn't meet Einar's eyes, too embarrassed at how naïve I'd been about Dune. "But still, I can't believe how off my judgment was about him. How could I have thought a male who spent his entire life bullying and belittling me could actually *love* me?" A bitter smile curved my lips. "I was an idiot then, but I'd be even *more* of an idiot now if I made the same mistake again."

Silence fell between us, stretching so long and taut that anxiety began to bubble inside me. Unable to take it, I looked at Einar, expecting him to be disappointed in me.

Instead, he was clenching his jaw, his golden eyes blazing with emotion.

"Adara." Einar dropped his second knee to the ground. My breath caught as he nudged my thighs apart so he could kneel between them, so close that his chest brushed against mine. I tried to lean back, but he planted his hands on either side of me on the stone bench, caging me in. "This Dune was using you for his own amusement as young, shallow males who don't know what they want often do. He may have stolen a few kisses in the dark, may have even shared a few of his secrets with you, but he's never fought by your side. Never helped you break into a temple, stormed a castle to rescue you, held you while you cried, or tended to you while you were injured."

Einar looked down at the golden cuff clasped around my wrist, the red primal stone in the center reflecting the last of the daylight. "I don't expect you to return my feelings," he said, his voice as raw as my insides felt. "But after all we've been through, I thought you'd think more highly of me than to compare me to a boy who is so clearly unworthy of you."

Guilt squeezed my heart, and I wanted to sink into the floor from shame. "Einar, I—"

"Hush." He reached out and brushed a finger along the mark on my neck. Heat rippled through me, and my mouth snapped shut as I fought against the sudden urge to wrap my legs around him and pull him into my heat. "You don't need to say anything. At least not until I've explained."

He pulled back to look me in the eye, and I braced myself, not sure where this was going. "Adara, I don't know if you know this, but dragons don't choose their mates. They are pre-ordained by the spirits. When a male dragon lays his eyes on the female that is meant to be his, a bond awakens between them that cannot be severed by anything, save death, or the female herself."

He paused, as if steeling himself for the next revelation, before continuing on in a rush. "That bond snapped into place the moment you woke me from my enchanted sleep. It's the reason you were able to break the spell when it should have lasted an eternity. The reason I haven't been able to leave your side, why I've protected you with my life even though doing so puts my people at risk. It's why I can always sense your moods, and the reason that you're drawn to me, even though you don't understand why."

He leaned in and blew a gentle stream of air against the mark, sending a full-body shudder through me. "A blood exchange, in addition to consummating, is what seals the bond between dragons. It's why I bit you... though you have to understand I didn't mean to." He lifted his head, regret shining in his eyes. "I lost control, and it's been tearing me apart ever since, because the last thing I wanted to do was influence your choice in any way."

"My choice for what?" I asked.

"To accept the mating bond... or reject it."

He flinched at the end of that sentence, the expression so subtle I wouldn't have noticed if I hadn't been so attuned to him. "You've probably felt drawn to me since the beginning, but that feeling will have increased tenfold now that I've bitten you because it's started the bonding process. Your body craves to complete it, which is why you want to bite me back, and why you're struggling with these feelings of desire. But you have to understand, Adara, that there's no going back on this. If we complete the bond, it's forever. Nothing save death can undo it, and even then..." He blew out a breath. "Let's just say I've seen plenty of dragons lose their mates in the war, and it changes them. If they had children with their mates they can continue on, but if not, they become a shell of themselves, living a color-less half-life."

"Is that what will happen to you if I reject the bond?" Horror sluiced through me, and I nearly recoiled from Einar at the thought. To think that Einar's happiness depended on my accep-tance of the bond... it was almost too much to bear.

The left side of Einar's mouth quirked up into a half-smile. "That would be convenient, wouldn't it? For me to say yes, and guilt trip you into accepting the bond that way?" He shook his head. "But no, that won't happen. I'll lose my one chance for a soul-deep bond with a female I love, and I'll never be able to have children. But I would get over it... eventually."

I let out a breath I hadn't realized I'd been holding, my shoulders slumping with relief. "Well... that's good, at least. But I don't understand why you didn't tell me about this until now, Einar. It seems like something I ought to have known from the beginning."

"I should have told you from the start," Einar admitted, "but I was too busy struggling with the idea myself, and to be honest, I was terrified of revealing the truth. While a dragon female has the power to reject a mate bond, the male doesn't. You could have forced the bond on me to control me, and there wouldn't have been a damned thing I could have done about it. I've seen that happen before, too."

"What!" I stared at Einar, aghast, my stomach turning sour at the very thought of manipulating *anyone* that way. "How... how could you think I would do something like that to you?"

"I don't think you would do that to me *now*," Einar said, a little impatiently. "But when you first woke me up, I only saw you as an enemy fae. I didn't dare reveal the truth about the bond, since I had no idea how much you might know about dragons and their mates. My strategy was simply to make you hate me—a task I didn't think would be difficult—so you would reject me, and in doing so, free me from the bond. But clearly, that didn't go as planned."

"Clearly."

I licked my parched lips, and his eyes flared as they tracked the movement. Tension thickened in the air between us, and I knew that if I leaned in even a little, we'd be locked in another stormy, passionate kiss, like the one that had led him to bite me in the first place. And even though we were in the gardens, where anyone could stumble upon us, I wasn't sure the threat of that would be enough to stop us.

In fact, judging by the gleam in Einar's eyes, I suspected he would very much enjoy Prentis stumbling upon us while I claimed him.

But did I want that? To claim Einar as my mate, and bind our hearts and souls together for the rest of our potentially very long lives? "It sounds like dragon matings aren't always loving partnerships based on what you just told me," I said. "Not if dragon females have a history of using the bond to manipulate males."

Einar laughed. "I have seen some miserable mate pairings, but those are few and far between." He took my hand in his again, stroking his thumb over my knuckles, his expression softening. "For most dragons, mating is one of the most joyous experiences they will ever have in their lives. The soul-bond strengthens our abilities, making us more powerful, and the security and stability that comes from that kind of partnership... well, let's just say it's something I secretly envied in my mated friends."

Grief shimmered in Einar's eyes for just a moment before he blinked it away, and I felt a wave of compassion for him. "You miss them, don't you," I said, squeezing his hand. "Your friends, your family."

He nodded. "Those who survived Aolis's shadow magic have gone to the realm Kiryan and I opened for them. I will never see them again, which was why I was so angry when you woke me. I didn't want to spend the rest of my life alone in this realm... but I'm not alone, not anymore. You may be a hybrid, but you are still a dragon, and that means you will always be kith to me. Even if you reject the bond."

A lump formed in my throat, and I looked at Einar for a long time, trying to come to terms with what he'd told me. I understood now why he was so territorial of me, why he'd never abandoned me despite his multiple attempts to drive a wedge between us. Why the idea of me marrying Prentis was so anathema to him, he'd been driven to mark me against his own judgment.

The rational part of Einar wanted me to choose him of my own free will. But the dragon inside him wanted to stake his claim, and to make sure everyone knew I belonged to him.

I wasn't sure whether that turned me on or frightened me.

"Is it the same for you?" I asked, touching the invisible mark on my neck again. "Have you been feeling these same... urges... the entire time we've known each other?"

"I've been doing my best to block out the bond," he told me. "If I allowed myself to truly feel the pull between us, I wouldn't be able to keep my hands off you. But sometimes, when I'm tired or when my guard is down, the connection opens up. Like that night in the cave, when I kissed you in my sleep." He glanced away, looking chagrined. "I still feel guilty about that."

"You shouldn't."

Surprise flashed in his eyes as they snapped back to my face. "Why not?"

"Because I wanted it," I said, shocking both of us as the bold truth slipped from my lips. "I couldn't accept that at the time, so I lashed out at you. But I did want it, Einar. I always have."

He grabbed my face and kissed me then, and I threw caution into the wind, wrapping my entire body around him and opening my heart to him. He growled his approval, his tongue sweeping past my parted lips to lick into my mouth, and I moaned at the taste of him. Fire swept through my body, igniting at my fingertips, but Einar didn't seem to care that I was singeing holes through the back of his shirt. He grabbed the back of my neck and angled my head to the side, deepening the kiss until my head was spinning, until my entire world reduced to the taste and scent of him, to the fusion of our mouths and the press of our bodies.

I trailed my hands down his back to slide them up the back of his shirt, but he broke the kiss before I could make contact with his skin.

"Not yet," he murmured, pressing his forehead against mine. "If we start down this road, I'll have you up against that statue with your clothes burned off before you can blink."

"And what if that's what I want?" I challenged, my chest heaving. I clenched the edge of the bench as he got to his feet, clamping against the urge to launch myself at him and make him finish what he started.

Something feral flickered in Einar's gaze. "You know what you have to do if that's what you want, but you're not ready." He closed his teeth around my bottom lip and gave it a wicked tug, then pulled away with a wink. "Come find me when you are."

He sauntered back into the castle, leaving me with curses on my stinging lip and a maelstrom of emotion churning in my heart. Because I did know—if I wanted Einar, I had to claim him fully, body *and* soul.

But if I did that now, I would lose Lady Axlya's support, and my chances of completing the ritual would go up in smoke.

And that wasn't worth the risk, no matter how much my body screamed otherwise.

23

Leap

The next two days at Angtun were torturous for Leap. Uncle Oren ordered Mavlyn and Leap to be put in separate rooms and kept under guard round the clock. They only allowed them to leave their quarters for short, supervised walks around the palace grounds, and never at the same time.

Leap knew why his uncle had done this—he didn't want the two of them conspiring to escape or undermine him, and he also wanted to punish Leap. He supposed he couldn't blame Uncle Oren—he had abandoned his house and family for a life of crime—but that didn't make this forced isolation any less miserable. The only bright spot in all of this was that his isolation meant that Ryker couldn't harass him. The bastard hadn't even tried to visit Leap, which he suspected was on Uncle Oren's orders as well.

He probably thinks that's part of the punishment too, Leap thought, rolling his eyes as he turned the page of the book in his lap. Reading wasn't exactly his favorite pastime, but the small collection of books on the shelf next to the fireplace was his only source of entertainment. This particular book was a treatise on the twelve wind spirits, which Leap was already familiar with, though he'd long since given up praying to them. He'd done so every night when he'd first come to Angtun, begging for them to bring his parents back. And while it had been an unreasonable request in retrospect, the fact that he'd only been given misery was proof enough that the wind spirits didn't give two squalls about him.

As far as Leap was concerned, he was on his own. Friends or no friends, in the end, the only person you could count on was yourself.

A knock on the door interrupted Leap from his musings, and he looked up to see Gale, the lightning rider who'd brought him and Mavlyn to Angtun, walk in.

"Time for my afternoon walk?" Leap asked, swinging his legs off the bed. "Have you got my leash ready?"

"Actually, Lord Oren sent me to fetch you," Gale quipped, not missing a beat. He mimed looping his hand around a leash and made a tugging motion toward the door. "He wants you to join him for tea."

"Tea?" Leap echoed, immediately suspicious. Uncle Oren didn't do 'tea', and especially not with Leap. He searched the lightning rider's face for any sign that this was a joke, but the male seemed dead serious. "Did he say why?"

"No... but I can guess." Gale said. He opened the door wide and ushered for Leap to get going. "Come on now, boy. We don't want to keep him waiting."

Gale disappeared into the hallway, and Leap hurried after him. "What do you mean, 'I can guess'?" he demanded as he followed Gale into the spiral staircase just a few steps from his door. They had placed him in one of the many tower rooms, this one fitted with iron bars on the windows so he couldn't escape even if he found a way to get his shackles off. "What do you know?"

"You know I can't tell you that." The stairs bottomed out into the palace's central courtyard, which had been converted into a maze-like garden. The tall hedges offered plenty of privacy for clandestine meetings and conversations, but they also offered an additional layer of protection should anyone attempt to infiltrate the castle. If a person didn't know which paths led to which of the many towers, and they couldn't fly, they would have a hard time figuring out where to go.

Leap knew based on the path that Gale picked that the lightning rider was leading him to the west tower, which was where Uncle Oren kept his apartments. That meant this was going to be a private luncheon, rather than one where his advisors and other members of court were present. That in itself was no cause for alarm, but based on the set of Gale's shoulders and the ominous way he'd spoken, Leap sensed his fortunes were about to take a turn for the worse.

As Leap expected, Gale led him into Uncle Oren's withdrawing room. His uncle waited for him in one of the wing-backed chairs clustered near the fireplace, a tea service laid out on the table before him, but Leap barely noticed. His attention zeroed in on Ryker, who sat in the chair next to his father. Both males had uncharacteristically solemn looks on their faces—in fact, Uncle Oren looked downright grim—but Leap didn't miss the almost gleeful look that flashed in Ryker's eyes when he'd walked into the room.

His life was *definitely* about to get worse.

Leap stopped just a foot shy of the table and clasped his hands behind his back. "Hello, Uncle." He inclined his head, the most respect he was willing to show under the circumstances.

"No hello for me?" Ryker raised an eyebrow. "How rude."

"I don't consort with murderers," Leap said flatly. He plucked a cucumber sandwich off one of the trays and popped it into his mouth, teeth coming down in an audible *crunch.*

Uncle Oren opened his mouth to chastise Leap, but Ryker spoke first. "It was an accident," he snapped, his yellow eyes flashing with annoyance. "Besides, it was an animal, so even if I'd done it on purpose, that still doesn't make me a murderer."

"You miserable bottom-feeder." Leap whirled on his cousin, teeth bared in a snarl. His power crackled to life inside him, pushing against the bonds on his wrists, but the manacles held fast, preventing him from unleashing it. "If I didn't have these blasted things on my wrists—"

Uncle Oren raised a hand, and a thunderclap ricocheted through the air just outside the room, loud enough to rattle the window and startle Leap and Ryker into silence. "That's enough arguing," his uncle said, his voice eerily quiet. "Sit down, Leap."

Leap did as commanded, a wary look in his eyes as he stared at his uncle. He'd expected Uncle Oren to shout or get angry, which was his usual response whenever Leap acted out. This grave side of his uncle was one he had never seen before.

Uncle Oren waited until a servant had poured tea for all three of them before he spoke, but when he did, he got straight to the point. "My informants have told me Tempest is dead," he said in that same quiet tone. "Bloodied scraps of her clothing, and the jade amulet she wore, were found at the border between Kaipei and Gaoth Aire. When the peasants in the nearby village were questioned, they admitted a female matching her description was attacked by shadow creatures in the forest and killed."

Horror and pity welled in Leap's chest. He'd never met Tempest, as she'd been shipped off to Kaipei as a hostage before he was even born, but he still felt sorry for his uncle's loss, regardless of the bad blood between them. Tempest hadn't deserved that fate—she should have been returned to her family after King Aolis's death, just like the others.

"I'm sorry," he said. "I wish I could have done something to save her."

"Yes, well, that would have required you honoring your loyalty to our family," Ryker said. A muscle worked in his jaw, and Leap clenched his armrests. "I bet you didn't even remember she was locked up in the castle when you rained your lightning and bombs down on it, did you, you—"

"I said that's enough!" Uncle Oren's yellow eyes flashed as he turned on Ryker, and Ryker's mouth clamped shut as the air between them crackled. He turned back to Leap, his posture stiff, his tone rigid. "I had planned to have you punished appropriately for your crimes, Leap, but Tempest's death has reminded me that safeguarding this family is my number one priority, next to safeguarding our realm, that is. Regardless of your recent behavior, you are still my sister's son, and she would be very disappointed in me if I wrote you off as a delinquent."

"What are saying?" Leap asked, cautiously optimistic. Could he have been wrong? Was his uncle actually going to throw him a bone?

"I'm giving you another opportunity to follow in your parents' footsteps," Uncle Oren said. "If you swear a blood oath that you will not abandon this family again, nor collaborate with any of the other fae races without my express permission, I will allow you to enroll at the lightning rider academy and rejoin our house."

"You want me to swear a blood oath?" Leap said, aghast. Blood oaths were old magic, and once made, could not be undone except by death. "But what about Adara and Mavlyn? They're my friends. I can't abandon them."

"Adara will have to rely on her own house for help," Uncle Oren said, his tone knife-sharp. "She's in Lady Axlya's care already, so I don't know why you're so concerned for her welfare, anyway. As for Mavlyn, I'll have her shipped back to Lady Mossi to be dealt with. I see no reason to keep her here."

Leap winced. He doubted Lady Mossi would welcome Mavlyn with open arms considering she was Adara's ally, while Mossi would be backing Slaugh's claim for the throne. As for Adara being in Lady Axlya's 'care', Leap knew exactly how it felt to be trapped in the arms of a royal house's bosom. If she was safe there, Quye wouldn't be urging Mavlyn and Leap to break her out right now.

However, Leap knew this was the most generous offer he could hope from his uncle. Following in his parents' footsteps and joining the Lightning Riders had been Leap's fondest wish at one point. He glanced over his shoulder to where Gale was standing guard at the door. The rider's gaze was inscrutable, and if he cared at all about the outcome of Leap's decision, he wasn't about to show it.

"I'll have to think on it," Leap said. "It's a big decision to make." He wouldn't just be turning his back on his friends if he did this. He'd also be indirectly swearing fealty to Ryker, who would one day take the house throne. And Leap wasn't sure he'd be able to bear that.

Ryker's lip curled into a sneer, but for once his cousin kept his thoughts to himself. "I see." Uncle Oren said, sounding disappointed. "I had hoped you would agree before I left, but perhaps the time away from me will allow you to think more clearly and make the right decision."

"Time away?" Leap frowned. "Where are you going?"

"I'm leaving for a summit tomorrow, where I shall seek restitution from Slaugh for Tempest's murder," Uncle Oren said. "Ryker will be in charge until I return."

"Wonderful," Leap said sarcastically. "I guess I'll be locked up in my rooms until then?"

"Actually, I'm going to give you free run of the palace," Uncle

Oren said. Leap's mouth fell open, and Oren smiled at his nephew's slack-jawed expression, mistaking it for gratitude. "You'll be allowed access to the library and the grounds, and to eat meals in the main hall with everyone else, just as you did before you left us."

"And what about these?" Leap lifted one of his manacled wrists.

"They'll come off as soon as you make the blood vow," Uncle Oren said smoothly. He rose from his chair, his half-finished cup of tea abandoned. "I need to prepare for my departure, but feel free to stay here and finish your tea, boys. Maybe you can even have a civil conversation and pretend you like each other."

He left the withdrawing room, shutting the door behind him with a snap. Leap expected Ryker to lay into him, but his cousin rose stiffly from his chair and stalked out through the opposite door, leaving him alone.

Leap blinked in confusion, then shrugged and sprawled out on one of the couches, taking the platter of sandwiches with him. "Tea?" he offered to Gale, who was still standing by the door.

The lightning rider rolled his eyes.

24

Adara

When I went to bed later that night, my thoughts were consumed by the day's events. I expected to be up all night replaying my conversations with Lady Axlya and Einar in my head. But the dream lily Einar had given me, which I placed on my bedside table, had lulled me to sleep the moment I hit the pillow, its spun-sugar scent tugging my mind into a hazy dreamscape filled with rainbow sunbeams and cotton candy clouds and kaleidoscopic butterflies. I drifted from dream to pleasant dream for the rest of the night, as weightless as a snowflake, and when I woke, I felt more well-rested than I had in a week. In fact, I was so cheerful when I arrived at the breakfast table the next morning, I almost didn't mind that I wasn't allowed to eat.

"You're in good spirits this morning," Cascada remarked as she buttered her toast. Half the water court had turned up for breakfast—Lady Axlya and her consorts, Cascada, Prentis, several of Axlya's advisors, and a male sitting next to Cascada I didn't know. "Quite a change from your display in the Hall of Mirrors."

"It's impossible not to be in a good mood now that Lady Axlya's given me permission to prepare for the ritual." I smiled at Axlya, pretending not to notice Cascada's not-so-subtle jab. "I'm excited to find out what my animal form is, and unlock my full powers so I can best serve the realm."

"Indeed," Axyla said, sounding somewhat amused. "And I'm excited for you to marry my nephew so you can best serve the realm."

A scowl threatened to wipe the smile from my face at Lady Axlya's not-so-subtle urging, and I had to hide it behind a sip of water—the only thing I could consume for the next ten days. I glanced over the rim of my glass at Einar, expecting him to be glaring daggers at either Axlya or Prentis. But he appeared to be unbothered, his intention focused on the arduous task of polishing off the kippers on his plate.

If I didn't know him so well, I would think he didn't care. But somehow, either because of the bite or because we'd spent so much time together, I'd become more attuned to his movements. I noticed the slight wrinkle that had formed between his brows, the way he'd gripped his fork a little tighter than normal, and the subtle tightening of his jaw.

My decision about whether I was going to marry Prentis was very much still hanging in the air like an axe above him, and he was bracing himself, waiting for it to fall.

Prentis cleared his throat, trying to break the tension that had thickened the air. "Now that Adara has officially begun the fasting period, I thought perhaps a trip to the water temple would be in order," he said.

"Are you sure that's wise?" Kalis asked. "The other clan heads will be arriving to meet Adara, likely tomorrow. It would be very unfortunate if she were absent."

"There is no reason Adara wouldn't make it back in time," Prentis said. "It's only a half-day journey. And besides, Adara needs to pay tribute to the temple and receive the priestess's blessing before the ritual can take place. She might as well do it now, before things get too busy here at court. Today may be our only opportunity to get away."

"Very well," Lady Axlya said. "I agree, Adara should visit the temple. Take Cascada with you too—the three of you can make a day of it."

"You mean the four of us," I said. When they stared blankly at me, I clarified. "Einar is coming, too."

Einar raised an eyebrow at me, and the others stared at me as if I'd lost my mind. "You do realize the Water Temple is under the sea, right?" Cascada said, speaking to me like she thought I was daft. "Your dragon protector will be useless down there. What's the point of even bringing him?"

"Useless?" Einar set his fork down, giving the conversation his full attention. "I may not be able to use my fire magic underwater, but I assure you the rest of my abilities are functional on land and sea." He flashed a fanged smile at her.

"Oh, really?" Cascada sneered. "Didn't both of my cousins have to rescue you from a kraken the other day?"

Einar folded his corded arms over his chest. "That was only because I was bound by those infuriating magical shackles," he protested. "You wouldn't have been able to fight back in my position, either."

"I would have never ended up in your position," Cascada said sweetly.

"Oh stop it, you two," Prentis snapped. "I'll have to fashion you a magical breathing apparatus, since I doubt you'll be able to hold your breath for that long, but there's no reason you can't come, Einar. Whether the priestess will allow you into the temple is another matter, but if Adara wants you by her side, then so be it."

"Thank you." Einar inclined his head. "That would be much appreciated."

I blinked, looking between the two of them. Were these the same males that had come to blows over me just the other day?

"I'm going to need a breathing apparatus too," I reminded Prentis. "I can hold my breath for quite a while longer than Einar, but still not long enough for a half-day trip under the ocean."

"Oh. Right." Prentis shook his head, looking a little befuddled. "You don't think you'll be able to use your gills again?"

"No. I already tried in the bath." I gave him a half-shrug, then glanced sidelong at Lady Axlya. "All the more reason for me to complete that ritual as soon as possible, am I right?"

Axlya huffed and made a shooing motion with her hand. "Be off with you before I change my mind."

She didn't have to tell us twice.

"**Y**ou didn't have to do that, you know."

I followed the sound of Einar's voice as I stepped out into the hallway from my bedroom, and found him leaning against the wall just a few feet to the left. He wore the same skintight, silver-scaled armor the water fae soldiers used, which was designed to be worn both on land and underwater. The armor was a bit too tight—water fae had leaner physiques than dragons, better suited for swimming—so it fit him like a glove, and I had to do my best not to let my gaze travel too far south.

"Didn't have to do what?" I asked as I pulled the door shut behind me, trying to pretend like I wasn't ogling him.

"You didn't have to intervene on my behalf." Einar's gaze

drifted down my body, which was clad in the same form-fitting armor he wore.

A blush rose to my cheeks as I realized my outfit was having a similar effect on him as his was having on me. My mind conjured a very similar image to the last time Einar and I were in the ocean together. Except this time, instead of sharing my breath with him in order to resuscitate him, we were locked in a passionate embrace, and instead of armor, we...

"Are you listening to a word I'm saying?"

I blinked, yanking myself back to the present. Einar was staring at me with one eyebrow raised, looking far too amused. "Sorry," I said blithely, clasping my hands behind my back to keep them away from his knowing gaze. "I tend to tune males out when they complain."

Einar smirked. "I wasn't complaining. Just saying that I would have followed you anyway." He moved to the side, clearing a path for me so I could walk ahead. "Now, do you want to get going, or do you want to stay here a bit longer so you can finish undressing me with your eyes?"

I rolled said eyes so hard, I was surprised they didn't get stuck in the back of my skull. "Don't flatter yourself." I stepped past him, gaze locked ahead so he wouldn't be able to see through my unaffected charade. The last thing I needed to do was encourage him.

Einar followed at my side, undeterred. "You could also just undress me with your hands. I find that more effective than using your eyes alone," he suggested.

"Oh, I don't know," I said in a sing-song voice as we traversed the staircase leading down to the great hall. "Hands are great, but I think I'd prefer using a different part of my body."

The mood between us shifted in an instant, the air charging with sexual tension. "What body part would that be?" Einar asked. The deep rumble of his voice sent a delicious shiver through me, and I tensed my muscles to keep from betraying my reaction to him.

I turned in the stairwell to face him, bracing my hands on the railings as I leaned in. My breasts brushed against his chest, and I allowed my lips the barest brush against his. "Maybe if you're a good boy, I'll show you sometime," I purred into his mouth.

Einar's golden eyes flared, and I spun away, my laughter echoing through the stairwell as I raced down the steps. His answering growl followed me into the great hall, and my whole body thrilled at the possessive tone. I wasn't entirely sure why I was baiting Einar like this when I knew I didn't have an answer for him yet, but something wicked and a little bit feral had awoken inside me the day he'd bitten me, a fiercely feminine beast that grew more outspoken with every day that passed. She knew exactly what she wanted, and she didn't give a damn about my misgivings.

The fact that I'd started fasting and was on edge from hunger probably didn't help...but I was going to need to do a better job of controlling her, regardless.

Einar caught up to me as I stepped outside to join Prentis and Cascada, who were waiting on the veranda. I felt all three of their eyes on me as I tilted my face to the sparkling sunlight, but I ignored them all, taking a minute to bask in the balmy morning air. The tang of a sea salt breeze teased my nostrils as it always did when I wandered the grounds. I wasn't sure of the water temple's precise location, but I knew from our arrival that the ocean itself wasn't very far.

"Adara." Prentis greeted me warmly, stepping forward so he could take my hand. He leaned down to kiss it, his lips lingering slightly longer than necessary. "Are you ready for our grand adventure?" he asked, his crystal-blue eyes twinkling.

"I should hope so," Cascada said before I could answer.

"We've been waiting for you for ages. I was just about to come looking and see if you needed help getting into the bodysuit." She gave me a critical once-over, her eyes lingering on my exposed wrists and ankles. "You're a bit too tall for yours, but at least you're not bursting at the seams like your dragon guard." Her lips twisted sardonically as she looked at Einar. "I'd avoid flexing those giant muscles of yours unless absolutely necessary."

"Noted," Einar said dryly.

"Are you always this pleasant to everyone?" I asked Cascada as the four of us fell into step together. "Or am I getting special treatment from you?"

"You'll have to forgive Cascada," Prentis said, a hint of annoyance in his voice. He walked to my left while Einar flanked my right, Cascada on his other side. "She's always had an acerbic wit, but it seems to have sharpened even more over the years." He shot his cousin a pointed look from beneath his brows. "Perhaps spending all those years living beneath that noxious cloud of shadow magic has robbed you of your manners."

Cascada shrugged. "Or perhaps living my life on the edge of a knife, not knowing if I'm going to be killed should my family do or say anything to anger the king, has made me realize that life is too short to care much about what other people think of me."

She caught my gaze, and I stared hard at her, looking for any sign of the shadow taint I'd glimpsed in her before. But the crystal blue depths of her irises were clear, not even a hint of the inky blackness I'd seen.

I remembered what Avani, the earth fae hostage, had told me when I'd met her. That even though everyone living in Kaipei Castle took regular doses of everbright potion to ward off shadow sickness, the taint continued to build up inside them due to round-the-clock exposure. Perhaps that was what had happened to Cascada, and now that she was home, she no longer had to fight the constant threat of infection.

"I'm sorry," I said.

Cascada scowled. "For what?"

"For being hard on you," I said, and I meant it. "You've been through a lot, and I...well. I haven't exactly been understanding."

Cascada huffed, turning away, but her countenance softened a little. It was entirely possible Cascada's misinterpretation of the events at Kaipei was through no fault of her own...who knew what effects shadow taint had on the mind? I saw first hand the toll it had taken on Mother, how she'd wasted away to a former shell of herself in only a handful of days. It stood to reason that Cascada would have suffered as well from such prolonged exposure.

Refusing to take her taciturn attitude personally, I turned my attention toward the adventure ahead as the four of us clambered into the carriage.

I thought we would go straight to the docks, but Prentis asked the carriage to stop in the port city, right outside the open-air market.

"It's customary for petitioners to bring a gift to the temple," Prentis said as we walked through the rows of colorful stalls. I listened to him with one ear as I took everything in—this place was ten times the size of Fenwood's weekly market, the air thick with the scents of spices and the buzz of conversations. "I thought we could kill two birds with one stone, and pick up the gift here while also allowing to do a bit of sightseeing."

"That's very thoughtful of you." I tore my gaze away from a jar full of butterfly wings to smile at Prentis. Einar had stopped at the stall next to us to examine some knives, and Cascada had wandered off to look at bracelets, so the two of us were alone for the moment. "What sort of gifts do petitioners usually bring to the temple?"

"It can be anything, really," Prentis said. "A garland of flowers, a stick of incense, or even a small parcel of food. Ideally, you should bring an offering you've prepared yourself. But the priestess will understand that you haven't had time, given the situation," he added at the dismayed look on my face. "Simply picking something from the market is good enough, so long as you put some thought into it."

"Great," I muttered under my breath. "No pressure."

We spent a good hour wandering the market, looking for something suitable. There were so many amazing things to choose from—bolts of silk, jars of tea and spices, crystals and charms and sweets galore. I would have been swept away by the dizzying array of choices if we'd just come to shop for ourselves. But the fact that I had to choose a temple gift, that first impressions were on the line, added a sense of urgency to what should have been a leisurely outing.

Eventually, I decided on a box of assorted candies. They were brilliantly colored and molded into a variety of shapes—stars, diamonds, hearts, marbles—and the watertight box was shaped like a little chest. It made me think of treasure chests full of jewels that an intrepid explorer might find in the belly of an undersea shipwreck, and I hoped the priestess would appreciate it.

"Finally!" Cascada exclaimed as we met her and Einar in the center of the bazaar. She had two bags clutched in her hands, and judging by the mountain of parcels Einar was carrying, it looked like that wasn't all she'd bought. "Let's get back to the carriage. My arms are going to fall off if I have to carry these packages for another minute."

Einar rolled his eyes from behind her. "You're a Greater Fae,

Cascada. You're strong enough to carry an entire kiosk worth of trinkets all by yourself."

"I don't know what you're talking about," Cascada said with an airy toss of her hair. She marched off to the carriage, pointing her nose to the sky, and I had to stifle a laugh as I caught Einar's disgruntled glare.

"Sorry about her," Prentis said. To his credit, he did genuinely seem to be chagrined. "It seems Cascada's time at Kaipei has robbed her of her manners."

"You mean she wasn't always like this?" I asked as he fell into step next to me.

"Well, she's always been a bit sassy," Prentis admitted. "But never outright rude, the way she's being to you now. Lady Axlya's granted her some leeway given that she's been a prisoner for nearly two decades... but I will speak to her about Cascada's behavior. This can't go on forever."

I mulled that over as we climbed back into the carriage and set out for the shore. Two decades of imprisonment at Kaipei Castle while consistently being exposed to shadow magic... that would do a number on anyone. But while I'd only known Cascada for a few brief hours during her time at Kaipei, something seemed different about her. The fae I'd met back then had been sassy and a little bit suspicious, but she'd shown none of the acrimony she was throwing at me now. I didn't know what to make of it.

I expected the carriage to lead us to the docks, but to my surprise, it pulled up to a private stretch of beach a few miles up the coast instead. "We're not taking a ship?" I asked as we disembarked.

"There's no need to," Prentis said, eyes twinkling. "We're going to ride the ocean current instead."

"Excuse me," Einar said, stepping up beside Prentis. He looked thoroughly discomfited as he glanced toward the ocean, and I knew he was remembering how just a few short days ago, he'd been dragged underwater and nearly devoured by a kraken. "But you haven't gotten to the part about how I'm supposed to breathe during this underwater venture."

"Ahh, yes." Prentis reached into his pocket and withdrew a small box. Inside was a slimy flower with purple petals and a yellow, star-shaped center, about the size of an eyeball.

"Gillflower," I said before Prentis could explain what it was. "It gives you the ability to breathe underwater."

"Yes." Prentis handed it to Einar. "Chew it thoroughly and swallow it all. It will give you the ability to breathe below water."

"Aren't you going to give me some, too?" I asked as Einar popped the flower into his mouth.

"I will if I have to," Prentis said. "But considering you could produce gills on your own the last time we were at sea, I'm hopeful you can do so again."

Nervous energy skittered across my skin from top to bottom as I looked out at the ocean. Yes, I had undergone a mini trans-formation when I dove into the water to save Einar, producing gills on the sides of my neck so I could give him air. But that had been under extreme duress. Would I really be able to do it again?

"Ugh." Einar screwed up his face as he swallowed down the gillflower, then gave a full-body shudder. "That was disgusting."

"Yes, I've heard the taste is most unpleasant," Prentis said, in that placid tone one might use when discussing the weather. He turned his back on Einar and offered his arm to me. "Are you ready, Adara?"

I pulled in one last deep breath of ocean air, and then nodded. "I'm ready."

We waded into the water together, the ocean lapping eagerly at my ankles as if it couldn't wait to drag me beneath its depths. Trepidation skittered up my spine as the water rose higher, sloshing against my calves, my hips, my stomach. Water never usually bothered me—I could hold my breath for far longer than the earth fae I'd grown up with, which was why I'd always sought refuge in the lake whenever Dune or the other children bullied me. But even I couldn't hold my breath underwater for the better part of a day.

As the water caressed the underside of my chin, I considered asking Prentis to give me the gillflower now.

But I had a feeling the priestess and the other water dwellers would be able to tell if I'd used it. And I didn't want to give them any reason to doubt my legitimacy as a water fae. Not when everything was riding on my completion of the ritual.

So instead of taking in a deep breath, like I usually would, I exhaled, then dove beneath the waves. Prentis's arm slipped from mine as I sank into the ocean's bluish-green depths, my eyes adjusting to the watery light. I spotted a large, colorful reef just a few yards ahead, teeming with a variety of ocean life, most of which I'd only seen in illustrations. I sucked in a delighted breath at the sight, but my joy was quickly drowned out as I inhaled a lungful of water.

"Adara!" Einar was beside me in an instant, clutching at my shoulder as I tried to cough the seawater from my lungs. Bubbles clouded the air between us as he shouted my name, and my vision began to swim from the lack of oxygen. There was nothing to inhale, nothing to feed my starved heart as it pumped weakly in my chest. Panic gripped me as I clawed at Einar's arms, my terror-stricken expression reflected in his eyes as I begged for help.

"Here!" Prentis tried to shove himself between us, the gillyflower in his outstretched hand. I let go of Einar's forearm to grab it, but to my surprise, Einar shoved Prentis out of the way, then yanked me against him and fused his mouth against mine.

Just as I had done for him when the kraken had pulled him overboard.

Instinctively, I sucked in the breath Einar pushed into my mouth. Giddy relief swept through me as oxygen filled my lungs, but before I could exhale, Einar pulled away.

"Try again," he told me, his voice sounding strange and distorted by the ocean water. "Let go of your fear, and try again. You can do this, Adara. And if you can't, Prentis and I are here to help."

He kept his hands on my shoulders, grounding me, steadying me amidst the weightlessness of the ocean. Closing my eyes, I let out the breath I was holding, and with it, the lump of dread and fear that had settled in my chest. Einar was right— even if I couldn't do this, he and Prentis were here, ready and waiting with gillflower and oxygen. Failure didn't mean death, at least not today.

But I wouldn't fail. I'd done this before. I could do it again.

I opened my mouth to take in a breath, and the sides of my neck began to tingle. Water rushed into my throat, and my gills opened, filtering the oxygen into my lungs and allowing the liquid to pass harmlessly through the flaps in my neck. Einar's golden eyes gleamed with pride as I pulled in another breath, then another, giving me the confidence to let go of him.

"I did it!" I yelled, spinning around and punching my fist skyward. I beamed at Prentis, who looked as though he wasn't sure if he should be pleased or annoyed. "I'm breathing underwater!"

"Congratulations," Cascada said dryly. "You've accomplished something the rest of us have been able to do since we were five."

Prentis elbowed his cousin in the ribs, who let out a yelp. "What Cascada means to say is that we're proud of you," he said, scowling at her as she rubbed the spot where he'd jabbed her. "Now if you're ready, let's get going. We have a current to catch."

"A current?" Einar repeated. "You mean we're not just going to swim there?"

"Swim?" Cascada laughed. "The sea temple is eighty miles west of here. Do you have any idea how long that would take, dragon?"

"Longer than I'm prepared to swim," Einar said dryly.

"Indeed," Prentis concurred. "Which is why we're not going to swim. We're going to ride the Orphyx current."

He pointed to a section of the ocean to the left of the reef, and Einar scowled. "I don't see anything," he said.

"That's because you're not a water fae, dragon," Cascada said with a roll of her eyes. "We're the only ones who can see the currents."

I squinted my eyes, trying to figure out what Prentis was pointing at. "Don't squint," Prentis told me when he saw what I was doing. "Relax, and open your mind."

I did what he said, allowing my vision to unfocus. The moment I did, three long, colorful ribbons of water appeared before me. Each was about twenty feet wide, snaking in different directions—a yellow-green one heading north, a steel-blue one southwest, and a purplish-green one that appeared to be going east.

"I see them," I whispered, a little awestruck. "Is it the purple one we're taking?"

"Yes." Prentis beamed at me with unmistakable pride. "The purple one will carry us to the temple."

He took my hand, and we swam toward the current, passing over the reef. Prentis allowed me a moment to take in all the sea flora and fauna—the spiny anemones, the rainbow coral, the striped fish and armored sea turtles flitting about as they searched for breakfast. But all too soon we swam past it, until we were directly beneath the current.

"Prepare yourself," Prentis warned. "This is a bit like being sucked into a vortex."

He kicked his legs to propel himself forward, dragging me with him. The current sucked us in, and I screamed as we shot forward, hurtling through the water at breakneck speed. I tried to look behind me to see if Einar and Cascada had followed, but the force of the current was so intense, I couldn't even turn my head.

"Relax!" Prentis shouted back at me. "You'll get used to it!"

My thundering heart disagreed, and I held onto Prentis's hand for dear life as we rocketed through the current. The water roared in my ears, drowning out my pulse as we tore past sharks, schools of fish, sea turtles, and a variety of undersea life. I even thought I saw two whales at one point, engaged in what looked like a mating dance.

We traveled like this for close to an hour before Prentis plunged his hand through the current wall without warning. The current spat us out, and I floated aimlessly in the water for a moment as I tried to catch my breath, the ocean spinning around us.

"Giant's teeth," I gasped, holding my stomach as I tried not to retch. "That was brutal."

The current spat Cascada and Einar out next to us, the latter looking quite a bit worse for wear. "I take it back," Einar rasped as he let go of Cascada's hand. It could have been the water, but his skin had a green tinge to it, and there was a dazed look in his eyes as he floated toward me. "I would absolutely rather swim than go through that accursed ride again."

"Oh, don't be such a baby," Cascada said cheerfully, slapping him on the shoulder as she swam past. She looked as fresh and rosy as someone who'd just stepped out of a morning bath. "The currents are a thrill ride! Surely it must be similar to diving through the sky."

"Not at all," Einar said, crossing his arms over his chest as he scowled. "When I'm skydiving, I'm in control. In that tunnel, I had to rely on you to get us in and out safely."

"Which I did with flying colors." She pinched his cheek, and I had to clamp down on the urge to growl at her as a wave of possessiveness filled me. "Now, are you two going to keep whining, or are you going to look at what we've traveled all this way to see?"

She pointed to something behind us, and Einar and I turned to look. My surroundings came into sharp focus, and I realized we were standing at the mouth of a valley. Two undersea mountains towered above us on either side, and nestled in the valley between was an undersea village that looked like something out of a storybook. Dwellings of coral and clamshell crouched in the mountains' shadow, their roofs thatched with kelp, and glowing lanterns illuminated the streets, though I couldn't tell from this distance what powered them. Beyond the village, perched on the edge of an undersea cliff, was a grand, domed building that I assumed was the water temple. But I hardly noticed it as I caught the telltale flash of a mermaid tail, flitting from one building to another.

I was in motion before I realized it, my legs kicking behind me as I eagerly swam toward the village. I thought Prentis would try to stop me, or offer a word of caution, but he said nothing as he fell in next to me, Einar and Cascada right behind us. Excitement bubbled inside me as we reached the village, but before we could pass through the arched stone gate, two merfolk bearing tridents swam forward, stopping our progression.

"Lord Prentis," the one on the left purred. Her ruby eyes gleamed with carnal hunger, and I raised my eyebrows as she gave him a blatant once-over. Hair the color of autumn leaves floated around her pale face and shoulders, only just covering her small breasts. Her milk-white torso flowed into the flame-red scales of her mermaid tail, which twitched in a manner that was somehow both eager and ominous. "It's been far too long since your last visit."

"Miriel," Prentis said, inclining his head. Was it just me, or had his cheeks turned pink? "Oranis." He acknowledged the other one, a male with sea moss-colored hair and a matching tail. "My companions and I are on our way to the temple. We'd appreciate it if you'd allow us safe passage through your village."

"Certainly," Miriel said. "What have you brought us as tribute?"

Prentis removed the pack he'd strapped onto his back, and withdrew an ivory tooth as long as his forearm. "A kraken tooth," he said, offering it to her. "I battled one of the sea creatures earlier."

The two merfolk exchanged glances, reluctantly impressed. "That's must have been quite a battle," Oranis said as Miriel accepted the gift. "Our queen will love to hear it."

"I will happily tell her the tale, and anything else she wishes to know, after we've completed our visit to the temple—"

"I don't think Queen Lethta will be pleased if she hears you and your company waltzed through her village without paying homage to her first," Miriel said. Her ruby eyes narrowed as she looked first me over, then Einar. "Speaking of your company, who are your friends?"

"My name is Adara," I told her, a little tired of being a spectator to this conversation. "And this is my companion, Einar."

"Companion indeed." A contemplative glint entered Miriel's eyes before she turned away with a provocative swish of her tail. "Come along, now. The queen has already been alerted to your arrival. We don't want to keep her waiting."

"So," I murmured as we followed the two merfolk into the village. "How many times have the two of you..."

"Don't," Prentis muttered. "It was a mistake, and not one I'm keen on repeating."

He refused to meet my gaze, and I wondered how much of that was true. Based on the curious and lustful glances Miriel kept shooting us over her shoulder when she thought we weren't looking, I didn't think she felt the same. And given what Prentis had already told me, and the sexual fluidity of water fae, it wouldn't surprise me to learn he had lovers scattered throughout the water realm.

Still, I found it hard to focus on any of that as we swam through the city. It appeared that the mermaids had repurposed an ancient city that the ocean had claimed, shoring up the sea moss-covered walls with shell and coral where they needed repair. A few bricks and cobbles still remained from the paved streets that had once existed, but the mermaids had let these go to the wayside since they had no need of pavement. Instead, they used lanterns powered by some type of glowing orb to mark the paths that wound through the city. The city streets were bustling with merfolk going about their day, and patrolled by merfolk riding giant seahorses, which I had to try very hard not to stop and gawk at.

The two merfolk led us into a grand building in the center of the city that looked to have been a manor house in its former life. It surprised me to see that the marble columns and floors were mostly intact, though the furniture had long rotted away, replaced instead by ocean-friendly pieces made from coral, shell, and rock.

I scarcely had time to take it all in before we were whisked into a receiving hall, where a mermaid with long, teal hair encrusted with shells and starfish waited in the center of a giant clamshell throne. Oranis and Miriel bowed swiftly, and I nearly did the same before I remembered that I was royalty in my own right.

"Your Majesty," Oranis said. "This is Lord Prentis, as you know, and his companions, Lady Cascada, Lady Adara, and Einar. They request safe passage through our kingdom to the Sea Temple, and as per the treaty, have brought this gift as tribute."

He presented the kraken tooth to the queen, who reached for it with long, talon-tipped fingers. Her citronella eyes glittered with delight as she turned the tooth this way and that, holding it up to the glowing orbs that lit the room.

"This is an excellent gift," she declared. "Our smith will be able to fashion a fearsome weapon from this. How is it you came by a tooth in such perfect condition?"

"I wrested it from the beast during battle," Prentis said proudly. "It pulled a passenger from my ship overboard, so we had to attempt a rescue. I would never attack a kraken unprovoked."

"Of course not," the queen drawled. Her gaze trailed over us, lingering on me for a moment before coming to rest on Einar. "I appreciate this gift very much, Prentis, but it appears you've brought me something else, something I want far more."

I stiffened as a sense of foreboding rose within me. "And what would that be?" Prentis asked cautiously.

The queen's smile widened. "Why, that would be the dragon, of course."

25

Einar

"The dragon," I repeated as the mermaid queen's avaricious gaze bore into mine. "You do realize I'm standing right here, yes?"

"Yes," Queen Lethta agreed. "You are, which is a marvel in and of itself. I don't believe a dragon has ever visited us before. I daresay this is a historic event."

"Einar isn't for sale," Adara said. Her entire body bristled as she stepped in front of me, and I couldn't help feeling pleased at the surge of possessiveness I felt through the bond. "He's a person, not an object for you to treat with."

The queen's eyes narrowed. "I'm sorry you feel that way," she said with a delicate shrug of her bare shoulders. "But your dragon is the price if you want safe passage through my kingdom."

Adara whirled on Prentis, fury blazing in her cornflower-blue eyes. "Why didn't you mention the mermaids required a tribute as well?" she hissed, grabbing his arm hard enough to bruise. "If I'd known this was a possibility, I wouldn't have brought Einar at all!"

"I didn't think it was important!" Prentis protested. He seemed distressed by the predicament, though I wasn't sure if that was because he was actually upset on my behalf, or because Adara was digging her fingernails into his bicep. "How was I to know the queen would ask for Einar? I thought the kraken tooth would be more than enough!"

Sighing, I stepped in front of the arguing pair and faced the queen. "Your Majesty," I said, bowing low. "It seems we are at an impasse."

"Indeed." The queen arched her eyebrows. "Will you be taking your leave, then?"

"Actually," I said, giving her my most charming smile, "I was hoping you would allow me to make a counter-proposal."

"A counter-proposal?" The queen fought to maintain a disinterested expression, but I could see from the renewed gleam in her eyes that I had her intrigued. "Surely you do not have a better prize to tempt me with than your own flesh and blood."

"Not quite," I admitted. "But I can offer the potential for entertainment. Set me the most difficult trial you can—the one that only the most elite of your warriors have ever been able to pass. If I pass it, you'll grant my friends and I safe passage through your kingdom both to and from the temple. If I fail, I will remain here and devote myself to you as your servant for the next thirty days."

"No!" Adara released Prentis so she could grab my arm. She tugged ferociously, trying to get me to meet her eyes, but I refused to break the queen's contemplative gaze. "Einar, don't! We'll find another way. Please."

"Very well." The queen's lips widened into a catlike grin that sent shivers down my spine. "I accept your terms. And I look forward to seeing you kneel at my feet."

"I cannot believe you agreed to this," Adara fumed the moment we were out of earshot. Muriel had shown the four of us to a guesthouse, then left us to settle in for the evening. The queen had been gracious enough to allow me one night of rest before the challenge, which was more than I'd expected.

"Of course I agreed to it," I said as I sat down on a large, round, backless sofa I was fairly certain was a giant sea sponge. Prentis and Cascada had wisely chosen to make themselves scarce, though I was certain they could hear every word of our argument from their rooms. "I'm the one who set the terms."

"And without even consulting me first!" she fumed, slamming her hand down on the low driftwood table in front of me. Her lavender-blue hair drifted around her head like it had taken on a life of its own, and her face glowed so fiercely I had no doubt she would be spewing fire at me if we weren't underwater. "Shouldn't I have a say in whether or not you offer up your life on my behalf?"

"You would if we were mated," I said baldly, and she blanched. "But we're not, so as it stands, my life is still my own to command. Besides, it's not as if she's going to kill me. Unless she doesn't have any gillflower for me. That might be a proble—"

Adara grabbed me by the front of my tunic and yanked me to my feet. "Stop being flippant," she growled, and I was shocked to see tears in her eyes. "If I have to mate the two of us to keep you from doing this stupid thing, I'll carry you upstairs to bed myself. But I can't let you do this. Not for me."

A wave of tenderness rippled through me at Adara's words, stronger even than the lust that pulsed through me at the idea of

Adara tossing me onto her bed and having her way with me. "My little firecracker," I said, hooking an arm around her waist to pull her close. "Do you really think I would do this for anyone else?"

"I—firecracker?" she faltered, her grip loosening on the front of my tunic. "Where did that come from?"

"Your eyes. They spark like firecrackers whenever you're mad." I brushed a soft kiss against her lips, smiling against her mouth as she trembled against me. "You've got a dragon's temper for sure, and that's sexy as sin. But I won't take advantage of this situation and allow you to mate with me out of a misguided sense of duty. When you choose me, I want it to be because you're ready and willing. Besides, you should have more faith in my abilities. I was the most fearsome soldier in the dragon army for a reason. How could you think for a second I'd fail tomorrow's challenge?"

She bit her lip, and a fierce urge to kiss her seized me. But she wrenched herself from my arms before I could follow through, distracted by the sound of movement. A moment later, Prentis swam into the living room. His eyes darted between us, but if he sensed the sexual tension in the water, he chose not to comment on it.

"You may be the most fearsome soldier in the dragon army," he said dryly, holding something out to me. "But if you want to best the queen's challenge tomorrow, I have a feeling you're going to want this."

"Merfolk of the Coral Kingdom," the queen announced in a booming voice, magnified by the large pink conch shell gripped in her hand. "We are gathered here today to witness Einar of the Dragons compete in our fiercest trial—The Robbing of the Kretos.

The merfolk who had come to watch cheered raucously. They'd formed a crowd about ten yards away from a deep rift in the ocean, Adara, Prentis and Cascada amongst them. I stood mere feet away from the opening, my body angled so I faced both it and the spectators. I didn't dare make the mistake of giving my back to the enemy—not after doing so had nearly resulted in death by kraken. I'd already spent several minutes peering into the rift, trying to get a glimpse of whatever horror I might face, but I couldn't make out anything in all that ominous blackness.

"The kretos is a giant sea serpent that terrorizes the ocean depths," the queen explained, more for my benefit than anyone else. "It usually prefers larger prey than mermaids, and rarely hunts our kind—however, its diamond-hard scales provide superior armor to any other material found in the ocean."

She turned to look at me then, a crafty smile on her face. "Your task is simple, warrior. Steal a scale from the kretos's hide. If you do so, I allow you and your friends to pass. But if you fail..." she trailed off, her smile widening. "Well, you know what will happen."

Without warning, she pressed the conch shell to her lips and blew, producing a long, clear note that pierced the stillness of the water. Bubbles began to pour from the rift, followed by a rumble in the ocean floor. A thrill shot through me that was part nerves, part battle fever, and I braced myself as a serpentine creature burst from the rift.

I stared in horror and amazement as the kretos coiled above

me, some fifty feet long, with glittering amethyst scales and eyes of pure silver. It was as beautiful as it was deadly, the malevolent look in its eyes sending shivers through me as it sized me up the way an apex predator did when facing challenging prey. The merfolk shrieked in terror and excitement as they swam away, retreating behind the rocks where they could spectate at a safe distance. I caught a brief glimpse of Prentis dragging Adara away, but I couldn't stare for long—the kretos was already bearing down on me, its giant maw opened wide to reveal four-foot long fangs and a forked tongue.

I propelled myself out of the way just in time as it struck, the force of the blow kicking up rocks and debris that clouded my vision. Fear pumped through my veins as I tried to swim clear of the murky water, but before I could, something long and slimy wrapped around my torso and yanked me forward.

"Oh no you don't!" I snarled, slashing at the kretos's tongue with my claws. It released me with a shriek, clouds of blood spreading through the water, and I kicked away again, thankful for the wetsuit. It was a little tight, yes, but it allowed me to cut through the seawater as swiftly as if I were flying, giving me full access to the same strength and speed I enjoyed on land and in the sky.

And then there was the other gift Prentis had given me. One I would never make use of if I couldn't get close to the blasted beast.

As the serpent reared back to strike again, I snatched a rock from the ocean floor and hurtled it toward its head with all my strength. It smacked the kretos in the eye, and it roared, thrashing its magnificent head this way and that. Thankful that it had no arms to attack me with, I rushed forward, but before I closed the distance, the sea creature slammed its tail into me, sending me flying through the water.

"You cantankerous bastard!" I shouted as I flipped end over

end, struggling to right myself. But the kretos got its bearings before I did, and it hurtled toward me, jaws wide open, fangs aimed straight at my chest. Unable to get out of the way fast enough, I did the only thing I could think of—I grabbed both fangs at once, then braced my feet on its lower jaw to keep it from swallowing me.

The creature shrieked in protest, trying to snap its jaws shut. My arms and legs shook as I fought to hold its mouth open, and I kicked away before it could ensnare me with its forked tongue again. But that dastardly tail was waiting for me, and instead of smacking me away like it did before, it ensnared me, coiling around my body in a tight grip that threatened to crush my ribs.

The kretos hissed as it brought me to eye level, its forked tongue flickering out between its still-bloody lips as it raked those malevolent silver eyes over me. There was no mistaking the gloating expression on its reptilian face—the bastard thought it had won.

And maybe it had won the battle, at least.

But I refused to let it win the war.

Without breaking eye contact, I yanked the kraken tooth Prentis had given me from the sheath I'd strapped to my thigh, then stabbed it straight through the kretos's hide. The beast let out an unearthly scream as the tooth pierced its tail, and I gripped the edge of the scale I'd loosened, ripping it free right before the beast smacked me away once again.

Prepared this time, I flipped through the air twice, then braced myself, preparing for an attack. But the kretos seemed to have had enough. Letting out one more infuriated shriek, it disappeared back into the rift, leaving a bloody trail in its wake.

Utter silence settled across the expanse as I turned to face the crowd. They stared back from behind the rocks with shell-shocked expressions, as if they couldn't believe what had happened. The queen looked particularly dismayed, not that I could blame her. I resisted the urge to sketch a bow—the gesture would come off as insufferably smug.

Adara was the first to jump up from behind the rocks, clapping and cheering with such enthusiasm, the rest couldn't help joining in. Before I knew it, the merfolk were swimming up to congratulate me, patting me on the back with their webbed hands and praising my performance. Even Prentis and Cascada seemed pleased—though not nearly as proud as Adara.

"You did incredible," she crowed, almost bowling me over with a hug. "I knew you could do it!"

"Did you now?" I teased. "I don't remember you saying that yesterday."

"I don't remember anything about yesterday," she said, breathless. "All I can see is you here, now. Alive and victorious."

The world faded away for a moment, and her head tilted up as if she were about to kiss me. But before our lips could touch, a hand alighted on my shoulder, and I turned to see the queen looking at me, a bemused expression on her face.

"I cannot decide if I am angry with you for using the kraken tooth or not," she said. "But it is plain to me that even if you agreed to serve me, it would be a service of the flesh alone. Your heart is devoted elsewhere."

"Yes," I agreed. "But it was an honor to compete in one of your traditions, nonetheless." Bowing my head, I offered her the scale in one hand, and the kraken tooth in another, but she shook her head.

"No, you have earned those, good warrior." She smiled, then stepped aside. "Now go, all four of you. And may the currents guide you to good fortune."

26

Adara

"**D**o you think the priestess will be angry we're arriving a day late?" I muttered to Prentis as we swam up the inclined path that led to the temple. The escort the queen had charged with accompanying us through the mermaid kingdom had mercifully abandoned us outside the gates, leaving the four of us to traverse the path to the temple on our own.

"Oh, most definitely," Cascada chimed in from behind us. "She's a fastidious creature, one of those types that prefers everything just so. And she won't appreciate that you've brought a dragon with you, either. Might have been better if you'd left Einar in the village with the mermaids after all."

"Cascada," Prentis snapped, shooting a glare over his shoulder at her before giving me an apologetic look. "The priestess won't be happy with our tardiness, but it's unavoidable given the circumstances, so she'll understand. Either way, Lady Axlya has commanded her to assist you with the ritual preparations, so it's not as if she's going to refuse you simply because we were delayed. The ocean is fickle, and no journey either under or across it is ever straightforward. She knows this better than anyone else."

Prentis held out a hand to indicate that we should stop, and we halted about five yards from the temple. It was a great silver dome, with small rectangular windows lining the base just below the roofline. Personifications of the five water spirits were carved into its walls, but the most interesting thing about it was the strange, purplish force field rippling through the water.

"We come with the tides," Prentis intoned in a deep voice, bowing his head.

I was about to ask who he was talking to when a figure stepped from the force field, as though conjured from thin... well, water, I guess. I stifled a gasp at the sight of a water fae dressed from head to toe in aquatic green armor, similar to the wetsuits we wore, except for the sacred symbols of the ocean currents stitched into a circle in the center of her torso. Her expression was serene in the way one might expect of a temple attendant, but the javelin she held in her right hand told me she meant business.

"Lord Prentis," she said in a voice like rippling water. "We expected you yesterday."

"My apologies." Prentis inclined his head. "We were detained by the mermaid queen."

The temple guard said nothing as she looked at each one of us, her piercing jade eyes scanning us from head to toe as if she were searching for any sign of corruption or ill intent. She lingered on Einar the longest, and I held my breath, wondering if she was going to deny him entry for being a dragon.

But after a moment she shrugged, then turned away. "Follow me."

She stepped through the force field as we followed, crossing through the barrier and into... fresh air. My gills vanished, and I sucked in a gulp of fresh air as the ocean water sluiced off us, pooling onto dry ground. The silver dome was still in front of us, but the illusion of bare ocean rock had given way to an herb and vegetable garden that appeared to spread across the entire circumference of the temple.

"What is this?" Einar asked, bewildered.

"An enchantment," a fae answered, stepping out from the temple's wide double door entrance. She wore aqua colored robes with the symbols of the currents embroidered across them in gold thread. An elaborate headdress rested atop her crown of robins-egg-blue braids. It appeared to be crafted from elements from all four of the water clans—cattails for the marsh fae, waves for the ocean fae, ovals for the lake fae, and snowflakes for the ice fae.

Her cerulean eyes fixed on me as she descended the temple's stairs with measured steps, and my skin prickled beneath the weight of her regard. "When we water fae built this place thousands of years ago beneath the ocean, we knew we could not expect our priestesses and temple attendants to spend the rest of their days breathing only ocean water. So we hired the witchlings to collaborate with the air fae and cast a special enchantment upon this place that filters the air from the surrounding ocean, and passes it safely into this space."

"So this force field is like a massive gill," Einar said, looking around. He pressed a hand to his neck, and his eyes widened as he realized his gills had disappeared. "What—"

"Worry not," the priestess said, her gaze flicking to him. Her mouth pursed in disapproval at Einar's presence, but thankfully, she kept her comments to herself. "We have gillflower on the premises to send you back with. You are not the first non-water fae to visit our temple... though you may very well be the first dragon." Her brows arched as she turned to look at me. "Was it necessary to bring him? What good is a dragon at eight thousand fathoms deep? Except as bait for frisky mermaids, I suppose."

I blinked at her. "How did you know about that?"

"The currents bring me news from all over the ocean," the priestess said. "I knew right away when the mermaid queen set her sights on your dragon. You should have given him to her. It would have simplified your life."

Einar growled low in his throat, and I ground my teeth together to keep myself from spitting out a barbed retort. "I realize you do not approve of our dragon companion," Prentis said hastily before I could get myself into trouble, "but he is here now, and we aren't very well going to send him away. Perhaps we can move on from this and focus on Adara's ritual preparations?"

"Very well." The priestess flattened her mouth. "Did you bring your offering, Lady Adara?"

"What?" I blinked, then fumbled for the pouch at my waist. "Yes, of course I did."

I withdrew the treasure chest of candy and held it out to the priestess for her inspection. She took it gingerly, as if I'd handed her a piece of dung, and inspected it before handing it back to me.

"Very well, this will do. Follow me, all of you—except for the dragon," she said, pointing a blue-tipped nail in Einar's direction. "He must remain outside. A fire breather cannot enter the water temple."

Outrage filled me, and I opened my mouth to tell her that technically, *I* was a fire breather too. But Einar caught my eye, and he gave a subtle shake of his head. *It's not worth it,* he mouthed.

I sighed, and swallowed my protests. *I'm sorry,* I mouthed back.

He merely winked at me, then took up a post next to one of

the doors, opposite where the temple guard was standing. She seemed annoyed that he was butting in on her duties, but she said nothing, and I swallowed a smile as we passed into the temple.

The priestess led us across the temple hall and to a raised platform in the middle of the room. In the center of the platform was a glowing pool, and as I drew close to it, I could hear a low, melodic hum emanating from the water. The tendrils of sound seemed to wrap around my mind, whispering of secrets just beyond my understanding, and before I realized it, I found myself kneeling at the water's edge, hand outstretched—

"Oww!" I yelled as the priestess smacked my hand, knocking it away before I could make contact.

"Stay your hand, child!" she snapped, and I heard Cascada snickering from behind me. "It is not yet time for you to commune with the Sacred Pool. She is the heart of our people, and only those who have purified themselves with the required ten days of fasting are permitted to partake of her waters. You are here to present your offering. Nothing more."

"My offering?" I stared up at the priestess. "You want me to throw it in the water?"

"I want you to *place* it in the water," the priestess corrected stiffly. "With *reverence*. Now repeat after me."

The priestess recited the lines to a water prayer in the old fae tongue, and I repeated them dutifully, only partially understanding the words. I seemed to be asking the water elements to open my heart to the universe and purify my soul of all unclean deeds, so I could make room for the sleeping beast inside me to awaken. Once I finished, I slipped the offering into the water, careful not to let my fingers touch even a single drop.

Bright golden light burst from the pool, and I flung my arm over my face to shield my eyes from the sudden flare. Power sizzled across my skin, and a fresh wave of energy surged through me. My eyes popped open to see my hands glowing with the same light as the lake, and I looked down to watch it spread across my entire body.

"Is this... unusual?" I asked the priestess, who was staring at me in wide-eyed shock. I looked around to see Prentis and Cascada staring at me too, as if they couldn't believe what they were seeing.

"It is unexpected," the priestess said in a clipped tone as the glow faded. "But not unheard of." She turned to Prentis and Cascada. "I need a moment alone with Lady Adara, to instruct her on the ritual preparations for the coming days."

"Of course." Prentis and Cascada made themselves scarce, the latter shooting glances over her shoulder at me as they walked away. The moment the temple doors shut behind them, the priestess's hand clamped around my forearm, and she pinned me with a stare far harder and more dangerous than her grip.

"You need to let the dragon go," she said.

"What?"

"The dragon standing guard outside," the priestess repeated slowly, as if I were a simpleton. "He is bound to you. You need to release him from that bond, or you will never ascend the Edirian throne."

"I don't know what you're talking about," I said stubbornly, even as my heart sank. Of course I knew what she was talking about—Einar had already explained the mating bond to me, that he was tethered to me, and would remain so unless I rejected the bond and set him free. I tried to tug my arm free, but she held fast, keeping me pinned beside the pool.

"You know precisely what I'm talking about," she said, her voice tight with controlled anger. "Your bond with the dragon is slowing you down, preventing you from reaching your full potential as a water fae. So long as your fire for him burns inside you, you will never convince the people of Lochanlee that you are one of them. Your selfishness is holding you back from achieving true greatness—and there is true greatness in you, Lady Adara, much as I'm loath to admit it." She skimmed her gaze across my skin, which still glimmered faintly.

"If there is greatness in me, it is *because* of my dragon heritage, not in spite of it," I snapped. I yanked on my arm again, and this time she let it go, allowing me to get to my feet. "I won't allow you to dictate what parts of me are acceptable to my fellow fae. They will get all of me, or none of me."

The priestess sighed as she rose, adjusting her headdress. "Those are pretty words," she said, "But if you are willing to let the world perish out of selfish desire, then you do not deserve to complete the ritual."

Icy fear crackled through my veins, and I desperately wished I could take back what I'd said. I couldn't afford for the priestess to reject me, even if she and I bore an instinctive enmity toward one another. "If it comes to choosing between Einar and the people of Ediria, I will choose the people," I said evenly. "But I do not need to make that choice today."

"Maybe not," she agreed. "But your time is running out, Lady Adara. And so is everyone else's."

27

Leap

Leap watched glumly from one of the central tower balconies as Uncle Oren and his advisors departed. The airship they boarded was sleeker and faster than the one that had carried him here from Angtun, the yellow and blue flag of House Reatha flying from its masts as it lifted off from the courtyard.

"Well, well," Ryker murmured from behind him as the ship picked up speed, getting further and further away until it disappeared into the cloudy winter sky. "Looks like it's just the two of us now, huh?"

Leap turned around to face his cousin. He hadn't seen Ryker since he'd stormed out of his father's rooms the other day. "I wouldn't say it's just the two of us," he said dryly. "We are in a palace full of guards and servants."

Ryker grinned. "Yes, but they all answer to *me*," he said in a gleeful tone that sent a shiver down Leap's spine. Leap tried to take a step back as Ryker closed the distance between him, but his cousin knotted his fingers into the front of his tunic, preventing his retreat. "There's no one to protect you now, Leap. No one to stop me from punishing you for running away."

Leap balled his hands at his sides to keep himself from attacking Ryker. Without his magic at his disposal, he didn't have a chance of winning in a physical altercation, and he knew his cousin was waiting for any excuse to give him a physical beat-down.

"Why are you doing this?" he asked instead through gritted teeth. "Don't you have better things to do than make my life miserable?"

"You mean do I have better things to do that punish the traitor who abandoned our family?" Ryker sneered. "Maybe. But I'm good at multitasking. I'm sure I can manage."

Without warning, he flung Leap away, sending the younger fae sailing through the air. Only years of training and agility prevented Leap from smashing the back of his head into the ground. He back flipped through the air, landing on his hands, then did a back handspring to get back to his feet. Lifting his fists in a fighting stance, he looked wildly around for Ryker as he prepared for another attack.

But his cousin had disappeared into the palace.

Bastard, Leap thought as he trudged back into the tower. He headed back through the central courtyard, picking his way through the maze until he arrived at the south tower. Leap braced himself for a confrontation with the guard posted outside the door, but the male said nothing, allowing him to open the door and go inside. He climbed the winding staircase until he reached the room he and Mavlyn had shared on their first night here.

"Mav?" he pounded on the door, half-afraid that Uncle Oren had moved her into the dungeons. "Are you in there?"

"Leap?" Mavlyn's anxious voice filtered through the door. "Is that you?"

Leap fished a knife he'd filched from the breakfast table out of his pocket and set to work at the door. In seconds, he had it open, and rushed inside.

"Giant's Teeth!" Mavlyn rushed over and scooped him up in a hug, squeezing so tight Leap feared his ribs would pop. "Thank the Radiants you're here! I thought your uncle had shipped you off to the mines, or worse, had you executed."

"He hasn't, but if you don't let go of me you're going to finish the job for him," Leap wheezed.

Mavlyn released him, an apologetic look on her face. "Sorry. I got a little carried away." She raked a hand through her auburn hair, which had seen better days. Judging by the disheveled state of her appearance, Leap guessed Mavlyn had gone into a bit of a depression. Guilt wracked him—she must have been worried sick about him over the last few days. "What's happening, Leap? I saw an airship leaving the palace through the window this morning. Did Lord Oren leave? And how did you get out of your cell?"

"Uncle Oren's left on a diplomatic mission," Leap said. "He seems to be feeling guilty, because he came to me yesterday and told me he'd pardon my crimes and allow me to join the Lightning Guard. Of course, that's only if I swear a blood-oath allegiance to House Reatha, and promise not to aid any of the other houses without his permission."

Mavlyn recoiled, a look of disgust on her face. "And you said *yes*?"

"Of course not," Leap snapped. "I may be a thief, but I'm not a sellout. What kind of person do you think I am?"

"Right. Sorry." Mavlyn scrubbed a hand over her face. "I'm just... I don't know." She sighed, dropping heavily onto the edge of the unmade bed. Books and miscellaneous items were strewn all over the place, drawers pulled out and upended. "I've been searching for a way to pick the lock on my shackles so I can get out of this forsaken place, but I haven't found anything." She gazed hopefully at Leap, but the light in her eyes died when she noticed the manacles still attached to his own wrists. "You can't get these off?"

Leap shook his head. "The locks are magical," he said ruefully. "Trust me, I tried. Uncle Oren's allowed me 'free rein' of the palace while I wait for him to return, but he wouldn't take the shackles off. He thinks if he gives me the illusion of freedom, I'll be more likely to agree to his demands."

Mavlyn shook her head. "Even if we escaped, we won't be able to break out Quye with these magical bindings. You have to find a way to steal the key or something, Leap."

"Trust me, I've been thinking of nothing else," Leap said. "Have you had any more dream visits from Quye?"

"No." Mavlyn bit her lip, worry shimmering in her green eyes. "I think the shackles are preventing me from receiving them. Or there's something wrong on her end. I hope nothing bad has happened to her."

"I'm sure she's fine," Leap said. Uncle Oren might treat Quye more like an object than a real person, but he would never allow anything to happen to her, and neither would her guards. As far as the air fae were concerned, Quye was practically a goddess— they wouldn't dare risk harming her for fear of being cursed by the wind spirits. "I have to go now, but I'll be back as soon as I can to break us out of here."

Mavlyn nodded. "Hurry. I have a feeling we're running out of time."

Leap used his stolen knife to shimmy the lock back into place, then returned to his own rooms. He needed time to regroup and figure out a plan, but the sight of Gale standing outside his door, leaning against the wall with his arms crossed, told him that would have to wait.

"What is it?" Leap asked wearily.

Gale shrugged, pushing off the wall. "Ryker's summoned you to the great hall."

A lump of dread solidified in Leap's stomach as he followed Gale to the great hall, where his Uncle Oren typically held court. He'd hoped to have a reprieve before Ryker dragged him out to make a spectacle, but apparently his cousin was unwilling to wait.

"Ahh, there he is!" Ryker cried as Leap and Gale entered the room. Leap stiffened at the sight of Ryker lounging on his uncle's throne, one leg thrown haphazardly over one of the arms as he dangled a wine glass from his free hand. The advisors were all absent, most having left with Uncle Oren, while the remaining ones had likely not been summoned for this farce. In their absence was a gaggle of Ryker's cronies and admirers—sons and daughters of the court who hadn't yet been assigned posts and duties by their families, and who were more than up for a bit of fun at Leap's expense.

The only actual adults in the hall were the guards stationed at the entrances, and Gale, who stopped a few feet away, leaving Leap to approach the throne on his own. He glanced back to see the lightning rider's reaction to all this, but Gale's expression was smoothed into an expressionless mask.

Ever the professional, Leap thought bitterly as he turned to face his cousin. He swept low into an exaggerated bow, gathering his false bravado around him like a suit of armor.

"How can I be of service to the court?" he asked.

"I thought you would never ask," Ryker said in that gleeful tone that always made Leap's skin crawl. He straightened to see Ryker looking not at him, but at the assembled crowd, all of whom were eyeing Leap. "My fellow courtiers, you may remember my dear cousin Leap. His parents were honorable members of the Lightning Guard, and we took him in when they were killed in battle. My father had high hopes that Leap would follow in his parents' footsteps, but he turned his back on the Lightning Rider academy and ran away, throwing his lot in with a band of thieves in Wynth."

The cronies gasped at the scandalous portrait Ryker painted, and Leap had to force himself not to roll his eyes at their theatrical reaction. Out of the corner of his eye, he saw Gale frowning. He wondered if he should even bother speaking up in his own defense, but he knew there was no use—he had already been judged and condemned. Ryker was merely laying out the sentence now.

"And that's not even the worst of it," Ryker declared. He paused to take a sip from his wine glass, then continued. "After Leap finished fleecing the hard-working citizens of Wynth of their coin, he left the city and joined up with a group of blood-thirsty harpies, who he's been helping by luring poor, unsuspecting fae to their lair!"

Angry shouts echoed through the chamber at this, but they were nothing compared to the outrage that flared to life inside Leap. "I never helped the harpies capture or kill fae," he said hotly, his fists clenching and unclenching at his sides. He took a step toward Ryker, but before he could say or do anything more, his cousin blasted him with a powerful burst of wind. Leap went flying across the room once more, and he braced himself for a collision, too stunned to catch his fall this time.

But instead of stone, he crashed into an armored torso instead.

Gale grunted as he caught Leap, his arms banding around the boy as he absorbed the brunt of the blow. Leap glanced up into the rider's face, shocked to see genuine anger blazing in the older male's eyes.

The lightning rider set Leap on his feet, then turned his flinty gaze to Ryker. "You can play your hazing games if you must, Lord Ryker," he said in a flat, emotionless tone. "But your father gave me strict orders to make sure Leap remains unharmed, and until his death, I answer to him, not you."

Ryker's face mottled with fury at not only being thwarted, but at having a set down delivered by a mere *guard* in front of his peers and friends. His throat worked as he searched for words, likely trying to figure out how to punish both the guard *and* Leap.

But the lightning riders, though they served the air realm at the behest of Lord Oren, were otherwise a law unto their own. Ryker had no power over Gale, and he knew it.

"There's no need to worry about Leap's safety," Ryker said, affecting an airy tone in an attempt to wrest control back over the room again. "I merely brought him here to tell him that since he refuses to make himself useful as a cadet, he can serve the realm by scrubbing the palace's floors." His thin mouth stretched into a gamine grin. "Starting with this one, of course."

A mop and scrub brush were produced, and Leap was forced to spend the next four hours scrubbing the great hall's floors on his hands and knees while his cousin continued to hold court. Ryker and his friends made sure to drop crumbs of food, spill droplets from their wine goblets, and even 'accidentally' knocked over his bucket so he had to stop and fill it with more soap and water. Their constant efforts to sabotage him made the process take twice as long as it should have, and by the time he left the great hall, he was shaking with suppressed rage.

"You shouldn't let them get to you like that," Gale said as he trailed Leap. The lightning rider seemed to have become his shadow, and Leap couldn't decide if he liked that or not. On the one hand, his presence curbed Ryker's cruelty, but on the other hand, Leap had no chance of escaping while having a guard in his presence twenty-four hours a day.

"Did Uncle Oren really assign you to protect me?" Leap asked, not looking back at Gale. His mind was stuck on the events that had taken place in the great hall, on the way the courtiers had pretended he wasn't there even as they tormented him, making him feel as though he had less importance than even the lowliest servant in the palace. They probably would have stepped on him, too, if Gale hadn't been there to monitor them.

His ears burned with humiliation at the thought that he had to be babysat after all these years of being self-sufficient. Was this really what he'd been reduced to?

"Not exactly," Gale admitted. "He ordered me to make sure you didn't escape, but he didn't say anything about you being hurt or injured. I'm sure he wouldn't approve of Ryker physically attacking you, though, so I don't feel bad about the lie."

"Right, but he has no problem with Ryker abusing me in other ways, is that it?" Leap asked sarcastically. "Forcing me to scrub floors and allowing his friends to tease and torment me is fine, so long as they don't actually lay a hand on me?"

Gale shrugged. "Hazing happens everywhere, Leap, even in the lightning rider academy." Leap could hear the frown in his voice as they crossed the courtyard. "Is joining the academy really so abhorrent to you?"

Leap stopped and turned to face Gale. "It would be an honor," he said, his voice uncharacteristically serious. "There was a time where I wanted nothing more, and would have jumped at the opportunity my uncle gave me yesterday. But that was before I met Adara, Einar, and Mavlyn, and realized that some causes are worth putting aside old grudges and boundaries for."

"And what causes are those?"

Leap took a deep breath, trying to gather his thoughts. "When I met Adara for the first time, she used her fire magic to cure one of the harpies of a shadow magic infection that would have killed her. This was after the harpies tried to kill her and take her back to the nest—and before you say anything," he added, annoyance creeping into his tone at the look on Gale's face, "—I *was* trying to stop that from happening. But anyway, Adara saved the harpy even though she had every reason to leave her in the snow to die. Einar, crotchety old dragon that he is, has stayed by Adara's side through thick and thin, even though he hates fae with every fiber of his being. Mavlyn—" the guilty knife lodged in his heart twisted a little at the thought of her— "left her hometown and her parents and everything she knows to help Adara, even though she knows Lady Mossi would punish her for it if she found out."

"The houses have been fighting for dominance for as long as fae memory can recall, even before the dragon wars. In all the stories I've heard about champions and heroes, I've never heard a single one where fae from all the realms banded together to fight a common enemy. But here we all are, risking everything for Adara because we believe she has what it takes to end the shadow curse destroying our kingdom."

Leap's gaze fell to the manacles biting into his wrists. "I let myself be dragged back to Angtun in chains, cut off from my magic, and left at the mercy of my asshole cousin, because I believe in Adara. I left my life with the harpies, risked my hide by returning to Wynth not once, but twice, and helped carry out an assault on the capital, because none of my problems matter as much as the shadow magic threat. There's no point in giving my uncle what he wants by taking the blood oath and joining the academy. The moment I turn my back on my friends, the shadow creatures will win. And no amount of training will be enough to save the kingdom."

"Well, I don't know about that," Gale huffed. He crossed his arms over his broad chest, looking both insulted and conflicted. "We lightning riders have been defending the border from the shadow creatures for nearly two decades now, and have done a mighty good job of it. Plus, we haven't had a single sighting of a shadow creature in close to a week since Adara killed King Aolis. Your uncle has already started pulling riders from the border—"

Leap's hand shot out, closing around the rider's arm. Gale stared down at the boy's small hand wrapped around his sinewy forearm, shocked speechless. "Please don't let my uncle do that," he said. "I know it seems like things are safe right now, but I saw that shadow demon with my own eyes. It's still at Kaipei Castle, still pulling strings, and if the shadow creatures have disappeared, that's somehow part of its master plan. Until Adara vanquishes it, we're still in danger."

A myriad of conflicting emotions—doubt, fear, skepticism—crossed Gale's face, but if Leap expected the lightning rider to change his mind, he was sorely disappointed. "I think you're just trying to convince me to help you escape."

Leap dropped Gale's arm with a sigh. "I'm trying to convince you to help me save the world," he said, turning away so he didn't have to see the look on the older male's face. "But I should have known better than to think I could convince you. Adults never take kids seriously, not until it's too late, and even then—"

He cut himself off, then turned and walked away. What was the point? This was an argument he would never win.

Adara

By the time I returned from yesterday's adventures, I was so exhausted I thought I would sleep until noon the next day. But my growling stomach woke me shortly after sunrise, and no matter how much water I drank, I could not quiet it enough to go back to sleep.

"Giant's teeth," I grumbled, tying the knot around my dressing gown as I stepped into the hallway. My footsteps were the only sound as I walked through the halls of the palace—aside from a few stealthy servants flitting around, everyone else was still asleep. Water fae didn't seem to be early risers as a general rule, which I was thankful for. I was in an irritable enough mood that I feared I would bite someone's head off if they tried to speak to me now.

Maybe I should just spend the entire fasting period submerged in water, I thought to myself as I made my way around the pond. When I'd been under the ocean, able to draw energy from the water, I'd felt significantly less hungry. It was a similar feeling to when I'd dipped my hand in the river water when Prentis's guards had loaded me onto the rowboat. But I had felt a hundred times stronger when I was completely submerged, the ocean's current flowing around me.

Wanting to test the theory, I toed off my shoes and approached the pond. My breath came out in frosted puffs as I slipped one foot in, then the other, feeling the cold ripple up my legs in waves. Another fae would have started shivering instantly, but I embraced the invigorating feeling, wading in until the water was up to my waist. The hunger pangs slowly faded, replaced by a tickling sensation in my feet. Frowning, I looked down, then let out a startled laugh at the sight of a golden koi nibbling at my toes.

"Well hello there, little guy." I crouched down, reaching through the water so I could pet it. It was the size of a small dog, and it wriggled happily as I stroked a hand along its golden scales, which were shot through with lines of lapis lazuli. "You're far more friendly than Lady Mossi's koi."

The sound of boots crunching on gravel alerted me to a visitor, and I turned my head to see Einar standing a few feet away from the pond. The morning sunlight backlit his tall, powerful form, and a now-familiar throb of desire surged from the bite mark.

His eyes flared, and my mouth went dry as I realized he could probably sense my need for him through the bond. But rather than comment on it, his gaze went to the koi fish rubbing on my legs.

"Are you talking to that fish?" he asked, his tone dry yet amused.

My lips twitched. "We were having a spirited discussion about aquatic politics before you interrupted." I stroked the koi's smooth scales one last time, then straightened up to face Einar. "Do you want to join us? It's quite refreshing."

Einar shuddered, shaking his head. "No thank you. I'm quite

comfortable watching you freeze your ass off while I stay nice and dry out here."

I grinned. "I'm not cold at all," I said, spinning around. Droplets of water arced from the sleeves of my dressing gown, catching rays of early morning sunlight as they hurtled away from me like tiny shooting stars. Einar yelped as a few drops hit him, and I laughed as he leaped back from the shore, well out of range. I wondered if it was my affinity for ice that made me impervious to the freezing temperatures, or if all water fae were built this way. Maybe that was something I could ask Prentis about.

"What are you doing out here, anyway?" I asked, sinking back into the water so I could float on my back. Serenity rippled through me as the water caressed my limbs—it wasn't the same heady rush I'd felt from the ocean, but a quiet bliss. It was almost as if each body of water had different emotional wavelengths, and I wondered what I would feel if I tried swimming in different ones. Would a babbling brook make me happy and bubbly? A rushing river fill me with a sense of urgency and direction? Why had I never stopped to think about this before?

"I followed you out here," Einar said, as if that were obvious. At my sardonic stare, he added, "The bond tells me how close or far away you are, so when you left your rooms, I felt it."

"Oh." A twinge of guilt pinched into me as I pictured Einar leaving his warm bed... followed by a rush of warmth as my mind's eye conjured a shirtless vision of him, naked skin and swirling tattoos and rippling muscles gleaming in the early morning light. I shoved the image from my head, trying to focus on the discussion at hand. "You should have stayed in bed, Einar. I'm perfectly safe out here."

"I know you are, but I was already awake," he said. A smile touched his lips as he added, "Besides, it's not a hardship to be out here with you. Not when I'm enjoying the view so much."

A blush rose to my cheeks as I conjured an image of what I must have looked like when he approached—dressing gown plastered to my curves, stiff nipples jutting through the fabric. "That settles it. I'm never coming out of the water."

Einar grinned, white teeth flashing in his darkly handsome face. "You're going to stay in there forever? Become a lady of the lake?"

"A princess of the pond," I corrected, sticking my tongue out at him. "They'll tell tales about me for ages--the temptress who lured males into the frigid depths of the water with the promise of wicked delights, only to give them a case of blue balls as their testicles freeze off."

Einar's laughter was cut short by the wailing cry of a child. The anguished howl wrenched at my heart, and I was out of the pond in an instant, shoes forgotten as I raced along the garden path. Einar's heavier footsteps pounded behind me as we followed the sound to its source, a servant boy of about ten years old kneeling in the grass.

"Ripples!" he wailed, and my heart sank at the sight of the calico cat sprawled on the ground in front of him. His small hands were buried in the cat's fur as he tried to shake it awake, but the animal was gone, its limbs stiff, eyes unseeing, bits of froth and vomit clinging to its mouth and whiskers. "Ripples is dead!"

A fae dressed in a maid's uniform rushed outside, duster waving in her hand as she ran to the boy's side. "Hush now, Elys. You're going to wake the entire castle!"

"B-b-but wh-why is he's d-dead!" the boy blubbered as she gathered him into her bosom. "I was p-playing with him-m in the k-kitchen this m-morning, and he was f-f-fine!"

I stood helplessly as the female tried to comfort her son, not knowing what to do. Einar, however, had wandered over to a patch of grass a foot away. "These look like cake crumbs," he said aloud. "Could your cat have eaten something that made him sick?"

I glanced over to where he was standing, and my heart froze into a solid lump in my chest. Scattered in the grass were tiny chunks of yellow sponge cake. Horror curdled in my gut as I looked up, my gaze climbing the palace wall until it found the open window some twenty feet above.

Bile rose up my throat, and I was suddenly glad I hadn't eaten anything. I would have thrown it all up... just like the cat tried to.

"Sick?" the mother echoed. "From cake?" She shook her head. "Ripples has gotten into cake before. He's never died from it."

Her words broke the spell of shock that had settled on me, and I sprang into action, grabbing Einar's arm and pulling him away from the scene. "That cake was in my room last night," I hissed under my breath once we were out of earshot. I felt bad about abandoning the boy and his mother, but this couldn't wait, and I couldn't afford for them to overhear. "Someone tried to poison me."

"What?" Einar's eyes went wide with shock, then narrowed, his entire face darkening with anger. "What do you mean, someone tried to poison you?

I shook my head, trying to get my panicked thoughts in order. "Last night, when I came back to my room, someone had left a slice of sponge cake on my dressing table. I was too tired to think clearly about it, and figured it was either a mistake or Cascada trying to sabotage my fasting. I just tossed the cake out the window and went to bed."

Einar glanced over at the spot where the dead cat had been found, then up at the window. "That's definitely your bedroom window." A muscle worked in his jaw, and the surrounding air steamed as angry heat rolled off him in visible waves. "I'm going to find the bastard who did this, shred them to pieces, and feed them to the koi."

I yelped as his wings exploded from his back, and before I knew what was happening, he'd yanked me against him and taken off. A few hard wingbeats later, we were in my bedroom, and he set me brusquely onto the bed before conducting a thorough search of my quarters.

"There are no unusual scents in this room," he growled, raking a hand through his hair. "And they've left no other traces of themselves."

"I'm not sure whoever it was would have brought the cake directly," I pointed out. "If it were me, I would have used a servant. Maybe we should question them all and figure out who asked them to bring it."

We spent the morning questioning the staff, but that turned out to be a fruitless lead. The maids and kitchen servants insisted none of them had brought the cake—they only cleaned the rooms in the mornings, and the one who had cleaned mine claimed that there had been no food when she'd left. That meant it had to have been placed while I was gone.

"Well, that rules out Cascada," I said crossly. "She was with us the whole day."

"It's possible Slaugh has spies planted here in the palace, and he's ordered them to off you," Einar said. We'd adjourned to an empty salon off the main hall to compare our findings. "That, or perhaps Prentis has a jealous lover who's heard of your potential nuptials."

"All this speculation is useless." I glanced at the clock on the wall, noting that it was nearly time for breakfast. "Should we tell Lady Axlya and ask her to open an investigation?"

Einar shook his head. "The assassin is most likely a member of the water court—telling Axlya will only alert him or her that we are onto them, which will make it even harder for us to catch them. Better for us to stay on high alert and be watchful for any further attempts. It's a good thing that you're not eating anything, and that I'm impervious to most poisons."

"Yeah, I guess that's one good silver lining about this fasting thing." My stomach growled, and I sighed deeply. "I think I'll skip breakfast this morning, if it's all the same to you."

"I don't blame you." Einar moved to the doorway, dropping a kiss on my forehead on his way out. The touch of his lips against my forehead sparked a different kind of hunger, but he moved out of range before I could act on it. "Try to get some rest, Adara. The other clan heads are arriving this afternoon, and you'll need your wits about you."

29

Leap

The next three days were miserable. Ryker had Leap up working from dawn until dusk, either scrubbing floors and toilets, or waiting on him hand and foot while his cronies fawned over him like he was their precious little prince.

"A little to the left," Ryker drawled, motioning with the wine-glass in his right hand while he pretended to read the ledger he held in his left. They were in the great hall again, Ryker sprawled on the throne while Leap sat on a stool, one of Ryker's feet propped up in his lap. One of the fawning females—Letta, Leap thought her name was—in Ryker's posse sat in the chair on his left, hand-feeding grapes while Leap massaged his cousin's manicured foot.

Leap scowled at Ryker as he adjusted his thumb, pressing rather harder than necessary into his cousin's arch. "Oww!" Ryker snapped, his leg jerking involuntarily. Leap tightened his grip on Ryker's foot to keep his cousin from accidentally kicking his face, then loosened the pressure from his thumb. "You did that on purpose," he whined.

"Or maybe you're just a sensitive little princess who can't handle a little pressure," Leap goaded. He pressed again, this time pushing against the top of Ryker's foot instead, and was rewarded with another whine. "I don't know what you're doing to make your feet hurt so much, anyway. All you do is sit on your lazy arse all day."

Ryker set the ledger aside, his face darkening as he pulled his foot from Leap's grip. "Say that again," he growled, ignoring the fresh grape Letta dangled in front of him.

Leap knew he should keep his mouth shut, but the injustices of the situation pressed in on him from all sides, pushing him to the edge of his patience. "I'll say it again using small words, since you didn't understand the first time," he said, every word dripping with sarcasm. "You. Are. A. Lazy. Stupid. Piece. Of shit. And you don't. deserve. To sit on. That throne."

Ryker exploded from said throne, tackling Leap from his perch on the stool. The two went down in a heap, rolling across the stone floor as they kicked and hit at each other, fighting for dominance. Leap came up on top and smashed a fist into Ryker's face. A fiery trail of pain raced across his knuckles as Ryker's teeth ripped into his skin, but it was worth the bright bloom of blood on the older boy's mouth.

"How dare you!" Ryker blasted him back, and Leap flew ten feet across the room. A feminine scream tore through the hall as he crashed into the wall, a thin tapestry the only cushioning between him and the brutal stone. The tapestry came loose from the wall and collapsed on top of Leap, the bolt it hung on cracking him on the head as he went down in a heap. Stars swam in his eyes as he flailed around in the billowing fabric, desperately trying to untangle himself, but there was no need as a familiar hand fisted in the front of his tunic and dragged him from the wreckage.

"What's the matter, little Leap?" Ryker taunted, his face twisted with cruel delight. His cheeks were flushed, his gaze blurry the way it always got when his cousin drank too much. Leap was dimly aware that a small crowd had gathered in the room to watch this unceremonious beat-down. "You're useless without your lightning magic, aren't you? Can't even throw a decent punch." He gave Leap a bloody grin. "What are you going to do now that your guardian isn't around to protect you?"

Leap stared hard at his cousin, willing the three faces that wavered before him to solidify into one. "You're jealous," he rasped, the realization ricocheting through him like one of his own lightning strikes. "That's why you've been tormenting me all these years, why you tossed my dog out of a three-story window? Because I can wield lightning magic, and you can't?"

Genuine laughter bubbled up inside him, but it cut short when Ryker closed his other hand around Leap's windpipe. "Shut your trap," he growled, the maniacal gleam in his eyes turning into something dark, verging on desperation. "I'm not jealous of your magic. So what if you can put on a little lightning show? You're still a cowardly little twerp who runs away from his problems instead of facing them like a real male would."

"Cowardly?" Leap choked out. He clawed at Ryker's hand on his throat, but his scrapes were as ineffectual as a chisel against a chunk of diamond. "That's rich, coming from the guy who likes to beat up on little kids."

"Ryker." Letta appeared at Ryker's elbow, her pointed face scrunched into a worried expression. "Maybe you should let him go. His lips are turning blue."

"What are you, his mommy?" Ryker spun around and shoved Leap into Letta's arms, surprising them both. Letta stumbled back as she caught him, and another one of Ryker's friends rushed to catch her before the two of them fell. "Take him, then, if you want him so badly. But don't ever show your face in my court again."

"Th-th-that's not what I was suggesting," Letta stammered. She let go of Leap, letting him fall on his ass as she rapidly attempted to distance herself from him. "I just don't want you to get in trouble with your father."

"Yeah, Ryker." The fae who'd caught Letta—a male called Kip—chimed in, shooting an uncertain glance at Leap. "Lord Oren won't be happy if he learns that you've been beating on Leap, after all the trouble he's taken to bring him back here."

"What father doesn't know won't hurt him." Ryker flicked an imaginary speck of dirt off his shoulder, then took a step toward Leap. "Unless one of you plan to tell him, but you wouldn't do that, would you?" he asked, his voice full of sweet venom as he looked each of his cronies in the eye.

Leap tried to scramble to his feet, to put distance between him and Ryker, but his entire body throbbed with pain, and the room spun, forcing him back to the ground. The manacles on his wrist didn't just prevent him from using his magic—they also stunted his healing abilities. He felt like a fish out of water, flopping around on the ground as his cousin loomed over him. Was this the moment Ryker would finally gut him?

The onlookers said nothing as Ryker planted a boot in the center of Leap's chest, pinning him to the floor. Panic burst sharp and bright beneath the pressure of Ryker's foot as he leaned in, pulling a small paring knife from his belt.

"I wonder how many times we can carve 'traitor' into your precious little forehead before we run out of space," he mused, testing the point of the knife with his thumb. A bright bead of blood welled from the tiny wound, and he flicked his tongue against it as he looked at the others. "Which one of you wants to do the honors first while I hold him down? Or are you all cowards?"

Leap's heart pounded so hard he couldn't even hear the voices of the others in the room. He barely registered when the doors to the hall slammed open, or the ringing of heeled boots against the floor. But he was dimly aware of shouts, of powerful arms yanking him off the floor, and the room came back into startling focus as someone slapped his face.

"Leap. Leap!" Gale's hardened face hovered before him, the lightning rider stooped to Leap's eye level. "Can you hear me?"

"Yeah," Leap croaked. He blinked hard, looking around to see Ryker struggling against the grip of two other lightning riders. The sight was so unexpected that he shook his head hard, but the vision before him didn't waver.

"Let me go, you disloyal dogs!" Ryker railed against the riders, his words slurring a little. "I'm in charge—you're supposed to answer to me!"

"You're in charge of the palace," Gale corrected, his voice as frigid as the winter winds that whipped around Angtun's spires. "Not in charge of the Gaoth Aire, and not in charge of the Lightning Guard. That honor still belongs to your father, and until he comes back to tell us otherwise, we will continue to act in his interests, not yours."

Gale jerked his head, and the riders released Ryker. He stumbled away, face bright red with anger and embarrassment. "You won't get away with this," Ryker fumed as Gale led Leap away. "My father will have you all thrown out of the Lightning Guard when I tell him about this!"

The riders ignored Ryker as they steered Leap out of the room. Leap allowed them to guide him out of the main tower, his feet moving mechanically as a haze descended upon him. The throbbing pain in his body seemed to have eclipsed him, drowning out his awareness of everything else. Next thing he knew, he was sitting in a chair in his room, the cold press of a glass bottle against his lips bringing him back to awareness.

"Drink," Gale ordered, and Leap swallowed. Burning liquid slid down his throat, and he sputtered and coughed against the acrid taste. He wanted to recoil, but the lightning rider forced him to drink it all.

"That's it," Gale said encouragingly when Leap had finished. He handed the boy a cup of water, and Leap guzzled it down, desperate to wash the awful taste from his mouth. A cooling sensation flooded his body, and the throbbing receded to half of what it was, allowing him to think past the pain. "There you are."

Leap pulled a face. "What in the Shadows was that stuff?" he asked, wiping the back of his hand against his mouth. "I've never tasted anything so awful in my life."

"It's a healing tonic," Gale said dryly. "You know, for those of us who don't have special healing powers."

Leap blinked. "You mean you have to drink this stuff every time you get injured?"

Gale laughed. "Not me," he said, stepping back to give Leap some space. "But not all lightning riders are Greater Fae, Leap. We all have the ability to wield lightning and ride spirit clouds, but we don't all have the benefits of extra strength, speed, and healing that you do. That's why potions and tonics exist."

"Oh." Leap frowned, trying to wrap his brain around that concept. "I didn't realize that. I thought all the lightning riders were like my parents."

"They are," Gale said. "Your mother was a Greater Fae, but your father wasn't. What he lacked in extra special abilities he made up for with sheer willpower and an unwillingness to give up." His smile faded away as sadness entered his eyes. "He would be very disappointed in me if he learned about what happened to you today."

A thick silence descended between them, heavy with the

weight of words unspoken. Finally, Leap asked, "So what do we do now? We just carry on with the status quo and pretend like the world isn't ending and Angtun hasn't been left in the hands of a spoiled psychopath?"

Gale sighed. "I don't know what I'm going to do. But I suggest you don't leave your rooms for the rest of the day. Ryker will be waiting for any opportunity to finish what he started this afternoon."

He turned to leave the room, one hand casually shoved into his pocket. As he pulled it out to open the door, a metal key fell from his pocket and clattered to the floor. Leap held his breath, waiting for Gale to notice, but the lightning rider appeared oblivious as he let himself out of the room, shutting and locking the door behind him.

Leap snatched the key up from the floor. It took him all of two seconds to get the manacles off, and he nearly shouted with joy as his magic rushed back to life inside him. Lightning sparked at his fingertips, and if he were outside, he would have stretched his hands above his head and released the surge of energy, lighting up the entire sky with his joy and fury.

The need for vengeance crackled in his veins, and it took everything he had not to rush out the door and fry Ryker into a crisp. Only the thought of his friends kept him inside his room, pacing back and forth as he waited for the sun to set and the inhabitants of the palace to fall asleep.

Eventually, the hour grew late, the ambient noises of the palace fading away until only the whisper of the winds remained. Using the same key he'd used to free himself earlier, he jimmied the lock of his door open, then rushed down the spiral staircase and to the bottom of the tower. The guard who kept watch just outside the tower door was conspicuously absent, and Leap darted into the garden maze, keeping both eyes and ears peeled. The crescent moon hanging in the sky offered only a sliver of light, ideal for keeping him concealed, but any guards on duty as well. He crept toward Mavlyn's tower, using the wind to check for any other fae lurking around corners or behind bushes.

But Leap encountered no one, not even a guard outside Mavlyn's tower. Cautious optimism unfurled inside him as he took the stairs up two at a time. He didn't even bother knocking, just used his key to force the lock and flung the door open.

"Mavlyn—" he announced, then stopped short, icy horror spilling through him as the scene before him unfolded.

"Hello, cousin," Ryker said pleasantly. He sat in the vanity chair in Mavlyn's room, legs crossed, a deceptively polite expression on his cruel face. "I had a feeling one of the Lightning Riders would set you loose tonight. Why don't you join us? Your friend has been waiting anxiously for you."

He flicked a glance to Mavlyn, who was hanging against the far wall, her body pressed against the stone and held up solely by wind currents. Leap could tell from the contorted look on Mavlyn's face that she was in extreme pain—that much extended pressure on her bones and joints had to be torturous. She opened her mouth to speak to him, but whatever words she might have spoken were snatched away by the wind and filtered straight to Ryker's ears.

"Ahh, how noble." Ryker smirked. "She's telling you to leave her and run."

Leap raised a balled fist, lightning crackling at his fingertips. "Let her go," he said. The voice that came out of him was not the high pitch of a boy, but the thunderous rumble of a man. "Let her go, or I'll kill you where you stand."

Power the likes Leap had never felt before pulsed through him, throbbing so intensely it was all he could do not to blast the entire room to smithereens. His entire body glowed with electricity, his skin and hair sizzling with it, and Ryker's eyes widened, momentarily shocked by the transformation.

But he recovered himself, smothering his surprise with a well-placed smirk. "You can try to kill me, but we both know that I'll snuff out her life before you can end mine." He picked up an object off the vanity and held it out toward Leap, and the fury in Leap burned even brighter as he realized it was a new set of manacles. "Now be a good boy and come here and put these on. I promise that if you do, no harm will come to your friend."

Leap took one slow step toward Ryker, then another. Mavlyn shook her head frantically the whole time, and Ryker grinned as she shouted soundlessly at him, enjoying every word. "There you go," he said, tossing the manacles to Leap when he was close enough. "You know what to do."

"Yes." Leap said. "I do."

He moved in a blur, clapping the manacles around Ryker's wrists before his cousin could catch on to his fatal error. The moment they closed, the air magic pinning Mavlyn dissipated, allowing her to collapse to the ground.

"Leap!" she cried, pushing herself to her feet, but he didn't look her way. He threw out a hand, firing a bolt of lightning at Ryker that blasted him out of his chair. His cousin's head smacked into the corner of the vanity, and his eyes rolled back into his head as he passed out.

"Ugh." Leap grabbed Ryker by the hair and pulled him upright. He gave his cousin a good shake, but he didn't stir. "You lazy, worthless bastard! How am I supposed to give you a beat-down if you pass out at the first strike?"

"Maaaaayyybe we just settle for torching the hair off his head, and get going," Mavlyn suggested. She rubbed her wrists as she walked over to Leap, shaking her head as she looked between the two boys. "Remind me never to get on your bad side, Leap. You're terrifying when you're angry."

Leap grinned at that, his anger forgotten. "I'm a force of nature," he said, letting go of Ryker's hair. His cousin's head thwacked against the vanity once more before he fell to the floor, and Leap decided that was satisfying enough. "Come on, let's find Cirra and get out of here. We've got an Oracle to rescue."

.

30

Adara

I watched from my balcony as Lochanlee's clan heads trickled into Usciete, each of them accompanied by a small retinue of personal advisors and servants. My stomach clenched as I remembered their scathing assessments of me, which doubtless had not improved after shattering Lady Axlya's ice mirrors. The impulsive action had felt righteous in the moment, but now that they were all here and I had them in person, it felt reckless and foolish.

These fae would decide over the course of the week whether they would back my claim to the throne of Ediria. That I was the clear successor to the throne didn't matter—if they got even the slightest inkling that I would not serve their interests, they would push to nominate one of their sons and daughters instead. And while I didn't care overmuch about ascending the throne, Lady Axlya did, and I needed her as an ally.

Lady Axlya had informed me she was throwing a welcome feast tonight, and she expected me to be there. "This will be your opportunity to correct the unfortunate first impression you made," she told me when I'd tried to beg off. Forcing someone to attend a feast when they were fasting seemed cruel—wouldn't the councilors understand? "These fae have come not just to navigate these tumultuous times with me, but also to meet you. If you hide in your rooms, they will perceive you as weak, and you will never earn their support."

My nerves gathered into a knotted bundle in my stomach as the hours passed, growing larger and larger until I felt like vomiting. Unable to stand it, I left my rooms and stole back into the garden again, hoping to catch a few more moments of peace in the lake. Surely none of the councilors would notice—they were all being settled in their rooms right now, or schmoozing with the other courtiers.

But I barely sank a toe into the water before I was interrupted.

"Adara." The feminine voice that came from behind me was as smooth as the surface of a frozen lake. Turning, my heart sank as I met a pair of wintry eyes set into a sharp, triangular face framed by ice-blue hair. It wasn't a face I'd seen in person before, but I recognized it all the same.

"You're Tamil, aren't you?" It wasn't really a question. She was dressed in winter furs that were a bit too warm for this seaside city, but doubtless served her well in the Bala Oighr, or Ice Wall, where the ice fae of Lochanlee made their homes. "The ice fae clan head."

"Actually, that would be my father, Tor," Tamil corrected. She took a step toward me, her gaze assessing but not unfriendly. "You're taller than I thought you'd be."

I fought the urge to hunch my shoulders. I'd always been tall for a female, and had only recently finished growing into my gangly limbs. "And you're shorter than I thought you'd be," I said.

Tamil raised an eyebrow at that, and I wanted to kick myself.

I was supposed to be making a good impression on these people, but I was failing miserably. "Why are you here instead of your father?" I blurted out, more to cover up my blunder than anything else. "Does he usually send you to represent your clan?"

"These days, yes," Tamil said. Her eyes flickered, revealing a quiet sadness in their depths before it disappeared, like a curtain being whisked over a window. "My father still rules Bala Oighr, but he is many centuries old, nearing the end of his life-span. It is difficult for him to leave his bed most days, nevermind travel across the realm to attend council meetings."

"I'm sorry," I said, withdrawing my foot from the water. I regretted it almost immediately as the sharp edge of my hunger returned, but I did my best to ignore the pangs in my stomach, turning my full attention to the ice fae ambassador. "It must be hard for you."

"Thank you." Tamil eyed my foot as I toed my slipper back on. "I didn't mean to interrupt your swim. I was passing by when I saw you, and thought I'd take a minute to talk to you before the other clan heads get their grubby hands on you." She took a step back. "I'll see you at the feast tonight."

"Wait." I said as she started to turn away. "Stay a minute."

Tamil paused. "Are you sure?"

"Yes." I sat down in the grass by the lake and skimmed my fingers across the surface—a piss-poor compromise, but it would have to do. Touching the water didn't remove the hunger pangs the way it did when I fully submerged myself, but it did take the edge off, allowing me to think more clearly. "You were the only fae at the council meeting who didn't judge or belittle me for my ignorance and lack of noble upbringing."

Tamil rolled her eyes. "The other clan heads are blinded by centuries of tradition," she said as she sat down next to me. The wind shifted, bringing me a whiff of Tamil's scent. She smelled of forest pines and freshly fallen snow, and I couldn't help but find the scent relaxing. "They're too stupid to realize a diamond in the rough when they see one."

I blinked. "I've been called a lot of things in my life, but 'diamond in the rough' isn't one of them."

Tamil chuckled, drawing circles in the water with her hand. Crystals of ice formed across the surface of the lake in the wake of her fingers, spiral patterns that seemed both random and intentional all at once. "You may be untrained and uneducated in the way of politics and court life, but there's no doubt that the royal bloodline flows in you. You defeated King Aolis in single combat, and you haven't even fully come into your powers yet. I'm almost terrified to think of how powerful you'll be once you complete your coming-of-age ritual."

My insides squirmed beneath her praise. "I wouldn't say it was single combat," I said, touching the golden cuff clasped around my bicep. I pulled the sleeve of my gown up to show Tamil the primal stone set into the precious metal, which I hadn't taken off once since the fateful night Einar had clasped it around my arm. "Einar, my dragon protector, gave this to me the night I killed Aolis. I used the decades of fire magic stored inside it to defeat him. I would have never been able to do it on my own."

But Tamil was already shaking her head before I even finished the words. "Most people would have disintegrated beneath the weight of that much power," she argued. "That you were able to channel it only proves my point—you are terrifyingly powerful."

I sighed. "If I'm so powerful, why won't anyone listen to me? Why won't anyone believe me when I say that the shadow creature threat is still here, and that we're all focusing on the wrong thing? I came here hoping that Lady Axlya would help me, and yet—" I cut myself off, remembering that even if we appeared to be alone, there were eyes and ears everywhere here.

"Lady Axlya's help often comes with strings attached," Tamil said, a knowing glint in her eye. "It wouldn't matter if you were a peasant from some no-name town or her first-born son—she never gives something for nothing. It's how she's maintained her iron grip on Lochanlee for close to a thousand years."

My eyes nearly bugged out of my skull. "She's that old?"

"She is," Tamil confirmed. "Lady Axlya has seen countless monarchs rise and fall, and has outlasted them all. To be honest, I don't know how the wily bitch has kept it up for so long. If I had as many consorts and children as she did, I'd probably die just to be rid of all their incessant whining."

A laugh burbled from my lips, and I hastily tried to turn it into a cough. "That's an irreverent attitude," I pointed out. "Do all the water fae feel the same way?"

Tamil shook her head. "The ice fae have always had a complicated relationship with House Usciete," she said. "We have felt strongly for many years that Bala Oighr should be a sovereign realm—we have very little contact with the rest of the water realm, or support from House Usciete, for that matter. Axlya, of course, refused to hear of it, and in fact tried to throw us a bone by marrying one of her nephews to my Great Aunt Mirielle some five hundred years ago. She was killed less than six months into their marriage, supposedly in a riding accident, though the circumstances were questionable. And to make matters worse, her husband refused to return the dowry."

"What?" I stared at Tamil, appalled. "Who was the nephew? Did Lady Axlya try to intervene?"

"No, she didn't." Tamil's mouth twisted into a bitter smile. "The nephew was Lord Tarlis. Prentis's late father. He was a favorite of hers, and she refused to hear anything against him."

I sucked in a sharp breath, feeling as if I'd been sucker

punched. "Prentis..." I shook my head, wondering what other skeletons lurked in my so-called betrothed's closet. This particular sin wasn't his, but who was to say he wasn't cut from the same cloth as his father, that he wouldn't try to have me murdered once I was on the throne he'd believed to be rightfully his?

Tamil sighed. "Lady Axlya to this day refuses to acknowledge the grievance, which has only heightened tensions between the ice and water fae even more." Her eyes grew hazy as she stared off into the middle distance. "The only water fae who ever sympathized with our cause was Olette."

I sat up a little straighter. "Did you know her? My mother?"

"Of course." Tamil smiled, genuine affection briefly driving the shadows from her face. "Olette always had a deep affinity for ice magic, so King Cyrian allowed her to spend the winters at Bala Oighr so she could train with us. She and I were fast friends, and she always told me that once she became queen, she would demand that Lady Axlya grant the ice fae our freedom." Her smile died at that. "Sadly, we both know that never happened."

I took Tamil's hand in mine, curling my fingers around her frigid ones. "I will take on my mother's promise as my own," I vowed to her. "If I become queen, I will grant your people their freedom."

"If?" Tamil raised an eyebrow. "Not 'when'?"

I sighed, my face falling. "Even if I convince the other clans to support me, I have to agree to marry Prentis. Lady Axlya won't back my claim to the throne unless I do."

"Of course she won't," Tamil muttered. Her upper lip curled in disgust as she looked back at the palace, her glare aimed at the absent house ruler. Her grip tightened around mine as she turned back to look at me. "I strongly advise against marrying Lord Prentis."

My insides seized up at the dire warning in her voice. "Why?"

"Because Prentis is far too ambitious to be content to sit by your side as a mere consort," Axlya said. "He will do everything he can to undermine you, and Lady Axlya will be whispering in his ear the whole time, coaching him as he acts as her eyes and ears. You will become a mere figurehead if you allow them to sink their claws into you, Adara."

I swallowed against the sour taste filling my mouth. I'd suspected Prentis would try to wrest power from me if I married him. After all, he'd spent the last two decades believing *he* was the rightful heir to the throne before the world became aware of my existence. But I'd imagined the two of us could work out a compromise, where he took on certain responsibilities from the monarchy while I took others. The sinister picture Tamil painted, one where I became a mere puppet for Lady Axlya, wasn't something I'd truly considered.

"I don't see that I have a choice," I said. "I need Lady Axlya's blessing for the priestess to perform the coming-of-age ritual. Without it, I'll never be able to defeat Slaugh and the shadow creatures."

Tamil withdrew her hand from mine. "Lady Axlya isn't the only one with a priestess up her sleeve," she said cryptically as she stood up. "If you need my help with anything at all, you know where to find me."

She retreated into the palace, her fur cloak whispering against the dying grass as she went. And I stared after her, inwardly grumbling about politicians and their machinations.

31

Einar

The entire water court had shown up at Castle Usciete. Six long tables were laid out in the ballroom for the welcome feast, every single seat taken by a water fae. Representatives from each of the four clans—lake, marsh, ocean, and ice—had traveled far and wide to be here, to confer with their fellow house members on how to deal with the potential power shift in Ediria, and to meet Adara, Ediria's long-lost princess and potential future queen.

I could feel Adara's anxiety through the bond, but to her credit, she hid it very well. Seated between Prentis and Lady Axlya, she was the picture of poise and grace as she schmoozed and made small talk with the other clan heads.

I wished I could hold her hand under the table, or offer her some small level of comfort, but Lady Axlya had insisted on placing me toward the end of the table. "It is imperative that Adara acquit herself as a water fae at tonight's feast," she'd told me when I'd tried to argue against it. "Your presence at her side will only remind the others of her half-dragon heritage."

"Or perhaps you're simply trying to give Prentis more time to win her over, since he can't compete with me," I'd said dryly.

She'd raised an eyebrow, but didn't bother to deny it. "Be grateful I'm allowing you to attend at all," was all she'd said.

So here I was, seated at the opposite end of the table, watching as Prentis made every effort to charm Adara, cracking jokes and telling her grand tales about their water fae ancestors.

The only clan leader who didn't seem to be actively taking part in the conversation was Tamil, the ice fae seated to my left, sandwiched between the two other members of her traveling party. She merely observed the goings-on at the table with a pensive expression, absently swirling a fingertip across the rim of her wineglass as she did. She was the only one here who didn't seem to be entirely comfortable in the lavish surroundings, and I felt a reluctant kinship with her.

Setting my own wineglass down, I leaned over a little so I could talk to her. "Are you going to actually drink that?"

Tamil's mouth kicked up at the corners. "I was wondering when you were going to speak to me," she said.

I raised an eyebrow. "Bold of you to assume I would speak to you at all."

She smirked. "We're the two outcasts at the table, Einar. It's inevitable that we would band together against everyone else."

"Outcast?" I snorted. "I hardly think that your peers would lump the two of us in the same category."

"Perhaps," Tamil agreed, her voice a low murmur, "but I promise, there is no love lost between me and Lady Axlya. In fact, I'm pretty sure that you are the only one in this room she likes less than me."

"Is this one of those 'the enemy of my enemy is my friend' speeches?" I asked skeptically. "Because I can promise you—"

"No," Tamil interrupted. "This is one of those 'the friend of my friend is my friend,' speeches."

"You would call yourself a friend of Adara?" I challenged.

"Her mother was one of my closest friends," Tamil shot back. "And I can see that like Olette, Adara's ice magic runs strong in her. She will always have friends at the Bala Oighr. And therefore, so will you."

Before I could think of a way to respond to that, Lady Axlya stood at the head of the table. "Members and allies of House Usciete," she called, the chatter in the room dying away. "Thank you for coming to Usciete on such short notice to discuss the dire matters facing our kingdom. As you all know, King Aolis has recently passed, which has thrown the matter of succession into doubt. He left no heir, and although Lord Prentis—" she briefly nodded at Prentis— "was the clear successor last time, we have recently discovered that the late Princess Olette left a child behind."

She paused for effect, then said. "I'd like to introduce Adara, daughter of Princess Olette and Prince Daryan, granddaughter of King Cyrian, and the prophesied savior of Ediria."

Adara slowly got to her feet and moved to stand by Lady Axlya, allowing everyone to get a good look at her. She wore a floor-length, sleeveless gown of forget-me-not blue that looked like it had taken an army of seamstresses to sew, a delicate filigree pattern embroidered in white thread across the skirt and bodice. A circlet of sapphires sat atop her crown of braided hair, and the dressmaker had sewn a gossamer cape into the shoulders that flared out behind Adara as she slowly turned around the room, giving her an unmistakably regal look.

"It's an honor to be here," she said once she'd finished meeting the eyes of every noble and courtier gathered in the room.

The silence stretched on for a few moments before someone spoke up. "Forgive me," Lady Ria said, a farce of a polite smile stretched across her sallow skin, "but this *is* the same Adara who murdered King Aolis less than a fortnight ago, correct? Do you really think that we can place a king slayer on the throne, regardless of her reasons behind the slaying?"

Adara flinched at the word *king slayer*—a barely perceptible jerk of the head, but one that a roomful of people trained to spot even the slightest weakness would have seen. "I did not murder King Aolis," she said in a voice of steel. "I defended myself from his attempts to enslave me, or kill me in the attempt, which unfortunately resulted in his death."

"Don't start," Tamil drawled when Lady Ria opened his mouth to chime in. "We all knew King Aolis was rotted to the core with shadow magic. We've been waiting for ages for someone to either off him, or for the shadow magic to kill him. Adara's done us all a favor, and you know it."

The ballroom erupted into a cacophony of arguments, some siding with Adara, others agreeing with Ria. Adara had committed a necessary evil to protect the realm, they all agreed on that. Even so, it was bad optics to put Adara on the throne after she'd killed the king. What kind of example would that set for the others? Wouldn't that encourage the other clans to challenge the monarchs to combat trials so they could steal the throne for themselves?

Adara was doing her best not to let the judgement of her fellow water fae affect her too strongly, but I could see in the tightness around her eyes, and the stiff way she held her shoulders, that their criticisms were hitting hard. Outrage on her behalf welled inside me, and the feeling turned downright murderous when Prentis surreptitiously took her hand and gave it a squeeze. Why wasn't the bastard leaping to defend her, instead of taking advantage of the opportunity to hold her hand like a pair of teenage sweethearts?

Eventually, Lady Axlya called the room to order. "That's enough," she said, her voice somehow melodic and firm at once.

"I did not bring Adara here to be put on trial for the death of King Aolis. Lady Tamil is correct—Aolis was corrupted by shadow magic, and while we will always be grateful to him for eradicating the dragons and bringing peace to Ediria, the fact remains that toward the end of his life, he could no longer serve Ediria the way he needed to. That's why he scoured our realm every year looking for a child of ice and fire—because he was convinced that Adara would be the one to do what he couldn't, to restore the balance to our kingdom."

She smiled fondly at Adara now, the way a proud parent smiled at their child when it was learning to walk for the first time. "I am confident that with Adara as our new queen, she will usher Ediria into a golden age the likes we have never seen before."

Adara smiled back, but I could see the doubts and uncertainties lurking in her eyes. I knew her well enough to understand that she didn't understand how Lady Axlya could brag about her with such confidence, while continuing to undermine her concerns about the shadow magic infection in private.

But it was clear as day that Lady Axlya didn't give two shits about the shadow magic threat, whether it was real or imagined.

All she cared about was that she remained in control of the throne, and whoever the kingdom put on it.

"Now," she said, her voice taking on a cheerful note, "before we tuck into tonight's sumptuous feasts, we have some entertainment. Each of the clans has volunteered one of their sons to demonstrate their magical talents tonight." She paused again, a conspiratorial smile on her face. "Whichever male gives the best account of himself will be granted a favor from the Lady Adara herself... and perhaps, if he is truly lucky, the chance to ask for her hand in marriage."

Shock rippled across Adara's face, her mouth opening as if she were about to protest. She pulled herself back at the last second, but I could see that she wasn't the only one who was unhappy about this. Prentis had gone stone faced next to her, the look in his eyes sharp enough to cleave Lady Axlya in two.

The house matriarch, of course, pretended to be oblivious to her nephew's anger, clapping her hands authoritatively. "Well?" she demanded. "Who is going first?"

32

Mavlyn

The winter winds howled around Leap and Mavlyn as they barreled through the skies of the Gaoth Aire, traveling as fast as they could to get to Windhelm. The two fae huddled together on the cloud for warmth, wrapping their cloaks around them and flattening their bellies to the cloud to avoid as much of the wind chill as they could. Frost clung to Mavlyn's lashes, and she feared she was mere seconds from losing the tip of her nose to frostbite.

Even so, Mavlyn would have traded a thousand nights of flying through frigid temperatures if it meant not being stuck in Angtun. And that wasn't just because every fiber of her being urged her to get to Quye. The city had been beautiful, to be sure, like nothing Mavlyn had ever seen, and under better circumstances, she would have enjoyed exploring it as a tourist.

But being trapped in the palace, at the mercy of Leap's psychopathic cousin, had been more than Mavlyn could bear. Her entire body shuddered at the memory of being pinned to the wall with his air magic, her very words stolen from her as she'd screamed and cried for help, then later begged Leap to run and save himself and Quye.

Never had she felt so helpless, so completely robbed of her bodily autonomy. Ryker had violated her, and had Leap left her at his mercy, she had no doubt he would have taken out his sadistic fantasies on her.

It was not something she would soon forget.

"A-a-are we there y-yet-t-t-t?" she asked Leap through chattering teeth, more to take her mind off the harrowing experience.

"I'm not sure," Leap said, his own jaw clenched against the cold. He squinted his eyes, trying to see through the foggy skies. "Cirra says we're approaching, but I can't see a damn thing up here."

"Have you considered using your wind magic to clear the way?"

There was a long pause. "No." He sighed, shaking his head as if he couldn't believe he was being such an idiot. "Gimme a second."

Mavlyn hid a smile as Leap sat up and lifted his hand, summoning a strong wind current. She couldn't blame him for being out of sorts after their ordeal with Ryker—for the most part, the two of them were grateful to have gotten away. But it had been hours since they'd left, and it was clear neither Ryker nor his guards were pursuing.

It was time to put the horror behind them, and focus on the reason they'd returned to the air realm.

Quye.

The wind howled in response to Leap's summons, whipping around them to form a mini cyclone that whirled through the skies, collecting wisps of cloud as it went. The early morning air cleared in its wake, gradually revealing the rocky silhouette of a fortress carved into a mountainside.

Mavlyn's heart beat faster at the sight of it. "It doesn't look very big," she said to Leap. "How many guards do you think we'll have to deal with?"

"Not many, maybe half a dozen," Leap said. "The number of guards isn't the problem—the real issue is the way it's positioned." He pointed to the edge of the terrace that the fortress rested on. "The fortress is inaccessible by land—flying is the one way to get in. Most of the fortress is inside the mountain, which has been hollowed out, but the outer portion, where the only entrance is, is so small that it's impossible to approach without being noticed."

An idea sparked in Mavlyn's mind, and she sat up so she could peer at the mountain fortress properly. "Is there any vegetation on the mountain?" she asked. "And how are the rooms inside ventilated, since I assume there are no windows inside?"

"I'm not sure," Leap admitted. "I was four years old when my parents brought me here, so I don't remember much. I know that there are some scraggly bushes and trees." He scrunched up his face, as though trying to dredge up memories from the recesses of his mind. "If I had to guess, I'd say there are probably air vents hidden amongst the rocks and stones on the mountain's surface that allow air to pass through to the rooms below."

"Perfect." Mavlyn brightened up. "That's our way in, then."

Leap directed Cirra to take them around the backside of the mountain, away from the prying eyes of the fortress battlements. The face of the mountain was terrifyingly sheer, normally only accessible by the most nimble of mountain goats. But while the winter winds had stripped the plants and bushes of their leaves, their branches remained. Mavlyn was able to use them as handholds, her magic strengthening the roots so they could support her weight. She hauled herself up the mountainside, allowing her earth magic senses to sink through the roots and into the ground so she could probe the terrain while Leap waited on Cirra, ready to catch her if she fell.

"Here," she said, pointing to a slim opening beneath a rocky outcropping. "There's a hollow spot under this chunk of rock. I think the vent is under there."

Leap flitted closer with Cirra, sticking his head out to peer beneath the rock. "Yeah, there is," he said. "But there's a grate fitted over it." He reached in and tugged on the bars, then shook his head. "It's too sturdy for me to move."

"Give me a minute," Mavlyn called to him. She made her way to the vent, skirting a few crumbling sections of the mountainside. Twice she almost slipped and fell, but she saved herself by leaping and grabbing onto another plant. She thanked each one profusely as it strained beneath her weight, giving it a tiny boost of magic in gratitude as she let go to grab the next one, until she was close enough to the grate.

Closing her eyes, she pushed her magic into the dead roots buried deep in the earth around the grate, willing them to respond. Slowly, they came back to life, unfurling their thick tendrils as they pushed up through the earth to taste fresh air for the first time in decades. They greedily latched onto the grate, and with several hard tugs, the piece of metal came free with a rusty groan.

"That's handy," Leap said as the roots tossed the grate off the mountainside. "But while I think I can shimmy in there, I don't see how you're going to fit under this rock."

"I didn't say I was done." Mavlyn smirked. She directed the roots once more, and they swiftly began to dig, widening the gap beneath the rock until it was big enough for Mavlyn to squeeze through. She thanked them with an extra shot of magic, then crawled under the opening so she could peer into the hole.

She couldn't see anything, but her senses told her it was a straight shot down.

"Uhhh... do you wanna go first?" she called back to Leap.

He snorted. "If you wanted me to go ahead of you, you should have let me crawl inside first."

Mavlyn rolled her eyes, then hauled herself over the opening so she could position herself feet first. Holding her breath, she lowered herself into the tunnel, bracing her hands against the earthen walls so she wouldn't free fall through the shaft.

She made it maybe ten feet down before she felt a brush of wind at her back. "You can let go," Leap advised her. "The wind will catch you."

Mavlyn glanced up to see Leap hovering above her. She scowled at the smug expression on his face, but she wasn't about to look a gift horse in the mouth, so she let go. A cushion of wind caught her, and she floated the rest of the way down the shaft, landing in a storeroom that appeared to be filled with old, discarded weapons.

"Well, isn't this handy," Leap said as he followed in after her. He picked up an old scimitar and held it up to the dim candlelight cast by the room's single wall sconce, eyeing the blade's rusty edge. "Could definitely give someone blood poisoning with this."

Mavlyn hefted a boomerang the size of her entire body. "This looks pretty nifty," she said. "If I was an air fae, I would totally use this."

Leap's eyes softened as he eyed the weapon. "My mother had one of those," he said softly. "I used to watch her throw it all the time when she and my father were at practice."

Mavlyn ruffled his hair in sympathy, then put the boomerang back in its place against the wall and pressed her ear against the door. Hearing no movement, she crept into a narrow, dark hall. She and Leap spent the next thirty minutes exploring the area, quickly realizing they were on one of the lower levels, where most of the fortress's storage rooms were. There were quite a few treasures and curiosities down here, but aside from a quick stop in the dried goods storage room to grab some jerky for the road, they kept moving until they found the staircase that led them to the upper level.

Mavlyn could tell there was more activity here—she could feel the earth vibrating with the footsteps of the fortress inhabitants. Even so, between her earth senses and Leap's ability to listen to the air currents, they were able to avoid the few people on this level. Most of the castle's resources seemed to be spent guarding the exposed section of the fortress and its gates. She doubted anyone expected an enemy to sneak in through the hidden air vents.

Something—Mavlyn wasn't sure if it was instinct or a hidden voice in her subconscious—tugged her persistently to the right. She followed that intuition through the maze of hallways until she reached a door guarded by a single soldier. The male's eyes widened in surprise, but Leap used his wind magic to cut off his cry for help, then struck with a targeted blow to the back of his neck. The man collapsed, and Mavlyn caught him before he hit the floor.

"Ruthless," she said, shaking her head as she dragged the unconscious guard away from the door.

Leap shrugged, fishing a sharp implement from his pocket. He jimmied the door open, and Mavlyn scrambled forward, leaving the guard in the hallway so she could hurry inside after Leap.

Her eyes went straight to the white couch in the center of the room, expecting to find Quye waiting for them there. But the couch was empty, and as Mavlyn spun around, taking in the bed, the tub, the chairs and rugs and couches, her heart sank.

"This has to be her room," Mavlyn said, trying not to let her voice quaver. "It's the same one I saw in my dream."

"Oh it is," Leap said dryly. "Look up."

Mavlyn glanced up at the ceiling just in time to see a white shape plummeting toward her. She shrieked as Quye pounced on her, enveloping her in a cloud of ivory fabric and incense.

"Got you!" the oracle shouted with unrestrained glee as she squeezed the life out of Mavlyn. Mavlyn was tempted to croak out something about not wanting her ribs broken, but her face was buried in the halo of Quye's riotous curls.

And if she was being truthful, she didn't want the oracle to let her go just yet.

Instead, she squeezed Quye back and closed her eyes, breathing in her incense and mountain pine scent and letting the momentary fear that had gripped her so tightly drain away.

"I'm so glad we found you," Mavlyn whispered, and Quye softened, her squeeze turning into an affectionate hug, her body melting against Mavlyn's own willowy curves.

"I had every confidence you would," she whispered back.

"You should probably let go of Mavlyn before you crack her in two," Leap said, sounding less than impressed by Quye's antics. He seemed unaware of what had passed between the two females as they reluctantly broke apart, which Mavlyn was grateful for. "We went through a lot of trouble for you to prank us like that."

Quye rolled her eyes. "Since when have you become such a party pooper?" she pouted, crossing her arms. Mavlyn frowned at the flowing silk robes Quye wore—they were hardly appropriate for a jailbreak.

Something dark flashed across Leap's face, and Mavlyn knew he was remembering their confrontation with Ryker in her tower room. She suppressed a shudder at the reminder of how, only a few hours ago, she'd been a few breaths away from losing her life.

"Let's just say the last few days have been difficult," he said.

"And the less time I need to spend in enemy territory, the better."

Quye's expression softened, her mouth bowing sympathetically. "I'm sorry," she said, pulling Leap into a hug. "I know coming back to Angtun and having to face Ryker was horrible for you, and that you did it for me, so thank you, and let's get out of here."

She didn't have to tell them twice.

Quye stripped off her robe, revealing the far more practical brown tunic, leggings, and boots she'd donned in preparation for their escape. She also fished out a small pack of supplies from beneath the couch, then swung it over her shoulder and crept out of her rooms with them. Mavlyn wondered how Quye had gotten hold of such items while being imprisoned, but she had a feeling she already knew the answer. The oracle was as charming as Leap was resourceful, and she'd probably sweet-talked her guards into sneaking her the items she needed under some pretext or other.

"Wow," Quye said when they'd climbed out of the ventilation shaft and out from underneath the rocky outcropping. She crossed her arms as the winter winds whipped around her, catching at the ribbons of her hair so they rippled out from behind her head like a banner. "You guys crawled through this claustrophobic tunnel so you could bypass the guards, even though you had no clue what was down here? I'm not sure if I should be impressed or horrified."

"I was a bit of both," Leap admitted as he climbed out after her. "Mavlyn was the one who came up with the idea."

"Was she?" Quye's eyes gleamed as she gave Mavlyn a once over. "Well, I shouldn't be surprised you're the real brains of this operation. It's like I said before—smart *and* beautiful."

Mavlyn blushed from head to toe. "I wouldn't have been able to do it without Leap," she demurred, looking at the air fae boy so she wouldn't have to meet Quye's eyes. She had a feeling that if she stared into them for too long, she'd melt straight into a puddle and slide off the mountainside. "His wind magic allowed us both to descend safely."

"Maybe," Quye said knowingly. "But as far as I'm concerned, you're the hero of this tale."

She winked, and Mavlyn gave her a helpless grin. "You're incorrigible," she said, laughing.

"Yes. But that's what you love about me."

Mavlyn knew Quye meant that casually, but her heart still skipped a beat. She was saved by having to respond when Cirra pulled up, and the three of them hopped on, grateful to get off the mountain. The cloud familiar expanded to make room for the three of them, but even so, Quye's knee brushed against Mavlyn's as they settled in. Mavlyn tried to ignore the warm, fuzzy feeling that spread through her at the contact, but it was hard, especially when Quye shifted, leaning her body more fully against her.

She didn't know why being in the oracle's presence made her heart beat faster, her head feel lighter, her body tingle with warmth and... other things. The two of them hardly knew each other—they'd only met once before, and had only exchanged a few words.

But Mavlyn couldn't deny she'd never felt like this about anyone before. She wanted to spend more time with Quye, and find out what lay behind those laughing eyes and mischievous smiles.

"All right," Leap said when they were well away from the mountain. "Where are we off to now? Back to Usciete, to help Adara?"

"Nope." Quye looked off into the distance, her sparkling gaze gone hazy as she beheld something neither of the others could see. "We've got an important stop to make first."

33

Adara

I rose with the dawn the morning after the feast, my mind sharp and clear, my hunger pangs all but gone. Sitting through the feast and watching everyone eat plate after plate of mouth-watering food had been torturous, though not as insufferable as watching the clan sons perform their various feats of water magic for me.

They'd all been vying for my hand, and had been roundly disappointed when instead of choosing one to be my husband, I'd crafted an ice laurel and crowned Lady Ria's son as the winner, then left the feast. But what could I say? His display of water swans sailing through the air had been impressive, but not impressive enough to marry him.

Padding to the window on bare feet, I opened the glass pane to let in some fresh air. The crisp morning air invigorated me, and as I stood there, scrunching my toes into the carpet, I realized I felt more clear-headed than I had in ages. The doubts and anxieties that had been plaguing me ever since I'd killed Aolis and taken on the burden of eradicating the shadow creatures had disappeared, leaving me with a sense of calmness and certainty.

It didn't matter whether I agreed to marry Prentis, or whether I loved Einar, or whether the others believed me about Nox and the persisting shadow creature threat.

The only thing that mattered was carrying out the mission the Radiants had given me. All these other problems and worries were distractions that Nox and Slaugh were counting on slowing me down so they could complete their plan to take over the realm.

If they succeeded, it wouldn't matter whether I'd promised to marry Prentis, or mated myself to Einar. Because the world as we knew it would end.

I turned and glanced at the dream lily, still floating in its bowl by my bedside. Its moonlit luster was only a third of what it had been when Einar gifted it to me, and I knew I only had maybe one more good night of use out of it. Smiling, I traced a finger down one of its soft petals, marveling at the thoughtfulness of the gift. I knew this flower and the sweet dreams it gave were a large part of the reason I felt so content and at peace with myself this morning.

A soft knock at the door jarred me from my thoughts. "Adara?" Prentis called, his voice pitched low so as not to disturb the other residents of this wing. "Can I come in?"

I shrugged my dressing gown over my pajamas, then crossed the room to let Prentis in. "You look like you're dressed for another undersea adventure," I noted, taking in the armored wetsuit covering Prentis's lithe form. My eyebrows rose as I caught sight of the second suit slung over his arm. "Are we going somewhere?"

"Yes." Prentis held out the garment to me, grinning. "We're going to the royal water park."

"Water park?" I echoed. "What's that?"

"A pet project of my mother's that's turned into something of an attraction for the city," Prentis said. "I can't explain more than that without ruining the surprise."

I glanced out the window at the sun that had barely crested the horizon. "It seems a bit early for an excursion," I told him. "I'm surprised you're not in bed like the rest of the palace, sleeping off last night's hangover."

Prentis chuckled. "I didn't drink as much as everyone else did... and besides, this is part of my master plan, to get some alone time with you before the rest of the court wakes up." He winked at me.

I hesitated, glancing at the door. "I should check with Einar, see if he wants to come with us. He'd be furious if he found out that I left without telling him." In fact, I was surprised he hadn't come barging in here already, considering that he was right across the hall.

"I see." Prentis's mouth flattened. "I didn't realize Einar was your keeper."

"He's not," I said, trying and failing to keep the defensive tone from my voice. "But he is my protector, and I know that if I were in his shoes, I'd be upset if I left without at least telling him. And if I tell him, I know he'll want to come with us."

"I'll tell you what." Prentis strode over to the small writing desk in my room, plucked a quill from its holder, then held it out to me. "Why don't you write him a note and slide it under his door? That way you can tell him where you are without disturbing his sleep."

"Prentis..."

He sighed, setting the quill back down. "Listen, Adara," he said, taking my hand. His touch didn't spark an electrical jolt in me the way Einar's did, but I couldn't deny the pleasant warmth that spread within me. "I realize you have misgivings about marrying me. If I'm honest, I'm not entirely sure about marrying you either. But I do know Lady Axlya is correct that a civil union between us is the best way to garner support from the realm for your claim to the throne.

"Is that why Lady Axlya offered my hand to the other clan leaders' sons last night?" I asked, a little more tartly than intended. "Because she supports this match so strongly?"

Prentis scowled. "She didn't mean that," he said, though I wasn't sure I believed him. "She hasn't been happy with my progress in courting you, and she wanted to remind me you have other options."

"I see." I pressed my mouth together to hold back the barbed words biting into my tongue. It was one thing to know that Lady Axlya viewed me as a pawn, another thing to see her dangle me amongst the courtiers of her house as a bargaining chip.

Prentis sighed at my expression. "You don't have to marry me if you don't want to, Adara. But before you reject me, don't you think we spend time with each other *without* our friends and family looking over our shoulders and eavesdropping on every word, so we can see if there's any compatibility between us at all?"

Genuine sincerity burned in his eyes as he looked at me, and I reminded myself that not long before he came in, I'd already told myself that I would do whatever it took to complete my mission. The most important thing was completing the ritual, and that meant going along with Lady Axlya's wishes, at least for now. If Prentis thought he had no chance of convincing me to marry him, he would tell her that, and she would call off the ceremony.

I couldn't allow that to happen.

"Of course." I squeezed his hand, giving him what I hoped was a sincere smile. "You're right. We should spend more time together, see if there could be something between us. Why don't you give me a minute to change, and I'll meet you downstairs in ten minutes?"

"Your wish is my command." He sketched a courtly bow, then gave me some privacy.

I changed into the wetsuit, taking a minute to unclasp Einar's cuff from my bicep so it wouldn't get caught on the material. I held the heavy gold piece up so it caught the rays of light streaming through the window, studying the ruby colored primal stone set in the center. The stone had been dull and lifeless after I'd drained its magic to kill Aolis, but it glittered with vitality now, sparks of magic swirling in its depths. I knew it no longer held even a tenth of the power it had gathered while Einar had been asleep, but it was good to see it had some reserves once more.

Once I pulled the sleeves of my suit on, I re-clasped the cuff over my bicep. It occurred to me that the cuff had replaced the magic-suppressing amulet Mother had forced me to wear all my life, though its purpose was the opposite. The first had been given to hide and protect me, the other had been given to empower and amplify my magic so I could protect myself.

But both had one thing in common—I never took them off. Not even to sleep.

Finished dressing, I crept into the hallway, my note for Einar clutched in my hand. I hovered outside his door for a moment, wondering if I should wake him up and tell him to accompany us. I could tell Prentis that the sound of me sliding the note under the door had alerted him, and Einar would be more than happy to insist that coming along was his idea.

But that was the coward's way out. Hiding behind others had never been my style, and I wasn't about to start now. Besides, the fact that Einar hadn't woken of his own accord meant he was deeply asleep. The poor guy had to be exhausted after the events of the last few days, especially since I'd woken him up early yesterday.

No, it was better to let him sleep. I could handle Prentis on my own. He was trying to marry me, after all, not kill me. And I could do with a break from their constant male posturing every time they were around each other.

I slipped the note under Einar's door, then went downstairs and met Prentis outside. Two kelpies—horse-like creatures who could assume different forms on land and water—were saddled and waiting for us, the morning light casting a golden tint on their shimmering ivory coats. The sight of them evoked a memory I'd nearly forgotten about, of me galloping away from the tryout fields on the back of Butterfly, Mavlyn's horse, leaving a trail of fiery destruction in my wake. I'd fled straight to my mother, hoping she would save me, hoping she would make sense of the maelstrom of confusion that had become my life.

Instead, I'd brought shadows to her door. And those shadows had been following me ever since.

"Are you ready to go?" Prentis asked, gazing curiously at me. His hand was outstretched, and I realized that I'd probably been staring off into space for several seconds.

"Yes, sorry." Shaking the memory free, I took his hand and allowed him to help me onto one of the kelpies. "I was just wondering why we didn't ride these to the temple, instead of the sea horses. Not that I'm complaining," I added as Prentis swung himself up onto his own mount. "That was an amazing experience."

Prentis chuckled. "It's a valid question from someone who's not intimately acquainted with the creatures of our realm," he said, urging his kelpie forward into a trot. My mount dutifully followed. "While kelpies and seahorses are both underwater creatures, their habitats are different. Kelpies are freshwater creatures, while seahorses prefer saltwater. A seahorse would not do very well in a lake, and while a kelpie can swim in the ocean for short periods of time, they can't travel as many fathoms deep as is required to reach the water temple."

"That makes sense." I stroked the side of my kelpie's neck, noting that its hide smelled distinctly of lake water. "I'm guessing that as leader of the lake fae, you prefer to ride kelpies?"

Prentis sighed. "Actually, though I do lead the lake fae, I have more of an affinity for the ocean," he said as we passed through the palace gates and into the city. The cobbled streets gave way to canals, and the kelpies smoothly transitioned into their water forms, their manes turning to fins and their hindquarters elongating into a mermaid-like tail as they sank until we were thigh-deep in the water. "My animal form is an orca, in case you didn't notice. Not exactly a lake dwelling creature."

He gave me a wry smile that didn't quite mask his frustration. "If you're an ocean fae, then why did Lady Axlya assign you a lake fae fiefdom?" I asked, frowning.

"Because that was the only one left, and as a Greater Fae who has decent control over all four of the water element aspects, I *am* qualified for the position." Prentis said. He tugged on his mount's reins, and we took a left turn, gliding beneath a bridge as we merged with a canal heading in a southwesterly direction. "I think she also felt a little bad that I was passed over in the line of succession for the Edirian throne in favor of Aolis," he added with a shrug. "But mostly, she put me there because that's where she needed me."

"I see," I said softly. Silence descended upon us, and I couldn't help feeling a little sorry for Prentis. It was clear he took his duty to the realm seriously, but had been given very little reward for it. Obviously, marrying me was a chance for him to finally break free of the stagnant, ill-fitting box his life had become. And while that wasn't an inspired reason to tie the knot with someone, I couldn't fault him for it.

We followed the canal for another mile or so before coming to a ramp that led out of the water and up to an archway that was made entirely out of water.

"*This* is a water park?" I asked, unable to hide my amazement.

"It is." Prentis's lips curved into a smug smile, obviously pleased with my awed reaction. The park was as impressive as it was playful, and it was immediately clear to me how this place had evolved from his mother's pet project to a city attraction. Iridescent mother-of-pearl tiles formed a curved shape on the ground that reminded me of a lagoon oasis, marking the outline of the water park. On the tiles themselves were several white stone statues in the shape of dolphins, whales, and massive turtles placed strategically around the park, each with a fountain shooting arcs of water into the air in time with one another. As the sunlight passed through the fountains, rainbows appeared in the sky like a glorious ribbon. Along one side of the park was a curved sea glass-like structure that rose as tall as the tallest statue and grew progressively shorter as it moved around the border of the park itself. As I looked harder at the structure, I noticed there was a steady stream of water flowing across the top and pouring out the bottom like a miniature mountain stream.

But all of that combined couldn't compare to the park's centerpiece. A beautiful mermaid statue was erected in the middle of the other statues, her tail acting as her base, with her arms and hair flowing upward as if she were moving gracefully through the water. She was encased in an orb of water that spun around her, the sunlight fracturing through the water to shimmer across her pensive stone face.

"Wow." I turned slowly as I took it all in, unable to disguise my childlike wonder. "I have to admit, this isn't at all what I expected."

"I hope you mean that in a good way," Prentis said as he deftly dismounted. He took my hand as I swung my leg over the side of my own mount, helping me to the ground.

"Definitely a good way," I mused as I took a step onto the tile. "This place is incredible."

"I'm glad you like it," Prentis said. He stepped up beside me and gingerly placed a hand on the center of my back. My muscles bunched against the intimate touch, but I forced myself to endure it rather than flinch away. "Though I hope you won't change your mind after this," he said, stepping away.

"After what?" I asked, turning to face him, then yelped as he shot a stream of water at me.

"Oh, you did *not* just spray me!" I shrieked as he darted away, laughing diabolically. Laughter bubbled up inside me despite myself as he shot another stream of water over his shoulder, but this time I ducked behind a turtle statue.

"Oh, I most definitely did," he called back, his voice full of mirth. "What are you going to do about it? Cowering isn't going to save you."

"Who said anything about cowering?"

I lunged from my hiding spot and threw an arm in the air, aiming for the dolphin next to him. Instantly, the water spouting from its mouth turned to hail, and he threw up his arms as the tiny ice pellets struck him.

Swearing and laughing at the same time, Prentis ducked and spun behind the turtle statue as the ice mixture flew right over his head. Undeterred, I scooped up puddles of water from the ground, using my ice magic to transform them into snowballs.

A movement caught the corner of my eye, and I turned, expecting Prentis to leap out from behind a statue and blast me with a spray of water.

But what I found instead was quite different.

A hulking monster rose from behind one of the mermaid statues, easily twice its height and four times as wide. Shadow magic swirled around its form, but I caught glimpses of something that looked like cracked earth beneath the shifting black smoke.

"W-what are you?" I stammered, taking a step back. The snowballs in my hands melted away, fire springing to my palms instead. Malevolent red eyes glared at me out of the darkness, and it followed me, black veins of corruptions spreading through the ground, cracking the stone floors and the statues as it walked.

"Adara?" Prentis called, rounding a corner. He skidded to a halt at the sight of the shadow monster, the mischievous light in his eyes replaced by a look of abject horror. "What in the name of the Radiants is *that?*"

"That" grabbed the nearest statue and wrenched it from its plinth like it was snapping a branch off a tree. I dove out of the way as it hurtled the marble mermaid in my direction, and a stray piece of shrapnel sliced my cheek as the statue shattered against the ground.

Swearing, I swiped at the trail of blood on my cheek as I leaped to my feet, blasting the creature with twin bouts of flame. Relief swept through me as the fire ate away at the cloud of shadow magic, revealing the hulking form of the monster beneath it. It looked like a troll that had been molded from clay, then baked in a kiln at too high a temperature, creating cracks all over its body.

"I think it's a golem!" I shouted.

"A golem?" Prentis shouted back, his voice rife with disbelief. "But that's an earth realm creature!"

He raised his hands and shot a powerful stream of water at the monster, no doubt intending to reduce it to a pile of mud.

But before the liquid could make contact, clouds of magic spewed from the golem's cracks, forming an inky shield around it. The water evaporated, and Prentis and I were forced to duck and run once again as the monster hurled more statues at us, grabbing one with each hand this time.

"This thing is ruining my mother's water park!" Prentis shouted as we ran. "We have to stop it!"

"You think I don't know that?" I dropped into a forward roll to dodge another flying statue, but I didn't watch where I was going and I nearly crashed into a statue that was still planted on the ground. "This thing is relentless! What are we supposed to do?"

"Try your fire magic on it again, and I'll follow it up with another water blast!"

I whirled around to face the golem and held out my hands, blasting it with another torrent of fire. Like before, my fire ate up the clouds of shadow magic, revealing the true form of the monster beneath. I glimpsed the glowing heart of black magic at the center of its chest—the true source of its power—a split second before Prentis called on a tidal wave of magic, assaulting the golem with blasts of water from the surrounding statues as well as his own hands.

For a moment, it seemed like the plan was going to work. The earth began to slough off the golem in waves of mud, and its steps slowed. But the black magic beating in the center of its chest flared, and shadow magic poured out, reforming the shield. Within seconds, the mud raced back up, solidifying around the golem once more.

"Fuck," Prentis said, echoing my sentiments perfectly.

The golem lumbered toward us, its form growing larger and more menacing with each step. Prentis and I closed ranks, summoning more magic, but my body was trembling with exertion. I hadn't eaten in days, and my reserves were severely

depleted. There wasn't much magic in the primal stone either—
it had only been a few days since I'd used it.

I was about to rally myself for one last attempt when a
massive winged shadow fell over us, blotting out the sunlight.
Every nerve in my body came alive, and I looked up even though
I already knew who had come to rescue us.

Einar. In all his dragon glory.

His fiery eyes flashed at us as he let out a sky-shattering roar
that was somehow both a battle cry and an admonishment. His
ruby scales flashed in the morning light, and my gaze snagged
on the enormous stone slab clutched in his massive claws. It
looked suspiciously like a rooftop that had been ripped off some
poor, unsuspecting building.

The golem looked up too, just in time for Einar to drop
several tons of stone on top of its body.

The golem collapsed beneath the weight of the slab, but
Einar wasn't done. He landed on the slab with all his weight,
smashing the monster flat like a pancake, then launching
himself skyward before the tendrils of shadow magic could
touch him. Prentis and I held our breath as the inky clouds
slowly began to dissipate, then evaporate into the air.

Einar circled the area a few more times, checking for other
threats. Seemingly satisfied, he made to land, but I held up a
hand. "Take the slab off him first," I said in response to his irri-
tated glare.

Einar did as I asked, removing the biggest chunks—the slab
had shattered beneath his weight—to the side so I could get a
good look at the golem. The monster had been crushed into a
million pieces between the two blows, but even so, I could still
see bits of earth trying to inch back together, encouraged by
tendrils of shadow. Gritting my teeth, I reached into the rubble
and pulled out the black primal stone that had acted as the
golem's life force, animating it and driving it to murder us. The

stone pulsed in my hand, sending shivers of revulsion through me as the evil magic tried to penetrate me.

Closing my eyes, I summoned my remaining fire magic and channeled it into the stone, gripping it as tight as I could. The corrupted primal stone crumbled beneath my fist and rained to the ground in ashes.

"There," I said as Prentis and Einar—back in his bipedal form—approached. "Now it won't be able to attack us again.

"Good," Einar said. He crossed his arms over his chest—his very *bare* chest—I realized, and raked the two of us with a look that could only be described as quietly murderous. "Now, which one of you is going to explain to me what the *fuck* happened here?"

34

Einar

And you're certain it was a shadow creature you fought?"

I fought the urge to roll my eyes at Lady Axlya's pointed question, which was neither directed at Adara, who had been shouting about the shadow creature threat from the rooftops since we arrived, or at me, who had actually defeated the damn thing. No, she was asking Prentis, as if his opinion on the incident was the only one that mattered.

"Absolutely," Prentis confirmed. He didn't seem to notice Adara's clenched jaw, or the barely concealed annoyance on her face as he answered the question. "It was a golem, but the black smoke cloaking it was unequivocally shadow magic. I could feel its noxious presence in the air, and the rotted lines it left in the marble..." He shuddered a little at the memory. "Well, let's just say I'm happy Adara used her magic to destroy the primal stone powering it. If not for her, I'm not sure we would have survived."

"I think the dragon deserves some credit too," Cascada said, surprising all of us. We were gathered in the Hall of Mirrors, with the clan heads and Lady Axlya's immediate family present, including Cascada and the consorts. "He did rip the roof of that building and use it to crush the beast, did he not?"

"I definitely wouldn't have been able to kill the beast if he hadn't smashed it to bits first," Adara said. She shot an apologetic glance at me, trying to catch my gaze, but I refused to look at her. I still hadn't forgiven her for the way she'd snuck off with Prentis without even *trying* to wake me up and tell me about it first. Instead, my gaze bored into Prentis, who in turn had been doing his best to avoid catching *my* eye.

I was certain he was the reason I'd slept through his and Adara's departure, and there would be a reckoning between us for sabotaging my duty and putting Adara in danger.

"Yes, yes," Lady Axlya said with an impatient wave of her hand. "Einar is to be commended for doing his duty and protecting his charge." The hint of sarcasm in her voice left no doubt that her comment was meant as a jab, but I kept my expression blank, refusing to rise to the bait. "But who sent this shadow golem, and how did it get into the city?"

"Aren't golems earth magic?" Kalis pointed out, a pensive expression on his face.

"They are," Tamil said. "And General Slaugh was a member of the shadow guard, who we all know were gifted shadow magic by King Aolis. He has every reason to want Adara dead, and the means to make it happen."

"But General Slaugh and the others don't have their shadow magic anymore," Cascada protested. Adara pursed her lips at that, but if Cascada was lying, she was a very good actress. The confusion on her face seemed genuine. "It disappeared when Adara killed the king!"

"My dear," Ilsa cut in, sounding both exasperated and sympathetic at once, "if that was the case, then where did that shadow golem get its powers from?"

Cascada's cheeks colored, and something dark flickered in

her eyes. An uncomfortable silence filled the room as the rest of the council members peered speculatively at Cascada, before Adara reluctantly broke it.

"Perhaps General Slaugh used shadow magic to muddle Cascada's memories of that night," Adara offered, trying to be charitable. "That could explain why her version of events is so different from mine and Einar's."

"Even if that were the case, that still doesn't explain why the shadow creatures have vanished from the rest of the continent," Lady Ria interjected. "I'm inclined to think Cascada's version of events is correct, and that this was just a fluke. Perhaps King Aolis kept some primal stones filled with magic, and Slaugh or one of his cohort saw fit to use them."

The rest of the councilors muttered at this, clearly torn on the issue. Prentis, Tamil, and the consorts seemed inclined to believe Adara, while the other two clan leaders and Lady Axlya seemed to favor Cascada. I suspected Lady Axlya's willingness to lean into her daughter's narrative had more to do with supporting the version of events that would allow her to maintain control over Adara and the throne than it did with what she actually believed.

After all, Axlya and the other house rulers had been navigating the shadow creature threat for the last two decades. Perhaps she'd grown so complacent about the threat that she no longer took it seriously.

Lady Axlya and the other courtiers bickered about the golem and its implications for a few minutes longer, before agreeing that yes, an investigation needed to be launched, and that Adara could no longer go anywhere without a guard to accompany her, at least not until after her coming-of-age ceremony.

"All right, this meeting is adjourned," Lady Axlya said. She turned to Adara as the others filed out of the room. "Come with me, child. The tailor will arrive any moment now to fit you for your ceremonial garb."

Adara froze mid-step, her body angled in my direction as if she'd intended to approach me. I tensed as our gazes met across the room—a clash of blue and gold, sizzling with enough pent-up emotion to charge a thunderstorm. For a split second, her courtly mask dropped, revealing a rawness in her expression that made me want to forget my anger at her.

But then she turned away, inclining her head to Lady Axlya. "Of course. Please, lead the way."

"Einar." Tamil's dulcet tones tugged me to a stop in the middle of the gardens. "Can I speak with you for a minute?"

I turned to see Tamil picking her way through a row of rose bushes, stripped bare of leaves in preparation for the coming winter. Her ice-blue eyes were guarded as she approached, but I couldn't blame her considering the history between our people. That she was willing to approach me alone, and she didn't regard me with veiled hostility and disdain like the other water fae, put her head and shoulders above her peers in my book.

"Of course," I said, abandoning my plan to return to my rooms. I leaned casually against a marble statue of a water nymph, and the cold marble reminded me of the battle with the golem. I'd seen the monster ripping statues out of the ground like blades of grass and hurtling them at Adara and Prentis from a distance as I'd flown toward them, pumping my wings as hard and fast as I'd ever done in my life.

I'd woken up sensing Adara's pain and fear, and I thanked the Radiants that the bond had led me straight to her. Under ordinary circumstances, I would have been confident in her ability to handle the golem on her own, but after six days of fasting, she wasn't at her full strength. I didn't know what would have happened if I hadn't gotten there in time.

Tamil perched herself on the bench opposite me and gave me a long look, as if weighing how much she should say to me. "I came here to talk to you about Adara," she said. "You're the only one here who seems to truly be concerned for her welfare, and who doesn't view her as a stepping stone to achieving power." She sighed, toying with the hem of her fur-trimmed sleeve. "I don't know if you're aware, but I was close friends with Olette growing up. And while she and Prentis were childhood friends, she never fully trusted him."

My eyes narrowed, and I sat up a little straighter. "And why is that?"

"Because Prentis's loyalty is too easily bought," Tamil said. "He was more concerned with doing whatever he could to curry favor with his betters, whether that was their tutors, or parents, or Lady Axlya. He worked as a spy for years for Lady Axlya before she gave him the lake fiefdom, and she plans to use him in that capacity again, but this time as Adara's king consort. If he marries Adara, her secrets will never be safe with him."

"I suspected as much," I said darkly. "Someone left a jar of incense burning outside my window last night, that had narcoleptic properties. It's why I didn't hear Prentis and Adara leaving this morning, even though I'm right across the hall, why I didn't realize Adara had left the castle until she was in danger." I gritted my teeth as my fangs lengthened, trying to force them back into my gums before Tamil noticed. "I'm pretty sure Prentis had it placed there so he could have some alone time with Adara."

"That sounds like something he would do." Tamil bit her lip, looking worried. "Have there been any other assassination attempts against Adara?"

I debated telling Tamil about the slice of poisoned cake, but decided against it. I didn't actually know her, and for all I knew, she was the assassin, trying to mine me for information to see if Adara and I were onto her.

"Nothing we've noticed," I said instead. "Thankfully with the fasting, we don't have to worry about food poisoning attempts, but I have been keeping close watch over Adara since we arrived at the castle." A grim thought occurred to me that made my stomach clench. "Do you think it's possible Prentis is the one who created the golem, or that he's in cahoots with whoever did?"

Tamil shook her head. "Prentis isn't above that sort of thing, but Adara is far more useful to him alive than dead. She's his ticket to the throne—if he was going to kill her, he would wait until she's produced at least one child, when he can safely assume the role of king regent."

"Over my dead body," I growled.

Tamil chuckled, though the sound held no mirth. "It would have to be," she agreed, turning more fully to face me. Her ice-blue eyes seemed to pierce my soul as she stared into my eyes. "You are attuned to Adara's whereabouts and emotions in much the same way Daryan was attuned to Olette's," she said baldly.

"Yes." I swallowed hard beneath her scrutiny, wondering if she knew about the dragon mating bond. Wondering if she was going to ask me outright.

Instead, she rose from the bench and shook her skirts out. "Olette and Daryan's story may not have ended well, but that doesn't mean yours has to follow the same path," she said as she walked away. "Don't give up on something before it's had a chance to blossom. Fight for her, Einar. Or we'll all lose."

35

Adara

"Push-ups? At this hour of the morning?"

I glanced up from my plank position as Einar stepped into the training room, looking well-rested and fresh as morning rain. Sweat dripped from my brow and into my eyes, and I blinked against the sting, then glanced back down.

"I'm losing too much muscle," I told him through gritted teeth as I pulled my elbows into my ribs. My arms shook as my chest brushed against the floor, and it took far more effort than it should have to push myself back up again. "I've probably lost five pounds since the tailor came to fit me for my ceremonial outfit. He's going to throw a tantrum."

Einar scoffed as he leaned down in front of me, offering a hand. "You've been fasting for eight days now," he said. "If the tailor isn't prepared to make alterations, he's an idiot."

I considered refusing it, but I knew that if I tried to do another push-up, I would collapse, and I would never hear the end of it. So I took his hand, trying to ignore the familiar jolt that passed between us at the contact. His skin felt impossibly hot against mine, and I realized that my own skin had gone cold and clammy.

Embarrassed, I tried to pull my hand away, but he held it firm, covering it with his other one.

"We haven't spoken since the battle with the golem," he said roughly. His head was bent slightly, and he looked at me through lowered lashes, a storm brewing in his golden eyes.

"I was hoping you'd forgotten about that," I said lamely. "You haven't brought it up, and it's been two days since it happened."

"You were reckless," he growled, his grip tightening on mine. But then he sighed, and the anger seemed to flood away from him, revealing the disappointment beneath. "But I understand why you did it, even if it hurts to know you didn't trust me enough to tell me where you were going before you left."

"I left you a—" *note*, I was going to say, then thought better of it. We both knew it was a flimsy defense. "It's not that I don't trust you," I said instead, squeezing his hand back. "It's that I know that despite your best efforts to give me space and adhere to my wishes, you would never have been able to stay behind. The mating bond would have forced you to come with us."

"Perhaps," Einar agreed. "But I could have followed at a distance." He ran a hand through his hair, glancing around at the training hall. The palace guards came here to do their daily combat training and exercises, making good use of the racks of practice swords and the grappling mats and the weighted balls and discs. "I'm surprised you're not beating on one of those."

He pointed to one of the training dummies lined up on the far wall, meant for striking. "I was tempted," I admitted, "but I can't do any kind of training or exercise that winds me. I tried to go for a quick jog the other day before you woke up, and nearly passed out."

"I was wondering why you looked paler than usual yesterday," Einar said, shaking his head. He dropped my hand so he could stroke a hand over my forehead. "You need to conserve your strength as much as possible. The water baths are only doing so much. And doing pushups won't stop you from losing more weight. In fact, I'm pretty sure you're only going to accelerate it."

"And I think you're just saying that because you don't want me getting better than you, old man." I stuck my tongue out at him as I stepped out of his reach, using the same insult Leap loved to toss at Einar. I could tell it hit the mark as his eyes flared, and a little thrill shot through me as he took a step in my direction.

"Better than me?" he echoed as he backed me toward one of the walls, a slow grin spreading over his face. "You think a few pushups are going to close the gap between us when I have decades of warrior training under my belt?"

My heart slammed against my ribs as I stepped sideways, preventing him from caging me in against the wall. We circled each other, my veins buzzing with adrenaline, bodies braced as we both searched for an opening. The phantom bite at my neck throbbed, and I could feel the bond between us pulsing like a living, breathing thing. The energy flowed straight into me, banishing the exhaustion, making my previously heavy limbs feel as light as a feather.

"What are you waiting for?" he purred, the words a challenge and a seduction all at once. "Come and get me, princess."

I pounced, coming in hot with a jab, but Einar was too quick. He ducked to the side, arms banding around my middle, and I squealed as he lifted me into the air and tossed me at the mats, which were thick and padded with straw and down. I skidded across the surface, then tried to backward roll into a crouch, but Einar was already on top of me, hips straddling mine, chest crushing me into the padded surface.

He leaned down, eyes glowing, the tips of his hair brushing

against my flushed skin. "Do you surrender?" he growled, the double meaning in his words unmistakable.

I arched my body against his in answer, sliding my hands over his shoulders and allowing my nails to scrape against his skin through the thin fabric of his tunic. His eyes slid to half-mast as a shudder rippled through him, and he leaned in further, his lips a hairsbreadth from mine.

I shifted back, then wedged my feet beneath his armpits and shoved his shoulders. He let out a yelp of surprise as he fell backward, and I shouted in triumph as I came up on top, reversing our positions flawlessly.

"You really thought I was going to let you have your way with me?" I crowed as I clamped my knees on either side of his hips to pin him in place.

Einar raised an eyebrow, a lazy grin spreading over his face. "Do you think that being on top means you're in control?"

He punctuated that last word by gripping either side of my hips with his big hands, then driving his pelvis into mine. I gasped as the friction sent a ripple of hot, wicked pleasure through me, the hard length of him pressing exactly against the right spot.

"Of course I'm in control," I panted, clamping my thighs around his hips to stop him from moving. My core throbbed, and I clenched my teeth against the searing wave of desire that urged me to move. I needed to get off him. Anyone could walk in on us—Prentis, Axlya, Cascada.

But the sensation of his body heat seeping into me was so *delicious*. And I found myself lowering my torso until I was flush against him, noses touching, breaths mingling.

"Mhmm," Einar said, and I nearly whimpered as the rumble of his voice sent vibrations down the length of his body and straight into my own. "Let's test that control of yours then, shall we, princess?"

His hands slid down my back to grip my ass, and I swallowed a moan as he dragged my core up his length, then back down. A bolt of pleasure shot through me at the increased friction, and my body went rigid against him.

"Still in control?" he purred, his lips brushing against mine as he spoke.

"Yesss," I hissed as he rocked my body into his. The word was a denial, an encouragement, and a plea all at once, and I felt my thighs loosening their grip, spreading wider so I could grind into him harder. His rumble of approval vibrated through me, making each bolt of pleasure that much more intense as he slid me up and down, up and down.

"That's it, princess," he growled as I began to move faster against him. His eyes blazed as he fisted a hand in the back of my hair, pulling my head back so he could expose my neck. "Let go for me."

He clamped his teeth around the phantom bite mark, and an explosion of pleasure rocketed through me, lighting my entire body up from the inside out. Einar clapped a hand over my mouth to muffle my screams as I came, rocking frantically against him to milk every ounce of pleasure from him. The orgasm ripped through me, so fast and intense, it left me breathless and shaking atop him.

"Good girl," he murmured, rubbing his hands up and down my back. I let out a shuddering sigh as I relaxed against him. A blanket of pure bliss settled over my mind, and I wanted nothing more than to lie here forever, listening to the steady tattoo of Einar's heartbeat while he ran his warm hands along my spine.

No male had ever made me feel like this before. And I wasn't sure if anyone else ever would.

"Lady Adara?" an unfamiliar voice called, and I bolted upright as one of the palace guards walked in. His blue eyebrows climbed to his hairline as he took in the scene before him, and I sat back, trying to act casual. After all, Einar and I were fully clothed, and we were on the training mats. "Lady Axlya sent me to find you. She needs you dressed and in the council chamber within the hour."

"Why?" I asked, brow furrowing. I sincerely hoped it wasn't for another meeting with the tailor, though I doubted she would bring him to the council chambers.

"Because Lady Mossi and Lord Oren have come to Lochanlee with a small army and they are demanding an audience," the guard said, shocking us both.

Einar and I exchanged loaded glances, then bolted from the room, leaving the bewildered guard in our dust. On unspoken agreement, we raced up the stairs not to our rooms, but to the highest tower in the palace. The topmost chamber served as the palace's war room, and the three guards manning it startled as we burst inside.

"Adara. Einar," Prentis said by way of greeting. He was standing on the far side of the room, right next to the panoramic window that stretched across the entire circumference of the chamber. "I'd hoped you'd come here once you heard the news."

He nodded toward the hillside just beyond the city limits, where two encampments had been erected. The flags flying from each of them were unmistakable—the blue and yellow of the Gaoth Aire, and the green and brown of Domhain.

"That isn't what I'd call a small army," Einar said as we approached the window. His golden eyes narrowed in thought, and I could see the calculations running through his soldier's brain. "They've brought around a hundred warriors each. More like an honor guard."

"Even so," Prentis said, his lips pursed. "That's two hundred too many, especially considering that they showed up without warning."

I only half-listened to them as I stared at the encampments, my mind racing. The guard had said Mossi and Oren were the ones who'd demanded the audience, but what about General Slaugh? Had he come as well, and if so, had he brought Nox? Was there some way we could sneak into the encampment and find out? Maybe if I could just get a minute alone with her, I could—

"Adara." Einar's hand curled around my shoulder, cutting off my train of thought. I looked up into his face, and swallowed at the sympathetic expression in his eyes. "It's too dangerous."

"What's too dangerous?" Prentis cut in, his eyes darting between the two of us.

"Nothing." I turned away from the window, avoiding his gaze. "I should get ready. I can't show up to the meeting looking like I just tussled with a mountain troll."

Einar followed me out of the room, waiting until we were well out of earshot before muttering, "I'll show you a mountain troll next time."

Despite everything, I smiled.

I took a deep breath as I approached the council chamber doors, nerves digging into my shoulders and churning in my gut. The three most powerful fae in Ediria, the leaders of the three noble houses, waited beyond those doors. One who wanted to manipulate me, one who had deceived me, and another who was unknown. Lord Oren was the only wild card waiting for me inside, but somehow, I doubted he was here as an ally.

No, the reason these two had come was because they'd heard I was here as a guest of Lady Axlya. And they wanted to head off any attempts to install me on the throne.

"Go on," Einar murmured from behind me. "I'll be right behind you."

I nodded, then squared my shoulders and stepped through the doors.

"There she is," Lady Axlya smiled warmly as I entered the room, as though I was a guest of honor. The seat to her right was occupied by Prentis, the one on her left clearly meant for me, and on the other side of the table were Lady Mossi and Lord Oren with their advisors.

"My apologies for keeping you waiting," I said, taking the empty seat. "I didn't know we were expecting company."

I let my gaze drift across the table, first to Lady Mossi, then to Lord Oren. The former was watching me with thinly veiled contempt, the latter with cool calculation. I sensed more than saw Einar settle into a shadowed corner of the room, close enough to intervene should someone attack, but far enough away as to not draw notice. We'd even dressed him in a guard uniform, hoping he would blend in with the others. After all, if Lady Mossi recognized him, she would likely demand he be thrown out.

"Allow me to introduce Adara, daughter of Princess Olette, and the rightful heir to the Edirian throne," Lady Axlya said proudly. "As a direct descendent of King Cyrian, she is the only one with a legitimate claim, as I'm sure you two agree."

"Actually, we do not," Lady Mossi said, the scathing note in her voice scraping against my nerves. "Adara may be Princess Olette's daughter, but she is also half-dragon, which weakens her claim."

"How so?" Lady Axlya asked breezily, as if she herself hadn't warned me of this countless times. "Olette and Daryan were joined in sacred matrimony, their union approved by the nation. Besides, she is engaged to my nephew, Lord Prentis, who we all acknowledged was next in line for the throne before we knew of

Adara's existence. Jointly, the two of them have the strongest claim of anyone else in the kingdom."

"And why is that?" Lady Mossi challenged. "Because the two of you are water fae?" Her upper lip curled, and the massive vase of flowers planted in the center of the table wilted, the edges of their petals blackening and curling inward beneath the onslaught of her anger. "I don't know how Lord Oren feels, but I, for one, believe that the water fae have held the throne long enough. It's time for another house to rule."

"Another house." Lord Oren scoffed, speaking up for the first time. "You mean *your* house."

Lady Mossi drew herself upright. "If you have a qualified candidate to present to us, by all means, bring him or her forward. But Slaugh has already made his claim, and he is a far more worthy candidate than Adara. He is a full-blooded Edirian who has served the realm faithfully for decades, and has far more experience than Adara. Besides," she added, tilting her head up in a manner that could only be described as *snooty*, "it's clear from the timing that Adara was conceived out of wedlock. Olette and Daryan couldn't have had time to consummate their marriage before he was killed—therefore, Adara is illegitimate."

I clenched my fists beneath the table as the three rulers bickered about legal precedents, as if I weren't sitting right here. A quick glance told me that Einar was just as enraged about these petty arguments as I was, and I had to remind myself that this didn't truly matter.

The most important thing was completing the ritual, which I would still do whether or not I became queen. The rest was just noise.

"I don't think you have any room to talk, considering how you earth fae breed like rabbits." A snide comment shot from Prentis to Lady Mossi drew me back to the conversation. "How many children have you personally popped out, both in and out of wedlock? I think the number of bastards you have are in the teens, at least?"

Bright pink blossomed beneath Lady Mossi's red clay complexion. "How dare you," she hissed, her jade green eyes glowing. The flowers on the table burst into violent life, tendrils skittering across the table in Prentis's direction. Prentis leapt to his feet, his water whip already unfurling, but I was faster. I slammed my fist into the table, and ice burst from my hand like a shockwave, spreading across the wood and stopping the approaching flora in its tracks. The vase and glasses exploded, forcing us all to duck beneath the table to avoid the glittering shards. When I lifted my head, the entire table had transformed into a block of ice, the flowers trapped within.

Oops. Guess I got a little carried away.

Absolute silence descended upon the room as the others emerged from beneath the table, surveying the damage I'd done. Lord Oren was shocked, Lady Mossi livid, Lady Axlya dismayed. I was one hundred percent certain this meeting was not going the way she intended.

I ventured another glance across the room at Einar, only to find his lips were twitching. I bit my lip as a wave of mirth hit me, suddenly realizing how absurd this entire situation was.

"Well," Lord Oren said as everyone resumed their seats. "If your fire magic is anything like your ice magic, then you're going to be absolutely terrifying once you've completed the ritual."

"My fire magic is even more formidable," I assured him. "And the ritual has always been my primary objective. It doesn't matter who sits on the Edirian throne if the shadow creatures take the realm."

"Shadow creatures?" Lady Mossi scoffed. "The shadow creatures have—"

"—vanished," I snapped, cutting her off. "Yes, everyone keeps saying that, and I almost believed it until a shadow golem tried to kill me yesterday." I braced my hands on the table and leaned forward, ignoring the sharp bite of the ice beneath my skin. "You wouldn't have had anything to do with that, would you?"

"Of course not!" Mossi exclaimed, but she'd gone pale beneath her dark complexion. "I wouldn't have sent an assassin after you—I may not believe that you are the right ruler for Ediria, but you are still the girl from the prophecy. I wouldn't dare risk the wrath of the Radiants by doing such a thing."

"Forgive me if I have a hard time believing that," I sneered, "seeing as how you were so willing to sell me out to King Aolis."

"That was different," Mossi said stiffly. "Aolis's intention was always to use you to fulfill the prophecy, not undermine it. I was merely accelerating the process."

"I believe we are getting off track," Lady Axlya said before I could respond. "The fact remains that as much as you might wish for General Slaugh to assume the throne, Adara is the rightful heir."

"Forgive me," Lord Oren cut in. There was a deep bitterness in his tone that sent a shiver of foreboding through the room. "But before we can continue to discuss the crown, I must bring up the matter of my missing daughter, Tempest."

An icy wind seemed to sweep through the room, and Lady Axlya and Mossi both stilled. "What do you mean?" Axlya asked carefully. "Was Tempest not returned to Angtun?"

"You know damned well she wasn't," Oren growled. He turned a baleful glare onto Lady Mossi. "Tempest was under the protection of King Aolis, and by extension, General Slaugh. Yet my sources tell me she was killed, while your daughter and Axlya's have both been safely returned to your bosoms!" He slammed a necklace onto the table—a jade eagle hanging from a golden chain, his yellow raptor gaze incandescent with rage. "This was found near my realm's borders along with Tempest's bloodied clothing, and reports that she was killed by shadow creatures. How can you expect me to support your nephew's claim to the throne, when he is the reason Tempest is *dead*!"

A thunderclap shook the room, and I sat down hard in my seat before my feet slipped out from under me. Lady Mossi was staring at Lord Oren as if she'd never seen him before, and Lady Axlya looked torn, as if she wasn't sure whether she should be pleased that Oren was not, in fact, throwing in his lot with the earth fae.

"I'm very sorry to hear that Tempest has passed," Lady Mossi said, sounding a little shaken, "but I can assure you, Slaugh is not at fault! He told me he let all the hostages go—"

"Without an escort?" Lord Oren barked. He bared his teeth, his tone positively venomous. "I don't know what kind of game you and General Slaugh are playing, Lady Mossi, but the disrespect you both have shown against my house is enough to make me consider declaring war against you, here and now!"

"All right," Lady Axlya said briskly, rising from her chair. "I think that's been enough talk for today. Tempers are running too high for us to have a productive discussion. Lord Oren and Lady Mossi, you are welcome to rejoin your encampment, and we will resume this meeting tomorrow."

"That's fine by me," Lord Oren said tightly. "Lady Mossi informed me General Slaugh will be joining us tomorrow, so that's perfect. He can answer for his crimes then."

36

Adara

T hat night, I tossed and turned fitfully in my bed. Anger coursed through me as I replayed the meeting over and over in my mind—the way the house nobles had argued over me as if I weren't present, and Lady Mossi's attempts to deflect her crimes back at me the most infuriating out of everything.

I knew my inability to control my temper was becoming a problem—this was the second council meeting I'd had a magical outburst at—but in my defense, Lady Mossi had also lost control. At least my show of ability had impressed Lord Oren, though just because he was angry with Lady Mossi didn't mean that he was on my side. And then there was Lady Axlya's announcement to the others that Prentis and I were engaged, even though I hadn't actually agreed to marry him.

Part of me wished I could knock all three of their heads together and make them see sense.

But I knew they didn't really care about the realm, or at least not at this moment. They only cared about making sure they maintained their grip on power.

I was just envisioning stringing Lady Mossi up by a rope made from her own plants when a knock at the door shattered my vengeful fantasy. Sighing, I pushed my coverlet back and padded across the floor to open the door, already knowing who was on the other side.

"Can't sleep either?" I asked Einar, leaning against the door-jamb. The moonlight filtering in through the corridor windows limned the outline of his tall, muscular form, and I swallowed as I realized he was clad only in a pair of pajama bottoms. Silvery light played over the planes of his handsome features, trailing across the dips and valleys of his muscles. My fingers twitched as I resisted the urge to follow the path they illuminated, from the broad plane of his chest down to his tapered torso, and...

"I could feel your frustration through the bond," Einar said by way of explanation. I snapped my gaze back up to his face, and the gleam in his eyes told me he'd guessed the direction of my wayward thoughts. The memory of our encounter in the training room rushed back into me, sending a flood of warmth straight to my core, and my thighs clenched together.

"Sorry," I muttered, glancing away. I wasn't sure if I was apologizing for my anger, or my lustful thoughts, or both. "I'll try to clear my mind so you can go back to bed."

I took a step back, but Einar placed a hand against the door-frame, preventing me from closing it. "Actually, I was wondering... would you like to go for a ride?"

I blinked. "Is that an innuendo?"

The corners of his mouth kicked up into a grin. "For once, no. I'm asking you if you want to fly with me."

I sucked in a slow breath between my teeth as I considered it. The last time I'd flown on Einar's back was when we'd run from Lady Mossi's griffin riders and crash landed straight into the Gaoth Aire mountains. So many things had shifted between us since that night, I could scarcely believe the events had occurred only a few weeks ago.

"All right," I said, holding my hand out to him. "But just for a little while, okay? We're not running away like a pair of star-crossed lovers."

Chuckling, Einar took my hand and led me through a series of unfamiliar corridors. His palm was warm and comforting against mine, and though the attraction between us still pulsed through the bond and into the phantom bite on my neck, it was a slow simmer rather than the raging inferno I'd felt earlier.

We didn't encounter a single guard on our journey, and after a few minutes, we emerged from the palace through what I suspected was a servant's entrance. "You've been mapping out the palace, haven't you?" I whispered as we snuck around the side of the building, heading for a section of lawn large enough for Einar to shift without destroying the carefully cultivated flower beds and trees.

"Of course I have," he said, sounding mildly offended. "You didn't think I was sitting around twiddling my thumbs while you've been charming politicians, have you?"

"I'm not sure 'charming' is the right word," I muttered. 'Barely tolerating' seemed to be more accurate, on their ends and mine.

I stepped back as Einar shifted into dragon form, watching as his large frame unfurled into the massive, winged, fire-breathing creature that still struck fear into the hearts of fae children during bedtime stories. But I felt no fear as I looked upon him, only awe at the way his ruby scales glimmered in the moonlight, shimmering with an almost divine iridescence. Wicked black spikes jutted along his spine, from the base of his neck to the tip of his tail, and matching claws curled from each of his toes, digging into the cold, hard ground. I knew that if he opened his mouth, I would find jagged teeth as long as my forearms and a long, forked tongue within.

But he didn't bare those fangs at me, or lash out with his claws or tail, and I knew he never would.

Einar was my protector, and I would always be safe with him, no matter what happened between us.

As if he'd read my thoughts—which he probably had—Einar stretched his neck out so he could nuzzle me with his reptilian snout. The gesture elicited a smile from me, and I stroked my hand down his snout before I moved around to his flank. There was a tender look in his fiery eyes as he lowered himself to the ground, wings spread out on either side of him like a ramp so I could climb up. I settled myself in between the two spikes closest to the base of his neck, wrapping my arms around the one in front of me and squeezing my thighs to let him know I was ready.

Without further ado, he took off, running a few short steps before launching us into the sky.

My breath caught as we climbed the starry sky, the freezing midnight air ripping my hair free from its braid so it could fly behind me like a banner. As always, I found the cold invigorating, a sharp contrast to the raw heat emanating from Einar's scales. I wondered if he felt the cold at all, or if his dragon hide rendered him impervious to it. I knew he hated the cold when he was on the ground in his bipedal form, but this high in the clouds, it had to be cold regardless of the time of year.

But that thought drifted away as we broke through the cloud cover and coasted through a sea of stars and darkness. It was hard to feel anything but wonder as we soared through the frosted night sky, and far too easy to leave my earthly worries behind on the ground.

I wished we could stay up here forever, where only the wind

could touch us. But more than that, I wished I could vault off Einar's back and spread wings of my own so I could fly alongside him. A vision of the two of us chasing each other through the clouds, zipping through beams of moonlight as we tried to outrun the dawn, unfolded in my head, and I felt something deep and primal stir inside me, lifting its head.

But all too soon, we dipped below the clouds again, bringing the world back into view. Still, it was spectacular as far as views went, shimmering rivers and waterfalls winking up at us from Lochanlee's rolling hills and valleys. Einar circled for a few minutes before alighting at the base of a sheer cliff and shifting back to human form. A massive waterfall rushed from the edge of the cliff and down into the roaring river below, infusing the air with shimmering mists that seemed to envelop us like the clandestine arms of a lover.

"Feeling better?" Einar asked as we perched atop a flat rock jutting out into the river.

"Much." I took a deep breath of the misty air, then let it out in a sigh of contentment. This place felt terribly romantic, with the moonlit waterfall on one side of us and the grove of trees on the other, cutting us off from the rest of the world. I thought Einar would use the opportunity to seduce me again, but he took my hand in his instead, a grave expression on his face.

"I know I promised not to kidnap you," he said. "But I think we should seriously consider leaving, now, before things get worse."

"Leaving?" I stared at him, my heart dropping at the deep lines of worry on his face. "Einar," I said, squeezing his hand, "we can't leave. I've nearly completed the fast, and things are getting worse. I can't afford not to complete the ritual."

"What good is the ritual going to do you if you're already dead?" Einar argued. "Two assassination attempts have already been made against you, Adara. *Two,*" he repeated, when I opened my mouth to argue. "Whoever is trying to kill you is only going to grow more desperate the closer you get to completing the ritual. You're not safe here, Adara."

"And where am I safe, exactly?" I cried, throwing up my hands. "Certainly not in the other two kingdoms. Lady Mossi would have me killed in an instant if I returned, and Lord Oren doesn't seem like he's on my side either. Lady Axlya is the only one with an interest in keeping me safe."

"No, *I'm* the only one interested in keeping you safe," Einar growled. "Lady Axlya is doing everything she can to turn you into a puppet, fastening each string to you one day at a time, gradually. By the time you're fully under her control, you won't even notice!"

He gouged deep tracks into the stone beneath us as he spoke, and I wondered if he even realized his claws had sprouted. "That's not going to happen," I said as calmly as I could. "The moment I complete the ritual, I'm going to go after Nox and end this. There won't be time for Lady Axlya to do anything else."

"Do you really think she's going to let you walk away like that?" Einar shook his head, frustration bleeding from his pores and saturating the surrounding air. "Adara, you're an investment, and as far as she's concerned, the two of you made a deal."

"We did not!" I said hotly. "She may have told everyone I was marrying Prentis, but I never agreed to it!"

"No, but she told you it was a condition for being allowed to complete the ceremony, and she's going to hold you to it," Einar said in a dangerous voice. "The priestess who's going to perform the ritual on you is likely the same one who performs marriages. Who's to say Lady Axlya won't try to force you into a wedding at the last moment?"

A chill raced up my spine, and my stomach turned at the

thought of Axlya bait and switching me like that. "I hadn't thought of that," I admitted. "Do you really think—"

I cut myself off at the look on Einar's face. Of course Lady Axlya would do something like that. She'd just announced an engagement I hadn't agreed to to the rest of the world. Forcing me to marry Prentis in exchange for my powers was exactly her style.

"Einar," I said slowly, weighing each word as I allowed them to drop from my lips, "if marrying Prentis is what I have to do to save the world, I'm going to do it."

He sucked in a sharp breath, and the sound was like a shard of glass pierced straight through my heart. My potential marriage to Prentis had always been the elephant in the room between us, and we'd broken our unspoken agreement not to discuss it tonight. The idea had always seemed so abstract, so far away, but Einar's words had driven home the reality of the situation. Panic gripped me, and my breaths grew shorter, the edges of my vision growing dark...

"Adara." Einar's hands were on my shoulders, and the next thing I knew, he was gently guiding my head down between my knees. "Breathe," he said, stroking a comforting hand up and down my spine. "It's going to be all right. Just breathe."

I sucked in one gulping breath, then another, forcing myself to focus only on the inhalations and exhalations, clearing my mind of all thoughts. Eventually, my breathing returned to normal, and with it, the soothing sounds of the wind rustling and the crickets chirping and the water rushing before us.

Sitting up, I scooted closer so I could lean my head on Einar's chest. Immediately, he curled the hand that had been rubbing my back around my waist, pulling me in against him. The warmth radiating from his body penetrated all the way to my core, driving out the chill that had nothing to do with the icy air around us, and everything to do with the idea of marrying Prentis.

"I don't know what I'm supposed to do," I said, my breath frosting in clouds around us. "If I had something I could use as leverage against Lady Axlya, I might be able to convince her to help us. But there's nothing, Einar. She holds all the cards."

"We could go to Mount Furian," Einar suggested.

"Huh?"

"Mount Furian," he repeated. "It's where all dragons go to complete the Umnar, which is our own version of the coming-of-age ritual. We take a special herb that opens our inner eye, then travel to the center of the mountain and tattoo the form of our dragon spirit using a combination of ink and our own blood."

He took my hand and pressed my fingers to the whorls of the tattoo that swirled from his left pectoral all the way down to his forearm. My breath caught as I traced the lines of ink—I could feel power humming in each one, like tendrils of living flame that had been preserved in ink and blood.

"What are you saying?" I asked, barely able to hear the words over the pounding of my heart. "Are you suggesting we go to Mount Furian, and I tattoo myself there?"

"It's worth a try," he insisted. "Especially since the shadow creatures have supposedly vanished. Now is a better time than ever to make the trek to Hearthfyre."

"We don't know that the shadow creatures have left Hearthfyre," I reminded him. "Nox probably commanded them all to retreat, and they're lurking in the one place in Ediria no fae dares to travel. Plus, what's the name of this herb, and where does it grow?"

"Esymoth," Einar said, then admitted, "I think it only grows in Hearthfyre."

"I've never even heard of it, and Mother forced me to study

herb lore for years." I blew out a frustrated breath. "If I thought this was a viable plan, I would pounce on it in a heartbeat, Einar." I turned into him so I could cup his cheek, wanting him to see the sincerity in my eyes. His stubble rasped against my palm, and the sensation sent a little thrill through me despite the heartache pulsing through our bond. "But traveling to Mount Furian is probably going to get us both killed."

Einar closed his eyes, turning his face into my hand. "I know," he murmured into my palm. The rumble of his voice vibrated up my arm and into my core, and I found myself leaning further into him, wanting to feel his mouth on other, less innocent parts of my body. "I'm just being selfish... because I don't want you to marry Prentis. I want you to marry *me*."

His eyes opened, and the blaze of love and desire in them made my heart sing and bleed at the same time. I wished with all my heart that I could say yes. That I could marry Einar instead, and the two of us could fly off into the sunset and leave these corrupt, desperate nobles and their twisted machinations behind.

Tears stung the corners of my eyes, and I shut them as I closed the scant distance between us, pressing my mouth against his.

Einar responded instantly, hauling me into his lap, one hand splaying against my lower back as the other one burrowed into my hair. He kissed me fiercely, and I opened for him, wanting to give as much of myself to him as I could. He tasted like wood smoke and cider and the crackling warmth of a hearth fire, and I clung to him, wrapping my legs around his waist and cradling his face like it was the most precious thing in the world.

His hands slid up the back of my shirt, and I shivered at the feel of his palms splayed across my skin. I could have allowed him to continue, to divest me of my clothes and give me another taste of the pleasure he'd given me in the armory.

But I didn't want to take. Not this time.

Breaking the kiss, I began to crawl down the length of his body, pulling up his tunic so I could trail a path along his skin with my mouth. Nervous energy crawled through me, making my fingers tremble ever so slightly as I slid them beneath the waistband of his trousers.

"Wait." Einar closed his hand over mine. His golden eyes glowed in the darkness, desire swirling in their depths, but confusion was stamped across his handsome face. "Are you sure?"

In answer, I slowly pushed the fabric down his hips, holding his gaze the entire time. His length sprang free into my waiting hand, and my fingers flexed around him, harder than I intended as I took in the size of him for the first time. His answering groan of pleasure emboldened me, and I began to slide my palm up and down, exploring the texture, the length.

"How can something be so hard and so soft at the same time?" I wondered aloud, and he let out a choked laugh.

"I don't know," he admitted, sounding both amused and on edge all at once. I squeezed him again, and his breathing grew more ragged. "That's just... how we're built."

"Mmm." I squeezed again, and delight rippled through me as he groaned again. Slowly, I increased the tempo, watching for any signs of discomfort. Though I'd heard the girls in my village gossip about this kind of thing, I'd never actually done it myself before. But though the muscles in Einar's face were taut with tension, fingers digging into the dirt, I could feel through the bond how much he was enjoying this.

"Adara," he gasped, bucking against my hand. "I'm going to—"

He didn't even finish the sentence as he exploded, shudders rippling through his body. Watching him surrender like this, his guard down, heart open, was the sexiest thing I'd ever seen in my life, and I wished I could give him more, wished I could give him all of me. Wished I could seal the mating bond between us so we could fully experience each other's pleasure and emotions, like the spirits had intended for us.

I couldn't do that... but at least I could give him this. And for that, I would always be grateful.

37

Adara

I drummed my fingers on the arms of my chair as I sat in the council chamber, waiting with Lady Axlya and Prentis for the others to arrive. A small selection of pastries, fruit, and coffee sat out on the table, but I wasn't even remotely tempted despite the fast. My stomach felt like it had been transformed into a lump of lead, and I had a feeling that if I even attempted to eat something, I would throw it right up.

"Adara," Lady Axlya said, a hint of censure in her tone. "You're going to drill holes in the chair if you keep that up."

"Sorry." I buried my hands in the folds of my skirt instead. "I just... the last time I saw General Slaugh, he tried to kill me. I'm not looking forward to meeting him again."

Lady Axlya laughed a little at that. "My dear, we have *all* tried to kill each other at some point," she said.

"You have?"

Her expression softened a little, but I wasn't sure if it was pity or sympathy she felt for me. "I sometimes forget that you weren't raised at court," she said. "If you're asking whether Lord

Oren or Lady Mossi have physically tried to harm me, the answer is no. But we have absolutely been undermining and attacking one another for centuries, even during the dragon wars when we were all supposedly aligned against a common enemy. We may all be part of the same kingdom, but we are not friends, Adara. You need to put this silly notion out of your head that you have to like your allies in order to treat with them. That's not the way the world works."

"Well, it should be," I shot back, crumpling the fabric of my skirt in my hands before I could think better of it. "Maybe the world would be a better place if everyone was honest with each other, and communicated with the intention of trying to understand and empathize, instead of trying to one-up each other all the time."

"In a perfect world, yes," Axlya said. "But we don't live in a perfect world, and the sooner you realize that, the sooner you'll be able to convince the others that you deserve to sit on the throne."

Prentis opened his mouth, looking torn—I wasn't sure if he was about to defend his aunt, or offer words of sympathy—but before he could say anything, the double doors opened. We all turned our heads to the entrance to see Lord Oren and his advisors stride in. Lady Mossi glided in behind him, and my entire body went still at the sight of General Slaugh walking arm in arm with her.

I expected to see the same male who'd captured me and brought me to Kaipei—the angry, sallow-faced warrior with shadow-blackened veins running up the sides of his neck and down his forearms. But the fae who walked into the room today was somber and reserved, no trace of the shadow magic he'd wielded either on his skin or clinging to his aura.

"Lady Axlya, Lord Prentis." He stopped in front of the table and inclined his head before his eyes met mine. "Adara."

I said nothing as I stared back at him, trying to peer past the serious, war-scarred soldier façade to the evil I knew lurked within. But the mask didn't waver as the others exchanged their greetings, then took their respective seats at the table.

"I must say," Lady Axlya said, "I'm surprised you didn't arrive yesterday with your aunt, General Slaugh. After all, we are here to discuss the subject of succession, and you have very publicly thrown your hat into the ring."

"I apologize for my tardiness," General Slaugh said gravely. "But as you know, Kaipei Castle has been in a state of chaos ever since Adara murdered our king. I was forced to pick up the pieces after she fled, and wasn't able to get away until yesterday."

I clenched my hands beneath the table—the bastard was sitting right here in front of me, talking about me as if I wasn't even here! My gaze flickered to the wall where Einar had stood yesterday, but I already knew he wasn't there. We'd both decided it would be for the best if he wasn't present for this meeting—instead, he stood guard outside the doors, where he could hear perfectly well.

"Too true," Lady Mossi said. "The entire country has been thrown into disarray by the king's death, not just Kaipei. That's why it's important that we install a new monarch as soon as possible, one who has the knowledge and experience necessary to lead our people."

"And you think that you're the best fae for the job," I said flatly, addressing Slaugh. "After everything you've done."

Everyone in the room turned to look at me, but I ignored them, keeping my gaze trained on my enemy. "It's true that I have done terrible things in the late king's name," General Slaugh said as he finally met my gaze. He was the picture of humility—his head slightly bowed, shoulders curved in, hands clasped almost as if in prayer. "But I was acting under the influence of his shadow magic, my will not my own. That is no longer the case, and now that I am free, I want to use my unique position and experience to undo the damage my predecessor has wrought."

"It seems contradictory for you to accuse Adara of murdering King Aolis, while indirectly acknowledging that without her interference, you would still be a slave to King Aolis's machinations," Lady Axlya said. The sharp glint in her eye belied the almost lazy way she spoke the words, and irritation flickered in Slaugh's eyes.

"Perhaps 'murder' is a strong word," Lady Mossi allowed.

"I disagree," Lord Oren said. He directed this comment at Slaugh, his brows drawn together like thunderclouds preparing to unleash a rainstorm. "I think murder is the perfect word to describe what happened to my daughter at your hands, Slaugh."

"At my hands?" General Slaugh raised his remaining eyebrow. "I don't know what you mean, Lord Oren. Tempest made a run for it during all the commotion, and she did not return to the castle. I'm very sorry she hasn't made it back to Angtun—I thought for certain that she would have tried to return home."

"Well, she didn't," Lord Oren seethed, "and she was in your care. That makes you responsible for her death!"

"I must agree that restitution is required, General Slaugh," Lady Axlya said primly. "And also that it is highly irregular that you sent all our daughters home without escorts. I realize you lost a number of soldiers during the attack on Kaipei castle, but surely you could have spared a few for such precious cargo?"

"That isn't the only thing that is irregular," I interrupted, before General Slaugh could spin some lie to cover his ass. "You all keep saying that shadow magic has disappeared from Ediria, but if that's true, then where is my mother, Gelsyne? Why haven't you brought her with you? You seem to forget that I was there that night, Slaugh—I saw the shadow demon take over my mother's form, saw it giving you orders. You're not fooling anyone, General Slaugh—you're just as under her control as King Aolis was when he was alive."

Pain flickered across Lady Mossi's features, and Slaugh sighed heavily. "Gelsyne was too weak after all the torture I subjected her to," he said. "Her body wasn't able to withstand Nox's occupation, and she perished."

His words slammed into me with the force of a hurricane, crushing my ribs and flattening my lungs. "No," I rasped, gripping the arms of my chair. Ice crept up the grains of wood, but I barely noticed as spots danced in my vision. I'd hoped that he would tell me otherwise, that Cascada had been lying when she'd told me my mother had been killed.

But even as I spoke, doubts crept into the dark spaces of my mind. Slaugh and Cascada had every reason to lie about this, but the pain on Lady Mossi's face was genuine. She might have been a manipulative bitch, but I remembered the way she'd talked about Gelsyne during our first meeting in the arboretum. She obviousy loved my mother, so much that she'd tried to trade me to King Aolis for both Gelsyne *and* Avani.

"Wait a minute," Prentis said. The suspicion in his voice snapped me out of it, and I turned to see him scowling at General Slaugh. "Cascada told us she killed Gelsyne, but according to you, she perished on her own. Which is the truth?"

"I—" Slaugh spluttered, losing his composure for a few seconds. "Yes, Cascada did end Gelsyne's life, but only to put her out of her misery. She was suffering from the shadow corruption, and there was nothing we could do to save her. Ending her life was a kindness."

"A kindness?" I echoed, incredulous. "You're the one who corrupted her in the first place, Slaugh!" I clenched my fists in my skirts to keep myself from lunging across the table and strangling him. "I want to see her body with my own eyes. Only then will I be able to accept that she's truly gone."

"We have already buried her," Slaugh said. "But if you insist, come to Kaipei, and I will unearth it for you."

There was a hint of challenge in Slaugh's voice, and I gritted my teeth. If my mother really was alive, then so was Nox, and returning to Kaipei would put me right where she wanted me. I couldn't afford to call him on his bluff—if it was one—and he knew it.

"Are we expected to believe that just because Gelsyne was unable to host the shadow demon, it's disappeared from our world?" Lord Oren asked. The skepticism in his tone mirrored the looks on the others' faces, and I could tell that distrust for Slaugh was spreading throughout the room. "Perhaps the rest of you are fooled by Slaugh's pretty excuses, but I consulted the Oracle recently, and she told me that the threat has not passed." We all started as he stood up, bracing his hands on the table so he could lean across it and rake us with a scathing glare. I stared as his hawk-like eyes landed on me, feeling like a mouse caught beneath a raptor's gaze.

"Even if General Slaugh is innocent, and my daughter is *somehow* alive, I cannot support his claim given the blood on his hands," he told me. "But neither can I support yours, not when you have not fulfilled the prophecy. As the others have said, you are inexperienced, and do not have the training required to lead our nation. Until you fulfill your destiny, and eradicate shadow magic from Ediria, I will not allow you to sit on the throne. In fact," he added, looking to Lady Axlya, "House Reatha is considering withdrawing from the Edirian Alliance altogether. We have shed the most blood in both the war and against the shadow creatures, sacrificing our soldiers for decades guarding the border to the Deadlands, and have received very little in exchange. This alliance no longer serves us."

The room erupted into a cacophony of shouts, all three house rulers arguing furiously. "The most blood!" Lady Mossi screeched. "Have you any idea how many tens of thousands of soldiers Domhain has lost in the dragon wars? And not to mention that it's *our* crops that have been feeding your lightning riders for centuries?"

"You would never have been able to grow those crops with such abundance if not for the regular rains my people have provided for you," Lady Axlya countered, her cheeks mottled red. "Lord Oren, I know times have been hard, but for you to withdraw from the kingdom now is foolhardy. This is not the time—"

I shoved back from the table and hurried from the room, unwilling to hear another word from either party. The others hardly seemed to notice, not even Prentis, for which I was grateful. I couldn't stand another moment in that room.

"Adara?" Einar fell into step next to me as I burst out the doors and fled down the hallway, his golden eyes shining with worry. "What happened? I could feel how upset you were through the bond; if Slaugh—"

"Not now," I bit out. "We can't speak freely here."

We rounded the corner, then skidded to a halt as we found a familiar figure standing in the center of the corridor—Tamil. A tall water fae soldier accompanied her, and my breath caught as I met his golden-green eyes.

"Kiryan," I said. "What are you doing here?"

"Getting you out of this mess," he said, nodding to the ice fae. "I'd hoped that Lady Axlya would have been sensible enough not to invite General Slaugh into the palace, but it seems her avarice has robbed her of common sense. It's no longer safe for you here, Adara."

"I can't leave, though," I argued, even though every fiber of my being wanted to flee from this horrid place. "Not with only one more day left until I can complete the ritual."

"That won't be a problem," Tamil said. She stepped forward, an earnest expression on her pale face. "I know we don't know each other well yet, and you have no reason to trust me. But there is an ice priestess at Bala Oighr, and she stands ready and waiting to help you complete the ritual. We have to leave now if we are to get to her, while the others are still distracted."

I stared at her hand as she held it out to me, feeling as though I was standing at a precipice, a sheer drop waiting below. Did I dare take this chance, when doing so meant losing Lady Axlya's favor forever? Or should I stay here, leaving myself open to attack from Mossi and Slaugh?

"I hate to say it," Einar said, "but even if we can't trust Tamil, we've always been able to trust Kiryan. He would never steer us wrong."

I looked up at Einar, into his pleading gaze. It was clear what he wanted me to do, and if I was honest with myself, it was the only choice that made sense. The only choice that wouldn't leave me trapped in a loveless marriage, bound to a house matriarch who only wanted to manipulate me, or left at the mercy of my enemies.

"All right." I placed my hand in Tamil's. "I'll come with you."

38

Adara

"Are you sure it wouldn't be better to wait until nightfall?" Einar demanded as Kiryan and Tamil led us down a series of stairwells and dark corridors. Judging by the consternation on his face, I gathered this was a route he hadn't used before, despite the amount of time he'd spent exploring the palace's back routes and service staircases. "Adara and I went on a night ride last night, and no one tried to stop us. I don't see why we couldn't do the same thing tonight."

"General Slaugh wasn't here last night," Kiryan reminded us. "He's brought a contingent of soldiers with him, including several members of the shadow guard, and is waiting for just such a moment as the one you're describing. The moment he sees a dragon taking flight from Usciete Palace, he'll send his men to shoot you down and take the both of you out. Better to flee now, while he is still preoccupied with the other nobles."

"I'll be even easier to see during the day, though," Einar argued. "How do we expect to get away if I can't fly?"

"You aren't going to fly us out of here," Tamil said. "Kiryan and I have planned everything. Thanks to his access to all the guard's memories, he knows every secret passage and tunnel. And I have a few tricks up my sleeve as well. Don't worry about it, Einar—we'll get the two of you out safely."

Einar grumbled a little under his breath, but didn't argue. After all, we *had* agreed to let Kiryan and Tamil help us. I suspected the real reason he was uncomfortable was because he wasn't used to taking the back seat and letting others lead.

"Thank you for risking your life for us," I said. I was thankful that my voice didn't shake, despite the fear jittering in my veins. "I know what will happen once Lady Axlya finds out you've aided me."

Tamil smiled grimly. "Axlya won't kill me, much as she might want to. Waging war on the Bala Oighr will cost her far more than she's prepared to lose, especially given the current situation. Even so, I would gladly pledge my life to yours, Adara. You're the kingdom's only hope for survival."

The gravity of that statement settled on all four of us like leaden weights placed upon our shoulders. Several floors above, I could hear a commotion—the thunder of boots pounding against stone, the clatter of armor and weapons. Lady Axlya had likely told her guards and soldiers to prepare for battle, and I couldn't blame her, with two enemy armies on her doorstep and all three nobles going at each other's throats.

Slipping out now while the guards were distracted was a good plan. I doubted anyone would be concerned with monitoring the secret passages right now.

"Almost there," Kiryan told us as we descended into the palace cellars. There was a warren of rooms down here, each stuffed to the brim with dry goods, pickled meats and vegetables, and alcohol. "The passage should be through here."

He led us into a large room filled with stacks of aged oak barrels. The pleasant scents of cedar and red wine mingled with the damp, cold air, but there was something else, too, a dark undercurrent that made the hairs on the back of my neck stand on end.

"Something is wrong." Einar threw out an arm to stop me from entering the room.

"What sharp instincts you have," a familiar voice said as someone stepped out from behind one of the larger barrels. I sucked in a sharp breath, my blood turning to ice—it was Cascada, a smug smile spreading over her face. There was something off about her—her eyes seemed too big in her skull, her pupils blown as if she were on some kind of drug. "Too bad they won't save you now."

She flung a hand in Tamil's direction, and to my horror, shadow magic crackled up her forearm and shot out of her palm, arcing like a lightning bolt toward Tamil's head. I jumped forward, trying to duck around Einar's arm so I could use my magic, but Kiryan beat me to it, shoving Tamil aside and taking the bolt straight in the chest.

His entire body convulsed, and he collapsed to the ground, eyes rolling into the back of his head. Black smoke leaked from his pores as his skin glowed, and I knew the radiant was using his own power to drive the black magic out of the poor guard's body before it could kill him.

"What is this madness?" Tamil demanded. Her face was pale with shock as she pushed herself to her feet, and I reached out to offer a steadying grip on her elbow. "How is it you're able to wield shadow magic, Cascada? Have you sold your soul to that demoness, just like Slaugh and the others?"

Cascada gave Tamil a wicked grin, and that sense of foreboding ran up my spine again. Her pupils expanded until they covered the whites of her eyes, eclipsing her soul in an abyss so dark and cold, I had to stop myself from recoiling.

"Cascada didn't sell her soul to me, not willingly." We all

started as Nox's voice poured out of the water fae's mouth, like black velvet rasping against bare flesh. "I simply planted a piece of myself into her shadow, and have been making some subtle suggestions that her subconscious has been more than happy to follow. Though now that I'm speaking through her to you, I have to say she does make a rather excellent conduit," she added, tapping a slender finger against Cascada's mouth. "I almost want to use her as a vessel instead of Gelsyne, except doing so would rob me of my ability to torment you, Adara. And we can't have that now, can we?"

She winked at me, and I stared at her as hope, of all things, began to blossom inside me. "Are you saying that my mother isn't dead?" Had Slaugh lied to me after all?

"Oh no," Nox purred, curling Cascada's lips into a diabolical smile. "Gelsyne is most definitely still alive. I'm afraid I won't be able to say the same for any of you, once I'm through here. Cascada's attempts to kill you were lukewarm at best, but I assure you, I'll be using something a little stronger than poisoned cake."

I barely had time to process the revelation that Cascada was responsible for that poor cat's death as Nox raised her hands, gathering power around her. Black lightning crackled down her arms, gathering in the palms of her hands as she prepared to attack again. I braced myself, summoning fire magic to my palms, and Einar and Tamil took up defensive positions, summoning their own magic.

I could feel the enormity of the shadow magic pulsing in the room, and doubt began to eat at the corners of my mind. Nox was powerful, even attacking from a distance, and I was weakened from the fast. I wasn't sure if my fire magic would be a match for her.

But just as she lifted her arm, the shadow lightning in her palms began to flicker, as if something was interfering with the source. "W-what is this?" Nox croaked, her pupils expanding and contracting, expanding and contracting.

"I think... Cascada is fighting back," Kiryan gasped from the floor. He seemed to have won the fight against the shadow infection, though it was clear from the way he struggled up into a sitting position that he'd barely managed it. "Nox is losing control."

"I haven't lost control of anything!" Nox snapped. Her black pupils slammed back into place, and she lifted her hands again, but Einar was already behind her, a small wine barrel clutched his hands. He smashed it atop Cascada's head, and she went down into a heap, eyes rolling into the back of her head much the same way Kiryan's had done just moments ago.

"Well shit," Tamil said as the four of us stared at Cascada's prone form. She lifted a questioning gaze to Einar as he crouched down beside the unconscious fae. "Did you kill her?"

He shook her head, his fingers against Cascada's pulse. "She's going to have a concussion, but she'll survive." He slid a hand beneath her back and lifted her up, then pointed to the ground beneath her. "This is the bigger problem."

We all looked to where Einar pointed, and I gasped. Along the left edge of Cascada's shadow was an inky patch about four inches long. It writhed beneath our collective stare, like a snake that had been staked to the ground.

"That's what Nox meant when she said she planted a piece of herself into Cascada's shadow," I said numbly.

"Yes," Kiryan said gravely. "By attaching a piece of her own shadow to Cascada's, Nox was able to manipulate her subconscious, altering her memory of the events at Kaipei and convincing her you were the enemy, Adara." He pushed himself to his feet and came to kneel by Cascada's side. "I can remove the taint, but doing so will tax this body to its limits. I will not be able to come with you."

"Do what you need to," I said, placing a hand on Kiryan's shoulder. I glanced down at Cascada's sallow face, guilt wracking me. All along I'd thought she'd turned traitor, when in reality she'd become another of Nox's victims, all because she'd jumped in to defend me against her and Slaugh. Her condition was partially my fault, since she'd risked her life so I could flee Kaipei... the least I could do was let Kiryan save her, even if it meant leaving without him.

"Let's go," Einar said. He steered me away as Tamil pushed aside a massive barrel, revealing the passage hidden behind it. "Before someone comes and finds us down here."

I snuck one last glance at Kiryan and Cascada, watching as the Radiant leaned over her, placing glowing hands against her forehead and torso. And then I followed Einar and Tamil into the darkness.

39

Einar

I expected Tamil to lead us into an earthen passage similar to the one Adara, Mavlyn, and I had used to escape Kaipei Castle. Instead, we followed her down a steep stairwell that seemed to go on forever. Then again, that might have had less to do with the number of steps, and more to do with the fact that they were slick with the icy moisture that clung to the air around us. Even using my fire magic to light the way ahead, we had to take each one slowly, lest we slip and tumble into the darkness beyond.

Eventually, the sound of rushing water drifted up the stairwell to greet us—faintly at first, but it grew louder with each step until there was no mistaking it. The stairwell bottomed out into a large underground river. I stopped and stared—the water glowed with some inner light, casting blue and green shadows onto the tunnel walls.

"Bioluminescence," Adara breathed. Her eyes were wide with wonder, ghostly light flickering over her pale features. "There are tiny creatures living in the water that emit a special light," she told me by way of explanation. "That's why the water glows like this."

"Oh." I stared hard at the rushing river, trying to see these creatures, but I couldn't spot anything. They must have been extraordinarily small. "Are they poisonous?" I asked, suspiciously.

"No," Tamil laughed. She wandered over to the edge of the river and hopped into one of the boats that waited for us, tied to a series of posts embedded into the riverbank. "And even if they were, we won't be swimming in the water, anyway."

Adara and I made to follow Tamil into the boat, but the ice fae leaned over the edge and plunged her hand into the water. Layers of ice rippled out from the spot, racing down the river and disappearing into the darkness of the tunnel beyond. Within seconds, the rushing rapids gave way to a thick, shimmering layer of ice, the tiny, glowing beings trapped beneath its frosted surface.

"You want us to skate our way out of here?" I asked Tamil in disbelief.

"Yes." She hopped lightly out of the boat and onto the ice. The frozen surface held her weight, and she slid forward a few feet before executing a perfect pirouette and spinning back toward us. "Is that going to be a problem?"

"I didn't bring skates," I grumbled.

"Neither did I." Tamil took a few glided steps toward us and held out a hand toward us. "Trust me, you don't need them."

"Why freeze the entire river?" Adara asked, casting a puzzled frown toward the boats. "Doing so must have taken an enormous amount of magic."

"Because the boats don't have oars, and my water magic sucks," Tamil said. "I can't control the currents to propel us through the tunnel like other water fae can. But I can freeze the river. Also, I didn't freeze the entire thing—I don't think even Lady Axlya has that much power. Just the stretch that leads through this tunnel. This river runs through half of Lochanlee—some people might get suspicious if the entire thing froze over now, when we are still weeks away from true winter."

With no alternative, the three of us set out across the river, gliding across the frozen surface and doing our best not to crash into the walls. Or rather, *I* was doing my best not to crash into walls. Tamil and Adara were obviously pros at this, skating across the surface as if they were born to it—which, I suppose, they had been. They cast graceful shadows on the tunnel walls as they moved, and I did my best to keep up with them even though I felt like a fish out of water.

Eventually, the ice gave way to water. Tamil created a small ice floe for us to stand on, using it as a raft as we coasted out of the tunnel and into a densely wooded area.

"Thank the Radiants—" I started to say, then stiffened as my senses went on high alert. Slamming my mouth shut, I grabbed Adara and Tamil and yanked them behind a cluster of trees, and not a moment too soon. Seconds later, a troop of earth fae soldiers marched past us, mere feet from our hiding place. My heart thundered in my ears, nearly as loud as the sound of their thumping boots and clanging armor.

"They're mobilizing their forces," Adara whispered as the sounds of their marching faded away. The blood had drained from her face, her knuckles white as she dug her nails into the bark of the tree she was hiding behind. "They're really going to attack the palace, aren't they? This is my fau—"

"Don't you dare blame yourself for this," Tamil snapped. She grabbed Adara's forearm, a fierce expression on her face as she spun the other fae around to face her. "You are not responsible for the designs Axlya and the others have set upon you, nor their petty squabbles. Besides, your presence is half the reason those three are fighting, anyway. The moment they realize you're gone, they'll stop fighting each other—"

"And devote their forces to finding Adara instead," I said grimly.

"Yes," Tamil admitted. "The sooner we get to Bala Oighr, the better."

40

Adara

I t took us the better part of a day to reach Bala Oighr. First, we had to make our way down the mountain the tunnel had deposited us out onto, which, unfortunately, happened to be the same mountain the earth and air armies had made camp on. We'd had to circumnavigate more than one troop of passing soldiers, and nearly ran headlong into army camps twice.

But even though the circumstances were stressful, I couldn't quite keep the smile off my face. I was finally free of that Shadows-damned palace and those insufferable courtiers, *and* I'd learned my mother was still alive! There was still a chance I could save her after I reached the ice priestess and completed the ritual. The thrill of impending victory spurred me onward, banishing my hunger and exhaustion.

By the time we made it down the mountain, the three of us were so paranoid about discovery that we didn't dare chance flying. Instead, we waited until nightfall for Einar to shift, then climbed onto his back and took to the midnight skies.

"I'm c-c-c-c-cold-d-d-d," Tamil chattered. She was sitting

right in front of me, bundled up in her furs. "W-why am I c-cold-d?"

"I don't know," I said, frowning. I felt the bite of the icy evening air, but as usual, I found it invigorating rather than cold. Feeling bad, I wrapped an arm around Tamil's waist and pulled her against me. "Here, you can have some of my warmth."

"Thank the Radiants," she sighed, leaning into me. Her entire body seemed to relax as she soaked in my body heat. "I don't understand how you're not freezing."

"And I don't understand how you're *cold*," I said, bewildered. I reached a hand behind me and pressed it against Einar's hide, feeling the warmth radiating from his scales. "Einar's body heat should be more than enough to keep you warm. He's like a furnace!"

"A furnace?" Tamil echoed. "Are you kidding? His scales feel ice cold! It's like they're leeching the body heat right out of me!"

I looked down at Einar's scales again, at the purplish iridescence shimmering atop their ruby surfaces, and something dawned on me. "Ironhide," I whispered.

"What?" Tamil said.

"Ironhide," I repeated. "Dragons have always been impervious to fae magic while in their beast forms, because of the iron in their scales. That's why you're feeling the chill, even though you should be impervious to the weather as an ice fae. His ironhide is nullifying your magic."

Tamil fell silent for a moment, tilting her head to watch as the stars hurtled past us. "It doesn't affect you, though," she finally said. "Because you're half-dragon."

"I never thought about it... but you must be right." I'd never felt any negative effects from riding on Einar's back, and it hadn't occurred to me that doing so would weaken a fae. I wondered if my mother had experienced the same thing Tamil was going through, or if she'd even ever ridden on my father's back before. Perhaps the mate bond between them had protected her.

The mate bond. I lifted a hand to my neck, brushing my fingers against the spot where Einar had bitten me. We were headed to Bala Oighr, where Tamil's ice priestess stood ready and waiting to perform the ritual. That meant I was no longer beholden to Lady Axlya's wishes—that I didn't have to marry Prentis.

That I could marry Einar instead, if I wanted.

I felt more than heard the rumbling purr that came from Einar's chest, almost as if he knew the direction my thoughts had turned. The vibrations traveled straight to my core, sending a flush of heat through my body, and suddenly, I wished I wasn't pressed against Tamil's back. The close contact seemed inappropriate, given the lustful direction of my thoughts, and I did my best to shove thoughts of Einar out of my mind.

I tried to stay awake through the duration of the flight, but I must have dozed off. One second I was staring at the silvery sea of clouds below me, and the next, Tamil was nudging my knee.

"Wake up, Adara," she said. "We're nearly there."

Blinking, I lifted my head from Tamil's shoulder, then let out a gasp. The rivers and lakes and gently rolling hills of Lochanlee had disappeared, giving way to a vast, rugged tundra. A massive wall of ice loomed beyond it, stretching from one end to the other as far as I could see and rising several miles above the ground to claw at the sky with its jagged edges. The sun was just beginning to crest the horizon, backlighting the wall with buttery yellow rays so it sparkled with the force of a mountain of diamonds.

"You'd better let us down here," Tamil called to Einar, pitching her voice high to be heard over the shrieking winds. "Otherwise the archers will try to take us out, and while your dragon hide will protect you, I'd rather not be turned into a pincushion this morning!"

Einar obeyed, setting us down a mile out from the wall. "This place is freezing," he grumbled once he'd shifted back into bi-pedal form. He hunched his broad shoulders against the stiff wind and rubbed his massive arms, which were clad only in the tunic he'd brought. "I wish I'd thought to fetch a cloak before we made our escape."

"We'll provide you with furs once we get inside," Tamil promised. Flakes of snow fell around us, disappearing into her white hair and frosted eyelashes. "Let's get going."

The three of us trudged through the snowy landscape, keeping our heads down against the wind. Einar did his best to bear the cold, but I could feel his discomfort through our bond, even muted as it was. I sidled closer so I could slip my hand into his, offering him what little warmth I could. He immediately tucked my arm into his, and a warm glow spread through my body, prompting a smile to tug at my cheeks.

"Thank you for flying us here," I whispered, leaning into him. I knew how tired he had to be after traveling through the night.

"You don't have to thank me for that." He turned his head to press a kiss to the top of my cheek. "I would fly through a legion of shadow creatures for you."

Tamil's eyes flickered our way, but she said nothing, allowing us the moment of intimacy. I wondered if she approved or not, and if watching us reminded us of the romance between my parents. Had she supported my mother? Or had she opposed the union like Prentis had?

"Who goes there?" someone shouted as we approached the ice wall. I craned my neck to stare up at the sheer face of the wall, to a lookout tower perched directly above us. One of many towers, I realized as I scanned the top of the wall. They were spaced about a dozen yards apart, each lit with torches and manned with a pair of archers. The one speaking to us now had his bow drawn, and I tried not to be intimidated by the arrow aimed directly at my face.

"It's me, Diren," Tamil called back, lowering her hood to reveal her face. "Tamil. These are my companions, Adara and Einar. My father is expecting us."

I started, having forgotten about Tamil's father. She'd mentioned that he was bedridden, hanging onto life by a mere thread. Did she find time to send word to him about our arrival, despite escaping on such short notice?

"All right," Diren shouted back after a long moment. "One second."

A large, rectangular section of the wall, about twice my height and five times my width, melted away, revealing a passage for us. Tamil led the way, Einar bringing up the rear, and I followed between them. The walls of the ice tunnel glittered around us, bathing us in a ghostly blue glow not dissimilar to the eerie light the underground river had given off earlier. While the tunnel was more than large enough to accommodate us, I couldn't help but be aware of the thousands of tons of ice above us, pressing in from all sides. Sweat crept along my temples as my mind threatened to conjure nightmarish scenarios, and I had to press my lips together to keep myself from urging Tamil to walk faster.

The ice wall isn't going to come crashing down on top of us, I reminded myself. *It has literally held for thousands of years.*

We emerged on the other side of the wall to find the two guards from the top of the wall waiting for us. "Lady Tamil," Diren said, confusion on his face as he beheld us. "The last I heard, you were at the war council in Usciete. How did you get here so quickly, on foot?"

"We didn't come on foot," Tamil said. She swept her hand

toward Einar and said, "Einar here is a dragon. He was kind enough to give us a ride... though as a fae, I don't recommend riding on dragonback unless you'd like to have all your magic siphoned out of your body. Please fetch us a few mounts from the stables. I'd rather not walk all the way to the fortress, or ride on dragonback again anytime soon."

She shuddered a little, and guilt wracked me as I noticed the shadows beneath her eyes and the gaunt expression on her face. She'd been putting on a brave face, keeping pace with us as we trudged through the snow... but then again, maybe she was only able to keep up because we were all tired. Einar had flown through the night, and I'd been fasting for ten days. None of us were in peak condition, to say the least.

"A dragon?" Diren's companion yelped. He reached for his sword, and Einar let out a low growl, shifting his body in front of mine. "How is that possible? All the dragons are supposed to be dead!"

"I've heard rumors of a dragon spotted in the attack on Kaipei Castle," Diren said. His eyes narrowed on me. "Are you the fae who killed King Aolis?"

I swallowed hard at the censure in his eyes, and looked to Tamil. I knew in the back of my mind that rumors about me had to be swirling through the countryside. Many of the Edirian citizens would look at me as a traitor rather than a savior of the realm, since they didn't know the truth about King Aolis and the shadow creatures.

"It's a long story, Diren," Tamil said heavily, "and I'm tired. But you know me, and you know our father. Would we bring a murderer into Bala Oighr?"

"No," Diren said. "Not willingly. But you might be tricked into helping one."

Tamil squared her shoulders and looked the soldier dead in the eye. "I realize you're being protective," she said in a steely tone, "but I gave you an order, and as the acting ruler of Bala Oighr, I don't owe you any explanation."

I expected the ice fae soldier to argue, but he snapped to attention. "Right away, my lady," he said, his cheeks pink from being chastised. He spun on his heel and strode toward a cluster of buildings, where I suspected the horses were kept.

The other soldier remained behind, staring curiously at me. "I heard some rumors about the attack on Kaipei too," he said. "That you're the daughter of our beloved late Princess Olette and that dragon prince she married. Is that true?"

"It is," I said.

He nodded. "If that's the case, then don't pay Diren any mind. Olette was as much an ice fae as I am, which means you're one of us. You're welcome here in Bala Oighr."

"Thank you." Relief swept through me, and I gave him a grateful smile. Not everyone in Bala Oighr seemed to be against me, which had to mean that there were others in Ediria on my side as well. I wondered what the villagers in Fenwood thought, if they would hail me as a hero if I ever returned, but somehow, I doubted it. I'd been forced to flee, since half the village had tried to turn me in to General Slaugh. I wondered if the other half who had defended me, including Mavlyn's parents, regretted their choice after learning I'd killed their beloved king.

The sound of hooves crunching on snow distracted me from my thoughts. I turned toward the sound, expecting to see Diren leading a trio of horses toward us, and a gasp flew from my mouth. It was Diren all right, and he'd brought us mounts—but the two massive creatures following him weren't horses. They were stags, their shaggy white coats and enormous crowns of antlers branching out from their magnificent heads a dead giveaway.

"They're gorgeous," I gushed, closing the distance between

myself and the magnificent creatures before I could stop myself. "Can I pet one?"

"Sure," Diren said gruffly. He held out the reins he clutched in his left hand toward me. "This is Silas. He'll be carrying you and your dragon."

"Silas," I cooed, stroking a hand down his great snout. The beast's thickly lashed eyelids slid to half mast, enjoying the attention. "It's lovely to meet you."

"If it's all the same," Einar said from behind me, "I think I'll follow you two from the air."

I glanced over my shoulder to see him eyeing the stags warily. "Are you afraid?" I asked, a little incredulous.

"I'm not *afraid*," Einar protested. "It's just, I've never ridden a stag before."

I glanced back at Silas, eyeing the saddle and harness strapped to him. "Seems like it would be the same as riding a horse," I said.

"I've never ridden a horse, either."

I swung around to face Einar, the stag forgotten. "Are you telling me that you, Einar, the fearsome general of the dragon army, have never received horseback riding training?"

He scowled, crossing his arms over his chest. "I'm a dragon," he said, as if that explained everything. "Why should I ride a beast of burden when I can ride the skies instead?"

Tamil snorted as she swung herself up onto her own mount. "That's a lot of words for 'I'm afraid of riding'," she said.

"Don't be ridiculous," Einar huffed, his wings snapping out from behind him as he transformed into his half-dragon form. "I'm not afraid. Flying means I'll be able to monitor any potential threats from the skies." He strode over to me as if to prove he was unafraid of the stag, then dropped a kiss on my forehead. "I'll see you at the fortress," he murmured against my skin.

"Okay," I agreed. "But it's okay to admit you're afraid."

"Maybe." His lips brushed against my ear, and I shivered. "But only to you."

He took a few steps back, then launched himself into the pearlescent sky, leaving me to stare after him. Dazed, I shook my head a little to clear it, then mounted Silas.

"Are you ready?" Tamil asked as I settled into the saddle.

I nodded. "Let's go."

We urged our stags into a trot, heading for the ice fortress looming in the distance. The fortress sat at the top of a mountain, and beneath it lay a sprawling city about an hour's ride away. The city was called Whitecrest, Tamil explained as we rode, but while it was the heart of Bala Oighr, it was hardly the only settlement in ice fae territory. We passed several smaller towns and villages on our way through the snowy landscape. Many of the dwellings were crafted from blocks of ice and snow, though there were a few log cabins. The villagers were all pale and snowy haired like Tamil, but while they did wear fur-trimmed cloaks, the fabrics of their tunics and dresses were quite thin considering the freezing environment.

"We don't actually need thick layers except in extreme temperatures," Tamil told me when I asked about it. She tugged at the fur trimmed sleeves of her own coat and winked at me. "I wore these furs to Usciete for show."

"I wish we had more time to explore," I told her as we passed by a colorful hot spring tucked behind a cluster of boulders. I could just make out the silhouettes of three fae reclining there within the clouds of steam. My tired bones and aching muscles cried out in protest as we continued past them. We'd passed three such hot springs, as well as majestic frozen lakes, incredible ice cliffs and formations, and other dazzling wonders. We'd also seen silver bison, white wolves, and snowy eagles, and once I thought I glimpsed a yeti peeking at us through a copse of trees.

"I'll give you a grand tour of the Bala Oighr once you've completed the ritual and defeated Nox," Tamil promised. "Your mother and I spent countless days exploring the many treasures of the ice realm. I'll tell you all about our adventures together."

"I'd like that," I said. A soft smile curved my lips as I looked at Tamil, and I added, "I'm glad I met you, and not just because you helped me escape. It's nice to meet someone who had a close relationship with my biological mother." Someone who could fill in the gaps and help me feel more connected with the female who'd given her life to bring me into the world.

Einar coasted through the skies above us, following closely so he could swoop in to the rescue in case any of the beasts or fae we encountered tried to attack us. But we ran into no threats, and he joined us on the ground when we reached the outer walls of the fortress. Someone had been alerted of our arrival, as a groomsman was already ready and waiting to take our mounts. We dismounted, then went inside, where a servant took Tamil's half-frozen cloak and offered the three of us hot mead to warm ourselves.

"Thank the Radiants," Einar groaned, taking a sip of the piping hot golden liquid. I nearly did the same before I remembered I was fasting, and reluctantly handed him my glass, which he downed in one swallow. "Sorry," he said, looking a little guilty as he set the glasses aside. "But I needed that."

"It's okay." I tried to smile at him through the sudden weight of exhaustion dragging at my limbs. "I'll be able to enjoy some mead after completing the ritual tomorrow."

"Tamil!" someone cried. We turned to see a group of ice fae spill into the foyer—a tall, handsome fae male, and three younger ice fae, one who resembled the male while the other two clearly favored Tamil. Heartfelt greetings and kisses were exchanged, and Tamil introduced them—the tall one was Havor, her fiancé, the other male Riven, his younger brother and the fortress's steward, and the twin girls were Lora and Nora, her younger sisters.

"It's a pleasure to meet you," Havor said, pumping my hand a little too enthusiastically. He didn't even seem put off by Einar, despite having his wings and claws out on full display. "We weren't sure if Tamil would be able to bring you back here, but we're glad she did."

"You weren't sure?" I glanced between Havor and Tamil. "Do you mean to say that you planned this?"

"Not exactly," Tamil hedged. "But after that initial meeting in the Hall of Mirrors, I gathered you weren't staying in Usciete Palace wholly of your own volition, and that perhaps you were tangled in one of Lady Axlya's many webs. As ice fae, we know better than anyone else about the prophecy King Aolis was obsessed with. He came to Bala Oighr every year to test each our children for fire magic, and we lived in fear that one of our babes would be stolen from us. But Lady Axlya never shared Aolis's obsession with finding you. She doesn't care about fulfilling the terms of the prophecy, only with making sure House Usciete maintains control of the throne. So I knew I needed to come as quickly as possible, and be there for you in case you needed to escape."

"You're even prettier than I thought you'd be," one of the twins said, smiling at me. "I think you'll make a great queen."

I blushed, the praise of a twelve-year-old somehow more impactful than all of Prentis's flattery combined. "I hope so," I told her, not having the heart to say that I didn't know if I was going to end up as queen at all. I'd thrown away all hope of controlling the succession when I'd fled Usciete, and if I were honest with myself, I didn't regret it.

Tamil's family looked like they wanted to question us, but Einar placed a hand on my shoulder. "If it's all the same to you," he said in that rumbling voice of his, "Adara is exhausted from her travels. I think she ought to rest, especially since she's still fasting."

"Of course," Tamil said, contrite. She turned to Riven. "Have the guest rooms been prepared?"

"Yes." He inclined his head toward me. "I've told the kitchen staff to prepare a feast in your honor, for after you complete the ritual. And we've sent a message to the priestess to make preparations at the temple."

"Preparations?" I turned to Tamil, hope rising in my chest. "Does that mean we'll be able to perform the ritual soon?"

"Yes." She grinned at me, the first genuine smile I'd seen since our escape. "Get some sleep, Adara. Your big day is tomorrow, and you need all the rest you can get."

41

Adara

I woke up to the sight of my mother staring down at me.

Not my actual mother, of course. That would have scared me straight out of bed—maybe out of the fortress entirely. But the white-haired female in the portrait hanging over the mantle was the late Princess Olette, according to the servant who'd shown me to this guestroom. The fae who stared back at me wasn't quite the same one who'd given birth to me, though. This portrait had been painted when my mother was only fourteen years old, her face still soft with the final echoes of girlhood, her hair loose around her face and adorned with a single white lily tucked behind her ear.

She'd chosen to wear an eggshell blue gown for the portrait, the high-waist empire cut hiding most of her still-slender figure, which hadn't yet filled out into curves. There was little of me in her facial features, but her tall, gangly frame was almost identical to my own teenage body before I'd blossomed into full adulthood. I wondered if she'd felt just as awkward and out of place as I had during those years, caught somewhere in the transition between child to adult, a stranger to my own body. And whether those feelings had disappeared once she'd completed her coming-of-age ceremony.

"Adara?" Tamil's voice filtered through the door as she knocked lightly. "Are you awake?"

"Yeah," I called sleepily, pushing myself upright. I let out a jaw-cracking yawn as she opened the door and padded in, then sat up straighter when a trio of servants followed in behind her, carrying makeup and jewelry and a gossamer gown made of some pure white material. "What is all this?"

"We're getting you ready for the ritual," Tamil said, as though it were obvious. She tilted her head toward the window, where the sky was just beginning to lighten. "I tried to let you sleep as long as possible so you'd have your strength, but we must get to the ice temple before dawn to begin the ceremony."

"I see." I swung my legs over the side of the bed, feeling a little uncertain. I'd crashed into a deep, dreamless sleep the moment the servant had shut the door behind me last night, and hadn't woken once through the night, not even to change out of my clothes. "I didn't realize we were beginning so soon."

"Are you not ready?" Tamil asked, eyeing me closely. She seemed in far better health than she had yesterday, a healthy pink flush beneath her pale skin, but a hint of shadow still clung beneath her ice-blue eyes. I suspected she hadn't gone straight to bed the way I had—as the acting ruler of Bala Oighr, she probably had many matters requiring her attention that had to be dealt with before bed. "The priestess has already begun preparations at the temple, but if you require another day of fasting—"

"No!" I hurried to cut her off, refusing to let anyone delay things. "No, I'm definitely ready." The morning rays of sunlight streaming through the window behind me seemed to suffuse my body with energy—I was practically humming with it, especially after nearly twenty hours of deep, restful sleep. "I had just woken when you knocked."

"Oh. Well, that's understandable." She smiled, looking relieved, then motioned to the servants. One of them veered off to the en-suite bathroom, while the other set down the dress and accessories. "Let's get you ready, then."

Tamil and the servants rushed me through the bathing and dressing process, styling my hair in simple waves that cascaded down my back, and fastening tiny diamond pins at my ears. The gossamer dress drifted around my body like layers of white mist, making me feel almost ethereal as I stood before the mirror.

Once I was dressed, Tamil led me out into the hallway, where Einar waited along with a contingent of ice soldiers. "They're here to escort us to the temple," she said as we started down the corridor. "I doubt Axlya's soldiers will get here in time to stop us, but we can't take any chances."

I nodded, her words barely registering as I locked gazes with Einar. His golden eyes shone as he stared at me, and I stood a little taller, fighting against the urge to preen beneath his stare. Not a word passed between us, but it wasn't necessary—the pride and affection swelling inside him was almost tangible, filling me with confidence and banishing my nerves.

I could do this. I was ready.

The ice temple was located inside a cave at the peak of the mountain, several miles above the ice fortress. Two sets of steps carved entirely of ice had been laid into the face of the mountain, and to my astonishment, they seemed to be moving, one set rippling up, and the other one disappearing into the mountain's base.

"Ingenious, isn't it?" Tamil said with a grin. She placed her boot on the first step, which started to rise, pushing her effortlessly toward the top of the mountain. "We call it the ice-calator. Saves a lot of time."

Einar and I exchanged dubious glances, but we stepped onto the moving staircase, not wanting to be left behind. I had to hold my skirts in my hand to keep them from getting caught between the moving steps, but this was still a lot better than trying to climb a mountain in this outfit.

Time seemed to slow to a crawl as Einar and I both kept our eyes locked on the mountain peak, our hands laced together. The platform rose higher, still, and I had to make a genuine effort not to look down as we stepped off, for fear of seeing the dizzying drop beneath our feet.

The path to the cave was wide and welcoming, lined with chunks of ice that were clear as crystal. The sun rays struck them, creating a kaleidoscope of light on the ground before us, and I felt like I was walking across a bridge made of rainbows. Tamil led the way, to the entrance, then paused, gesturing for us to go first. Einar sucked in a sharp breath as he took the first step forward, and I kept pace with him, one hand still in his, the other holding my skirts so I wouldn't trip.

The entrance was simple, the walls of ice arching over us like a tunnel with intricate loops and spirals carved into them. Ice crystals grew overhead, dripping down from the ceiling like stalactites. They exaggerated the kaleidoscope effect of the sunlight filtering through the ice.

A wide staircase brought us down from the entrance into the temple, which had to have taken years to carve. The floor mimicked the same spiral patterns seen in the tunnel, but on a grand, intricate scale with never-repeating individual snowflake patterns woven into the spiral from the center that I admired upon our descent. From the ceiling hung an ice chandelier with geometric crystals containing twinkling lights in violet, cerulean, and white. The cool light illuminated a series of ice sculptures in the shapes of bears, elk, and foxes, all of which stood regally along either side of the temple, like frozen guardians forever bound to protect this sacred place.

A tall fae clad in ice-blue robes stood in the center of the main hall, surrounded by half a dozen white-robed acolytes. Her bluish-white hair was bound into a mass of tiny braids and gathered at her nape into a queue, and her regal features were marked by tiny snowflake tattoos, starting from one end of her brow to the other, almost like a tiara made of stars.

"Welcome, Adara," she said, her serene voice echoing through the temple. "My name is Tuliana, and I am the priestess of this temple. It's an honor to have you here."

"The honor is mine," I said, bowing my head. "I'm indebted to you for agreeing to perform the ritual with me on such short notice." My heart beat faster with anticipation—after almost two weeks of fasting, interspersed with political battles and assassination attempts, this was finally happening.

The priestess laughed, the sound like ice crystals tinkling in the wind. "My dear child," she said warmly, stepping forward to take my hand. "You are the girl who was promised by the spirits themselves to save us from this curse of darkness. I assure you, it is my honor to be the one to empower you, to give you the weapons you need to fight back against these shadow demons who are so intent on destroying our home. Now come," she said, before I could argue. "There is much to do."

She led me into the temple's inner sanctum, leaving the others to wait behind. I cast one last anxious look at Einar, who gave me a reassuring smile, before the doors shut behind me, sealing me into the chamber with the priestess and her acolytes.

I expected to see some kind of altar or slab, but instead, a circle of ice crystals awaited me, each of them lit from within by a different color on the light spectrum. The rays of light fractured and bounced off the walls, creating a kaleidoscopic rainbow that seemed to swirl around the room. I stood there for a long moment, transfixed by the colors, before Tuliana tugged on my sleeve, drawing me toward the circle.

"You must enter the circle alone," she instructed me in a gentle voice.

I did as she said at once, not wanting her to doubt my readiness. The moment I stepped within the ice crystal circle, vibrations traveled through my body, from the soles of my bare feet all the way to the top of my skull. It was as though I could *feel* the lights emanating from the crystals, as if their wavelengths had taken on a tangible form.

A floor pillow awaited me in the center of the circle, along with a small, steaming cup of tea. I sat down on the cushion and took the cup in both hands, inhaling the fragrant steam. The scent was like nothing I'd smelled before—it reminded me of dreams and starlight and wide open spaces, as if the tea leaves themselves held all the endless possibilities of the world.

"Am I to drink this?" I asked Tuliana. She and the other acolytes had settled into cross-legged, seated positions around the edge of the circle, forming a protective barrier around me. The sight was somehow both unnerving and comforting. I was still unused to such focused scrutiny from a large number of people, but at the same time, it was nice to know that I wouldn't be alone in this.

"Yes. The tea will put you into a special trance that will open your mind, allowing you to see the threads that connect you to the rest of the universe. This will enable you to find the inner beast that lurks within you, so she can awaken." The priestess held out her hands to either side of her, and she and all the acolytes joined hands, sealing the circle. "While you are doing so, we will chant the ritual hymn. The words will guide you, but there's no need to focus on them too much—simply let the hymn flow through you, and your mind will follow."

Nodding, I swallowed back my nerves, then lifted the cup to my lips and downed the tea in one go. The hot liquid was bittersweet, and as it slid down my throat and into my stomach, my skin began to tingle.

The priestess and her acolytes began their hymn, and I did as she asked, closing my eyes and allowing the words to drift through my mind. The hymn was in the ancient fae language, so I couldn't understand it. But I felt something within me unfurl, as if the map of my life was opening up to show me a glimpse of the future.

The tingles that spread throughout my body shifted, fading away in some places while intensifying in others, like myriad tiny hands tugging my body in different directions. I opened my eyes, and nearly gasped aloud at the sight of dozens of glowing strings emanating from different points in my body— an ankle here, a knuckle there, the crook of my elbow, the tip of my ear. They seemed to disappear into infinity, but when I focused on the one tugging at my pinky, the others faded away. An image coalesced out of the kaleidoscope of colors bouncing around the room—a dragon male and a fae female holding hands and staring at me, love brimming from their eyes.

"We're so proud of you," they said, their voices echoing in the ice chamber.

"Mom. Dad." There was no doubt in my mind it was them. I'd never seen a picture of Daryan, but the cuff clasped around the wrist of the male was identical to the one wrapped around my bicep. The female was a dead ringer for the girl whose portrait hung in my room, her curves filled out, the softness in her face given way to high cheekbones and a sharp yet feminine jaw. I reached out to touch them, but the moment my fingers made contact, they dissipated into a cloud of smoke, and the other strings winked back into existence.

Disappointment welled inside me, but the feeling drifted away on the melodic refrain of the hymn, replaced by a natural curiosity. One by one, I mentally reached for the other strings, looking to see where they led to. Each one conjured visions of people and places—some obvious, like Mother and Mavlyn and Fenwood Village, while others belonged to people and places I didn't recognize. I wish I knew whether they were from my past or my future, but the universe didn't seem to differentiate between different points on the timeline.

I supposed the truth would reveal itself to me, in time. If I even remembered all of this when it was over.

I looked down at my palm and noticed there was another string, this one not attached like the others, but laying contentedly in my palm, as if waiting for me to tie it to myself. I lifted my head as I followed its ember glow, and sucked in a sharp breath at the sight of a flaming red and gold dragon hovering before me. Our eyes met, and my heart sang in recognition. This was the metaphysical incarnation of Einar's soul, and the string that flowed from the tip of his fiery tail into the palm of my hand was the representation of our bond. It wasn't connected to me, not yet. But it could be, if I wanted it to.

I closed my hand around the thread, and a comforting pulse of warmth traveled up my arm and into my heart. Smiling, I tucked the thread into my pocket for later, when the time was right.

And then I reached for the thread that was tied to my chest.

The moment I touched it, a bluish-white orb appeared in front of me, emanating a light so fierce I had to squint my eyes against it. Tears blurred my vision as the orb unfurled into a long, sinuous shape, and when I blinked them away, I found myself staring at another dragon.

But this wasn't the fiery spirit I'd seen earlier. This dragon was carved out of ice—it shimmered in the rows of crystal scales that flowed over her muscular form, glinted sharply in the icicle-like spikes jutting from her spine. Her cornflower-blue eyes glowed with an inner flame that called to something within me, and I knew in an instant that she was me, and I was her.

This was the spiritual manifestation of my beast.

I'd found her.

As our eyes locked, something within my chest began to open, like blossoms unfurling to greet the rising sun. My inner fire ignited within my chest, the way it did when I was about to call it to my palms. But so did the icy river that also snaked within my soul, pushing frosted power into my blood. The two veins of magic rushed into the air before me, visible to my naked eye for the first time, and I watched with wide eyes as they clashed, expecting an explosion of energy as the warring elements fought for dominance.

But though steam and spitting sparks filled the air, something began to shift. I stared down at my palms to see a strange, golden-green light spill from my skin, softly at first, then brighter and brighter until I was forced to turn my palms away to keep from blinding myself. The power swelled inside me until I felt I was about to burst, and I reached for my beast at the same time she reached for me—

Shrill screams ripped me from the vision before we could make contact, throwing me unceremoniously back into reality. I blinked hard, trying to make sense of the pandemonium—hulking soldiers in black armor, white-robed acolytes flying, deep red blood spattering on the rainbow-dappled walls.

But before I could reconcile it all, someone grabbed me by the hair and yanked me to my feet.

"Well, well," a familiar voice, one I never thought to hear again, sneered in my ear. Shock rippled through me as I twisted my neck to stare into the face of Dune Terran. His hair and eyes were pitch black, his skin the color of obsidian, but the face of my childhood bully and the fae I'd once fancied myself in love with was unmistakable despite the shadow corruption that had warped him. "Look what we found here."

"Dune?" I spoke the name uncertainly, not entirely sure if this was yet another vision. Something cold and hard clamped around my wrists, but I barely noticed, my mind still whirling. "What is this?" His fingers dug into my scalp, preventing me from turning to look at him. "Let go of me!"

"Not a chance," he said, a wicked grin lighting up his rugged features. He loosened his grip on my hair enough to spin me around, and my stomach lurched as I took him in. He wore the black regalia and armor of the shadow guard, and a dark aura pulsed around him, more potent than General Slaugh's and nearly as sickening as Nox's power. "Not after all the trouble I've gone through. Your dragon may have saved you from my golem, but he won't be able to protect you now. It's time for me to finish you off."

42

Einar

"How much longer do you think she's going to be in there?" I asked Tamil as we stood guard outside the inner sanctum.

The aquamarine light shimmering from the cavern walls played across Tamil's pale face as she turned to give me a wry look. "Sometimes it takes a few hours. Sometimes it takes days. I think the longest recorded coming-of-age ritual was just six hours shy of being a full week long."

"A week?" I nearly shouted the words before remembering that Adara was just on the other side of the door. "I'm not sure we have that kind of time. General Slaugh and the others will find us long before that."

Tamil rolled her eyes. "That's the worst-case scenario, Einar. It's not going to take a week. No one I know has taken longer than a day. Besides, don't your own rituals take just as long?"

"Anywhere from one to three days," I agreed gruffly. "But the fate of the world doesn't usually rest on them."

I glanced at the double doors to the inner sanctum,

wondering how Adara was faring. She'd been in there close to five hours already. If this was anything like the Umnar, she would have ingested a hallucinogenic tea to open her mind, propelling her into the spiritual journey that would lead her to her inner beast. I wanted her to experience the same intense rush of power and unshakable sense of self I had when I'd connected with my dragon form for the first time.

I just wanted her to do it a little faster.

"Do you hear that?" Tamil asked as a rumble shook the cavern. Dust particles rained from the ceiling, and we froze at the sound of alarmed shouts. A wave of dark magic rippled through the air, and I automatically shifted into my half-dragon form, wings bursting from my back.

"I'll go check it out," I growled. Tamil shouted after me as I ran forward, but I launched myself in the air, clearing the switchback stairwell in a few short wing beats. I landed inside the mouth of the cave to find a full-scale battle taking place just outside. My mouth dropped open at the sight of ten shadow guard soldiers tearing into the small group of ice fae Tamil had posted outside the cavern entrance. How had they cleared the ice wall and gotten all the way here without raising an alarm?

But a sickening realization lurched through me as I remembered how General Slaugh had taken Adara. He'd opened a portal using shadow magic, then grabbed her and yanked her through it before any of us could stop him. The shadow guards must have used the same magic to get here.

These thoughts all flitted through my head in a split second, and then I was charging forward, picking up a fallen sword as I ran with one hand, a massive fireball already building in the other. Tamil's soldiers fought valiantly, but the shadow soldiers were tearing through them, using their tainted magic to crumble their ice shields and strike at their hearts. I ran up behind one as he stood over a terrified ice fae, boot on his chest, mace swinging down toward his head, and drove my sword straight through his back. His death scream rent the air as another shadow soldier ran toward me, and I blasted him with the fireball in my free hand, sending him flying down the mountainside.

"Einar!" Tamil appeared at my side, an ice javelin clutched in her hand. Fury blazed in her ice-blue eyes as she threw the weapon, aiming for a tall, dark-skinned shadow guard ten yards away. This one was different from the rest—he wielded raw shadow magic rather than the tainted elemental powers of his fellow guards, using it to destroy his enemies where they stood. Without even looking away from the fae dangling from his fist, he caught the ice javelin with his free hand. The elemental weapon melted instantly, raining onto the stony ground at his feet while the fae in his other hand rotted away, skin, hair and eyes consumed by the black magic permeating his veins.

"What is this madness?" Tamil shouted as black spikes burst from the ice fae's skin. "What are you doing to him?"

The shadow soldier turned toward us with a grin, and my stomach lurched as I recognized him from Adara's description. "You're Dune. The earth fae boy who broke Adara's heart, then tried to turn her in to General Slaugh."

"At your service." He sketched a mocking bow, releasing the ice fae as he did so. To the mutual horror of both Tamil and me, the fae turned in our direction with a snarl, baring sharp fangs dripping with inky venom. There was nothing left of the person he'd been inside the soulless eyes that glared out of his mottled black face—only a deep-seated, animalistic hunger.

"As for what I'm doing... I've turned him into my slave," Dune said nonchalantly, as if reducing fae to mindless monsters was no big deal. "Mistress Nox ordered me to kill you and Adara, but I don't see why I should have to do all the dirty work myself."

He snapped his fingers, and the fae bounded forward with terrifying speed, an unearthly scream tearing from his throat.

Tamil and I dove out of the way, the ice fae dropping into a forward roll while I took to the skies, beating my wings hard to gain altitude as quickly as possible.

"Go after Adara!" Tamil shouted as I conjured more fireballs to rain down on the beast. "I'll handle the creature!"

Tamil slammed her fist into the ground, sending a wave of ice across the battlefield just as the shadow creature charged. It shrieked as it lost its footing, skidding sideways across the ground to slam into the mountainside. The other shadow guards started flailing as well, their armored boots not made for icy terrain. The remaining ice fae soldiers rallied, and Tamil conjured another javelin, stalking toward the creature as it regained its feet.

Tearing my gaze away from the scene, I dove through the cave entrance and arrowed toward Dune, who was halfway across the temple floor, a handful of shadow guards in tow. He turned just in time for me to body slam him, letting out a surprised grunt as I took him to the ground. I tucked my wings in to protect them as we rolled across the slick cavern floor, my claws shredding his armor like paper and leaving deep gouge marks in his skin. Black blood seeped from the wounds and into my skin, and a wave of nausea swept through me as I felt the shadow magic permeate my body.

Even so, I refused to let go. Not until the bastard was dead.

"I'll never let you touch her," I snarled, closing my scale-armored hand around his throat. "Even if it means sacrificing my own life."

Dune grinned up at me, his expression tinged with madness. "That can be arranged," he croaked even as I squeezed his windpipe. My claws sank into the soft flesh of his neck, black blood sluicing over my fingers, and—

Pain exploded in the back of my skull as one of the other shadow guards struck me from behind. Stunned, my grip on

Dune's neck loosened, and the next thing I knew, I was flying through the air. My wings crunched as my back slammed into the wall, and I roared in pain, trying to blink away the stars dancing in my vision so I could find my enemy.

But there was no need to look—Dune was right in front of me, a maniacal gleam in his fathomless dark eyes as he pressed the palm of his hand into the center of my chest. The dark magic in my veins spread faster, clouding my mind with bloodlust and rage. Suddenly, I no longer knew where I was, what I was doing, or why I was there.

I only knew the monstrous need for murder.

"You'll be sacrificing your life all right," Dune said, his voice distorted and far away as the shadow magic took hold. "But for me, not Adara."

43

Adara

My mind spun as Dune hauled me out of the inner sanctum by my hair, his shadow guards trailing behind him. My feet dragged through pools of blood, but I could barely feel the horror of it because I didn't have full control of my body. The visions had disappeared, but the tea was still doing its work, weakening my mind-body connection so my limbs felt heavy and numb.

I could hear the sounds of fighting coming from outside the cave, but down here it was deathly silent, the cavernous space littered with the dead bodies of acolytes and ice fae soldiers. Four more shadow guards waited for us, and my heart sank at the sight of the sagging male on his knees, his upper body held up between two of them.

"Einar," I choked out, my eyes filling with tears. Fury pumped fresh strength through my limbs, and I grabbed Dune's arm, forcing him to a stop. "What have you done to him?" I demanded.

"Done to him?" Dune smiled as he released my hair, sending

me stumbling backward a few steps. "That's a funny way to thank me for sparing your lover's life. I could have had him killed, you know, but here he is, waiting for you to return to him."

A rumbling growl filled the cavern, and trepidation skittered down my spine as Einar lifted his head. My insides froze at the sight of the black veins running across his face and into his eyes, eclipsing his golden irises. That growl turned into a terrifying snarl as black spikes ripped through his skin, and he leaped to his feet, throwing off the grips of his captors.

"No," I said, voice shaking as he took a menacing step toward me. "Einar, please."

He paused, and the hesitation gave me hope. "I know you're still in there, Einar," I pleaded, taking a tentative step toward him. "Fight this, please."

I looked down at the palms of my hands, willing the golden magic from earlier to come to the surface. But though I could feel it churning inside me, it refused to come out, trapped behind the dragon part of my soul that hadn't fully awoken. Flames sprang to my hands instead, flickering weakly as though they were oxygen starved.

"Don't listen to her," Dune snapped, irritation flickering over his features. The ugly look in his eyes made my stomach turn— how had I ever been attracted to him? "She's fae, the enemy— her ancestors have slaughtered thousands of your kind. Don't you want to make her pay?"

Einar threw back his head and let out a roar that shook the cavern. Ice crystals rained down from the ceiling as he charged me, and I dodged, barely moving out of the way fast enough. Drawing from the last reserves of my strength, I hit him with a blast of ice magic, freezing his feet to the ground to buy myself time. But the ice melted away almost instantly, the dragon hide encasing his lower legs nullifying my power.

"Why are you doing this?" I cried, tearing my gaze from Einar to look at Dune. The sickening glee on his face as he watched Einar and I fight turned my stomach. "Why are you being so cruel to me, after everything you've already done?"

"Everything *I've* done?" Dune's smile dropped as his lip curled into a sneer. "You're the one who killed our king, Adara, and forced our kingdom to the brink of civil war. You're the reason everything is careening out of control. The Mother of Shadows told me that killing you would help restore the balance, and I'm more than happy to oblige. Besides," he added, the smirk returning, "you never put out, Adara, even after I spent all that time and effort trying to woo you. This is my way of getting the pleasure I'm owed."

An unholy amount of disgust filled me at those words, but before I could respond, Einar rushed me.

"That's it," Dune crowed as the male I loved rammed his shoulder into my midsection. "Kill her and take your revenge!"

The force of the blow threw me backward. If I'd been at full strength, I could have back flipped through the air and landed safely, but my limbs were still uncoordinated, and I crashed into the ground instead. Einar was on top of me in an instant, his clawed hand wrapping around my throat. Weakly, I scrabbled at his chest, but my strength was ineffectual, and the edges of my vision began to darken.

Sagging into the ground, I looked up into the face of the male who had promised to protect me. I knew I should feel hurt and betrayal, but I only felt sadness that this was the way our story was to end. That I would die by his hand, and he would live out the rest of his days as a mindless shadow slave. That we had never completed the bond, never fully realized the potential of our relationship.

"I love you," I whispered, reaching up to touch his face. If I could do nothing else, I wanted to say those words to him at least once before I died.

Einar froze as my fingertips brushed his cheeks. His eyes flickered from pitch black to fiery gold, back and forth, back and forth, and his grip on my throat loosened. Another growl rumbled from his chest, and hope sparked inside me as I realized the real Einar was still inside, still trying to fight for me.

"What are you doing?" Dune shouted from somewhere nearby. "Finish her, you idiot!"

Einar's hand flexed around my throat, as if he couldn't decide whether to let go or squeeze harder. I tightened my grip on his head, pulling him closer to me, as if I was going to kiss him. The hand on my throat loosened further, his body trembling against mine, and my teeth ached as a familiar warmth swept through my body.

"I love you," I said again, and I struck.

Fangs punched through my gums and into the flesh of Einar's neck, and he let out another earth-shaking roar as pure white light flared between us. The light was so blinding that I had to close my eyes against it, and I heard Dune and the others stumble back, hissing. Einar bucked against me, but I wrapped my arms and legs around him, holding him fast as I sucked on the wound. The shadow magic pulsing in his veins poured into me, and the golden magic inside me went to work, disintegrating the black corruption before it could take hold.

But the shadow magic wasn't the only thing I took from Einar. I also drew on his strength, pulling his fire into me to bolster my flagging reserves. Heat and light and magic flared between us as the bond opened wide, and I gasped against his neck as pure energy rushed into me. I took as much as I could, then allowed some to filter back into him, mingling a bit of my life force with his.

"Adara," Einar whispered, and my heart swelled with joy at the sound of my mate's voice. "I'm so sorry."

I opened my mouth to say something, but before I could, someone ripped Einar from my arms. I leaped to my feet as Dune and the other shadow guard attacked, fire racing up my arms as I blasted the closest two. They screamed as they went up in flames, my fire eating through their armor and devouring their flesh.

"Your pathetic fire magic won't save you!" Dune shouted. He struck Einar with a pulse of shadow magic, and I cried out as it slammed into Einar's chest. But though the blow sent him stumbling back, the magic itself seemed to bounce harmlessly off him, as if it couldn't find purchase.

Einar's eyes widened, first with surprise, then delight. "Well, well," he said, a wicked grin spreading across his face. "It looks like I'm immune to shadow magic now."

Dune gave him an ugly smile. "That may be so," he said as the other shadow guards took up position around us. "But you're severely outnumbered."

I glanced around at the twenty or so guards, my heart sinking a little. Even with Einar's magic coursing through me, I wasn't at full strength, and neither was he now that I'd taken power from him.

"If you surrender," Dune said in a soft voice, "I'll spare the rest of the ice fae. No one else has to die tonight."

I clenched my fists. The sounds of fighting had died away from outside. I didn't want to think about what that meant, didn't want to think about the fact that Tamil wasn't here, didn't want to consider that after everything, Einar and I could still lose this.

"You're lying," Einar snarled. "Even if you show them mercy today, the ice fae will still die by your shadow mistress's hand eventually. Sparing them now won't save them from that fate."

Dune opened his mouth, but an unearthly screech drowned out his words. We all turned toward the mouth of the cave just in time to see Leap shoot through the entrance on the back of his cloud, Mavlyn and the Oracle with him. I gaped at the small army of harpies on his tail, the sound of their wingbeats and battle cries filling the air as they dive bombed the shadow soldiers.

Einar and I exchanged amazed, bewildered glances, then charged into the fray. I fired off a barrage of ice stakes in Dune's direction, and he dodged, but a well-aimed air blast from Leap sent him stumbling straight back into my path.

"Kill that slimy bastard, Adara!" he shouted as he attacked a pair of shadow guards. The harpies were tearing into them with knives and claws, Mavlyn using her vines to yank them off their feet and slam them into the ground. Even the Oracle was in action, using her wind magic to trip up the soldiers so Einar could slash and stab at them. It was a beautiful, violent choreography, and my battle spirit rose inside me, banishing the last of my fear and exhaustion.

"Adara," Dune croaked as I advanced on him. Tiny flames sparked to life across the surface of my skin. "Please. We have a history."

I laughed darkly, my steps quickening as the fire spread, enveloping me in its orange glow. I could see myself reflected in his eyes, the blue-white heart at the center of a towering column of fire.

"We may have a history," I agreed as I backed him up against one of the temple pillars. "But I'm not the same girl you knew, Dune."

I pressed my body up against Dune's, the way I'd once done when we were teenage lovers, when I'd been infatuated. The flames jumped from my skin to his, and I leaned in to whisper in his ear as his flesh began to smoke.

"I'm Adara, princess of Ediria, daughter of dragons and fae. And I'm going to make you pay."

Dune screamed as my fire tore into him, eating both at his flesh and his shadow magic within. He struggled against me, tried to buck me off, but I held him fast against the pillar, looking into his eyes as I let my magic do its work. I refused to turn away even as his flesh melted, as his blood steamed away, as his bones crumbled away into nothingness.

Only when he was reduced to nothing but the flecks of ash coating my skin and hair, did I finally step back.

The sounds of the fighting rushed back in from around me, and I turned to see Mavlyn use her vines to rip the arm off a shadow guard soldier. The rest of them were either dead or dying, their bodies lying next to the acolytes they'd murdered. A few harpies had joined the numbers of the dead as well, but most of them were still standing, helping my friends make short work of the remaining enemies.

"Adara?" Quye approached me, her eyes wide with concern. I knew what I must look like, my hair a wild mess, my skin and clothes covered in the ashes of my former boyfriend. "Are you all right?"

"I'm fine," I told her even as she laid her hands on my arms. A cool wind whispered up my body, brushing away most of the ash. "But what are you doing here? Aren't you supposed to be in the air temple?"

"Oh, that place is overrated," Quye said with an offhand wave. "It's far more exciting out here in Bala Oighr."

Leap snorted as he came up to us. "What Quye really means is our Uncle Oren wasn't happy about how easily we breached security to get to Quye last time. He thought cutting her off from the winds and hiding her away in a mountain fortress was the best way to deal with that."

"Luckily, Leap and I were able to figure out where she was,

and we busted her out." Mavlyn looped an arm through Quye's, smiling. "And it was a good thing, too. Without her, we wouldn't have been able to convince the harpy queen to lend us her warriors."

"I would have come even if Queen Makani had refused her help." One of the harpies said as she stepped forward, and I started—it was Amelie, the one whose life I'd saved using the golden apple I'd filched from Lady Mossi's orchard. She smiled, exposing her serrated teeth. "Well met, Adara."

"Well met," I agreed, looking around the room. But whatever joy I'd felt sputtered out as my gaze landed on the body of the dead priestess, still lying a few feet away from the door.

"Where is Tamil?" I asked.

A rustle of wings alerted me as Einar—who had flown to the cave entrance to check for any remaining shadow guard—landed. My heart sank straight into the soles of my boots at the sight of Tamil's limp body in his arms, her furs soaked with blood.

"No." I rushed over as he sank to his knees, placing her on the ground. I dropped hard next to her, my hand slipping into Tamil's as her gaze fluttered. "No, Tamil. Please."

Tamil coughed, black blood bubbling over her lips. The blood vessels in her eyes were turning black, matching the ones creeping up her neck. "I'm sorry," she croaked. "I tried to hold him off, but he was too strong."

"Don't speak." I squeezed her hand, trying not to let the panic show on my face. "Just hold on. I'm going to save you."

Minutes passed as I tried to draw on the golden light from before. But it was nowhere to be found—I'd used everything I had on Einar.

"Adara." Einar's hand curled around my shoulder, and I looked up to see him staring at me. A lump swelled in my throat at the heart-wrenching look in his eyes. "We have to end this for her."

One of the soldiers handed a dagger to me. I stared at the blade in my hand for a long moment, then down at Tamil's chest.

Tamil's eyes fluttered open, her gaze locking on mine. "Do it," she whispered.

I nodded, then sank the dagger into her heart in one swift motion. Her eyes opened wide as she let out a last gasp, and tears coursed down my cheeks.

"Goodbye, my friend," I murmured as her eyes slid shut for the last time.

A tomb-like silence settled over the cavern, and everyone bowed their heads. The memory of Tamil's fiancé and sisters greeting her with such joy flashed through my mind, and white hot pain lanced through me. How would they look at me once they'd realized Tamil had sacrificed herself to save me, and that it was all for nothing?

"I failed you," I rasped, dropping her lifeless hand. Tears dripped from my face and onto hers, but she didn't stir as the cold droplets hit her skin. "I've failed everyone."

"No," Einar disagreed. He took my shoulders in his hands, offering me strength and comfort I didn't deserve. "It's we who've failed you. We should have planned for this, should have had more soldiers guarding the cave, should have fought harder to keep Dune from reaching the inner sanctum. None of this is your fault."

The tortured sound in his voice tore at me, and I shook my head, anger and despair clawing at me from the inside. "There must be some way to make this right," I insisted. "Some way I can still complete the ritual and defeat Nox."

"There is." Quye's shadow fell over us, and I looked up. The

Oracle's expression was uncharacteristically grave as our eyes met. "But it's not going to be easy."

"What do I have to do? Should I go back to Lady Axlya and ask?" Maybe I could still convince her to let me marry Prentis...

But even as that thought occurred to me, the bond between Einar and me pulsed softly, as if in reminder of what we shared. It was stronger now—I could feel the current of energy running back and forth between us, melding our abilities. It was why I was able to draw on his strength when I needed it, and why he was now immune to the effects of shadow magic.

How could I marry Prentis, when I was practically bound to Einar already?

"Oh no," Quye said, and the next words she spoke tilted my world on its axis. "You're not going back to Axlya. You're going to Mount Furian. And you're going to ask the dragons."

To be continued...

Adara and Einar's story will continue in Caged in Shadow, Book Three in Of Dragons and Fae. Head over to www. jasminewalt.com for more information on where you can find it!

P.S. Did you enjoy this book? Please consider leaving a review. Reviews help authors sell books, which means they can continue writing sequels for you to read. Plus, they make the author feel warm and fuzzy inside, and who doesn't want that? ;)

ABOUT THE AUTHOR

NYT bestseller **JASMINE WALT** is obsessed with books, chocolate, and sharp objects. Somehow, those three things melded together in her head and transformed into a desire to write, usually fantastical stuff with a healthy dose of action and romance. She also writes under Jada Storm.

Her characters are a little (okay, a lot) on the snarky side, and they swear, but they mean well. Even the villains sometimes. When Jasmine isn't chained to her keyboard, you can find her practicing her triangle choke on the mats, spending time with her family, or binge-watching superhero shows. Drop her a line anytime at jasmine@jasminewalt.com, or visit her at www.jasminewalt.com.

ALSO BY JASMINE WALT

The Baine Chronicles Series:

Burned by Magic

Bound by Magic

Hunted by Magic

Marked by Magic

Betrayed by Magic

Deceived by Magic

Scorched by Magic

Fugitive by Magic

Claimed by Magic

Saved by Magic

Taken by Magic

The Baine Chronicles (Novellas)

Tested by Magic (Novella)

Forsaken by Magic (Novella)

Called by Magic (Novella)

Dragon Riders of Elantia

Call of the Dragon

Flight of the Dragon

Might of the Dragon

War of the Dragon

Test of the Dragon

Secret of the Dragon

Her Dark Protectors

Written under Jada Storm, with Emily Goodwin

Cursed by Night

Kissed by Night

Hidden by Night

Broken by Night

The Dragon's Gift Trilogy

Written under Jada Storm

Dragon's Gift

Dragon's Blood

Dragon's Curse

The Legend of Tariel:

Written as Jada Storm

Kingdom of Storms

Den of Thieves

Printed in Great Britain
by Amazon